The Third Buddha

Jameson Currier

Currier once again targets the big themes of modern gay life: identity, faith, homophobia, romance, and the complexity of relationships, but at the heart of *The Third Buddha* are the little acts of random kindness that continue to astonish in times of crisis and war.

Jameson Currier expands his richly detailed storytelling to an international level, weaving together the intertwining stories of the search for a missing journalist in the Bamiyan region of Afghanistan with a young man's search for his older brother in Manhattan in the aftermath of 9/11. The result is a sweeping, multi-cultural novel of what it means to be a gay citizen of the world.

Jameson Currier is the author of two novels, *Where the Rainbow Ends* and *The Wolf at the Door*, and four collections of short fiction: *Dancing on the Moon; Desire, Lust, Passion, Sex; Still Dancing: New and Selected Stories*; and *The Haunted Heart and Other Tales*.

Also by Jameson Currier

Dancing on the Moon: Short Stories about AIDS

Where the Rainbow Ends

Desire, Lust, Passion, Sex

Still Dancing: New and Selected Stories

The Haunted Heart and Other Tales

The Wolf at the Door

The Third Buddha

Jameson Currier

Chelsea Station Editions
New York

Book design by Peachboy Distillery & Design / Design Serrano
Cover illustration by Peachboy Distillery & Design

Published as a trade paperback original by
Chelsea Station Editions,
362 West 36th Street, Suite 2R
New York, NY 10018
www.chelseastationeditions.com
info@chelseastationeditions.com

ISBN: 978-0-9844707-2-3
Library of Congress Control Number: 2011928389

First U.S. edition, 2011

To the survivors and the heroes,
the lost and the missing

There is a reason for all things
and all things have a reason.

One

"I'm not convinced two men can have an honest relationship," I said. I had not said anything at all during dinner, remaining quiet and listening to the mix of political and sexual banter bounce between the other guests and our hosts, as Eric delivered one elaborately prepared dish after another to the table. My neighbors Eric and his lover Sean, a gay couple in their mid-fifties, threw little soirées biweekly in their Chelsea apartment for a combination of their single and coupled gay friends, in order to be matchmakers or therapists as the necessity of their friendships required. I was twenty-four that summer and staying in my older brother's apartment down the hall; it was often impossible to escape Eric's attentions as I came and went from the building, and I once amusingly accused him of installing a spy cam because he was so knowledgeable of my comings and goings—or lack thereof—particularly my desire for hibernating for long stretches on the sofa watching movie after movie, the titles of which he also seemed to know.

But it was my comment on the inadequacies of gay relationships that immediately stirred up my host that evening.

"Of course they can!" Eric answered me. "You've just had a bad experience." And then to his other guests: "Teddy is just talking nonsense. He's too young to really believe that."

"Think about it," I continued. "Two men. In a relationship. How much truth can there be?"

"As much as you can accept," Eric answered. "Not every relationship is the same. And sometimes just because a man has secrets, doesn't mean that he is not an honest man and truthful to his partner. Sometimes it's a matter of compromise, not truth."

"Maybe you just haven't met the right man," Stan said to me. Stan was a friend of a friend of Eric's. He worked in a foreign-service program and had returned to the States and New York because of "family business," which none of us had asked him to elaborate on, respectfully considering it another off-topic issue that evening. "Family business" could mean either a parent's illness or a sibling's marriage or divorce. Or it could be a deeper secret, a way to disguise one's own truth. Perhaps Stan had been in some kind of legal or financial trouble. Perhaps he was bisexual and married and had a child—or had fathered an illegitimate one. It was a mystery Stan was not ready to explain or reveal to anyone that evening.

But I was grateful that I didn't have to elaborate any further on my own disastrous personal experiences and that the others around the dining table were now drawn into the conversation.

"Or perhaps you're too focused on sex being an equivalent of love," Sean said to me, jokingly. Sean was a psychiatrist, so everyone always gave his words more weight than those of his stockier partner, though Eric, a respected commercial photographer, relished being the foolish and more socially frivolous of the two. "I certainly had that problem when I was your age," Sean added. "Of course, I'm wiser now because my sex drive is not what it once was. But I don't think that sex should be the sole basis of a long-term relationship with another man. Too much disappointment."

"Are you saying I'm not sexy?" Eric whined across the table. "Or lousy in bed?"

This was followed by nervous laughter from everyone.

"Of course, as Eric said, every relationship is distinct," Sean added.

I was glad the topic soon shifted back to Stan, who until recently had worked in Afghanistan, and as dinner progressed from drinks to salad to entrees to dessert, the tale of Stan's work in a clinic in the Bamiyan province unraveled as he recounted his experience aiding a television journalist who had been injured in an accident. The journalist was a mutual friend of Eric and Sean. And in the odd set of connections and circumstances of those at dinner that evening, the journalist Stan had helped had once lived in my brother's apartment, before my brother had assumed the lease. Eric was particularly proud that he was able to join together all the pieces of this puzzle over a three-course meal.

I was tired that evening and after a rich and heavy dessert of Dutch apple pie and ice cream, I excused myself from the party and the other guests and went back to my apartment. I had found it increasingly difficult to be social with other guys, which Eric had noted, of course, and which had been the catalyst for the dinner invitation. That week I was also watching another neighbor's dog, Joe's black cocker spaniel named Inky, while Joe was away in Los Angeles. Inky was a beautiful dog, a princess who padded about softly and tossed her curly head and floppy ears at me; one of her unacknowledged blessings was that she pulled me in and out of the apartment so that I did not completely lose contact with the outside world. I was greeted with a whoosh of affection as I stepped through the apartment door, tiny paws landing just below the faded white of the knees of my jeans. I snapped on her leash and we went to the end of the hallway to wait for the building's sluggishly slow-arriving elevator.

As it finally arrived, Stan was leaving Eric and Sean's apartment and I held the elevator door open while he said good-bye to the two men with handshakes and kissed cheeks. He joined me for the ride to the ground floor and Inky's brisk sprint through the lobby to the sidewalk.

I liked Stan. Unlike our hosts, who were forever filling empty spaces with nonsensical chatter and opinions, he was not much of a talker. He was a tall, handsome, masculine man, a guy's guy who always seemed to be well put together and admired, about three or four years older than I was, so I felt a more generational bonding with him than I had shared with our older hosts, who had, in the eleven months I had lived in my brother's apartment, tried to step into the roles of mentor, parent or guide for me. There was also a quiet modesty to Stan, as evinced by the personal story he would not disclose at dinner—he had been as vague in many of his statements as I was that evening about my ruinous love life—and there had been not an ounce of bravado when he had recounted his assistance to Eric's friend in Afghanistan. I admired the fact that he had boldly stepped into foreign service after graduating college, something I had not been able to do myself, and I envied him for having already amassed a handful of anecdotal adventures that he could recount to strangers over a meal. But it had also made me feel rather inconsequential in the fabric of gay life and that perhaps I had been wasting my life in the city. In the elevator I was bashfully shy—or rudely uninterested in him—but Stan gruffly complimented Inky's beauty and funneled me questions about her and her owner which kept both of us looking down at the curly black mop of her and not at each other.

It was a warm summer night, mid-July, and the day's heat still seemed trapped close to the sidewalk. I broke into a light sweat as I moved away from the air-conditioning of the building and into the city air. We walked silently together to the end of the block and were about to shake hands as we reached Eighth Avenue where Stan would head towards the subway stop to begin his journey back to Long Island.

On the street, a bike messenger—an Asian guy about our age in a tank top and bright green cycling shorts—suddenly rode across a pothole he had not seen in his path. He went flying over the handlebars and landed on the street, unconscious. From the angle where we were standing we had both witnessed the accident. The messenger had not been wearing a helmet for protection. Stan touched me on the shoulder as the guy was rising up in the air, over the handlebars of the bike and onto the pavement, as if to keep me in place and out of harm, and once the fellow had landed on the ground, Stan rushed into the street to aid him.

"Do you have a cell phone?" There was already blood on his shirt from where he had leaned into the Asian boy's head to check his wound.

I did, but not with me. I stepped farther away from Stan and the accident and stopped another guy who was walking by and talking on a cell phone, and I tapped him on the shoulder and asked, "Could you call nine-one-one for us?"

He was a beefy sort of guy, wearing a formfitting T-shirt and carrying a shoulder bag, and I gathered he must have just been at one of the gyms that dotted the neighborhood. He nodded at me, hung up on his call, and called the emergency line and explained to the operator where we were.

Before he had hung up, a police car arrived, followed by an ambulance, and soon the messenger was being lifted onto a stretcher.

I thanked the beefy guy, and he disappeared as the officers and emergency workers arrived, and Inky's restlessness tugged me to one end of the block and back so she could sniff around and do her business.

When the ambulance and officers left and the street was cleared of gawkers, it was just Stan and myself and the dog. Stan's clothes were soiled and his hands were dirty with grime and dried blood. The messenger would be all right—more blood and broken bones than serious internal damages, the medical workers seemed to think. His blackout had only been for a minute or so. But he was being taken to the hospital for stitches and further tests.

"You can't get on the subway like that," I said to Stan. "You can wash up and take one of my brother's shirts."

We walked back to the apartment building and self-consciously waited for the elevator. I tried to commend Stan on his quick actions, but it felt strained and awkward and I was tired and ready to be on my own for the night, and Inky was restlessly tugging at the leash because she knew she would soon get a treat when we were back in the apartment.

In the elevator I unhooked Inky's leash and she leapt down the hall when we reached my floor. Inside the apartment, I pointed to the bathroom—the layout was not much different from Eric and Sean's apartment—and went to give Inky a treat and then find a shirt for Stan to wear.

A few minutes later he emerged bare chested and asked if I had a plastic bag he could use to carry his soiled clothes back to Long Island. It was impossible not to take in his body's military athleticism—thick, muscled shoulders and arms and a nicely developed chest covered with black hair curving into a thin, dark line that traveled down the middle of his solid stomach and widened again above his navel. I handed him the shirt I had found in my brother's closet and went into the kitchen to find a bag.

Stan was in the living room wearing my brother's shirt when I handed him the plastic bag and, as he stuffed the soiled clothes inside it, he asked, "Do you think they were trying to set us up?"

"I know for a fact that they were trying to set us up."

He nodded and smiled and stepped a little closer to where I was standing.

"You're a nice guy," he complimented me. "It would be a shame to disappoint them."

I smiled and bowed my head, accepting the approval, and he kissed me on my forehead.

He was a big guy and it was a brotherly gesture, but it made me feel vulnerable. I lifted my eyes up to him, which was when his kiss fell against my lips.

Slowly, clumsily, as if being awakened from a deep sleep, I put my arms around his waist. His hands slipped around me and settled at the belt loops of my jeans, where he hooked his fingers as I moved my hands beneath his shirt and around to his chest. I had wanted to kiss him since I had met him at Eric and Sean's and I held my lips open as he forcefully moved his tongue into my mouth, as if to prove that he had been interested in me, after all.

He tugged the bottom of my T-shirt and slid it up over my arms and tossed it behind him, and his hands moved to my waist as he pressed his mouth against the center of my chest. His lips rode up my neck and I let him linger there till the pleasure was unbearable, and then I took the edges of his shirt and pulled them towards his head.

We stood bare chested now in front of each other, deep-tonguing and stroking each other's bodies. I rubbed his nipple between my thumb and forefinger while he moved a hand to my crotch and grasped the erection beneath my jeans. Then he unzipped my fly, pressed his hand inside and clutched my cock through the fabric of my underwear.

My hands moved to unbutton the top of his khaki pants and as the zipper gave way his trousers fell off his hips and puddled at his knees. He was wearing a pair of light blue boxers, tented from the head of his cock, and I reached my hand to his thigh and slipped my fingers under the hem of his boxers until I found its wide, mushroom-shaped head. His cock was warm and hard and I clutched it and gave a few strokes, then found his testicles and cupped and squeezed them.

He pulled away from me as if to find his balance and breath, and I took the opportunity to slip out of my jeans. He sat on the arm of the couch and undid the laces of his shoes and stepped out of his trousers. He had a nice smile and I leaned over him and kissed him, and we fondled each other for another few moments, then I drew him up by his arms and he followed me into the bedroom.

We were rougher now, stroking, kissing, tweaking, nibbling. In the darkness of the bedroom I could see his smile and he made soft noises of astonishment as we twisted and rolled around. I expected him to withdraw from my rising intensity, but he accepted it and pushed it farther. I wanted him to love me because I found him, in spite of whatever secrets he might possess, a good, honest man—and to love him in a way that could transcend the need for sex but would also embrace its deepest desires. I thought that if I could prove to him that I was a good sexual partner then he would also see that I could be a good boyfriend or husband for him, a mistake I continually made with every man I found my way into a bedroom with.

He asked if I had lube and condoms, and I rolled away from him and found them in the drawer of the nightstand. I thought he wanted to fuck me, but it was the opposite. I took it slow, fingering him till he was ready to accept my cock. He gasped and his chest flushed as I entered him and I pulled out until he hungrily urged me back. He wanted to hold my neck as I fucked him and I obliged until I realized I could curve my spine and take his cock in my mouth as I remained inside him. I felt entirely innocent and genuine with him, as if this were the first time I had ever done this with a guy and we were to do this together the rest of our lives. He was full of puffs of astonishment and I could feel the muscles of his stomach clenching and shifting and I kept at him, unrelenting.

He pushed my lips away as his orgasm arrived and I withdrew from him and finished myself off. I left him and toweled myself off in the bathroom, regarding the satisfaction of my smile and the raw, red patches on my shoulders and neck where the stubble of his jaw had burned my skin. Back at the bed, Stan toweled himself off, and there followed a long period of lying together cuddling, holding each other, rubbing our hands and fingers along skin and hair. I mentally reprimanded myself for pushing myself so emotionally into the sex and for stepping into what I really knew was to be another one-night stand. I knew it wouldn't go any farther with Stan than this pleasurable moment, and I felt the hurt and disappointment of it before he had even left the apartment.

"You must have been starved for affection there," I said, as I lifted myself out of his embrace, referring to his time working in Afghanistan.

"No," he answered. "Just the opposite. There was a local boy," he said, then quickly clarified, "...young man. He was a handsome young man."

He rolled over so that he looked out the window, away from me, and I followed him, wrapping my arms around his waist in an effort to keep us together. I could feel his voice vibrating through his skin and into my fingers as he talked. "It began innocently enough. Eye contact. Flirting. Holding hands."

"Holding hands?" I said and lightly laughed.

"Casually," he explained. "It's a gesture of friendship between men. Muslim men are openly affectionate towards each other in a way that would be regarded as odd—or gay—here, and it's easy to fall into their habits."

"I was working at the clinic," he said, after a pause, as if he had been reviewing a memory before he attempted to describe it. "Dispensing medicines at the makeshift pharmacy. Tending to walk-in emergencies. Trying to patch up all these problems with aspirin and Band-Aids."

Now he laughed as I had, lightly, then continued. "The young boy showed up one day looking for work. I shooed him away because there was nothing for him to do but get in the way, and there was nothing to pay him with. But he returned about an hour later. He was really looking for food and I gave him some bread and a chocolate bar I had saved since I was in Kabul. He was ecstatic. He knew a little English. They all know a little English there."

"Hello, Meesturh," Stan mimicked the accent. "I lihcke you. You lihcke me?"

We both laughed at the imitation, and Stan continued. "Like I said, it started with flirting. He was always smiling at me and he had a terrific smile—dimples on his left cheek you just wanted to drop your tongue into. He was always happy to help me with whatever I was doing. He made me smile. I gave him food every day. Bread I had taken from the guesthouse where I was staying and taking my meals. I would be grumpy in the mornings until he showed up, ravenous, and I watched him eat. He was sleeping in the caves up on the cliffs."

"The caves?"

"The grottoes on the hillside, carved by the Buddhist monks centuries ago. Where the ancient giant Buddhas had been. They were cold, nasty places, and I have no idea how he stayed warm at night, because it could get very cold. There were many families living in the caves and I can only imagine that their body heat was what was warming them—when they had food to fill their stomachs. The boy had been separated from his parents at a refugee camp, and he was staying with his older sister's family—her husband and a little baby girl. He was tall and slender, bony from hunger, as if you could see him growing right before your eyes into a hungry young man. He wouldn't eat all the food that I gave him. There was always something that he tucked away in his pocket that I knew he would give to one of them later. It was heartbreaking if you stopped to think of it, but there was so much to think about, that this was only one minor thing. Every day there was another casualty or a patient with a problem—an abscessed tooth or a broken toe. *Something.* It was such a cold, harsh place. Beautiful. But *hard.*"

He continued. "One night I was able to bring him to the guesthouse to dine. It was owned by a local Muslim man and he had always objected to my suggestion of the boy eating with us, in spite of my offer to pay extra to have him there, then one night the owner changed his mind. The boy ate with us—the rest of the MSF staff in the clinic and a few of the Red Cross guys who were also in the house—and they all knew him and were glad to have him with us. He helped the owner carry out the dishes of food and clean up—we ate on the floor, sitting on pillows and using our hands most of the time. There were three or four of us staying in each of the rooms and instead of having the boy walk back in the freezing dark to the cliffs I had him sleep beside me on the floor. It was a simple, polite gesture. I was just trying to be a good Samaritan, but I knew it would create trouble for me one day. He stayed with me every night after that. Each night he slept closer and closer until we were sleeping together. It was just so natural. One day I knew I was in love with him."

"This was the fellow who drove the van?" I asked. "To the hospital. To Kabul?"

"Yes," Stan said. His body was tense, frozen into thought.

"How old was he?"

"I don't know."

Then again, after a pause, he added, "It was part of why I left. He was too young. I wasn't sure what I could give him. So I ran away."

"You ran away?"

"I left him in Kabul. I told him that I had to return to America for a while, because of a family problem; that I would be back soon. He took it okay, because I convinced him that I was coming back. There was no family problem."

"Are you going to go back?"

"I've gotten a new assignment. Working in India."

He lay still for a while, breathing slowly in and out. Then we both rose and showered together, stroking each other to another orgasm beneath the warm flow of water.

Clean, exhausted and back in the bed, I drifted off to sleep in his embrace. I sensed him stir hours later, rise out of bed and begin to get dressed. The activity roused Inky in the other room, and I groggily stayed awake until Stan was dressed and at the door.

"Good-bye and thanks," he said, as he left. "I hope you find him."

I nodded and closed the door, petting Inky and groping my way through the darkness of the apartment and back to sleep. I was by then too tired to miss him, but I knew I would in the days that followed.

Two

The explosion knocked the van into the air. It flipped onto its roof, trembled and swayed, rolled over twice, and settled on its side. The engine stopped with a choking groan. The front right wheel had struck an unmarked land mine left behind from the Soviet invasion. The van had just passed a gray-bearded man wearing a small round cap and a dust-covered black jacket over a light-colored shalwar kameez. He was prodding a bag-laden donkey along the dirt road with a long stick. The driver of the van had leaned his head out of the window and spoken harshly to the old man, his hand movements displaying his irritation. He had been driving for more than eight hours along an unpaved route through the mountain passages. In the van were a professor, a journalist, and a cameraman. Ahead, on the northern side of the valley, was a panorama of sandstone cliffs, the entrances of caves and grottoes blackening its façade like bullet holes through a gold curtain. It was the spring of 2002. They were in the Bamiyan province of Afghanistan on a quest to discover the third Buddha.

The explosion was deafening, bursting through the metal floor. Fragments pierced the journalist on his right side, from his calf to his shoulder, tearing through his clothing and just missing his neck. His hearing stopped. He tumbled through a cloud of dust, a burning pain streaking across his lower legs. François Dupray, the elderly professor and an archeologist, was dead at once, a leg severed in the blast, a crater where he had been seated in the front of the van. In the back seat, the journalist wiped his eyes and climbed over the cameraman's unconscious body. He pushed open the door, struggling to breathe in the dust. He pulled the cameraman out of the van. The cameraman's turban unraveled from his head as the journalist dragged the heavy, lifeless body across the dirt field. The journalist fell to his knees, his blood dribbled into the dirt, his mind flashing: *Why? Why? Why? Why?*

The driver was able to open his door and climb out of the van. He stumbled into the sunlight and wobbled on his feet. His eyes met the journalist's before the van exploded into flames. The driver ran in the direction of the village. The journalist lost consciousness.

The explosion sent the donkey running, his hooves stirring up more dust. The old man chased the animal, too frightened to look back. The sound and the funnel of dust into the bright blue sky sent a crowd of men hurrying out of the village in the direction of the accident. The first to arrive at the scene, a bearded man on a bicycle, riffled through the journalist's pockets, taking his wallet, watch, passport, and press card. He unlaced the cameraman's boots and quickly biked away. Other men arrived, scavenging through the victims' clothing and the smoking contents of the van. Money belts were located, unhooked, and removed. The burned and melted filming equipment was taken; cameras and videocassettes and lenses and lamps and batteries were hidden beneath jackets and long-hanging tunics. The smoke from Dr. Dupray's books and maps and laptop was smothered and the items stowed out of sight. The picks and shovels the professor was bringing from Kabul were used to dismantle the van's doors and seats and wheels.

Finally, a bearded man atop a horse arrived and shouted orders to the men. The bloody and burned pieces of Dr. Dupray's corpse were covered with the deep blue cloth that had been the cameraman's turban. Two men lifted the journalist's body onto the back of the horse. The cameraman was carried to the village on what had once been the vinyl covering the back seat of the van.

The three bodies were taken to the hospital in the village, abandoned a year before by its medical staff after the Taliban raids. A few rooms had been rehabilitated by relief workers for birthing and tending the ill. M'sheem, the journalist, was carried in through the clinic entrance and placed on an oilcloth on the floor that in better times was spread out for a large family feast. A dark-eyed young man, barely out of his teens, a local worker who helped with the foundling pharmacy, arrived in the room to help a clean-shaven man—a non-government organization worker—wash away the clotted blood. Slowly, they removed the metal fragments from M'sheem's body, or at least the visible pieces of them, and sewed the wounds closed. They worked on their knees and with the dim light of a kerosene gas lamp, even though outside the room the day was still bright. There was seldom electricity used in the clinic. The gas generator was used only a few hours a day for the hospital ward—if there was gas. There were no intravenous antibiotics or pain killers for M'sheem at the clinic. No blood transfusion was possible at the hospital. Unless there was a military chopper at the makeshift air strip at the western end of the valley, which today there wasn't, the nearest operating base and hospital was a backbreaking nine-hour drive through mountain passages—the reverse route the archeologist and his companions had embarked on that morning.

The archeologist's body was left in an alley off the courtyard. The NGO worker—Stansel Chartoff from Huntington, Long Island— examined the corpse. Stan was Jewish, a dedicated Democrat, and a methodical twenty-eight year old inexperienced in medicine. He was in the last days of his two-year stint with Médecins Sans Frontières and had spent the long winter in the Bamiyan province helping establish the pharmacy. He was now ready to leave this cold, war-torn Muslim country behind for another assignment. He would write a report later about both men. Dr. Dupray's clothing and flesh were blackened together by burns so that it was difficult to tell where one started and the other ended. The left leg was severed at the thigh; portions of flesh were missing from the right chest and shoulder. Dust and dried blood clogged the ears and nostrils and lips; uneven rows of yellow teeth were exposed in a snarl.

Stan spoke to another NGO worker in French. They were both dressed in western attire—shirts and slacks with vests and pockets from which they could pull notebooks and pens and eyeglasses and knives and tools.

M'sheem had not regained consciousness. He needed fluids and blood. To the workers, he was not known to be a journalist. He was clean-shaven, a Caucasian, and clearly a foreigner who required immediate treatment. The archeologist had been expected to arrive a few days before. The news of his death was already circulating through the village. Stan told the other NGO worker that he would drive M'sheem to the Red Cross hospital in Kabul in the hospital van—a white Land Cruiser supplied by UNESCO—along with Dr. Dupray's body. Stan would not return to Bamiyan. He would take along Ali Hassad, the Afghan teenager who assisted him in the pharmacy, who would drive the van back with supplies and medicines and another relief worker from Kabul.

There was a small argument first. The other NGO worker advised Stan to wait. It was growing dark. The Afghan boy was too young and inexperienced to drive the route. It was suicide to try to navigate the mountain passages at night. Stan protested. They would proceed cautiously and slowly—he was no fool—and if he needed to stop for the night he would. He would take water and food and warm blankets. And an ambush was less likely to happen at night, traveling in the dark.

Stan spoke softly and urgently to two men in his broken and halting Dari—telling them to use a stretcher to carry M'sheem's body carefully and quickly to the van. He told Ali Hassad to make sure there was enough gas for the trip. Two other men wrapped more cloth around the doctor's corpse. These local men—all bearded and turbaned and decked out in a combination of Afghan and western-style clothing—would make more money assisting here, at the functionless hospital, than they could begging in the bazaar. The foreigners had arrived to help and they were willing to help the foreigners.

◇◆◇

Ari, the cameraman, was dark skinned and black bearded. He was dressed as a native. His white shalwar kameez was bloodied by M'sheem's wounds, though he had no visible, open wounds himself. He was bruised on his thighs and chest and forearms and forehead, the more painful ones beginning to darken into red and purple blotches. Dirt was caked in the creases of his neck and at the corner of his eyes. His beard was scraggly and filled with more dirt, even though it had been neatly trimmed days before. Sweat and dust and the impact of the turban had sculpted his hair into comical waves and curls. He arrived at the hospital last, almost an hour later than M'sheem and the doctor's body, because the men carrying him had stopped to inspect and swap their pillage. Ari was taken in through the entrance of the hospital ward, to a little used inpatient room on the second story and placed on a rug on the floor. He was covered with a small blue blanket that had been airdropped into the village by a relief agency. He was left to die, or expected to die. Hours later, he sputtered into consciousness with a coughing spree. His head was a lump of red-hot pain; any attempt at raising it caused him agony. He rolled to his side and looked at the room, his head aching from the movement, as if his temples were being battered by white-hot hammers. There were three other men lying on the ground near him, also on rugs and covered by blue blankets, either unconscious or sleeping or dead. By the door a man sat cross-legged, bowing and chanting beside a patient as if he were reciting prayers. He was dark eyed and dark bearded. When he caught sight of Ari's movement, his eyes widened with surprise. He began speaking to Ari in a language Ari did not understand, full of fierce-sounding syllables and phrases. Only when Ari did not respond, returned to lying on his back and breathing heavily through his mouth, did the man stand up and approach him.

More words were spoken in the strange language. Ari looked up at the man. He was exhausted and wanted to sleep. Even a shrug was impossible. He smelled dirt and smoke rising up from his clothes. The pain in his forehead was excruciating and he tried to roll his head to the side, only to experience more pain, startling and burning up from his neck.

Ari fluttered his eyes and lost consciousness, only to feel, minutes later, his head being elevated and his eyes struggling to stay open. The dark-eyed man was trying to get Ari to drink from a small, battered tin cup. Ari turned his head to refuse the drink. There were stabbing pains at the base of his neck. The man pushed the cup to Ari's lips and forced him to drink. It was cold tea, weak and bitter.

The liquid at the back of Ari's throat was soft and refreshing. It eased the burning sensation his coughing had created. Pain radiated across his legs and arms. He wanted to sleep but the man wanted him to drink more. Ari could not remember anything about the accident, and the man who tended him did not know he had been in the archeologist's van. Ari did not remember his own name. He did not know where he was. He did not know where he had been going or where he came from. He could not understand anything the man said to him. Finally, when the man felt enough tea and attention had been given to Ari, he placed Ari's head back down on the rug. Ari was covered with another rug, something thicker and warmer than the thin blue blanket he had been using. He felt the room growing colder. He felt his body forcing him into sleep.

Stan Chartoff did not choose the easiest route. He was headed for Kabul, where he would finish his reports and make arrangements to travel to Pakistan via Jalalabad and the Khyber Pass, passing through the risky and unstable tribal regions in order to reach Peshawar, where he would meet up with other NGO workers and hopscotch back to New York, plane after plane after plane. He told Ali Hassad to take the northern route through the Shibar Pass. They would head for the NGO hospital in Anabah in the Panjshir Valley instead of the Red Cross hospital in Kabul or the military base at Bagram. The Anabah staff were better equipped for the type of surgery the patient in the back of the van might require if he survived the trip.

Stan did not know anything about the identity of M'sheem, other than he was Caucasian and appeared to be in his thirties or forties and had been traveling with the archeologist. He imagined the patient was probably another archeologist, or a translator, or a geologist, or an engineer. Maybe a Frenchman, like the elder professor. The Anabah hospital staff would be able to alert the military at Bagram and arrange an airlift of the doctor's body to Manas Air Base in Kyrgyzstan and back to his homeland. They could also assist with identifying Stan's dying patient in the back of the van; they were better equipped to navigate the mires and morasses of embassies and governments then he could do on his own. And Stan did not want to deal with the military.

The drive was slow and uncertain, Stan mistrusting Ali Hassad's speed along the dark, dirt path beside the Bamiyan River. The boy was tired and restless, unhappy that Stan was leaving the hospital and Bamiyan. They stopped at Bololah where Ali Hassad smoked a cigarette and Stan said he would drive the ascending cliffs. Stan was full of fear, wondering if it was a mistake to do this tough journey in darkness, no light at all except the moon and stars and the front beams of the van. Finally, exhausted, they reached a plateau. Stan parked the van and checked on M'sheem. He thought the patient stirred momentarily as he slid open the door. The patient's pulse and breathing were steady but he must have gone into shock in order to negotiate the pain and the rocking, unstable journey of the van. Above, the blackness of the sky made Stan feel small and worthless. He knew almost nothing of science or medicine. He'd only seen this position as a possible adventure. A chance to learn something after college. *War.* This was what he had learned: *His country had forgotten about war.* He felt certain that instead of arriving at Anabah with one dead body, he would be arriving with two. What kind of strength must this man have in order to survive such wounds and an exhausting trip? Stan opened a canteen and dribbled a small amount of water onto the patient's lips. He had no idea if this could help. It was the only thing he could think of to do.

Ali Hassad leaned his head against the car door and fell asleep. Stan fretted and worried and tried to relax, stirring Ali Hassad hours later when the first touch of sunlight began to appear over the snow-capped peaks. The young man washed the sleep from his eyes with the brisk cold water of a stream. He asked Stan if he would change his mind, return to Bamiyan. Stan shrugged his shoulders and said, "I must go."

They arrived in the Panjshir Valley two hours later, the lush green fields of grass looking like hope.

At the hospital M'sheem was treated immediately, whisked out of the van and into an operating room. Stan did not intend to stay to see if the patient survived. He could not afford to make that kind of emotional commitment. There had been too much already with Ali Hassad. Stan filled out as much paperwork as he could about the archeologist's body while Ali Hassad smoked outside by the van. They were both gone before M'sheem was out of surgery.

The next morning Ari woke cold and sore. He struggled to sit up, then struggled to stand. He decided it was best to sit. The light in the room was dim, the air stuffy, the floor cold and smelling of dirt. The dark-bearded man brought him a tough piece of nan which Ari chased down with tea. The small piece of bread made him hungry. His head began to ache. The dark-bearded man helped Ari walk to another room. This room was cleaner, brighter. The walls were peppered with bullet holes and the window covered with a plastic sheet that flapped at the bottom corner from a breeze. Ari drank more tea and slept on another rug. When he woke there was another man with the dark-bearded man who spoke to Ari in the strange-sounding language.

Ari shook his head to indicate he didn't understand and responded with *"Où? Où suis-je?"*

The man wore a khaki shirt with many pockets. He lifted his eyebrows and said, *"Français? Êtes-vous la France?"*

Ari did not know the answer to the question. He responded in French that he was in pain. *"Douleur. Mal de tête."*

The French-speaking man left and returned with a small pill. Ari swallowed it with more tea. He lay back down on the rug while the man continued asking him questions in French. "What is your name? Where is your identification? Where are you from? Why are you here? In Bamiyan?"

"Bamiyan?"

"Afghanistan. Are you with the Red Cross? UNESCO? Division des Sciences Sociales et de l'Archéologie?"

"I don't know."

"The Buddhas? Are you here because of the Buddhas?"

"I don't know."

"You must be someone."

"I don't remember."

The French-speaking man left and arrived a few minutes later with another one, who asked the same questions. Ari gave the same answers, but this man checked his pulse and examined his bruises. He shone a tiny light into Ari's eyes which made Ari blink. "You must rest some more," this man said to Ari. "And you must help us find out who you are."

The man spoke to the bearded man for a few minutes in the strange-sounding language. Ari struggled to remember how he had gotten the bruises, how he had gotten to this dark room of mud-brick walls. He struggled again to stand on his own and took a few steps towards the door. The three men watched him. Ari looked out at a bright courtyard full of dust. A great sadness overcame him. Something had gone wrong but he did not know what it was.

◆◆◆

That afternoon a woman arrived at the hospital. She spoke with Ari. Estelle was dressed as the NGO men had been—khaki shirt, vest, and trousers. She was older, her eyes pale gray, her peppered hair cut close to the scalp. She was from Nydalen, Norway. She had joined the Red Cross after finishing training as a nurse, then found her way to the People in Need Foundation and the World Food Program. She had come to Afghanistan in December 2001 with the United Nations, and stayed on in Bamiyan when the Red Cross decided to rehabilitate the hospital. She asked Ari the same questions the men had asked him. Again he had no answers. She asked him his name. He did not know it. His memory was gone.

She furrowed her brow and asked Ari if he was Muslim. He could not tell her. She asked about his pain and his bruises. He told her which were worst but said he had no idea how they had happened. She told him a French archeologist had been killed the day before in an accident. She asked if they had been acquainted. Again, Ari had no memory of knowing why he had come to Bamiyan.

She sat with him while he ate more bread and drank more tea. She had a comical smile that made Ari at ease.

"Do you speak English?" she asked.

"Yes," he answered.

She asked him where he was born, where he lived. He could not remember either.

Ari's English was good. Estelle told him he might be a translator. She explained they must develop a plan. It was impossible for Ari to stay at the hospital. There were no resources for him. It was too cold at night. There was little food at the hospital. There was no security or protection. If he were an important foreigner, there was a risk of kidnapping. He needed to eat and sleep and grow stronger without fear. "There are lots of opportunity to work here for someone strong," she told him. "But the weak are at the mercy of many."

She spoke to the dark-eyed, dark-haired man who had assisted Ari the day before. The man nodded and bowed. "I will inform the Americans and the foreign workers about you," she said to Ari. "And have them send word to the French embassy in Kabul. We will try to discover who you are and why you are here. Until then, you will stay with Haatim and his family on the mountainside. Haatim will help you make the climb. I'll send you with a good supply of rice and daal and raisins. They will feed you. When you are strong enough, come back down to the village and find me. We will send you where you belong or find you a place to work."

"Barâdar," Haatim said. He stretched out his hand and clasped Ari's.

"Brother," Estelle said. "He will call you brother."

At Anabah, M'sheem was hooked up to an IV and given fluids and antibiotics and painkillers. A blood transfusion was scheduled. His skin was washed and cleaned of the dust and grime that still remained from the accident and the journey to the hospital. Stan Chartoff and his Bamiyan assistant had done a good job of removing most of the metal fragments from M'sheem's wounds. An X-ray revealed a small fragment had pierced a tendon in the leg and was lodged in the bone. Surgery to remove it and repair the tendon lasted almost two hours. Amputation was not necessary, though the operating surgeon was concerned that the lapse of time since the accident might have created a greater risk for infections. M'sheem was operated on by a gray-bearded man from Milan who had set up the charity hospital eight years before. He was kept in a recovery room for the remainder of the day. There were more fluids and antibiotics and painkillers. Tubing was placed at his nostrils to help him breathe.

Late in the afternoon M'sheem regained consciousness for a few minutes. A fortyish nurse from Wales tried to get him to respond to questions, but he slipped into sleep before he could answer. She checked M'sheem's vital signs—pulse, blood pressure, heartbeat—and changed his IV bag before taking a smoking break. She would not allow herself to fret over the unknown patient. Her cigarettes helped keep her disconnected and focused on her work. She had worked at this hospital for four years. This patient was not one of the worst. The worst were the ones with lost limbs—hands or feet blown off by land mines. The screamers, she called them. The ones who arrived shrieking with pain. The ones who needed surgery, amputation, prosthetics, rehabilitation. Months and months of pain and treatment. Not this one. This one was tough. She could tell. He would survive. She wasn't worried about this one.

Barâdar followed Haatim and his uncles, Nadeem and Siraaj, out of the village. His stride was slow and deliberate. His feet were swollen. His arms felt like they carried weights. Along with the food supplies, Estelle had given Ari a woolen pakol and a used pair of boots. Both were too small. He tried to keep the cap balanced on his head. He tried to walk so that the boots did not pinch and tear at his heels. His headache had not gone away. It had shifted to another point, reminding him of the bruises along his legs and chest. Outside the hospital they were followed by four young boys carrying sticks, their clothes too big and hemmed with patches of different fabrics. As they headed towards the cliffs, the men teased the boys and the boys stirred up the dust with their sticks. They reached a large empty niche carved into the side of the cliff. It was filled with rocks and rubble. The boys were sent away. The men pointed skyward at a path along the cliffs.

Haatim and his uncles had thin beards, round faces with high cheekbones, small noses, and narrow eyes. All three men had bad teeth and big smiles and a fierce strength they liked to display by helping the taller Barâdar navigate the dusty slope. They shoved their hands beneath Barâdar's arms, lifting him over rocks he could not manage on his own. The clutching and grabbing and boosting caused Barâdar a great amount of pain. He felt unsteady and breathless. At one point he had to force Haatim and the uncles to stop. The climbing was slow and exhausting. The altitude was making it difficult for him to breathe. His head was throbbing.

Barâdar sat and gathered his strength. Below, dusk was settling over the valley. The lush green patches of farmland were disappearing with the light. Ahead, white ribbons of smoke threaded out of some of the openings of the caves. A few had makeshift doors of salvage from cars or crates. At one opening, a woman leaned out and gathered up clothing she had stretched out to dry. At this height Barâdar heard the sputtering of a generator in the valley, the rush of a faraway stream, and the clanking of a metal pot landing against a rock.

The men helped Barâdar up to his feet. He followed them up the slope, into a cave, and down a small staircase carved into the rock. They entered a hollowed-out corridor which led to several small cave-like rooms. Inside the rooms families were huddled around fires or seated on rugs. A young boy stood in a doorway and watched Barâdar limp and stoop through the dim corridor. At the entrance to one room, the men removed their shoes. Barâdar was glad to leave his own behind. Inside, an elderly woman was working at a tiny black stove that was tucked into a corner. She disappeared behind a small wooden screen when Barâdar entered with the men.

She was coaxed out by Haatim. She acknowledged Barâdar with a slight nod of her head. She spoke to the uncles with a hushed annoyance even Barâdar could detect. Roonah was married to Nadeem. She wore a dark-patterned shawl that covered her hair and the sides and back of a blue chintz dress. Over this she wore an embroidered purple waistcoat. A pair of mis-sized blue corduroy trousers showed beneath the skirt. Nadeem responded to his wife by handing her the clothing and the new supply of food that came with their tall, dark-eyed guest.

The walls of the cave were covered with soot. The ceiling was low, but the room was large. An old trunk was nearby. A straw broom and two guns leaned against the stone wall. Barâdar had a vision of an apartment filled with books and shelves of mementos and pictures, his first flare of memory. He did not know where it was. As he struggled to recall more, Haatim prodded him to sit on the floor.

Barâdar watched the men sway and pray. Roonah passed out bowls of rice for them to eat. Barâdar waited for some kind of utensil—another sign he took that he did not belong. The men used the fingers of their right hand to scoop the rice into a ball at their palm and break it away when it reached their mouths. Roonah sat near the stove, away from the men, her face bowed towards her lap and plate.

Barâdar imitated his hosts. The scooping and palming was a tiring process, but the taste of the warm food made him realize how hungry he had become. After he had finished two small bowls, he wanted nothing more than to sleep. The men sat nearby and tried to talk to him, pointing to their items of clothing or the rug or a cup. They pronounced the words in their strange language and motioned Barâdar to respond in French, which made them all laugh. Barâdar's answers arrived in both French and English, and one item, "socks," he answered in Italian, "*calzini.*" He was glad when the men passed around hot tea and talked to each other. He understood that he remembered nothing significant from his past but that he would not forget anything about this night in the cave with this family. He was wakened some time later—he had fallen asleep with his head against the side of the cave—and was moved to a rug near the entrance of the room and given a blanket. He used his pakol cap as a pillow.

Hours later he woke feeling feverish and ill. He groped his way out of the cave and along the cold stone walls of the dark corridor, following the moonlight that shone through the top of the staircase. He made his way down the sloping cliff looking for a spot to relieve himself, his hot breath condensing in the chilly night air. At a landing he inched over to a small platform, his woolen socks snagging on the rocks. His skin was burning. He gathered up the ends of his tunic, unbuckled his trousers and squatted, the fiery rush of his bowels making him dizzy and light-headed. Ashamed and tired, he used his socks to clean himself, hiding them beneath a pile of rocks. He wondered if he would survive in this cold, foreign world, barefoot, alone, sick, and hungry.

M'sheem woke from a dream. It had been raining and he was trying to reach shelter. The rain was thick and gritty. It wasn't water; it was falling dirt. In his dream he could hear the dirt-rain landing on the ground: pounding, thumping, splattering. Like a monsoon. Deep in his chest. *Rackety-rackety-rackety-rackety.* He was trying to reach an awning where he could escape the sound. The sound of the rain grew louder and heavier until it was so loud he was aware it was silent. He blinked his eyes open out of fear.

Something was wrong. Awake, the light was too bright for his eyes. There was tubing at his nose and an IV needle in his right arm. He was stiff and thought he was paralyzed. There was an emptiness inside him. Something was missing. His vision blurred when he squinted and looked around the room. Nausea rose up from his stomach. Instinctively, he lifted his hand to his forehead to stabilize himself, but the weight, the pain, and the IV tubing stopped him.

His movement caught the attention of a woman who was tending another patient. When she left the room, M'sheem detected the blur of her blue head scarf and deep purple skirt. The emptiness was sound. The absence of sound. He could not hear anything. Instead of panicking, he closed his eyes to sleep.

He woke smelling smoke. Something tugged at his arm. At first, he thought an animal was biting him. He jerked his arm to save himself. Above him was a woman with short red hair and a freckled complexion. She was wearing a nurse's uniform beneath a green sweater. Beside her was another woman wearing a blue head scarf. They both leaned towards his face, asking him questions. He could not hear their voices. He turned his head away, frightened. He closed his eyes to go back to sleep but the red-haired woman tugged his arm again. He opened his eyes and watched her lips moving. He tried to hear her voice. He turned away again, but she persisted in asking him questions. The tubing had been removed from his nose. The smell of smoke was coming from her clothes.

He watched her lips move. He felt like he was underwater, aware of vibrations and waves but only able to move slowly. He felt the dirt rain again. *Rackety-rackety-rackety-rackety.* His memory of the accident came back to him in small flashes. The tumbling through the cloud of dust. His blood dripping into the dirt. *Rackety-rackety-rackety-rackety.* His eyes darted away from the red-haired woman and around the room. He was in a hospital. "Ari?" he said, not hearing himself speak but feeling the vibrations rise up from his stomach and lurch through his throat. "Ari?"

Barâdar slept through morning prayers. Exhaustion kept him beneath his blanket. A light fever lingered and made everything slow and indistinct. He could not follow a train of thought for more than a moment without it collapsing into surreal and disconnected events. He kept seeing himself as a shadow without detail. The men spoke in hushed voices and left the cave. Barâdar woke feeling thirsty and dirty and cold.

The old woman brought him warm tea. His "*merci*" made her smile girlishly. Her teeth were stained and crooked, but her smile was warm and engaging. She gave him flat pieces of bread which he chewed slowly. There was no door to the cave. He sat by the opening and stared at the bright green fields and mud-brown buildings of the village below. A breeze made him feel stronger and hopeful.

The woman was never idle. She knitted coarse strings into a zig-zag pattern, stirred a bucket of yoghurt, and lifted chunks of dung to feed the fire in the small stove. She left Barâdar alone in the cave many times—first, to wash scarves and trousers in a stream at the base of the cliffs, which she dried by the fire in the cave or by placing them on the rocks near the cave's opening. She fetched water in battered plastic buckets and balanced bundles of sticks on her head. From the opening of the cave Barâdar could watch her descend and ascend the cliffs with the other women from the caves. He admired their balance and strength. He studied the outline of the small, muddy-brown buildings in the valley below for some sign of familiarity, but there was nothing that triggered his memory. He imagined himself soaring above in the cloudless sky as if he were in some kind of movie. *A movie*, he thought, *something else that meant he did not belong here.*

He slept more. He woke and looked at the sooty ceiling. There were faint drawings on the walls, in the higher recesses. He tried to remember things about himself but there were only small things. A faint tan line on his left arm where he had once worn a watch. A beard which felt new and scratchy and uncomfortable. He could add numbers up in his mind. How could he remember how to add and subtract but not remember his own name? Or the face of his mother? The bed he slept in. *Yes, a bed. He slept in a bed.*

Afghanistan. Bamiyan. Why here? What in the world has brought me here?

M'sheem's throat was dry. He was given a small cup of purified water. He tried to explain that his hearing was gone by cupping the palm of his hand against his ear but it involved too much movement. He started first with, "What? What? What? What?" Then, deliberately, distressingly, said, "I can't hear!" And then louder, as if to prove the point to himself, "*I can't hear! I can't hear!*"

The red-haired nurse brought an older man into the room. He was the gray-bearded surgeon who had operated on M'sheem's leg. He examined M'sheem's ears and eyes and asked him questions that provoked more anxious responses of "What? What? What? What?"

They experimented with levels of pitch and volume. M'sheem discovered he could hear their shouts as mumbling sounds. Slowly, loudly, the doctor told him the hearing loss—ruptured eardrums—could be assessed and treated elsewhere. But first he needed to rest. Recuperate from the surgery on his leg. And they needed to know who he was.

He looked at his leg. It was stitched and scarred and scabbed. He tried to write, but his right hand stiffened from pain. He drank more water, complained about his hand, then proceeded with a mixture of writing and talking.

His name was James, or Jim as he was called by the military personnel, and Mr. Jim, or M'sheem by the Afghan locals. James MacTiernan. He was an American reporter for the International Broadcast Network. He was based in Rome. He had been in Afghanistan for a week and had been expected to leave in a few days. He was on an assignment in Kabul when he met a French archeologist. He had agreed to go with Dr. Dupray to Bamiyan to do a news piece on an undiscovered Buddha. A large, reclining Buddha the professor believed was buried in the valley at the foot of the cliffs.

He remembered small bits about the van hitting a land mine as they approached the village, which the doctor said accounted for the metal fragments and Jim's hearing loss. Jim asked about the cameraman, the professor, and the driver. The doctor informed him that the professor's body was in the morgue at the hospital. The American military and the UN had been contacted. The doctor and the hospital staff knew nothing about the cameraman or the driver. Jim remembered seeing the driver running away. And Ari, the cameraman, lying in the dirt field, his turban unraveled. Jim was convinced Ari was still alive. Ari had been unconscious, but breathing. He wasn't dead. Which is what he told the doctor and the red-haired nurse. "Ari Sarghello," he wrote on a small piece of paper. "Please tell them he is missing, not dead."

The surgeon explained how Stan Chartoff, an NGO worker from the Bamiyan clinic, and a tall Afghan boy had delivered Jim to the hospital in Anabah. Now that they knew Jim's identity, they would contact the medical staff at the American military base in Bagram to see if Jim could be transferred there for better medical treatment. A better evaluation of his hearing loss. Perhaps a hearing aid. Rehabilitation for his leg. He could be flown back to Rome. Or America, if he wanted.

"What about Ari Sarghello?" Jim persisted. "How can I find out what happened to him?"

"Rest," the red-headed nurse yelled at him. "You must rest."

Jim's eyes flickered around the room, wondering how he might escape. Return to Bamiyan and find Ari. He was wearing a long cotton shirt. Flimsy hospital trousers. His shoes were nowhere in sight. He was defeated but he refused to accept it. He pointed to the line on the pad of paper where he had written, "Ari Sarghello. Please tell them he is missing, not dead." He tapped it repeatedly with the stubby end of the pencil till his point was made. "Please contact the IBN," he said. "Please speak to Simon Bosewall. Tell him Ari Sarghello is alive and must be found."

Three

I was in my first weeks of law school in Philadelphia when the planes hit the World Trade Center in September, 2001. I was already knee-deep in reading and study groups, struggling not only with the lessons and the law but with whether my choice to pursue them was a mistake. I had realized very quickly that I no longer had the enthusiasm for more schooling, burned out from finally getting a dual bachelor's degree in history and American studies only a few months before, and I had a professor who had singled me out for abuse within my first days of classes. "Mr. Breed-gees," he purposely mispronounced my name, "I doubt you have the depth of understanding to be a criminal attorney. I suspect if you last the entire semester, you should consider one of the corporate fields. Something less ambitious and career defining."

The truth was that I was longing to be anywhere but in a library reading and studying and arguing case points. Instead of Philadelphia, I should have volunteered for one of those adventurous foreign jobs, like building a hut in Kenya or helping flood victims in China, something more absorbing and engaging and "hands-on," but I was also not yet ready to admit that my law school decision might have been a big mistake, even though it was clear to others that it already was. At issue was also the respect I wanted of my parents—they had encouraged me in this path and I did not want to disappoint them by giving up on it so soon.

Within minutes of the impact of the plane on the South Tower, my father had called me on my cell phone. He had been unable to reach my older brother, Philip, who worked as a broker at the World Trade Center, and there were news reports that a fire had started in the upper floors of the building. I was seated in a classroom at the time, nursing a cardboard cup of coffee as the professor was beginning a lecture on "criminal structures," when I felt the vibration of my cell phone and saw my father's phone number tick across the screen. My heart tumbled; I knew something was wrong. My first impression was that it had everything to do with my mother—why else would he be calling me so early in the morning? I let the call go into voice mail, saw the little envelope appear on the screen indicating a message had been left, and fidgeted and sweated and worried as I listened to the lecture and attempted to take notes. About the same time, I noticed another student across the room checking his cell phone, then a student who worked as a part-time secretary in the administrative office burst in through the door, saying, "The Trade Towers have been hit!"

I knew instinctively that this was a moment I would always remember as the girl lifted her hands to her face to show her horror. Where were you when the news broke? How did you hear about it? What were you doing? What was your reaction?

The professor, a former district attorney and a Second Circuit court judge, briefly cross-examined the student-secretary in a hushed, calm manner—Trade Center? New York? Wall Street?—and then quickly dismissed the class. I knew now in my gut that my father's phone call had nothing to do with my mother and everything to do with my brother.

I was not estranged from my brother, but we were also not close; our lives had very little orbits around each other. Philip was thirteen when I was born, entering his teens and an older, adult world, and I often fantasized when I was growing up that I was an only child, only to be startled by a comment from one of my parents about something Philip had said to them and the realization that somewhere out in the strange world beyond St. Louis, I had an older brother who lived and studied and worked and loved and had life issues. He was not out and open about his homosexuality with my parents, or at least I was not aware of it until I turned twelve and I caught my mother crying on the stairs one morning, her head bowed towards her lap. When I asked her what was wrong, she said, "You brother is just giving us some problems, Teddy. We'll be alright. Your father will talk to him about it."

Later, I overheard snippets of my parents' conversation with each other and felt a deep shame about my brother's sexuality, even though I understood little of what it was about. I had read about "gay men" and the "growing rate of AIDS infections" in the books and magazines in our neighborhood library and felt a deep fear not only for my brother but also for myself. What if I was the same sort of man as he was? Weren't we related, after all, made up of the same genetic framework? If he were gay, what did that mean about me?

My brother was not a sissy, or at least I have no memory of clues to that. He did not lisp or flap his hands when he spoke or play with dolls. To my knowledge he never dressed up in my mother's clothes or tried her make-up on while she wasn't looking. He did not fit the stereotypical image of a gay man that I held in my mind from having watched TV sitcoms and re-runs as a boy. Philip was incredibly bright—in high school he had aced chemistry and physics and was president of the Math Club, though he was also not a geek. He played trumpet in the school band, which made him popular with both jocks and girls, and was co-captain of the tennis team, a sport which demanded little practice so he could do other things. My parents were always quick to let me know that something I was doing—or choosing—was also something that Philip had enjoyed doing—or not doing. He had organized paper drives for fundraisers for new gym equipment, sold doughnuts door-to-door to raise money for new band uniforms, and once he had gotten his driver's license, volunteered with a library cart at a nursing home not far from school.

I had stumbled my way through high school. I had done poorly in geometry and worse in economics, though I had enjoyed World History and Civilization. I was slow learning to use a keyboard on the computer and was too uncoordinated to do gymnastics. I hated going to church or Bible camp or practicing trombone, which I gave up my sophomore year because I thought I could play football. I made the team as a receiver and played the first two games—until I kept dropping the ball too often and sat on the bench for the rest of the season and never tried out for the team the following years. After school, I held various jobs at the nearby mall—a cashier at a fast food restaurant, a clerk at a vitamin store, and a waiter at a small café. But it always seemed that my ambitions were small when compared to my brother's achievements.

But more than that I resented my brother's intrusions into the simple organization of our lives—we had to miss the broadcast of *The Breakfast Club* to meet him at the airport, dine as a family at the Red Lobster instead of shooting pool with my friend Brian in his basement, drive together to the nursing home to visit my grandmother instead of sitting with Craig in his bedroom listening to music. By then I was a self-absorbed teenager, wanting only to go in my own direction or that of my friends. That my brother only appeared during the holidays was often a relief—he showed up alone, smoked cigarettes in the driveway, and drank bottles of wine he sneaked into in his bedroom in a knapsack—and his interaction with the family was awkward and strained. My mother was desperate to know details of his life, though she did not wish to hear of Philip's dates or boyfriends or anything to do with his being gay or having sex with other men. She asked him about seeing plays and Broadway musicals, the exotic trips he had taken, while my father tried to pin him down on investment advice, which he was always reluctant to give. Once Philip made a casual remark about dating an older man and I saw my mother's face fluster and redden and she excused herself from the room, but later I heard her tell Philip that "We haven't told anyone about it outside of the family. We thought it should be kept private." Whenever I heard a classmate call another one a "fag" or "homo" in jest or ridicule I felt a deep burning shame because I could not step forth to defend my brother either. But the true fact of it was I studied my brother on those visits home—I watched the way he held his fork and chewed his food and swallowed, admired the way his hair was cut and styled, memorized the words and phrases he used to describe something he liked as *fab-u-lous* or *marv-e-lous*, and the way he cleared his throat and laughed at something he found ironic or funny. His characteristics were eerily similar to mine, but he had seemed to sail through his teenaged years without all the strife I was experiencing. After he left to return to his own world, I would spend hours in his bedroom snooping through the stuff he had left behind when he first left home for college and which my mother had never cleared away or discarded—his old sweaters and jackets, the weathered science fiction paperbacks, the messages written in the corners of the photos of his yearbook from his friends—"Philip, I would never had made it through calculus without you sitting in back of me. You are a true friend and I will really miss you and hope we stay in touch, Love, Marci." and "That was a great time we had together on the band trip to Chicago. You rock! Steve."

I avoided "coming out" to myself and my parents in the same way my brother had done for so many years, to avoid seeing and hearing their disappointment. But being like my brother did not make us any closer. I was twenty-three years old on the day the Towers fell. I had only slept with two men. There was not much to tell about myself, except that I had a deep fear of who I would find when I started to look.

When I stepped out of the classroom and called my father back, I heard the strain in his voice immediately. "Teddy, you've heard?" he asked.

"I don't know all the details," I answered. "Did you hear from Philip?"

"No," he answered. "Your mother wants you to get to New York as soon as possible." My mother was always complaining that Philip and I were not close enough, as if by bringing us together in the same physical space she might be able to accept more readily the secretive details of his life. She had encouraged me to visit him in New York during the summer months before I began law school, but when I had asked Philip about staying with him, he had given me some excuse about being in Africa for a vacation and I dropped pursuing the idea, though a week before the terrorist attack he had sent me an e-mail that he was planning to be in Philadelphia for a business conference and did I want to get together for dinner and we had set a tentative date.

But I was angered by the realization that Philip was not recognizing the possibility that I was also gay—that he seemed so uninterested in *my* life—or my life when it only intersected with *his*. The Prodigal Son and Good Samaritan wasn't a decent brother to his own brother.

"Why?" I asked my dad. "What's going on?"

There was a pause in my father's voice as I heard him say something to my mother. They were watching a television news program, most likely on the small set with the worst reception in the den of our house.

"Do you remember what floor Pup said he worked on?" my father asked me. Pup had always been my brother's nickname; since a boy he had demonstrated a handsome, masculine, playfully personality—the kind of guy ready to go out to play tag football or wake up early to head to the creek to fish. "Pup" seemed to fit him perfectly. My parents had visited Pup in New York two years before and they had gone to see Philip's office and dine at Windows on the World, the restaurant on the top floors of the North Tower. I had heard a lot of details of that visit from them because I had not been on the trip—going instead with some college friends down to New Orleans on a Thanksgiving break.

"No," I answered, because it was not something I would have remembered. "Why?"

"Your mother wants you to check on Philip."

"I'll keep calling him till he answers."

"No, she wants you to go to New York. She's—"

"Is it safe?" I interrupted.

"She wants to know he's okay."

"Dad, that's not possible. I have classes."

I heard him sigh and admit to himself that bad news would be arriving. "Tad, your mother doesn't want me to leave her to go to New York. We need you to get to New York to make sure Pup is okay." "Tad" was the nickname I had been given since I was a baby because I was the "tadpole" of the family, and as hard as I tried to leave it behind, my Dad would yank it out every now and then to remind me.

"I'm sure he'll call," I said with a tone of irritation. "Did you try his cell phone?"

"He's not answering."

"Did you try his apartment? Maybe he's at home."

"No," my father answered tersely. "He's not there. Get up to New York as soon as you can."

"Where am I going to stay when I get there?" I asked my father, a bit too snidely. He knew of Philip's eluding my visit.

"At Pup's."

"How? I don't have a key."

"Your mother thinks she has the number of one of his neighbors. Get enough cash to pay a locksmith or call the police. Just till we know he's okay and then you can get back to school."

"Dad, this is crazy. You want me to rush to Manhattan to make sure Philip is okay just to turn around and come back to Philadelphia?"

"Tad, your mother is in tears…"

That did it, of course. The spasm of guilt, nine hundred miles away. When I hung up, I tried Philip's cell phone but the call did not go through. It simply vanished into cyberspace and I turned furious. Once again, my errant and absent brother was making a huge change and impact in my own plans. For all I knew—and my father knew—Manhattan could be annihilated before I reached it. It was a seriously crazy idea.

I walked over to my dormitory, where a group of students were huddled around a television set, and I watched the South Tower collapse into a column of gray and black smoke. I knew in my gut that that was the end of my brother and I stepped awkwardly into a hallway and heard my cell phone ring. I knew it was my father calling again, though I could not get the courage to answer his call. I was moving through my own stages of shock.

I used an ATM machine to withdraw as much cash from my account as I could—a couple of hundred dollars that was left from a student loan—and in the parking lot behind the dormitory, I flagged down a guy to see if he could give me a ride to wherever he was headed. His name was Will and he was going to Princeton where his father taught classes and we listened in silence to the news updates on the radio until he dropped me off at the train station off Highway One. I learned that there were no trains running, though there were a lot of people driving in and out of the parking lot, asking questions of each other and callers on their cell phones. It was as if I had stepped into one of my brother's sci-fi paperback plots where everything was out of sync. I was ready to give up, call up my Dad and admit defeat. I was now stuck in the middle of nowhere. Then, a woman who was waiting said that her husband had made it across the Hudson on a ferry and was stranded in Hoboken. Another woman offered to drive this lady there because her own husband had made it to a PATH station where all the trains had stopped. I asked them both if I could hitch a ride—mentioning that my brother worked in the South Tower and had not been heard from that morning. Both women were in their early thirties, impeccably dressed and seemed to radiate high incomes and a suburban stylishness and I could tell they were both wary of a stubbly young man with jeans and a T-shirt and long wild hair. I tried to give them as many details on my brother as I could in the space of our two-minute negotiation by looking them squarely in the eye and wiping the nervous sweat from the sides of my face. Something changed in both women as I told them I was trying to locate my brother, a flicker of compassion, trust, assistance, courage, and their acceptance of me seemed to give more credence to my insane mission.

There was a surreal comedy to the beginning of this adventure—it was a strangely beautiful day—the sky a brilliant blue ceiling above us. The leaves on the trees were a thick, translucent green from the bright sunlight, the grass which grew on the banks of the highway was still lush from summer, but a crisp dryness hovered in the air, a hint of a chill, of the immense change of fall arriving.

It felt like a slow trip through a foreign country, studying every highway sign as if it needed to be translated and considered a possible route. Two hours passed on the highway, each minute seeming like an extra hour. The husband of the woman driving worked as a lawyer and had been on his way into court when his train was delayed and then canceled. The other woman, with a stranded husband in Hoboken, was from Austria and spoke with a light German accent. Her husband worked for American Express, located in the Winter Garden building across the street from the World Trade Center.

The women thought my idea of getting into New York was crazy. The news reports on the car radio suggested travelers remain at home. Manhattan was sealed off to incoming traffic. Every building in lower Manhattan was being evacuated. This was not something small, but huge and worrisome. The reporters on the scene sounded confused and overwhelmed by background noise.

The traffic was heavier when we finally reached the exit for Hoboken. One street had been turned into a one-way route for emergency vehicles; an alternate route was hindered by delays. The woman with the stranded husband was relaying directions from her spouse to the driver. When we encountered another delay, I asked the woman to see if her husband was within walking distance.

"Too far," she answered.

"But how far?"

"Forty-five minutes, an hour, maybe?" she told me, after asking her husband.

"I'm going to walk it," I told the women.

"No, you can't," they both protested. "It's too far."

"This traffic may never move," I answered. "I can make it there faster on foot."

I opened the car door and thanked both women—Jessie and Aria—and suggested that they park on the other side of the street and wait for their husbands to make their way to them. They nodded, seemed to consider the suggestion, but Jessie said she wanted to press on a little farther.

On the sidewalk, on my own, I made better time. My eyes were tired from the bright sun and I wanted something cold to drink because I was feeling dehydrated, but I didn't want to stop. I wanted to reach the waterfront as quickly as possible and try to get across to Manhattan before it was impossible. The noise from the traffic— honking and sirens—increased as I made my way closer to the piers. As I came around a corner to cross another highway, I could see the evacuation ahead. Rivers of people—men and women—were flooding into the street; emergency vehicles were parked end to end with flashing lights atop them.

As I moved into the crowd, I began to ask where the boats were docking. Some men and women were covered with a white powder— their suits and briefcases and hair and eyelashes dusted with ashes. Many were crying or sitting on the ground, their eyes glazed over with shock. I made it to a ramp where a ferry was unloading passengers, squeezing through the police and medical teams, where I finally got a view of the Hudson River—the waterfront full of small boats making the crossing, many with flashing lights and sirens and announcements being shouted over public address systems. And I also saw, for the first time, the smoking gray funnels that had once been the World Trade Center.

I waited until the ferry was emptied of passengers, then asked a guy my age who was working on the deck if the boat was going back across for more passengers.

He nodded to me, but I was suddenly lost to a group of firefighters who were boarding the boat, and I followed them on board as if I belonged with them.

No one questioned me once I was on board, and I sat near the prow, trying to remain inconspicuous. The crossing was swift and determined. I sat at the edge of the group of firefighters—it seemed that they had come up from somewhere in South Jersey—and they were all speaking on cell phones or walkie-talkies, yelling to each other things such as "Joey said the Marriott collapsed," and "Sy says there's debris as far as Chinatown," and "Trust me, this was no accident. This was premeditated. An act of terror."

My cell phone rang, and I opened it to see that it was my Dad calling again, but I turned the ringer off, aware that I had caught the attention of several firefighters. I did not have any belief that I was throwing my own life in peril by attempting to make my way into New York. I was only doing what my parents had asked of me and channeling my anger and confusion towards my brother.

At the docking in Manhattan, I followed the firefighters off the boat, surprised that no one was questioning an arriving student with a backpack, though I knew that I could keep myself inconspicuous as long as I looked as if I belonged with them. There was more bedlam on this side of the Hudson—impromptu triage sites, more policeman and medical teams, and another line of emergency vehicles waiting at the curb. Two army helicopters passed by overhead in a deafening roar that made everyone stop and watch them fly by. But I was shocked by the look of horror and desperation and frustration on the faces of those men and women waiting to take the ferry across to New Jersey and now I could detect a strange scent in the air—burning metal and wire, it seemed—and a thin layer of white ash on the ground, as if it had snowed only moments before.

I began walking northward along the West Side Highway. A park had been built near the water and I followed the trail uptown, as others were doing, around the pockets of other men and women trying to evacuate the island or return to their uptown homes.

I walked until I reached a large sports complex that had been built within giant airplane-sized hangers which a man who was passing by told me stretched up to Twenty-third Street. I crossed the highway and began walking west through Chelsea, stopping at a deli that was open and buying a bottle of water and a sandwich, which I ate as I continued to walk crosstown. There was a nervous pace to everyone out on the sidewalks—pedestrians darting from one side of the street to the next, cell phones pinned to their ears—but the city also seemed suspiciously empty and haunted.

My father had been calling Philip's apartment regularly, the calls disconnected or unable to go through, and when they were connected, they were quickly dumped into voice mail. My father had given me the name and phone number of one of Philip's neighbors, who I was to try when I got to his building.

It was close to three in the afternoon when I reached Philip's building. I buzzed Eric in apartment Four-R from the lobby, and heard a staticky voice on the intercom speaker as the door buzzed and I pushed it open. I waited for what seemed to be an interminable amount of time for the elevator to arrive and when I stepped out onto the fourth floor minutes later, a short, stocky man with a ring of white hair around a balding scalp gave me a wave with a hand.

He was standing half in and half out of the doorway of an apartment and when he saw me his eyes widened and he said, "Teddy? I spoke to your mother earlier..."

He stepped out of the doorway and met me mid-hallway and shook my hand and said, "I don't know if this key will work. It belonged to the guy who lived in the apartment before your brother moved in. Years ago. We were good friends. Still are. But I don't think Pup ever had the lock changed."

It was odd to hear a stranger call my brother by his family nickname. He held the key up to me as if I were to examine it. I nodded and followed the man down the hallway to where my brother's apartment was located. "Let's knock, first, just to see if he's here," Eric said. He was trying to be cheery, but I could see the nervous strain on his face that my presence had created, and I knew my own expression was beginning to form a scowl.

There was no answer to the knocking, and Eric slipped the key into the lock and it opened the door. He held the door for me as I stepped inside. I heard him remove the key from the lock. He reached it out to me and said, "Here. You hold onto this for a while."

I took the key and we awkwardly looked into the apartment, keeping the door open, as if Philip might arrive at any moment behind us and ask, "What's up?" The main room was clean and tidy, as if it had been straightened up just for the purpose of our discovering it. I had always thought my brother had good taste and it showed. There was a small dark brown leather couch and a matching chair and ottoman. A series of vintage European travel posters hung on a wall. Remote controls for the stereo and television equipment were evenly lined up on a glass-topped coffee table. Only the magazines at the side of the chair looked disorderly, as if they had been dropped there after reading.

"Did you eat?" Eric asked me after a moment to break the silence. "Are you hungry? Could I get you something?"

Before I had a chance to answer, the phone in the apartment rang and we listened to the four rings before it stopped. I waited to hear an answering machine click into place, but the apartment fell into silence. Philip's phone service must have also included a remote call-answering feature.

"I should let my parents know I'm here," I said and lifted my cell phone out of my pocket to dial. When my father answered I told him I was at Philip's apartment but he was not at home. My father told me that a triage site had been situated outside a hospital in Greenwich Village and that a hotline had been set up to report the missing. I wrote the information on the back of a takeout menu that I found in Philip's kitchen. When I hung up Philip's neighbor asked, "Do you need company? Do you want me to stick around? I can help—"

I mentioned the hotline and the triage site and that I should contact both. When I tried the hotline number all I got was a busy signal. Eric had wandered back into the main room and had turned on the television set and was watching a newscast. He turned the volume down low when I came into the room but we were both startled to hear Philip's phone ring again and we looked at it until it went silent.

"You can't watch this forever or it will drive you mad," Eric said, nodding to the news broadcast. "We can walk to St. Vincent's. That's where they are taking victims."

"Victims?" I answered. It sounded so fatal and final to me and I had only just arrived. I wasn't ready yet for bad news. "Is it far?"

"No, not really. Only a few blocks."

I nodded my head and said, "Okay."

"Let me lock up my apartment first," he said. "And I have a spare key I can give you for the downstairs door so you can come and go as you need to."

A few minutes later we were standing in the hallway waiting for the elevator. Eric had a camera strap draped across his chest and a large camera in one hand. A belt around his waist carried a photography bag. He had been wearing a large T-shirt and baggy shorts when he first met me and now with a baseball cap on his head and his dusty white sneakers he looked like a tourist who had wandered into the building by mistake.

"I've been conflicted all day," he said, giving me a sheepish look with his arched eyebrows.

"Conflicted?" I echoed back to him. I found it an odd choice of words to keep a conversation going.

"I used to be a news photographer a long time ago—when I was about your age—I traveled a lot—tail end of the Vietnam conflict, Cambodia, Thailand, Japan. But it was hard work and you always had to be on call and I just fell into the conclusion that I wanted something easier and I was tired of being alone doing it. This morning when I saw the footage of the impact of the plane, my gut instinct was to grab my camera and run downtown and start snapping at whatever I saw. But I haven't done that in years. And I was intimidated by my own desire to do it and the horror that it was happening where I lived—not where I was covering as a journalist."

I nodded as if I understood all that he had said and, as we stepped into the elevator, he described some of the other events he wished he had covered, including the demonstrations at the Presidential conventions in 1988, which led to a string of expletives against Ronald Reagan for never having mentioned the word "AIDS." When we reached the lobby of the building, Eric introduced me to a friend of Philip's who was arriving home—a handsome man about my brother's age—who hugged me and said, "This is horrible, truly horrible," before he stepped in the elevator and disappeared. It was then that the dread began to consume me. On the walk down to the Village, Eric continued talking about his photography career, as if to dispel my anxieties and make our mission more entertaining for me, but it was hard not to regard the others out on the sidewalk, darting uptown, talking on cell phones and searching the sky. Eric shifted to talking about his partner Sean, whom he had been with for twenty-four years, slightly longer than I had been alive, and how they had met one night at a gay bathhouse not far from his apartment. "We messed around in the showers and decided we weren't through with each other, so I brought him back to my place and he never left. Of course, that kind of sex stopped years ago, but we're still both open to any sort of adventure that might come our way."

It was odd to hear an older man talk openly about gay sex and his relationship and I flushed out of embarrassment; I knew so few who were out and open—or adventurous—at any age.

At St. Vincent's there was a line of parked ambulances and a crowd of watchers behind a set of wooden barricades that had blocked off the street. I edged my way through the crowd, leaving Eric as he began to snap photographs of a distraught woman who held a picture of a man whom I took to be her husband. When I reached the front of the crowd I stepped up to a policewoman and said, "My brother. My brother is missing. How can I find out if he's been brought here?"

She looked at me with a pair of large, brown teary eyes and said, "You have to stay behind the barricades, sir. We're addressing the situation. You have to be patient."

❖❖❖

I slept fitfully that night. When I returned to Philip's apartment that evening after having only been able to give information on my brother—and not receive any news of him—I had called my parents and felt their worried disappointment when I said Philip had not returned home. I tried over and over to admit that he was not dead, listening to any movement in the hallway in hopes that it was him arriving home. I lay down on the couch and fell into a deep sleep which was punctured by the ringing phone. The phone rang throughout the night, as Philip's friends in the city and across the country began to realize and remember that he had worked in the South Tower. I refused to pick up the phone and talk to anyone—I didn't want to enter my brother's personal space, but I also didn't want to confirm his friends' fears and get sucked into their hysteria and grief. I had my own uneasiness to grapple with. I tried to read for a while, but the textbook I had brought with me felt too theoretical and I was more compelled to turn on the television set for news updates; then late that evening—or early the next morning, when I realized that everything I was hearing was just the repetition of prior facts, I turned down the sound and fell back asleep.

In the morning the phone began again, early, before seven o'clock. It startled and unnerved me so I unplugged it from the wall and searched through the cabinets of the kitchen for a way to make coffee. I found a jar of instant—unopened—and boiled some water and poured it into an "I Love New York" mug that I found on a shelf. The caffeine awakened me and I began to inspect my brother's kitchen with a keener mission to uncover the mysteries that he had kept hidden from his family. He wasn't much of a cook or a chef. There was little food in the cabinets or the refrigerator, certainly nothing to even make an omelet. My brother must have eaten out regularly or ordered take-out because there were menus from neighborhood restaurants stuffed into a kitchen drawer, and from the look of them he had relied regularly on a few favorite Thai and sushi places. On his refrigerator door were souvenir magnets from San Juan, Amsterdam, Barcelona, and other places, and photographs of him with groups of men in swimsuits clutching drinks on a beach or on a float in a parade. Pup had a wide, toothy smile and the sleek, butch look of a bull mastiff puppy—a short forehead, small nose and dark brown eyes, but a wide jaw pebbled with a dark beard always in need of a shave. On the upper corner was a picture of our family taken when Philip was fourteen or fifteen, his jaw already swarthy and darkened by thick sideburns and looking a lot like our dad. I was one or two years old and sitting on my mother's lap, my mouth wide open with a laughing expression and my eyes tilted up towards my brother. I had a copy of this same photograph in a frame in my dorm room—years before, Mom had had dozens of copies made, and a large one hung framed at the top of the staircase in our home in St. Louis.

I called my Dad to tell him Philip had still not returned to the apartment, and listened to him describe a hotline that had been set up for the firm where Philip worked—Dad had been able to get through and speak to someone who had not been in the office yesterday and had been phoning employees for updates, but no one had any news on Philip. I wrote the number down to call later, along with a list of hospitals where victims had been taken. I booted up the computer that was in Philip's bedroom and looked at his browser and e-mail accounts. His bookmarks had a lot to do with financial and investment sites—he must have worked at home often—but there were also ones for chat rooms, porn galleries, and gay travel groups. In his download folder were pics of guys he must have met online—some facial portraits, but mostly shirtless or displaying their endowment or fetish. Philip seemed to have a preference for dark, handsome looking guys like himself or who were larger, more muscular or bearish, though there were plenty of exotic, slender Asian youths as well. There was a general e-mail account—PhilipKBridges, which was the one he had given me—but a few others set up under aliases—ChelseaPup, Built2Play, and Pup10011. I signed onto his e-mail account—he had embedded his passwords in the software—and looked at the ChelseaPup messages he had sent a day or so ago, but was interrupted with an instant message from a user named HungryMuscl who wrote, "Pup, thank God, I thought you were in trouble!"

I was horrified at the thought of being uncovered and snooping through my brother's stuff, and I immediately signed off, unable to send out the unhappy news about my brother failing to arrive home. And I was still uncertain whether Pup was missing or just out of town. I had tried to broach that subject with my father, but he had handily dismissed it. "He always tells your Mom before he leaves for a trip. He's been back from Africa for more than a month."

I scrolled through some news Web sites, looking at photographs of the Towers, the planes, the collapse, the evacuation, hoping to recognize my brother in one of them, then got up from the desk and walked to the bedroom window and looked down at the street below. The view was partially blocked by a tree that grew south of the entrance to the building, but the sidewalk was empty until a man walking a cocker spaniel exited the front door of the lobby and disappeared down the block. *Pup*, I thought, *why were you such a mystery? Don't you understand we are hurting now? Where are you? What has happened?*

I looked randomly through his closet and clothes drawers. There was nothing out of the ordinary such as leather chaps or vests, though there were plenty of expensive shirts and an assortment of black urban outfits, the sort he always appeared in casually when he was visiting in St Louis. In a bottom drawer I found a stash of X-rated videocassettes, condoms, lube, dildos, and butt plugs. I closed the drawer quickly, not wanting to enter that private space either, but knowing I would have to visit it sooner or later.

My face was still grimy and sweaty from sleep and I went to the bathroom to piss, the coffee now rushing through my system. I rinsed my face and dried it on a towel, accidentally inhaling a scent that must have once been on my brother. On a shelf was a small basket that held an assortment of sample colognes, small tubes of amber or clear liquid, glued or fastened to a card from Barneys or Saks Fifth Avenue. In the medicine cabinet I read through the prescriptions on the vials—Xanax, Ambien, oxycodone. I found a stash of about twenty cheap toothbrushes, something I thought was odd until I realized it must have been a stash ready for Pup's impromptu guests. I tore off the plastic wrapper of one and brushed my teeth, feeling a bit more human to be cleaner, then stepped into the shower, where I lingered longer than usual, thinking of scenarios of Philip's return which evolved into more tragic images of confronting my mother with the news that he would not be coming home.

I raided Pup's drawers for underwear, socks, and a T-shirt, but put on the jeans I had worn the day before, the warm, dusty smell of them offering both comfort and dismay. I used my cell phone to call my roommate in Philadelphia—I wasn't that fond of him, I found him stuffy and opinionated, but I told him that my brother had not shown up yet and learned that the dean had not canceled classes and that I was certain to fall further behind. Law school now seemed like an impossibility to me and a rush of relief passed through my mind that I now had a viable excuse to withdraw.

I was looking through Philip's checkbook—he had a healthy investment portfolio and a hefty savings account—when there was a timid knock at the door. It was Eric, the neighbor I had met the day before. With him was a taller gentleman, graying and distinguished looking, wearing small wire-rimmed glasses and an outfit that can only be properly described as "preppy"—a button-down cotton shirt and khaki pants. He reminded me of one of my law school professors. Eric introduced him to me as Sean, his partner. "You look just like your brother did when he moved in here ten years ago," he said.

"Eleven," Eric corrected.

"*Eleven*," Sean repeated, adding an inflection of displeasure at being corrected in front of a stranger.

"I told you the resemblance was remarkable," Eric said to his partner, then asked me, "Any news on your brother?"

"Nothing yet, really," I answered.

"Have you eaten anything?" Sean asked.

I shook my head "no."

"We'll get something on the corner, then," he said. "The diner is open. We can go there first before heading downtown. Eric has printed some photographs we can start handing out."

Eric handed me a sheet of a stack of about one hundred pieces of paper that were in a folder. On it was a picture of my brother with his name below it and the word "Missing" in large capital letters. I had never seen this picture of my brother before—it was a cropped close-up of his face, the left corner of his lip lifting into a smile, and it made him look rather impish.

"I used him a lot when I needed a hand model for ad work," Eric added. "When he would let me. He had great hands. Strong, the dark hair etching his wrist. He probably could have made a career out of it. This was just a test shot I did one day as I was setting up the lighting. He was talking about a trip he had taken with some friends to the Caribbean."

I nodded and handed the sheet back to Eric. I was grateful that someone had a plan but I was frozen into place by the fear of it.

"Get your keys and some paper and pens," Sean said to me. "Let's go find your brother."

Four

They were in Turkey the day the Towers fell, in Doğubeyazit, a village near Mt. Ararat. They were interviewing local residents and the members of a multi-national expedition for a special that would air months later. They had met the descending climbers on the slope. Ari carried the camera and Jim backpacked their equipment, water, and supplies. The expedition was returning from a search for the resting site of Noah's ark. The climbers were a consortium of Italians, French, Greeks, Canadians, and Brits—historians, geologists, and theologians with an auxiliary detachment of seventeen people which included mountaineer-rescuers, musicians, painters, and a documentary crew. Jim and Ari were working on a news report about the expedition, partially funded by the British and Greek governments.

Jim was forty-five, easy-natured and sociable, a child of the American suburbs and pop culture re-energized by Europe's history and sophistication. His face was sunburned and creased with dirt, his blonding-brown hair matted with sweat, but on camera he could still produce a lopsided smile and a dimpled charm. He was shorter than he appeared on the daily newscasts, filmed at angles that gave him credibility and compassion. His unusual green eyes seldom went unnoticed, pale at the center and ringed with darker edges.

Ari was taller and younger: thirty-two, an American of Italian-Iranian descent. He was dark eyed and dark haired, his deep-set eyes and black stubbly complexion gave him a foreboding, menacing appearance. Ari was observant and persistent, never willing to back away from his opinions. That week he had canvassed the Turks hired by the expedition as laborers and found that they were underpaid and had not consented to the filming. He lobbied the documentary producers to correct the oversight, which annoyed the team of archeologists and led them to complain to Jim and refuse interviews. Jim was forced to remind his cameraman that they had been sent to Turkey to film the news and not to try to improve the labor conditions of others.

There were other disagreements between the two news partners over establishing shots, sound cues, light readings, and fade-outs. Jim had a director's eye. Ari had a reporter's desire. Lately their partnership had soured after Jim accused Ari of filming him from an unflattering angle. On the replay of a broadcast Jim noticed he appeared to be all forehead. A wide, shiny, aging receding hairline. Ari justified the angle because Jim had insisted he be filmed on a sloping road in front of a building entrance. Ari could not keep the camera frame steady while squatting and filming.

"Your job is to make me look as convincing as I can be," Jim said. "Even when I am blatantly at fault."

"Convincing or vain?" Ari asked.

"*Both.*"

But the source of their confrontations went deeper. Ari was eager to make a stronger mark with the news bureau; after more than three years of tagging along with Jim he was frustrated that he was still the guy behind the camera and not the one fielding the questions and calling the shots. Ari's contacts were deep in activist organizations and non-governmental charities, causes for world hunger, AIDS, poverty, and third-world health concerns. Jim did not consider himself a political reporter. He shied away from the high-profile pieces and assignments that Ari would have preferred them to cover. Jim was an arts reporter. He worked on cultural pieces, profiles of musicians or celebrities or actors in Europe, occasionally filing a travel-related piece of interest to British tourists or a soft news report on the success of a foreign film. Sometimes he did an investigative report on an out-of-the-way museum or an overlooked artifact or a forgotten antiquity which involved speaking with an embassy representative or a government bureaucrat. Beyond this, Jim had no ambition to cover breaking news.

They were a competent team with good ratings and a strong recognition factor. The network saw no reason to break them up to cover other stories. Ari felt otherwise. He wanted to cover a war—*any* war other than their own.

Jim received the news first about the collapse of the World Trade Center towers, by cell phone the following morning, in a call from Simon Bosewall, their producer in Rome, where Jim and Ari were based. "No one is sure how it will escalate," Simon told Jim. "No need to change your plans. But keep in touch."

Ari had spent the prior evening with a small clinic staff, trying to gather information on health concerns and governmental benefits, only to find himself swept into the misery of a woman giving birth without the aid of a midwife, and he had returned to the hotel feeling tired and uneasy. He was sleeping when Jim received Simon's phone call. Jim woke Ari and told him the news of the Towers. They spent the morning dialing numbers on their cell phones and watching the fuzzy television screen in their hotel lobby for more news of the disaster in New York, neither of them understanding the Turkish broadcaster and waiting for English soundbites to keep them updated. They were not due back at the bureau in Rome for another week. They were joined in the lobby by two crew members from the documentary team and an overactive British historian, who theorized the attack was a Muslim-inspired jihad of Al-Qaeda. Ari started an argument with him over terrorist training camps that were said to be hidden in the mountains of northern Pakistan. The historian thought it was highly improbable because the region was too isolated for supplies to get in and out without some kind of notice from the authorities.

Ari wanted to file some kind of news footage of the day. He suggested to Jim that they film the reactions of the villagers and local politicians. Jim discouraged this, reminding Ari of their language barriers. He did not want to stir up local animosity or point out a suspicion of guilt to anyone; after all, they were Americans citizens traveling abroad and working for a media empire that could cast suspicion on anyone with the least calculated move. The network had not asked for any footage from them.

Jim was relieved they did not have to report on an event such as this; the early estimated casualty figure in Manhattan was close to ten thousand victims. The sudden tragedy reminded him of the years when he had lived in Chelsea, and he tried several times to reach Eric and Sean, two friends in Manhattan he still kept in touch with, but he had been unable to connect with them.

Ari also had strong ties to New York. He had been born in the borough of Queens, where his large family of uncles, cousins, sister, mother and other relatives still lived and worked. His mother's family ran a carpet import business, which Ari had made a great effort to extricate himself from. "In our bedroom, my cousin and I could hear the jets leaving the runway and we always dreamed that it would be our way out of the family," he once told Jim. The morning they heard of the World Trade Towers tragedy, Ari paced and complained until he finally reached a cousin on his cell phone. His family was well and all accounted for, but his cousin saw it as a bigger tragedy. "We will all be under suspicion," Ari's cousin said to him on their brief call. "We are never considered true Americans."

Ari immediately agreed. "Civil rights are only what a government grants a citizen," he said. "Privacy can be easily lost to legislation— or force."

Ari had also been unable to reach Eric Hinton—he had once worked as Eric's photography assistant. And he'd been unable to track down Eric's neighbor Philip Bridges, who worked at the Trade Center.

"Pup's cell phone has gone dead," Ari told Jim. "What do you think that means?"

"Too many calls?" Jim answered. "Everything is jammed. I can't reach Simon now."

The next day Jim and Ari boarded a bus to Kars where they took a train to Istanbul. Jim was finally able to reach Eric and learned that Pup Bridges was among the missing victims. Ari took the news stoically, then suggested to Jim that they film reactions to the attacks outside the American embassy. He was unhappy being so disconnected from what was happening in the rest of the world and couldn't remain idle. "I need to do *something*," he said to Jim, his face turning dark with anger. "*We* need to respond to this. People want to talk and be heard and we can give them a forum."

"Filming someone vent is not news," Jim said. "Nor is it our job to do it."

Jim suggested that Ari fly back to New York when international flights to the States resumed so he could spend time with his family. "Stop trying to deconstruct this," Jim said. "Take a break and see your parents. Your uncle would appreciate the gesture."

"He'd only take the opportunity to make me feel guilty and try to lure me into the carpet business. They don't understand that this is my life, not theirs, and that I want to be independent—not dependent on them."

In spite of his belief that he had disentangled himself, Ari had not completely disassociated himself from his family's footprints; in fact, he had volunteered to spend a day with one of his uncle's carpet suppliers in Istanbul to examine and inspect a storeroom of rugs his uncle might import, and the tragedy in New York had done nothing to cancel or rearrange Ari's promise.

"He's a good man," Ari told Jim, when he set out to make the appointment. "A good uncle. He always provided for me. I do this because he's my family."

"What about Pup?" Jim asked.

"What about him?" Ari answered.

"Isn't that the real reason why you're upset?"

"What can I do when I am so far away?"

In Istanbul, Jim and Ari learned of the Al-Qaeda and Taliban connection to the World Trade Center attack and the anticipated American response in Afghanistan. Osama bin Laden was rumored to have trained terrorists in the mountains near Pakistan. Jim's years of cultural reporting had given him a broad view of world history and politics; he knew of the Taliban activities in Afghanistan because he had assisted on a news report six months earlier on the destruction of the giant Buddha statues in the central mountainous province of Bamiyan. For the broadcast he had helped to create a graphic of the seventh-century Chinese Buddhist monk Xuanzang's route along the Silk Road between China and the Middle East. Xuanzang, a religious pilgrim who detailed his journey in a diary, had written of his impressions of the statues and the painted grottoes and the Buddhist monastery in the Hindu Kush mountains. At its height from the fourth to the seventh centuries as many as five thousand Buddhist monks had once lived in the grottoes of the cliffside at Bamiyan, carving a labyrinth of hollows, caves, niches, passages, and porches. The map which Jim had helped create, along with archival film footage of the two large Buddha statues taken in the 1970s before the Russian invasion of Afghanistan, were assembled by the London bureau and added to the footage of the Taliban demolishing the giant Buddhas in the cliffs above the Bamiyan valley—the larger statue, one hundred eighty feet tall, the smaller, at one hundred twenty-five feet. Both statues had been built between the third and fourth centuries.

The day the bureau acquired the footage of the destruction of the Bamiyan Buddhas, Ari viewed the film with Jim at his desk computer. "The Taliban are worse for Afghanistan than the Russians," Ari said. "They've thrown the country backwards—women have to remain covered in public. Government is by mob rule. And Afghan culture is being erased." Jim had always been impressed by Ari's knowledge of both world history and current affairs. Ari also knew the back story of how the cameraman from the news agency *Al Jazeera* had captured the footage of the bombing of the Buddhas.

"The Taliban didn't permit reporters to see the destruction," Ari explained to Jim. "The cameraman disguised himself as one of them—using a fake long beard, turban, and robes—and snuck into Bamiyan. He hid his camera beneath his tunic and coat. If he had been caught, he would have been imprisoned, tortured, and executed."

"It was a smart way to cover the story," Jim said. "But I doubt you would have sat back and watched that sort of thing happen."

"I would have tried to stop them," Ari said. "That would have been the right thing to do."

"And lose your life?"

"And you? What would you have done?"

"You're always quick to cut me short. I'd do what any reporter would do," Jim answered. "I'd tell the truth. Let the guilty become guilty and not worry about the consequences."

Jim learned second-hand of Ari's plans. They had shot establishing footage of Istanbul from Galata and done interviews with American cruise-ship tourists shopping at a bazaar and trying to pretend that nothing was out of synch in the world. The only news that was being reported was reactions to the Trade Center attacks, but Jim wanted them to adhere to their schedule, the reason they had come to Istanbul. Jim was researching a report about the disappearance of several pre-Greco-Roman artifacts from an Istanbul museum and was using the bazaar stalls as a stepping-off point to discuss the black-market trading of antiquities. Ari had begged off filming for the rest of the day to do another errand for his uncle, visiting another storeroom of another rug exporter. Jim had already secured permission from the director of the museum; he filmed the interior himself, carting the heavy camera through the sweltering crowded streets in a backpack that made him sweat and question his sanity. His afternoon was spent bending over glass cases till his back ached, trying to get a good shot. He was more patient than Ari would have been with this, but Ari wouldn't have fretted over whether there was a glare from the glass case—he would have known how to adjust the camera to deflect the light.

They had arranged to meet later at a bar that several of their news colleagues also frequented. Jim had time to return to the hotel and shower. As he was leaving his hotel room, his cell phone rang. It was Simon Bosewall.

"What's going on?" Simon asked. "Is Ari out of his mind?"

"What do you mean?" Jim asked.

"He said he has an offer to work for *Al Jazeera*. In Pakistan. He's trying to strong-arm me into reassigning him to another bureau. He suggested New Delhi so he could get into Pakistan through our connections."

"I'll talk to him."

"Did you know of this?"

"Promise me you won't reassign him. Tell him he can do some kind of on-camera report."

"You two need to talk," Simon said. "I don't need him on camera."

Jim and Ari were lovers. They lived together in a small flat in the Parioli neighborhood of Rome, not far from the news bureau offices where they worked. They had met four years earlier in Cannes. Jim was on an assignment covering a Greek singer attending the film festival. Ari was hitchhiking through Europe, looking for work and a career that was independent of his family's carpet-import trade. He had been trying to obtain a position with a non-governmental relief agency in Paris. Their meeting had been arranged by a mutual friend, Eric Hinton, four thousand miles away in New York, sending a postcard to Jim that Ari was hitchhiking his way through Europe and looking for work.

When Jim heard of Ari's plan to be reassigned to New Delhi so that he could sneak into Pakistan, he felt more betrayed than angry. Four years before Jim had convinced Simon to take a chance on Ari as a freelance cameraman. He had not disclosed their relationship to his boss. Simon, in his early fifties, had been a political correspondent in Washington before he became a foreign bureau editor. He was more interested in election coverage and political commentaries than weather-related disasters such as record-breaking rainfall and if Mount Vesuvius was active again. But he did have a soft spot for Italian cinema and opera; he had championed Jim joining the bureau after a series of articles Jim wrote on the unseen treasures of the British Museum and an on-camera interview to promote the stories.

In Ari's job interview, Ari's politics had immediately impressed Simon. Ari knew the backstory of political bribes in the Italian parliament, as well the celebrity movement behind "Free Tibet" campaigns and the Greek government's campaign to have the Elgin marbles returned to Athens. "He's a sharp guy, a bit passionate and hot under the collar about a few things," Simon had told Jim, "but that can be good in a newsman."

When Simon got wind of Jim and Ari's personal relationship—in the first months after Ari had been hired as a permanent staff cameraman—he was irritated and perturbed. Jim had pitched him into an ethical business problem. Simon, himself, was in a long-term gay relationship with another news professional—an arts reporter for *Le Monde*—and he had purposely overlooked his lover for Jim's position years before.

Simon did not admonish or demote or fire the team. He didn't want to disrupt the newsroom (nor did he want his own lover campaigning again to work for the bureau). With Ari's arrival at the bureau, Jim had developed an on-air enthusiasm that was noticeably apparent to Simon and others at the network. Jim and Ari had filed reports from Paris, Berlin, and Prague. They covered the film festivals in Deauville and Venice, the book fairs in London and Frankfurt, the opera seasons in Milan and Vienna. They were efficient and reliable, never going over budget. Simon felt no need to change their arrangements. And now, with the relationship out and open and common knowledge at the bureau, Simon arrived at his office desk with notes from his lover Will to Jim. "Be sure to cover Octoberfest," Will would write and Simon would pass along. "And don't overlook the new exhibit at the Louvre."

Jim was drunk when Ari arrived at the bar in Istanbul where they had arranged to meet. He could not hide his distress. "*Why?*" he asked Ari.

Ari was sullen and silent. He ordered mineral water, knowing he would need to maintain a professional—and personal—composure.

"I want the experience," he said. "I want to see what it's like. If Simon doesn't work out something with New Delhi I think I can get embedded with the troops the U.S. will send. I've got a few feelers out."

"But working for who?"

"Whoever will take me."

"Why haven't you talked about this to me before? Why didn't you tell me first?"

"I knew what your response would be."

"Is this it? The end?" Jim asked.

"No, I don't want it to be. But I want to see if I can do this."

Jim took a sip of his drink and looked around at the bar. It was small and dark and poorly decorated. "Does any of this have to do with Pup?"

"No," Ari answered. "And yes."

Ari flickered his eyes around the bar, as if he were looking for help. "I can't erase the past," he added. "But this has nothing to do with *us*."

"It has everything to do with *us*," Jim said, and then after a pause, added. "We could use a break. It's beginning to show." He held himself together, though he knew he would let it all out later, in private, while Ari was asleep. He hated confrontation and melodrama. He hated being right or wrong or forcing the issue of a compromise. He hated being pushed into this kind of childish behavior.

"I need you to support me on this," Ari said.

"You want me to sign your death warrant? I'm not going to do that. I'd rather you tell me you're leaving me for another guy."

"But I'm not," Ari answered. "I'm not leaving you. This isn't over."

Jim pretended not to hear. Or react. "Maybe I'll go back to New York for a while." he said. "Or visit with my mom."

"Is that what you want?" Ari asked.

"Me? You've already decided it's over. What do you care what I think?—or want?"

"You don't understand me at all," Ari answered. "You don't understand that I *do* care."

They returned to Rome at the end of the week. Ari's offer from *Al Jazeera* was a bluff. He was passed over for the embedded Afghanistan position in favor of another cameraman with more military experience. Simon Bosewall refused to help him be re-assigned to New Delhi or another IBN bureau. They both spoke with Eric Hinton in New York. Pup Bridges was missing and presumed dead, a victim of the September 11th terrorist attack. His younger brother was living in Pup's apartment, slowly breaking down. Jim put off his trip to New York. He and Ari both requested to work with other partners, though more times than not, they continued to work on assignments together, mostly pieces now on the empty airports and lack of tourists and cancellations of events. At home, sadness haunted both men. They ate together and slept together, but beyond this they did not share much. A fissure had split them. They moved in silence through the apartment—each in his own space—reading, sitting in front of the television, working at a computer, their bonds frayed and unraveling.

By October, the American troops were in Afghanistan. Jim contributed two news pieces on anti-war demonstrations in London and Berlin. Ari produced a spot on Europe's most vulnerable terrorist targets. Ari tried again to get an assignment in New Delhi but was turned down once more. Then Simon asked Ari to pitch him story ideas. He allowed Ari to be a segment producer of a report on the increased security measures on Italian transportation, from ferries to train terminals to border checkpoints. Jim had to shift his reporting to more topical issues. "It's a different time," Simon explained to Jim. "I can't ignore the rising tensions and the public's interest in them. I need you to pitch in on these. I'm trying to keep you in a zone where you feel comfortable."

Comfortable? Jim thought. Just when it looked like he could relax because Ari was not to be part of the in-place coverage of the military operations in Afghanistan, Ari was suddenly calling the shots on their reports. Ari was pleased with the turnaround; he felt Simon was finally taking his work seriously.

Then Simon took Jim aside with another request. Ari had pitched a news trip to New York City—among the storylines he wanted to cover was the impact of the terrorist activities on the local Italian and Greek communities of the city. "I don't want anything about Ground Zero," Simon said to Jim. "Every half-assed reporter is doing that as a sob story and I don't need any more of them. I want to see how this is impacting the small business owner—deli owners, cab drivers, chefs, barbers—but on a local, national, and international scale. What they've lost. A piece on the impact on the tourism, the economy, and holiday retail industries on both sides of the pond would work, too. If you don't want to take the assignment—and I understand why you wouldn't—I can send Ari and have him work with the bureau staff in New York."

When Jim hesitated, Simon added, "Make a stopover in London or Paris. Do something on the impact on the British Museum or the Louvre. Something you want to do to make it worth your while."

Five

Grief is an unshakable thing, a flooded river that arrives suddenly and without warning and swells over its banks and disrupts everything held in place. In the first month I lived in my brother's apartment I had failed to draw a complete portrait of him and I could not bear to speak to my parents, pulling away from them inch by inch because there was nothing to report except the quiet chaos within a city too large to remain still. Yes, there were details about the cleanup at Ground Zero, the removal of debris, the fires still burning, the quality of the air. My parents called me with names of agencies and phone numbers to reach out to—counseling services, city workers, a help line at a division of such-and-such in Albany. Somehow there was a group of survivors from my brother's firm—men and women who had been out that Tuesday, sick, traveling on business or planning to arrive late, tending to a child's illness or a trip to a doctor. I met a few of them in a loft in Soho one night at the urging of my parents, hoping within the sobbing mess of this I could find some kind of clue to my brother's last day. In my own mind I had imagined Pup waking that morning and stretching out of his sleep—yoga poses to keep him calm and focused—he would have shaved and showered, dabbed a spit of cologne at his wrist or jawline, straightened his tie in the mirror and headed out to the subway, bought a token and waited on the downtown platform. He'd be wearing a silver-gray suit, lightweight because of the warm weather, but something that made him look exceptional, and he would have gone to one of the coffee shops on the lower level of the Trade Center and ordered something sweet and jolting, a triple latte mocha express with extra foam and sprinkles. He'd have started a conversation with a co-worker at the elevator bank, a nod to the heavy rainstorm that had happened the night before that might have segued into a brief nod at what the weekend might bring. "*September*," he would have emphasized. "I love this kind of weather. Reminds me of home."

At his desk he would have checked the messages on his phone, booted up his computer, gone to the toilet for a piss and a rinse of his hands, then sat at his desk and planned the accounts that needed attention that day, reviewing the trades of the day before, the movement in the overseas markets, waiting for the exchange bell to ring. The disruption would have startled him, the thunderous noise of the first plane hitting the North Tower, the building lightly swaying, the sudden confusion and disruption in the office. He would have gone to the window to look, first down to the ground to see if he could spot debris, then around to the other side of the office where the windows were facing the damaged floors.

He would have been one of those to remain calm, calling Security, trying to get a handle on whether the office staff was safer where they were or if they should be evacuated. He would have thought about calling Mom, then decided against it because it would only worry her. It would have been an extraordinary sight, looking at the gaping hole in the North Tower—the smoke, the ring of flames, the sudden confusion of what was falling to the ground. Then, the horrified gasps, and the sense of doom arriving as a shadow suddenly crept through the sky, something approaching *their* building. He would have become a Boy Scout then, calming everyone, coming up with a plan. I was certain this was the kind of man my brother was, even though he hadn't been that kind of brother to me.

"I hope it was instant," a woman said to the rest of the circle of survivors the night I attended that office support group. Her husband was one of the missing. "I hope he didn't suffer."

No one I spoke to at that meeting could confirm that Pup had gone to the office that morning. "It was early," a twenty-something woman told me. "And I wasn't on that part of the floor." She worked as a broker-trainee, and had made it to the office late that morning because she had been dropping off her two-year-old son at day care. She had noticed a lot of police activity around the lobby of the North Tower, but it hadn't registered that it was serious accident. In the elevator she had heard others comparing stories, and when she had gotten to her desk she had called her husband and told him she was leaving for the day—it seemed too risky to stay put. Of the others who had worked in the office that day, none could place Pup's whereabouts.

Later, a man approached me as the room was beginning to clear. He was about fifty and Latino and introduced himself to me as "Miguel."

"I had lunch the day before with Pup," he said. "Falafel place he loved. He was in a good mood. Said he'd been to the beach over the weekend."

I nodded and thanked him, putting another little chip of my brother into the box of puzzle pieces I had collected. On my way out the door I told myself that I wouldn't make another one of these meetings. I wouldn't be able to swim through this kind of grief again.

I could testify that I experienced both the best and worst of New York City—the bureaucratic nightmare of every step, the generous patience and assistance of strangers. An international violence had been disclosed to me and I saw a world that was treacherous and suspicious. The city was overwhelming—it seemed to grow larger and larger block by block, as one micro-neighborhood became another and another— Hispanic bodegas blending into Ukrainian meeting halls giving way to Indian restaurants and then to Chinese food markets. Most days I felt lost and overwhelmed and alone, particularly as I exited the subway and found myself in my brother's neighborhood, walking along on Eighth Avenue in the heart of Chelsea. When my brother had arrived in Manhattan after college the neighborhood was a growing cluster of gay-friendly bars, restaurants, and small businesses, but now, eleven years later, Eighth Avenue had grown into a gay Mecca that was flamboyantly referred to with an array of monikers from "Homo Mile" to "Swish Central." And there was always a dizzying selection of guys to look at—coming and going from the gym, the office, their apartments, walking dogs, carrying bags, talking on cell phones. Chelsea boys. Muscle clones. Gym bunnies. Of course the best-looking guys were always speaking to the other best-looking guys, stylishly dressed, even as the weather became colder and jackets and scarves only fetishized their muscled body mass. I felt both an outsider and a voyeur, trying to overhear little snippets of their conversations to see if I understood their lives and could appropriate their attractiveness. What I heard always had to do with desire and was infused with a campy irony I strained to understand myself—"Well, have you seen her *since*?" or "Pink was *def*-initely not her color." And I could witness lust shift from eye to eye, from man to man—one guy crossing the street could eye another and immediately change his course, but I found it hard to do it myself—that complex bravado required to meet a stranger's stare and follow through with a hook-up; instead, I would never let my own interest linger, always bashfully deflecting my eyes, always wondering how to make the next move.

My brother's apartment building was its own microcosm of this mischievous community. The Chelsea Rose—nicknamed by its tenants "The Chelsea Ho"—had been built in the mid-1950s, the pink stone bricks shipped in from Pennsylvania via the new turnpike, and rumor had it—according to Pup's neighbors Eric and Sean—the leasing company had given a young, closeted real estate agent the task of renting out the new apartments, and bachelor after bachelor signed lease after lease. Over the years, these "professional men" morphed into disco bunnies and the like, and there had been as many legendary stories associated with the building as with the Chelsea Hotel, a few blocks uptown, though not quite driven by that location's star power and glitz. The Chelsea Ho was home to the more practical and playful. Sean particularly loved to tell the story of a man who one night picked up a hustler and threw him out of his apartment minutes later and the young man then went door to door, floor to floor, telling the other tenants that he was "John's roommate" on "the floor above" and he had "lost his keys" and needed to borrow "five more bucks to pay the locksmith." According to Sean, tenant after tenant had readily contributed funds to help defray the boy's misfortune.

And it was a genuinely big-hearted place, with a congenial and collegiate atmosphere. My brother had been well regarded and there was always a guy ready to crush me with a hug as I waited in the lobby for the elevator to arrive. And there was a gathering rush to collectively mourn Pup, which happened one evening in Eric and Sean's apartment.

"I don't think any of us can wait years for closure on this," Martin had said to a crowd of about thirty of Pup's friends and neighbors one night in early October. Martin was Pup's age and had known him for more than seven years and lived in an apartment on the ground floor, so like Eric, he knew of most of the comings and goings of the building. The room fell silent as Martin toasted my brother. "And this is not closure, because Pup will always be in our hearts, and we don't know for certain what has happened to him. But we're here tonight because we need to come together as a collective community to express our outrage and sadness and at the same time celebrate a special guy who touched all of our lives and let the spirit of him—wherever that bad ass is floating and having a fucking good time—know that we miss him and wish him the continued joy he brought to all of us."

One by one, friends lifted their glasses and added a comment or relayed an anecdote about my brother. It was maudlin and sentimental and funny and outrageous and it was hard for me not to be impressed and overwhelmed and depressed by the experiences because I was aware that I knew so little of Pup and here were more pieces for me to place into a box and carry and shift and try to find its complete picture. Martin told an anecdote about Pup mooning a police officer from a bus in Acapulco, and Eric said he never knew a guy who had so many ex-exes, which meant he wasn't serious about dating, only more serious about continuing with the sex. Wayne told about Pup being a volunteer at the finish line of the Gay Games marathon and slowing down a few of the racers with offers of his phone number. "He thought that would make them want to finish faster," Wayne laughed. "But it made them stop dead in their tracks because everyone wanted to know Pup!"

I tried to stay on the outer rims of the conversations, but his friends drew me into *their* family bonds with my brother, telling me how proud they were to be a marshal beside him in the Pride Parade or how much fun they had together driving down to Rehoboth and singing show tunes at the top of their lungs. I smiled and nodded, knowing I smiled and nodded as my brother had done with them, laughed in the same voice and pitch, and fretted over the same honesty and disclosure as he had—the fact that I would not be able to relay any of the ribald tales of my brother to my parents and would now possess more hidden history about Pup that I could not explain.

My parents had resigned themselves to the diminishing facts of Philip as well. They had called me one night, late, saying that there had been friends over from the church and that the minister had stopped by, and I knew that this must have acted as a wake for them, their way of expressing their own joy and sorrow and saying good-bye to my brother. My parents had no desire to come to Manhattan and try to make their way to the smoking rubble downtown or navigate the bureaucratic nightmare it had created, and the possibility that Philip would emerge from the debris was so unlikely now that we were more focused on whether any remains of him might be found at all. The officials working the scene had released little identification of any of the victims to their relatives—tests would take months they said; items were being carted from downtown to a site somewhere in New Jersey or on Long Island. I made trips to the Family Assistance Center looking for news of Philip, first to the Armory, and then when it was relocated to the Hudson River pier. I stood in line with plastic bags holding Philip's toothbrush and combs. I had my mouth swabbed for DNA and handed out flyers with Philip's photograph to anyone who would take one, usually some woman who wanted only to hug another person and cry. I could not bear to have such grief heaped upon me when all I wanted was news and facts. And I did not move with much hope. Philip had worked on the eighty-first floor of the South Tower, within the impact zone of the hijacked Flight 175 that had been headed from Boston to Los Angeles. By the middle of the second week, when I had made my way to a hotel on Forty-second Street to get into a meeting for victims' families that my father had heard about, I desperately wanted a closure to all this, to be able to know and accept Philip's death so that my family could move on with our grieving and healing. And I wanted to get on with my own life. But there was still more to do, and Philip's life—or death—kept mandating the direction of my own life. I returned to the pier to apply for his death certificate, only to find the expedited process required more waiting and waiting and waiting, and I would arrive back at Philip's apartment frustrated, finding flowers left by the door by a neighbor or a casserole dish with a note taped to the tinfoil that read, "For later."

I don't know how I made it through some days, the depression consuming me, the fact that my life had stopped as my brother's had, that I was treading water about my own uncertainty. Law school was no longer an option—I had given up on that because my full-time job had become to find out all I could about Pup. but at the back of my mind there were the thoughts—*What's next for me, what should I do when all this is over? Do I stay here? Do I look to find myself elsewhere?* Some days I felt that I held my brother's body on my shoulders, trying to drag myself into the bathroom with his extra weight, trying to carry him out of the apartment and into the city, down into the subway with him still on my shoulders, waiting in line to fill out another form or speak to another counselor. Complicating all this was the fact that Philip's friends had readily accepted me as a gay man in a way I had not accepted myself. They asked me if I was dating someone, what

clubs I went to in Philadelphia, what I did in my free time. *Free time?*
I wanted to cry out, *I don't know, I don't know anything about free
time—or about being gay.* No one ever gave me an instruction manual
on how to be an openly gay man and not feel mysterious or ashamed
about it—because the truth of the matter was, no matter how open
and out and active and happy my brother was in Manhattan, he was
not that way in our home in St. Louis. He was a gay man who had
to leave home to find himself, not a gay man who had found himself
within his own home. And once again, I was just like him.

As time passed and hours became days and days became weeks and
weeks could be clumped into a month, I began to get the sense that
everyone—friends, tenants, neighbors, co-workers—wanted to put
this awful, irrational tragedy behind them, not just Pup's death, but
the paralysis that had afflicted the city. By mid-October I could sense
the desire of the other tenants in the Chelsea Rose to return to their
normal, urban, harried lives, their lives before the terrorist attacks,
and I was aware of them drawing away from me. Now, waiting for
the elevator, I noticed neighbors lingering longer at the mailboxes,
excusing themselves to run back outside to do another errand instead
of acknowledging my persistent grief and commiserating with me
over the loss of my brother.

I handled it all stoically. Somehow I had convinced myself that
I was destined to go through my life as a single, solitary unit. A
boyfriend seemed both impossible and improbable. And then one
afternoon as I was walking up Eighth Avenue from the subway exit, I
heard a voice yell out in my direction, "Pup! Pup?"

I turned and saw on the west side of the block a large, bald
muscular man in a white T-shirt and jeans wave at me and cross
against the traffic. "Pup!" he yelled again at me as he drew closer,
then, as he came within a few steps said, "Sorry, I thought you were
someone else."

He had a familiar look to him—sort of like the giant guy in the Mister Clean television commercials except with more piercings and tattoos—his left arm was full of a colorful, swirling design that traveled down to his wrist. I recognized him as one of the guys in the photos on my brother's refrigerator. He looked at me again and then said, "You know him? Have you seen him? He hasn't been calling me back. You know Pup?"

I tried to say that he was my brother, but the man, so large and intimidating, drew in closer and stared at me, so that all I can remember saying is "Yes," and deflecting my eyes to the ground.

"Oh god, no," he said with a horrific sob in his voice. "You're the brother, aren't you? Where's Pup? What happened to Pup?"

I looked up off the ground and met his eyes and in that moment, he understood why Pup had not called him back. He reached out his hands and framed my face with them, sobbing louder as his face compressed in anguish, "Oh god, no, no, *no*. It's not possible. Tell me it isn't possible."

He took my face and pushed it against his chest, his arms wrapping tightly around me as if I were going to flee at any moment, and I heard and felt the sobs pushing from his gut to his throat. He was a solid frame of muscle and sweat and tears and hysteria and I knew that he was creating a scene—a dramatic but honest one—and that passersby were stopping and giving us consideration. I maneuvered us out of the middle of the sidewalk so that the large man was pressed against the brick wall of a building, and I slowly extricated myself as he covered his face with his hands and continued to sob. He kept this up for a few minutes, and I stood awkwardly in front of him, bending down to whisper over his giant back and into his ear, "It's okay. It's okay. Do you need something? Should I call someone? Water? You need water?"

He finally straightened his posture—he was a good eight inches taller than I was—used his fingers to dig away the tears in his eyes, and said, "I gotta go." His hand clutched my shoulder and gave it a squeeze, and without any other regard he turned and began jogging away from me. I was still in a state of shock from having been caught up in such an immediate tornado of grief, and I leaned against the building and tried to calm my breathing. I continued to catch stares, but fewer and fewer of them as people who had not witnessed the exchange began to replace those who had hurried away from it.

The following day, the man was sitting on the flat rise of bricks outside the Chelsea Rose. When he noticed me approaching, he stood up immediately and I saw that he had a large unwieldy bouquet of sunflowers in his hands.

"Listen, I'm sorry about yesterday," he said and held out the flowers towards me. His voice was deep and raspy, as if he had just been at a football game yelling and smoking a pack of cigarettes. As I took the overlarge flowers from his extended arm he began to sob and rub his fingers at his eyes to stop his tears. "He meant so much to me. I loved him. I loved him like my brother."

He began to openly sob again and he sat back down on the brick stoop and covered his face with his hands and cried. If I hadn't been so caught up in the drama I would have laughed at how absurd he looked, this huge muscular man crying on the sidewalk.

I was saved by Sean exiting the building. "Chris," he said when he saw the sobbing giant at my side. "Eric has been trying to reach you for weeks. Where are you living now? No one has been able to find you."

"Me?" he looked up at Sean and gave him a weary smile. "I'm always a mess, you know that."

"Your cell phone number is *de-listed*," Sean said. "How can we reach you if you don't stay in touch with us?"

"This is not my fault," he said.

"And no one is blaming you. We're as upset as you are. We thought you were missing too."

"I was in L.A. on a shoot and everything got fucked up. It was canceled, I couldn't get back, then I didn't have the money, then the shoot was on again, then it was off."

"Where are you staying?"

"With Bruce."

"Again? That can't be good for you."

"He told me about Pup. I didn't believe him. What am I going to do?"

"What we all do. We grieve. We build up our lives again, piece by piece. Just like Teddy is doing *now.*"

"Teddy?" he asked.

"This is Teddy," Sean answered, tapping my shoulder. "Pup's brother."

"I'm Chris," the man said and dug his fingers again into his eyes. "I loved your brother, man. Your brother was a god to me."

Chris followed me upstairs to Pup's apartment, crowding into the elevator and towering over me as we began our rocking ascent to the fourth floor. He wanted to know all the details I could tell him about what might have happened to Pup. "How do you know for sure?" he kept asking me over and over, squinting his eyes and flushing red. There wasn't much for me to say, except that Pup was lost and had not been found.

In the apartment he settled on the couch, but only as a butterfly would, or perhaps a giant Dalmatian, lightly perched as he asked me about guys from Pup's gym that I might have heard from. A few of the names were familiar to me, but others weren't, and after I shook my head once or twice too many times, he jumped up and sort of grumbled and went to the shelving unit where the TV was located and which framed most of the interior wall of the room. On the top shelf and close to the ceiling was a glass and metal hookah. It had a camel painted on the frosted glass and its dual hoses lent a sexual suggestiveness as it perched above the room. Chris easily lifted it off the shelf, saying as he did so, "You know we got this in Morocco this summer. Clever little thing."

He held it in front of his chest, his face reddening with frustration. I thought he would drop it to the floor and watch it smash, or worse, throw it against something and create a larger mess for me to clean up, but instead, he uprighted it, so that its snake-like tubes hung down like the tendrils of an octopus. He took the base of the glass unit and as he twisted it off I noticed that there was a large, square metal base below it. The glass unit was detached from the base and a hidden spring revealed that the square was a box. From the box he lifted out a plastic bag and I realized at once it was a hidden stash of marijuana. I was dumbfounded because for the weeks I had lived in the apartment and I had never known it was there, even with all my looking and snooping through Pup's stuff.

"You don't mind, do you?" he asked me with a raspy growl. "I can't think straight right now."

He settled the hookah and its boxy base on the floor and sat back down on the couch and opened the plastic bag. I was mesmerized as he rolled a joint in less than a minute, found a lighter in a wooden box that sat on the same shelving unit, and lit up.

"I bet he hardly even got to try this stuff," he said. He took a long, deep toke and reached the joint out for me to take.

I shook my head. As much as I wanted relief from all my misery and frustration, I still felt I needed to keep my wits around this guy.

"You look just like him, you know," he said. "Well not exactly, but close enough."

He took another toke and frowned. "This is gonna fuck me up big time," he said. He looked at me and added, "You can't let this fuck me up big time."

My expression must have belied my anxiety, because it seemed clear to me that I could not prevent this giant from doing anything, and then he squinted and began crying again, breathing in through his mouth and heaving his chest up and down in an overly dramatic fashion. It played itself out in a moment and as he wiped his eyes, he said again, "You know we got that in Morocco this summer," as he looked at the bong. "Damn, I'm gonna miss him, you know? He was like a brother to me."

He seemed to relax a bit after this, as if the pot had created a calming effect, and he asked me when I had arrived in the city. I gave him an abbreviated account of my adventure from Philadelphia to Hoboken, and he seemed to gather this all in, saying as an aside here and there, "Yeah, Bruce told me this," or "I could never have done that, you're a much smarter dude than I am," and I was glad when his cell phone rang and he dug his fist into his sweatpants and checked the caller ID. "Man, I don't have the energy for this," he said, and snapped the phone shut without taking the call.

He rose up off the sofa and replaced the hookah and its base on the top shelf and said he was hungry and asked if I wanted to order Thai food.

"Pup loved the spicy stuff," he said, "Massaman beef, curry crap, that kind of shit. I like the noodle stuff. Wet and slurpy and clears your sinuses pronto."

I followed him into the kitchen, where he opened the drawer where Philip kept all his take-out menus. He seemed dazed and shaky, as if the marijuana had had too strong an impact on his senses, and he stood wobbly in front of the refrigerator with the takeout menu in his hand, not looking at the menu, but at the photographs on the refrigerator door.

I leaned across him and pointed to a photograph of Pup with a darkly attractive, taller and younger man that was taped to a corner of the refrigerator. "Who is this?" I asked him. "I haven't met him."

"A friend," he answered. "Well, a sort of friend. Ari—this guy," and I looked at the dark, attractive man I had pointed out—"was one of Pup's boyfriends. Although Pup never had boyfriends, he had a long thing going with Ari. You should never try to box a guy in. Big mistake there."

He lifted a finger to the refrigerator door and moved it along the photos and settled at another one, where the dark-haired guy was beside

Chris and Pup and another man. "This is Jim," Chris said. "Ari's partner now. This was in Morocco. At the house we rented this summer."

I asked him about some of the other photographs, which he identified from a gay cruise to the Caribbean and a drive along the coast of California, and he settled into a short anecdote about another picture of the two of them in front of a tiny pagoda, when Pup had gone to Tokyo on a business trip and Chris had tagged along. "It was the hardest place to find someone to play with," he said. "Coffee was twenty bucks a cup at the hotel, and no one would look you in the eye. We finally met a prissy Australian dude who turned out to be hung like a horse and a real wild guy when it came down to having some fun." He seemed to get lost in the memory of it as he silently regarded the take-out menu which was still in his hand. Then after a bit, he said, "We should order. I'm starved."

I let him choose the items and place the order, and when it arrived at the apartment door almost a half hour later in the hands of an annoyed Mexican fellow, Chris was smoking another joint and mentioned he had left his wallet at Bruce's apartment, and I paid for the food and the tip.

As we ate at the table off to the side of the kitchen, he asked me, "You got someone special? Boyfriend? Buddy? Or a girl? You bi?"

I shook my head, hoping I indicated none of the above without having to explicitly detail my inexperience in all of those kind of relationships.

"I know some guys I can hook you up with. What are you into?"

"Into?"

"What kind of guys you like?"

When I hesitated, he asked, "Girls? You into girls?"

I became flustered at having this persistent, bold conversation with someone I barely knew, even though other friends of Pup's had also tried to pin me down in exactly this manner—and my experience with that should have at least given me some sort of glib and practiced answer. But I still fumbled at a response. "Eric knows a guy he wants me to meet," I said.

"Eric? You mean he wants to fix you up? On a date?"

I nodded. The curry sauce Chris had picked out was making my sinuses run and I excused myself to turn away from him and blow my nose.

"I like Eric," Chris said. "Good guy. Been nice to me. But some of his friends are real losers. They're all so serious. You should come out and party with me some night. You'd have lots of fun."

"Where?"

"All over the place. There's this thing happening uptown tomorrow night. Guy from the East Side I know is putting it together. Getting a DJ and everything."

When I didn't eagerly jump in and say that I wanted to tag along, he said, "What gym you go to?"

"I haven't joined any."

"Why not use Pup's?"

"A lot of his... stuff was lost," I said. "It didn't seem right."

His cell phone rang again and he pushed himself away from the table to dig into his sweatpants and check the caller. This call he took, saying, "Hey!... Yeah!... I could do that in about a half hour."

When he hung up he told me it was a client, though I did not ask him what services he provided because I already had an idea of them. He swept some of the plastic utensils and sauce packets into the plastic bag and said, "I'll give you a call. We can do the gym together. I can introduce you to some guys. I'd know they'd have a lot of fun with you."

At the door, he surrounded me with a hug and kissed me somewhere in my hair, and in the hallway I waved good-bye to him, thinking he might not be the dim-witted muscular giant he seemed to be as he took the interior stairs down to the lobby, instead of waiting for the lethargic elevator to arrive.

Six

And then I was caught up in the whirlwind of Chris. I didn't hear from him the following day, but the day after that he phoned me early and suggested I meet him at the gym a few blocks away. It was a gray, chilly day and I had nothing else I wanted to do. He had secured a pass for us through a "friend of a friend," and I followed him from the lobby to the changing room, peppering him with questions about Pup—I had had time to think up plenty for him.

"Were you dating him?" I asked.

"Dating?" he answered and screwed up his face, as if he were trying to translate the word into another language. "No, wouldn't call it that."

"Why did you do so much together? Were you lovers?"

"I told you Pup never liked labels."

"Partners? Boyfriends?"

"He wasn't that sort of guy."

"What kind of guy was he?"

"The smartest one I ever knew."

"Smart? In what way?"

He seemed annoyed with me for attempting to pin him down about my brother, and he asked another guy in the weight room if he would spot him doing bench presses. I left him and took the stairs to a set of stationary cycles that overlooked a running track and a basketball court. I did about three miles on the cycle, then went and worked through some exercise machines on another floor, but I did not find Chris in the weight room later, nor in the locker room, when I was ready to ask him more questions, and I knew I had blown the chance of making a friend—and I wondered why Chris had even asked me along. If I had not been my brother's brother, I would have had nothing in common with Chris.

I showered and when I was ready to leave the gym it was pouring rain. I had not brought an umbrella with me and I could have dashed the few blocks and gotten to the apartment soaked and changed into dry clothes, but instead I stood on the steps and under the eaves of the building and watched the rain come down, feeling thwarted and defeated. I had wanted Pup's friends to like me for who I was, not because I was his brother, and I had hoped the same of Chris and once again I had failed.

"Pup! Pup! There you are!" I heard someone behind me yelling.

It was Chris. I turned and said, with too much bitterness and anger, "I'm not my brother!"

I heard the annoyed tone flare through my voice and felt the frustration lodged in my throat, and I turned away from him and began to cry. It was a silent, wincing sort of whimper at first, as if I were ashamed to be caught displaying a resentful emotion, but the more the tears flew out of me the stronger and more gasping they became.

"Tad, Tad, dude, I'm sorry," he said, and he stood behind me as I continued to sob and patted my back.

After a minute I collected myself and apologized. "Everybody keeps mentioning how much I remind them of him, but I hardly even knew him. He was a rotten brother."

"You don't mean that, man."

"He didn't care."

"He did. Maybe he didn't show it, but he did."

"What did you hate about him? Tell me something you hated about him."

"I didn't hate him. I never hated him."

"No one ever hated him. Except me."

"He could be a grouch. Like you. If he didn't get his way."

"Did you ever get pissed off at him?"

"Yeah, sometimes. He could never be lazy. But he was the universe to me. He was the reason why I'm still here."

Chris was an any-drug addict and an alcoholic-sexaholic. "There's nothing I haven't done," he boasted at one twelve-step meeting I attended with him. "Or wouldn't do again. And if someone thinks there's something I haven't tried, well, I'm willing to try it. I have no will power 'cause I'm an easy fuck."

Chris was HIV-positive and said that his diagnosis fifteen years earlier hadn't been a turning point to better organize his life, as it had been for some men. "Man, it was the end," he said. "I took a bottle of something and woke up days later at St. Luke's. I didn't ever think it was a second chance for me. Hell, I was positive—and it was the worst thing that could happen and still be alive."

He'd met Pup when my brother was a buddy to one of Chris's ex-lovers during his final months battling AIDS. "Pup was a saint," Chris explained. "He'd arrive at Bill's apartment and wash dishes or change the IV bag or something like that. And he was a good listener. He would just sit and listen. And every guy who ever met him had the hots for him. And Pup hardly ever turned down a guy. He just hated them being needy and jealous because he was seeing someone else. I witnessed a few cat fights over him. There was one summer in Fire Island he was pissing off everyone in his house because he was sleeping with all of the guys."

And in the years that my brother had known him, Chris seemed to have moved from one vague job to the next. He had done some porn videos and worked as an escort from an ad that appeared in the back pages of the bar rags. Eric had used him as a body model for various ad campaigns for gay bars and party clients, and for a while Chris had been a personal trainer at an upscale East Side gym. He never had a permanent address—crashing with someone for a few months or a few nights, sometimes in Manhattan or Brooklyn, sometimes in West Hollywood or with a guy in the Castro in San Francisco, and I got a sense that Chris had always had family money to rely on to move about wherever he wanted to be, even though he always moaned that he was hard up for cash. At one point he had trained as a professional masseuse, using Philip as a guinea pig to practice on to pass the certification. "We'd always end up fooling around," Chris said. "Pup could have made a killing doing massage. He was always showing me what I was doing wrong."

Years ago Chris had struggled through bouts of illness—he'd gone through night sweats, pneumonia, blood transfusions, and at one point he intimated he was down to eight T-cells, which he had named after Snow White and the Seven Dwarfs, and he had been a part of a drug cooperative—he had gone to Mexico a few times to bring back drugs that were not available in the U.S.—"but I had to stop it," he told me at dinner one night. "I always got too fucked up when I went down there. It's amazing that I'm still alive after all the shit I've put my body through." But his drug connections, while supplying him with a steady supply of recreational drugs, which he freely admitted pimping to other guys on the club circuit—had also benefited him; he was one of the first test cases to use the drug-cocktail therapies that would turn around his health. "There was a gastroenterologist on the Upper East Side that everyone was going to. I was lucky that I had heard about the therapy before he had, so I was able to work out my own mix."

I never knew if anything Chris said was really the truth. He was an overcomplicated man who could often veer out of control. At another twelve-step meeting he admitted, "I'm powerless to change my life. I'm just a rushing river. One day I'll reach the sea and that will be the end of it."

He was always looking you in the eye as if challenging you to pay attention or ignore him. And he was fiercely strong in the strangest ways. "I almost used last night," he would say to me when he got me on the phone, and then launch into a tale of walking up Eighth Avenue to

Hell's Kitchen to score some crack from a dealer who worked outside an adult bookstore, only to decide to go inside the store and to find himself invited to a sex party in Harlem where there was some "deep fisting" going on. "Those dudes were really whacked out," he added. "You know, I just want to go to South Beach and lie on the sand and sweat and feel the breeze from the water. I'm really sick and tired of all this craziness."

He seldom asked anything about me, what I was feeling or who I had heard from about the terrorist attacks or what the city had told me about the identification of the remains of the victims, but he was able through a "friend of a friend who knows a firefighter" to get us access to a building that overlooked the work going on at Ground Zero, or "the pile," as I had often heard it referred to. One morning we took the subway as far downtown as it would go, made our way through security checkpoints with ease and into a building where we took an elevator to one of the top floors.

Chris left and I sat in front of a window and watched the cranes lift steel beams from the pile that had once been the two giant office towers, as men as small as ants looked into empty spaces while the debris floated to the back of a truck. I sat there thinking about how little I knew of the world—of finance, construction, security, relationships, health—how an engine works, what makes electricity run, how rain begins, why the body is allergic to some things and not others. There were other relatives of victims that day in front of the windows watching as well—the wives and mothers of firefighters and policemen who had responded to the first call, managers of a firm that had been housed on one of the lower floors, the brother of a street vendor who had been missing since the day of the attacks.

"They're not giving any of this to the press," I overheard one of the wives whisper to another. "They're not letting the guys from the station work the pile anymore."

This seemed to ignite a heated discussion between the two women, and, as I looked away from the window, I overheard a man in a business suit tell an older man, "We're not saying that there are no whole bodies to be found, but we don't expect to find many. Everything's decomposed. *Vaporized.*"

My parents did not want me to empty my brother's apartment until there was some concrete confirmation of Philip's death—and we'd arranged with the management company to continue the lease. The assets in Philip's bank accounts were able to cover the expenses—and once I had told my dad that I had no intention of returning to law school he had encouraged me to stay in Pup's place for a while until things found an order. But I was at a loss for something to do besides searching for Philip and waiting for more news to break. Some days my head would be burning with anger and indecision and I wanted nothing else but to escape as Chris had suggested, to throw it all to the wind and end up somewhere on a beach.

On the few nights that Chris was not involved with a "client" or out at a party, he tried to escape his craziness by showing up at Pup's apartment with an old movie he had found at the video store on Eighth Avenue. "Man, this is the wildest movie," he would say and load it into Pup's video machine. "Bette Davis's face looks like a road map in this," or "I'd never let Redford get away from me."

I understand now that those days when I was struggling to decide whether to remain in Manhattan and walk in my brother's shoes were my crash course in understanding and appreciating gay culture. And Chris was the mentor and guide that my brother had not been for me. I knew from my clandestine reading as a teenager about what a "tit clamp" and a "butt plug" were, but I didn't know what they felt like or what a "safe word" was, and I learned these from Chris—not directly, always, but through one of his rambling tales of being high on something and having sex with more than one guy at a time. I had never seen *The Way We Were* or *Pink Flamingos* or *The Boys in the Band*. As we watched those movies Chris would lie on my brother's couch and drape his arm on my leg or across my shoulder and fondle my crotch. I was startled and resistant the first time it happened, but he paused the videotape and rasped back at me, "We both need this, Tad," and I succumbed to the intensity he directed at giving me a blow job because in my mind by accepting it, it somehow made me feel more gay.

Sometimes Chris would stroke himself or allow me to jerk him off in return, though he wouldn't let me provide him with any oral reciprocation, something I was willing to try because I had had so little experience with it. "Dude, I'm a cesspool," Chris would say and push my head away from his lap and then bring himself to a climax, dry his fist off with his T-shirt, and we would continue with the movie. I had never been so freely and openly sexual with another man in this way—or even a woman for that matter—and some nights when Chris wasn't headed elsewhere he would fall asleep on the couch and find me in the bedroom later, awakening me as he settled his large body around my own.

In a very short space of time I got to know the feel and heat of him, understand the mood that he arrived with and what he expected or wanted, what he thought was funny or sexy or "just plain crap from the Republicans." I didn't know what to make of any of this at the time—or of anything else for that matter—and Chris would often remark, after rewinding the movie or as we were crossing Eighth Avenue to return the tape to the store, "Tad, we need to find you a good buddy to hang out with. You're too good to get stuck with a mess like me."

And then one morning—it was November—there was a videotape still left in the machine. Chris had not been around for several days. I had tried the cell phone number he had given me, but there was a message saying the customer was no longer using the service. I called Eric to see if he had heard from Chris, and when he said "No," he paused and said, "I can call Bruce, if you want me to. See if he knows where he is." Bruce was an on-again, off-again lover of Chris's whom I had never met but had heard things about, such as "Bruce loves this scene," or "Bruce would know that other movie he was in." And Eric knew that Chris had been spending time with me in Pup's apartment. A few minutes later Eric called back and said that Bruce had mentioned that Chris was in Palm Springs.

"Palm Springs?" I answered, shocked to find that he had left town without telling me.

"Something about a job or a client," Eric said, then, when I made no other remark, asked, "You need company?"

"No," I answered, gathering up my defenses. "He left a tape here a few days ago. It's probably overdue."

I tried to make some small talk, but I couldn't, I was too weak with depression, and when I hung up I went to lie on the couch. Later that night, when I was aware that I was going to be alone, I took the tape back to the store on Eighth Avenue. As I was dropping it back in the return bin, I noticed a sign taped on the door that said, "Help Wanted. Desk Clerk. See Manager."

I asked at the front counter for the manager and found that he was only in during the afternoons. I left my name and number about the clerk position and the next day I received a message on my cell phone asking me to drop by the store and fill out an application. I had forgotten about leaving my information and I decided that I didn't want the job, but late in the afternoon, after rising from a nap, I walked over to the store. Video Bang occupied a retail space shared by a card store and an adult novelty business of sex toys, lubricants, and X-rated reading material—magazines, calendars, and coffee-table books filled with the spectacular physiques of nude men. It was emblematic of a lot of other gay stores I would visit in years to come—selling items like rainbow flags and pride decals, Tom of Finland T-shirts, and a wide assortment of dildos within a haze of incense mingled with the scent of leather and rubber. There was a wall of dog-eared porn magazines—the new ones were for sale at the counter—and a case of cock rings and a rack of leatherwear. A portion of the video store was sectioned off with X-rated DVDs and tapes behind a short wall-like barrier that shielded the customers looking at the titles, and there were always more guys wandering in and out to check the latest releases than there were looking at a shelf of gift cards or teddy bears.

I found the manager in a room no bigger than a closet that was behind the cashier. There was a small desk, a computer, and shelves of videos and books and DVDs, all at lopsided angles and in piles, looking as if they would tumble over at any minute.

There was no chair in the office other than the one behind the desk, where the manager was seated—a tall, handsome man named Karl with a clean-cut military look. I had seen him in the store several times before when I had been there with Chris to pick out or drop off a tape. I filled out an application and when I stood in front of his desk, he looked at the application and told me I was overqualified for the job without meeting my eyes.

It occurred to me that I was obviously not his "type"—he had that sort of macho attitude that leathermen affect for only their own kind.

"I know," I said, "Sorry to take up your time," and as I turned to leave, he looked up from my application and asked me, "Are you any relation to Pup Bridges?"

"My brother," I answered.

"Where has he been?" the manager asked, suddenly brightening at the fact that I was related to Philip, or perhaps as if he were regarding me decked out in a harness and chaps. "I haven't seen Pup around here in weeks."

I was surprised that he had not heard about Philip and even though I had explained his absence many times and in many ways to many different people in many scenarios, it was never easy for me to release the news. "He worked in the Towers," I said and reached for the door to leave.

"Wait!" he said and stood, and asked, "Pup?"

I knew, of course, that the man must have been one of my brother's many admirers. His face turned a bright red and he said, "Stay, stay," and waved me back to where I had stood in front of his desk and he told me his full name and we shook hands.

I stood there in silence for a few minutes as he pretended to regard my application with deeper interest, but I knew he was looking for a way to absorb the news and ask me for more information about my brother and to maintain his cool regard of me. Finally, he said, with a weary sounding tone of someone who had done retail for far too long, "Can you do evenings? I need someone responsible here in the store till we close."

Seven

They planned eight days in New York working out of the news bureau office in Midtown. Jim felt the change when they arrived at the airport—a somberness tinged with anxiety about what might happen next. Ari was questioned at immigration though he possessed an American passport, explaining the purpose of his visit was dual—business and visiting family. There were problems with the luggage—a suitcase was lost—and Jim's cell phone coverage disappeared. Ari's cousin met him at the baggage claim. Jim headed into the city alone.

They intended to maintain separate schedules while not working together. Ari was staying with his family in Queens, Jim at a hotel near Penn Station. Jim had booked interviews with the director of the Met using another cameraman. Ari scheduled a management-training session with the Human Resources department of the network. Jim had a list of potential theater and gallery openings he could attend in the evenings, some possibly for an expanded arts coverage. Ari had agreed to meet with his uncle at the family's warehouse to go over inventory. They both were avoiding a dinner with Eric and Sean, until Ari called Eric and asked for details about Philip.

"Nothing new," Eric said. "Nothing has been recovered. His brother is here—staying in Pup's apartment. Why don't you and Jim come down and meet him? I can have you all over for dinner."

"It would be too awkward," Ari said.

"He's not Pup," Eric said.

"I don't want to put Jim into that position."

"Jim and Pup got along fine this summer, didn't they?"

"It's not them," Ari said. "It's us."

Eric called Jim for a better explanation.

"We're exploring alternatives," Jim explained.

"Does that mean you are ignoring your friends?" Eric asked.

"No," Jim answered. "I can see you whenever you want."

"Ari too?"

"I can't answer for him," Jim said. "He makes his own decisions."

In Queens, Ari was pampered as the prodigal son. His aunt cooked his favorite foods. His cousins listened in awe to his travel adventures but bragged about their girlfriends. He spoke to his uncle about the rug merchants and weavers he had visited and the import costs. But he also felt boxed in. He missed having Jim around. Abdul had always disregarded Ari's relationship with Jim. Ari's homosexuality was swept under the table. His uncle suggested it was time to consider marrying and raising a family.

"There is a daughter of one of my buyers who would be right for you," Abdul said. "She would keep a good home."

"I would not be a good husband," Ari answered, though he felt he already was, something he had fought time and time again to prove to Jim.

"Nonsense," Abdul said. "We did not raise you to say this."

Ari's mother echoed his uncle's desire to have Ari closer to the family. Ari slowly pushed the idea away. He offered to do a news piece on the family business—a clear conflict of interest he knew both Jim and Simon would notice. A story about importing goods from Muslim countries—what it now took to bring a rug from a small village in Afghanistan to the Queens showroom.

His uncle was flattered but did not want attention focused on the business at a politically sensitive time. He countered by asking Ari to become a buyer for the company—he could stay in Rome or manage the process from New York. Ari did not accept or reject, only thanked his uncle for the offer.

Jim had escaped his own family guilt when his father had refused to recognize his son was gay. "We didn't raise you to be like that," Jim's father said. Jim had believed that he had always been a good and ethical man—a man of both mistakes and generosity, something his father had not seen in him.

Home had always been an elusive concept ever since Jim left Virginia for college. He preferred to think of himself as a man with many friends and a lot of work to do, which had worked well until his roommate Frank blurred the lines.

Frank had been considerably older than Jim—twelve years his elder—and their entire relationship had been focused on Frank's battle with AIDS. They had lived in the building in Chelsea where Eric and Sean lived. Jim was conscious of his life breaking now into chapters. Before Frank. With Frank. After Frank. Before Ari. With Ari. And now the possibility of After Ari. "I don't regret any of it," he told Eric the night he met him for dinner. "But what do I do next?"

Jim had taken an afternoon off to meet with an agent who repped on-air talent for CNN and MSNBC. They lunched at a restaurant near Rockefeller Center. The agent, a fast-talking, overweight blonde woman, told Jim he was too old to start over as a beat reporter for an American outlet, but he could easily shift to another news agency in the European market because of his recognition factor. They discussed the possibility of him relocating to Paris or London and the goal of Jim becoming an anchor. Jim felt uneasy maneuvering behind Simon's back. He missed being able to complain to Ari about the ageist treatment he was receiving or seek his advice if this was the right move to make.

"Do you understand what you would be giving up?" Eric asked Jim. They were eating at one of the new restaurants in Chelsea, admiring the waiters and customers.

"It would be fewer hours," Jim said. "Better benefits."

"Not the job."

Jim looked away, unable to answer.

"And I'm not talking about the sex."

Jim took a deep breath, looking over Eric's shoulder at two young men at a nearby table, probably out on a first or second date. He was aware that he was both jealous and sad.

"To have that kind of closeness with someone," Eric added. "That kind of intimacy and history and understanding. You know how hard it is. You want to throw yourself out into the dating pool again?"

"Of course not," Jim answered. "But every relationship reaches a stage where it reinvents itself or plays out. I think we've reached the end."

"You *think* you've reached the end? What about Ari? Is that fair to him?"

Jim had always believed that his relationship with Ari would be short lived.

"I've broken up with Sean so many times in my mind," Eric said. "But in reality I could never do it."

"If you are unhappy," Jim said, "why stay?"

"He listens to me. I listen to him. He cares about me. I care about him. Do you know how hard that is to find? We're not two straight people with a desire to procreate and start a family. We're two gay men with issues and egos and complexities. We compromise."

"So you are saying that all this is my fault."

"No," Eric answered. "I'm saying listen to him. You still love him, don't you?"

Jim twisted the corner of his lip into a smile because he did. "Ari put you up to this, didn't he?"

"Of course," Eric answered. "He doesn't want it to end."

❖❖❖

"I admire your career," Ari told Jim the first day they met. It was the summer of 1997. They were eating lunch at an outdoor café on the Croisette in Cannes. Ari was twenty-eight and dressed in a striped blue-and-white T-shirt, the kind a gondolier in Venice might wear. It made him look extraordinarily handsome, or so Jim thought. He was twelve years older than Ari.

"My career?" Jim replied.

"Very heroic." Ari added.

"Heroic?"

"About who you are," Ari said.

Jim had a busy schedule while in Cannes. He had had to reschedule meeting Ari several times. He was only meeting with the young man as a favor to Eric. Later, Jim had an afternoon of screenings and interviews and that evening working a party—certainly nothing heroic in that.

"You've never shied away from talking about your life," Ari added. He deflected his gaze away from Jim, fumbling with a small camera which had been hanging by a strap against his chest.

"My life?" Jim answered, and laughed. He hoped he did not come across as condescending. "Not many people have been interested in *my* life. They've been more interested in telling me about *theirs*."

"You've always been open about who you are in your pieces."

"I have?"

"I read all the articles Eric had by you at his studio."

"Eric's a sentimentalist. He should have thrown those out long ago."

"True, he *is* a romantic," Ari said. "But those stories are historically valuable. They're about things people weren't talking about."

"A lot of people were talking about AIDS," Jim said. "It was all over the news. You couldn't escape it."

"But so many people were avoiding writing about gay men with AIDS. You humanized it in those interviews."

Jim deflected the compliment. It hadn't been a happy time to write about. He thought of Frank and became sensitive about his age and surviving. "Were you even born then?" he asked in a lightly bitter tone.

"It was a scary time," Ari said. "I was just coming out."

"It *was* a scary time," Jim added softly.

In the years since Frank's death, Jim had moved first to Athens, then to the bureau position in Rome. Seven years went by. He dated a few guys now and then, boyfriends who might last for a few weeks, an attempt at a relationship falling apart sooner or later because of Jim's work schedule or his need to leave to cover a story out of town. In fact, Jim was grateful for the solitude—it kept him focused on work and avoiding the heartbreak of another lopsided relationship.

Ari's relationships had also been insubstantial, a trick or perhaps a second date, but seldom a long-term affair, unless he counted Philip Bridges, the man who had moved into Jim's apartment when he left New York after Frank's death. Pup had only wanted a playmate, not a boyfriend, but after so many times together the lines began to blur—or at least they had to Ari.

They also had Eric in common. Eric—friend, mentor, guide, busybody, matchmaker. Ari had worked as Eric's photography assistant while he was still in college. Frank and Eric had been best friends long before Jim had moved to Manhattan.

"You shouldn't have any problem finding work," Jim said at lunch. "Eric said you were good. Lots of photography opportunities here. Do you speak French?"

"And Italian."

"That's right," Jim nodded. "Eric said you had a doctorate. A Ph.D. in..."

"European history."

Jim nodded. The young man seemed bright and intelligent and opinionated, but lacking the confidence or experience of an overeducated academic. There was a restlessness about him, as if he wanted to be somewhere else.

"So you can always teach. You have that to fall back on."

"I'm not ready to teach. And I do have a problem finding work."

"Why's that?"

"I'm too outspoken."

"So be an activist," Jim suggested.

"People don't hire activists," Ari added.

"No," Jim answered. "But they do find them interesting."

It was impossible to avoid even the slightest news update on the missing, or the grieving, or the impacted, or the shocked and appalled and angry. And it was impossible to avoid Ground Zero. They did exactly what Simon had told them not to do—taping an emotional segment at the smoldering downtown scar. Ari's cousin knew the brother of a firefighter. They suddenly had access to the towering mounds of steel, replaying the tragedy before an audience. Jim, standing in front of the debris, looking at Ari behind the camera, thinking how silly their own feud was when placed against this bigger picture.

Anyone willing to be interviewed spoke first of where they were when the planes hit and how they heard the news.

"I heard a loud thump when I got out of the shower," one restaurant worker in Little Italy said to Jim. "I just thought it was everyday traffic. Then the sirens began. And never stopped."

Jim reported on the international efforts to locate the missing— British and Italian citizens lost in the collapse of the Towers. It had been Ari's idea. Ari had searched for details on Philip Bridges and his firm since the day they had arrived in Manhattan, though he had avoided reaching out to contact Pup's brother or family. Ari also co-produced a segment on relief services available for displaced workers and survivors. When Ari had brunch with Eric and Sean on the weekend before he was to return to Rome, he asked about Pup's family—how they were handling the news that he was missing and presumed dead.

"His brother has been here since September 11th," Sean said. "Trying to piece together Pup's life."

"That can't be easy," Ari said.

"You should meet him," Eric said. "Help him understand a little better what kind of guy Pup was. I daresay Chris has left a good impression."

"Chris? Chris Radnor?"

"He roared into town to grieve—just like you—and then left. He charmed Teddy the way Pup charmed others."

"That's so not like Chris."

"Charm is probably the wrong word to use," Eric added. "Harmed is more appropriate."

"Teddy is young," Sean added. "He doesn't have Pup's cockiness."

"All the more reason for me not to meet him," Ari added.

"Why is that?" Eric asked.

"It would be something else that Jim would hold against me."

"Jim's not that kind of guy," Sean said. "You know that better than any of us."

"What happened this summer with you and Pup?" Eric asked.

"Nothing," Ari answered. "It was a visit. We met him in Tangier for a weekend. With Chris."

"And nothing happened?"

"I didn't say that. I just said it was a visit."

Eight days after their arrival in New York, Jim was at the international terminal at Kennedy airport waiting for his flight to Gatwick. He had finished a short visit in Virigina with his mother and sister and was traveling alone to London, where he was going to do a story about a British dance troupe that had cancelled and then reinstated their international tour. Ari was flying directly to Rome the next day. Jim would use a cameraman from the London bureau to do the piece. They had not spoken to each other since Jim left Manhattan impulsively to visit his family.

Jim's cell phone rang and he immediately hoped it was Ari. Instead, it was Abdul Ramati, Ari's uncle.

"I'm disappointed in you," Abdul said.

Jim recognized the voice. He had spoken often with Ari's uncle at the bureau or at the apartment—often relaying messages to Ari when he refused to be drawn to the phone. "How is that?" Jim asked.

"You left without visiting us."

The last time Jim had spent time with Ari's uncle was seven months before, an uncomfortable business dinner in Rome with Abdul and two of his carpet suppliers and their spouses. Jim had been invited, but only if he and Ari arrived with "beards"—female companions who could mask their homosexuality and their relationship from Abdul's clients. Jim had refused the invitation. Abdul would not take no as an answer. He insisted Jim and Ari attend—and agreed they could come without dates. He introduced the couple at dinner as "business partners on an assignment in 'bella Roma.'"

Jim was a familiar face to Abdul's Italian and German clients—his news pieces were broadcast into their homes and discussed in their offices. They had watched his recent interview with an Italian actress hoping to run for political office, an idea the men found as ridiculous as their wives found it encouraging. Jim gave Ari credit on helping out with the segment, describing the special lighting and make-up arrangements the aging actress-politician had demanded. "Ari knew her movies better than I did," Jim told the dinner guests. "But I remembered a gown she had worn at the Venice Film Festival. She figured the two of us out before we even started the interview. I think that's why it came out as good as it did."

Abdul had been displeased by Jim's tale and the not-too-subtle reference to his relationship with Ari. Even Ari was surprised by Jim's admission, but knew it had a lot to do with his uncle's insistence on masking Ari's relationship with Jim. Jim's activist instinct had been a defensive counter. Ari had remained uncharacteristically quiet that evening, in deference to his uncle. And this had annoyed Jim.

"I had a busy schedule this time and wanted to make sure Ari could spend more time with his family," Jim said to Abdul. He was suddenly uncomfortable, sweating; the terminal was stuffy and overcrowded. He looked at the ticket counter, hoping his flight would start boarding and he could avoid this conversation.

"We think of you as family, too," Abdul said. "You've been a good influence on Ari. We're counting on you to keep him grounded. If that boy had wings, he would fly."

"So he's told you, too?"

"I might understand if he wanted to fight. Fight in a war for a good cause. Independence. Justice. Freedom. But to experience it? Just to cover it? See it? Talk about it? Analyze it? Doesn't make sense to me."

"I don't understand it all myself," Jim said. "But I do know what it's like to want to change. I've been there. It happens."

"I know it happens. And I know he won't stop till he gets an assignment to cover the war. Watch his back for us. For me. You're his family. And that makes you ours. He needs you now more than ever."

Back in Rome, they settled into an expectant relationship—each maintaining a non-combative stance, waiting for something to happen that would set them on a different course. They worked on news pieces together and separately, kept separate personal schedules that only converged in the evenings to share a bed. Both men looked at ads for new apartments and new jobs and battled the depression of inertia or change. Stupidity and resentment made frequent visits. Ari ate out most evenings; Jim had a cocktail or two after work at a neighborhood bar. Sometimes, after the sheer exhaustion and anxiety of avoiding each other, an unexpected comment—or the brush of a hand across a shoulder or the small of the back—would send them tumbling into each other, pants tugged down, shirts lifted, lips forced apart by tongues. Loving each other was expressed through physical proof. Disgusted and pleased by their need for each other, they would briefly fall into their familiar loving routines—lying on the sofa together to watch a movie—or into an argument about discrimination or poverty or unfair legislation.

In early March, Jim flew to London. The New York agent had arranged an interview with the BBC for a European anchor position. The following week, an offer was made. Jim approached Simon about a counteroffer from the IBN—an anchor position—something steady, stable, and without travel.

"Does Ari know about this?" Simon asked.

"Not yet," Jim answered, and added that he was trying to keep Ari out of the equation.

"You wouldn't leave Ari. You'd both be devastated. You can't be serious."

"The position was offered to me," Jim said. "Not to us. I would have to leave him. Whether it would be a temporary or permanent break for us is still up in the air."

An hour later Simon arrived at Jim's desk with an assignment for Afghanistan. Jim would report on the humanitarian response. He would be traveling with a French team from UNESCO. The report would be about airdrops of food and supplies to isolated regions or those hurt most by the war.

"This isn't the solution," Jim said. He had been deliberating how to tell Ari about the offer from London.

"It's high profile," Simon answered. "The network would promo it. And you."

"What are the logistics?"

"Fly to Kyrgyzstan, then south with the UNESCO team," Simon explained. "You'd have escorts and translators the whole way. There would be other journalists and other networks involved. You'd have access to the military but only with certain personnel and in certain zones. You'd have some time in Kabul to report the rebuilding efforts there. Then back. It's strictly a charity report. Nothing about any military actions. Everything safe as it can be. I can give you a week or longer if you want. Two weeks, tops. You can opt to stay a little longer if there is something special you want to cover that's non-military. The UN will get you out when you're ready."

"Who would shoot the footage?"

"You've got your pick of talent. We just have to clear credentials."

"You're not setting me up?"

"Nope. You were *requested* on this one. The timing is just coincidental. Your call on the cameraman."

"He's got the languages—French. Italian. That does help."

"You want to tell him?"

"Seven days," Jim said. "I want it all mapped out. No detours. Let him think it was your idea."

Eight

On the third morning Barâdar woke with the men and joined them in their prayers. He knelt on the carpet and closed his eyes, trying to remember something of his past. Words and phrases came to him: "*Béni celui qui s'est tourné vers Toi et s'est hâté d'atteindre l'Etoile du matin des lumières de ta face,*" and "*Béni celui dont toutes les affections se sont tournées vers l'Aube de ta révélation et la Source de ton inspiration.*" These did not match the prayers of his hosts. He did not belong in Bamiyan. Or Afghanistan.

He left the cave with Roonah, carrying down the slopes a battered tin bucket and empty plastic bottles to fill with water. His feet were more comfortable in the boots without the thick socks. His headache was gone, replaced by a dull cloud that sat at the front of his skull. At the stream, he went northward, away from where Roonah and the other women who lived in the cliffside caves were hunched over their buckets, washing clothes by pounding and kneading them against the rocks as if they were wet dough.

He squatted and balanced himself on a rock, tapping the cold water against his face. *Béni celui qui s'est tourné vers Toi et s'est hâté d'atteindre l'Etoile du matin des lumières de ta face.*

He did this several times, until his skin adjusted to the temperature of the water, each time lifting more water against his face, which he wiped dry against the sleeve of his tunic. Phrases of other prayers—he was sure they were prayers—came into his mind. *God sufficeth all things above all things, and nothing in the heavens or the earth but*

God sufficeth. He filled the tin bucket and carried it out of sight of the women, removed his tunic, smelled his rank skin, and washed his chest and armpits.

He returned to the river for another bucket of water. The giant cliffs hung over him. He felt small and unimportant: *Thou art the Remover of every anguish and the Dispeller of every affliction.* English. These were *English* prayers. He had a knowledge of both languages. Could he be an American? Or was he French?

He used more cold water to clean his groin and ass, hopping and squirming because of the icy water, thinking, *My God! How did I ever get to this?*, knowing that in his other life, the forgotten one with the prayers, he had not had to manage as he was doing now. *There was a toilet. And a shower. And soap.* He was a foreigner. That was certain. A fact.

Back at the cave he tried to help Roonah stack twigs, but she waved him away. He slept some more, woke, and ate a small bowl of daal. He studied the view, trying to solve his mystery and grew frustrated. "Mamère," he called Roonah. He gestured towards the village and said in French, "Mamère. I will be back soon."

She shied away from him, briefly acknowledging him with a flustered wobble of her head. He went through a corridor of the caves and put on his boots. He climbed down the sloping staircase to the valley. Each time he did it it seemed paradoxically easier and longer, a journey to nowhere because at its conclusion he knew nothing more of himself.

At the base of the cliff was the burned-out shell of a tank. It was coated with dust. Rust circled the cannon and grew between the metal seams. He walked up to it and touched the site, trying to determine if the sun heated the metal. It was cold and hollow to his knocking. He wiped the rust against his pants and followed the path to the old village, nodding at the men who carried provisions towards the cliffs. In the village, many of the buildings were crisp shells of baked mud, gutted by fire or explosions. Charred stumps remained in a few; in others, the outer walls were pockmarked with holes and scars.

A boy rushed up to him as he approached an empty street of mud-brick buildings that led to the hospital, asking him in English for "money, money, for my mah-der," which he realized he understood. Barâdar held out his hands, palms up, to show he had nothing to give the boy. The boy followed him and persisted, then abruptly gave up.

The hospital was at the edge of the destroyed blocks, away from the new village that was being built by foreigners—military and non-governmental workers overseeing groups of local men.

Barâdar watched an elderly, bearded man speaking to someone through the pharmacy window. His hands were brown and dry and he used them with pleading gestures as he leaned into the building. Barâdar walked the length of the building to the back entrance through a gate. In the second-floor room where only days before he had been left to die he found Haatim rolling up a prayer carpet. There was a stuffy darkness to the room he had not remembered. Haatim was surprised and pleased to see him. Barâdar asked him, "Estella? Madame Estella?"

Haatim walked Barâdar down the stairs and out to the bright courtyard. He pointed to a door and patted Barâdar on the shoulder. Barâdar thanked him and shaded his eyes from the bright sun.

Through the door was a hallway which led him to a large room where Barâdar found Estelle seated at a makeshift desk. There were three other desks, a dented filing cabinet, a small bookshelf, and a computer, with cables running through a window. She greeted him as Haatim had, with surprise and pleasure. There was a small stove in one corner of the room with a row of kettles. On a shelf was an assortment of cups. In French, Barâdar asked Estelle, "Please tell me again where I am."

She took him to a yellowed map that was pinned into place on the wall. She flattened out a curl in the lower left of the map, then pointed to a spot at its center and said, "Bamiyan. Valley of the Gods." She explained the borders of the country of Afghanistan. "What is now Afghanistan is a network of passes between China and central Asia,

India and the west. The intermingling of cultures here in Bamiyan was bound to be extraordinary."

He became dizzy and nauseated. He stopped her while she was explaining the location of Pakistan. "*Médecine?*" he asked her. "*Quelque chose pour la diarrhée?*"

The journey from Anabah to Bagram roused and rocked Jim in and out of consciousness. Sedated and lying in the back of another van, he felt the vibrations of the engine and the dips and climbs of the wheels along the rocky, unpaved road. At the triage site at Bagram, a front gate medic classified him as a minor casualty, moved him to the hospital barracks, and scheduled him to be shipped out with the next more serious casualty that would require an emergency evacuation to Landstuhl Regional Medical Center in Germany.

Jim was asleep during the intake. Examining the chart clipped to the end of his bunk when he woke, he hobbled down the corridor of beds using his IV pole as a crutch, the pain in his left leg so unbearable he breathed through his mouth. "You can't do this without my permission," he yelled at an army specialist visiting another patient on the ward. He waved the clipboard in the air to catch the soldier's attention; even though Jim could not hear his voice, he kept it authoritative and self-confident, as if he were in front of a camera. "I could turn this into a legal matter. One violation after the next."

The specialist flickered his eyes around the room. He caught the attention of another soldier. Jim detected the alliance. He struggled for breath, turned and yelled at the other soldier, "I have to get in touch with the IBN. Simon Bosewall at the IBN in Rome."

The soldier, a private first class named Baxter, trotted down the aisle to block's Jim's progress. Jim saw that his disturbance had reached a male nurse in a corner of the room, who was scrambling to alert another soldier. The specialist was headed in Jim's direction. Jim knew he had to connect with someone; the only way he would be taken seriously was if he found an ally. "I've got to find my cameraman," he said to Baxter, a young man with a worried brow. The specialist tried to steer Jim back to his bunk, but Jim turned to the private and caught him by the wrist. He looked him in the eyes. "You understand that, don't you? You'd go back for your buddy. Tell me you wouldn't leave him to die if there was a way you knew you could save him."

They were what remained of an Imami Shia Muslim family that had lived on a farm four miles outside of the village. Their cattle were slaughtered when the Taliban seized control of the region. "So many lost," Haatim told Barâdar through Estelle. The Sunnis had driven them off their land, burned and destroyed their qala. Haatim's mother, father, and brother had been killed by the Taliban, shot in the first raid on the farm. Haatim and his wife's two uncles—Nadeem and Siraaj— had returned from the village to find what meager furnishings they had owned burning to ashes and the women in tears.

They were Hazaras, descendents of warriors of Genghis Khan. A second and third raid had led them to abandon their home. For three years they had lived in exile in the mountains, barely surviving on what rations they could locate. Haatim's wife had fled the house during the first Taliban raid, survived the massacre by hiding in a ditch. In the mountains she died in childbirth; her newborn daughter died not long afterwards. His wife's aunt, Roonah, had cobbled together meals to keep the family alive, melting snow for water and digging up roots to cook and leaves to chew on. When the Taliban were driven out of the valley, they had returned to Bamiyan to live in one of the hillside grottoes carved out of the sandstone cliffs by the monks centuries before. Four of them eating and sleeping in a cave the size of a cart. Nadeem and Siraaj found work helping NGO aid workers restore demolished buildings in the old village. Haatim was helping at the rehabilitated hospital, clearing debris, setting up equipment, saying prayers for the dying, training to be of assistance.

"An old proverb goes that if Allah wants to make a poor man happy he first makes him lose his donkey and then allows him to find it again," Haatim told Barâdar through Estelle's translation. "I have lost my wife and child and brother. Allah has brought you to me as a brother. Next he will give me a new wife and a child. There is a reason for all things and all things have a reason."

Barâdar could not remember his own family, whether he had a sister or brother, or if he had ever been married. He studied the faces of everyone he met at the hospital, looking for a key to unlock his past. Sometimes an image of a street or a block of stores would flash across his memory. A narrow alley. A flight of stairs. An elevator door that did not open. Sometimes a combination of feelings emerged that he could only partially deconstruct: trust and hurt, ambition and compromise, faith and confusion.

In the cave his eyes burned from the bright light that shone in through the large cliffside opening, ached from the strain of looking at dark walls in the dim light of the caves. He paid too much attention to some things and none at all to others. He used his fingers to massage his forehead and fold together into prayers.

"Who am I?" he asked the faint image that was still visible on a curve of the ceiling, a seated Buddha without a face, only the surrounding halos. "Where am I from? What am I doing here?"

Jim felt childish demanding so much attention. The private first class, Michael Baxter, a baby-faced soldier from Mississippi who had been in Afghanistan three months, contacted the press corps who were living on the base. Wade Quinlan, a tanned, chain-smoking reporter from the CBC based in Paris, had known Jim for several years, sharing junkets to Cannes and Venice early in his career until he could land hard news assignments with his bureau. He sat beside

Jim's bunk at the hospital barracks and advised Jim to get out of Afghanistan.

"This isn't your beat," Wade said, shouting at Jim to be understood. "Everyone is at odds."

On a pad of paper Wade wrote, "They only want good stories coming out of the war. Can you imagine that? It's been very sticky for some of the British press. We're all guests of the American military."

"Can you get me into the press tent?" Jim asked.

"Simon Bosewall wants you back in Rome."

Wade had e-mailed Jim's boss when he had heard that Jim had been admitted to the Bagram hospital.

"Had he heard anything of Ari?"

Wade shook his head. Simon wanted to keep Ari's disappearance under the radar, fearing if Ari was alive and kidnapped, he might be tortured or ransomed, and the network was trying to avoid Ari's disappearance from becoming news or escalating into an international crisis.

"I can't leave without finding Ari."

Wade had met Ari several times when he and Jim had covered the same events. He had tried to treat Ari with professional respect, though Ari had drawn a battle line between them. Wade had been married for twelve years, had two girls in junior high in Brampton, a suburb of Toronto, but had developed an affection for younger male companionship while away on assignment. Jim and Ari had drinks with Wade in Athens a year ago, shortly after Wade had spent a week's vacation in Naxos with a local boy he had taken up with, and Ari had called Wade out on the closeted, duplicitous life he was leading—both personally and professionally.

"It doesn't do anyone any good to live one life and hide another," Ari had argued. "It's hypocritical."

"Hypocritical or smart?" Wade had responded. "I'd lose my job if I lived my life the way you do."

"Then your employer needs to change," Ari said. "There are legal protections in place."

"It's not just my employer," Wade answered. "It's my beat—what I cover, what I report about. A gay man would not be given access to the information I am privy to from sources. I'd be considered a risk."

In the hospital ward, Wade shouted at Jim. "This isn't the place for you guys. You should get out of here as soon as possible."

Jim's eyes flickered around the barracks in alarm.

"Get me into the press camp," Jim said. "I'll file whatever happy story I have to."

"It won't be easy," Wade answered loudly. "There's a quarantine on base right now. Some kind of stomach bug hitting the barracks. Rumor is that even the SAS has been sequestered."

Jim reached out for Wade's pen and pad. "E-mail Ari's uncle, Abdul Ramati, at this address. Tell him Ari is missing. Ask him if he can help."

Barâdar wondered if he was a translator. Other foreign words came to him—*"vitello," "formaggio," "prego"*—which Estelle told him were Italian for "veal," "cheese," and "please." At the hospital, he studied his face in an old, cracked mirror, but he saw nothing of his past, only a confused man with a short, scraggly black beard. He couldn't see his mother or his father in his features. He wasn't even sure how old he was.

But he felt certain that someone would locate him. Someone from his past was trying to find him. He knew this instinctively. He was not alone. His father would be wondering about him. His mother would be worried. If they were alive. Were they? Someone would be concerned. A girlfriend? A wife? A boyfriend? A lover? He ran his thumb across the finger where a wedding band would be worn, but no memory came to the surface. A friend? A co-worker? Could I have been a translator? An engineer? An archeologist? A soldier, even? Someone must be thinking of him.

He had his photo taken and sent to UNESCO. He felt protected. Blessed. Each day he grew a little stronger. He napped on the floor of the hospital when Haatim had no chore for him to do or he sat and spoke with Estelle. He asked her what Norway was like.

"Cold and beautiful," she said. "In summer, the valley where I lived is beautiful, right out of a fairy tale."

Barâdar asked her about her family. Were her parents still alive? ("Heavens no, they died many years ago.") Was she married? ("Once, but he died long ago, too.") Any children? ("Two sons, both working for the government as engineers.") Did she still have a home in Nydalen? (Yes, she rented it out to her neighbor's daughter and her husband.)

"What does it look like?"

"Stucco painted yellow," she answered. "Warm yellow. The last time I went back it seemed so small. When you're here, in a place like Bamiyan, with such a giant blue sky draped above you, other places seem so tiny."

Barâdar tried to imagine a yellow house, but all he could find in his memory was the dull amber glow of a lampshade. This was followed by a beige blanket. Or a couch. Then a room of books, which is what he told Estelle.

"And outside?"

"Outside?"

"Through the window of the room. *Think*."

"A city."

"Paris?" she asked.

He did not respond to this, then asked. "Was the archeologist alone?"

"There was another Frenchman, badly wounded," she said. "They were taken to Kabul."

"Why Kabul?"

"Injuries," she said. "He'd lost a lot of blood. If he survived he must have lost his leg."

"What was his name?"

"There was no identification on him. He wasn't recognized. He was brought in through the clinic. MSF took him to Kabul as quickly as possible. Airlift was impossible. There was no one at the landing site that day. So they left that evening. Drove out of the valley in the dark."

Barâdar asked about the accident. Where it had been. What had happened.

"Were you with them?" she asked.

"I don't remember," he answered. "I don't know how I came here."

He asked Estelle about other accidents. Why hadn't the landmines been cleared? Why were the buildings in such bad condition?

She explained about the Taliban raids. The destruction of the Buddhas in the cliffs. The planes hitting the World Trade Towers in New York. The world response and presence of the U.S. military in Afghanistan. She told him of refugees who had been hiding out in the mountains.

"Why has there been no one here to help before this?" he asked.

"We are at the center of the world, but the hardest place to get to. In winter, it becomes even more difficult."

"But the landing strip. I saw a helicopter there yesterday. Can't aid be flown in?"

"Flown in, trucked in, we are doing what we can now that we can do something. Were you with the refugees? In the hills? Did you follow them into the village?" she asked. "Were you sent to help them?"

"I don't remember," he said again.

In the afternoon, he walked with Haatim to the new bazaar, built just below the plateau and a short distance from the area destroyed by the Taliban. Haatim stood inside a small stall, talking with men who approached him and described some sort of malady or pain that he or a relative had. Haatim distributed a pill to each of them from a knapsack that he had carried from the hospital. When an argument between two men began, Haatim waved them both away. Haatim and Barâdar left the stall and walked through the bazaar. Haatim used a pill to bargain for a sack of nuts and dried apricots and another pill for some dried meat.

The men circled to the rear of the bazaar, where a grid of streets and new homes was being built. Haatim talked and pointed at the buildings, chinned himself up and looked over a wall. He spoke to a young boy who was playing in a courtyard, then a woman spoke to him from the shadow of a window.

At the end of the street, they found Siraaj and Nadeem sitting against the wall of a building. The four of them greeted each other and took the path that led to the cliffs. The men draped their arms around Barâdar's shoulder, patted him on the back, and smiled their big toothless smiles for him. The men talked lively amongst themselves. Barâdar knew it was not an argument, but some kind of plan being hatched by Haatim, who seemed to be trying to convince his uncles of something.

Barâdar was coated in dust, which radiated from his clothing as he walked. His eyes were tired and dry. But he was happy, even if he was lost. He was surrounded by care. He had food, friends, people concerned about who he was. Each night that he returned to the cave he felt the joy of finding a family—Roonah smiling and taking his bundles of sticks or wool or bags of rice and offering him a small cup of food, Siraaj or Haatim pouring him tea or goat's milk, candles glowing and flickering in the breezes. They spoke to him in Hazaragi, taught him words and phrases, "*baaleh*," to mean "yes," "*mamnoon*," for "thank you," "*khoda hafez*" as "good-bye." He answered them in French, smiling and bowing politely with each lesson, responding with "*oui*," "*merci*," and "*au revoir*."

The next morning at the hospital Estelle offered Barâdar a ride to Kabul; two NGO workers were going for supplies and would be back in three days. In Kabul, Barâdar could visit the embassies and the Red Cross and the United Nations. He could ask for help in finding out who he was. He would always be in their care. He could stay in Kabul with the NGO workers or return to Bamiyan.

Barâdar refused the offer. He could not leave Bamiyan. The thought of being alone, uncertain and unidentified, worried him. He had no papers, no documentation, no passport, no nationality. What if he had done something wrong? What if he were arrested? What if he were wanted for a crime? Some day he might go, but not now. Kabul was too uncertain to him. It was best to remain here, where he had been lost, where he might be found. Here, in Bamiyan, there was work and food and a family to keep him company.

He told Estelle he was strong enough to work. He asked her about the archeologist who spoke French and who was excavating near the cliffs at the eastern end of the valley.

"Will the archeologist pay me?" he asked. "I must help out my family."

For two days Jim made bargains with God: *"Bring Ari back and I can live with the silence. Bring Ari back and I can go without walking. Lord, take away my sight, too, but keep Ari alive."* His hearing was gone. He could not move his right leg without pain. But his mind was healthy and alert. He could not stop replaying the accident. *Rackety-rackety-rackety-rackety.* He heard it over and over. *Rackety-rackety-rackety-rackety.*

On the third day, when Jim woke, he heard a whining noise in his left ear. It was the sound of the small engine of a fan. He stifled his pleasure, hoping this was not an answer from God that Ari was not coming back. That Ari was lost and alone, or dead somewhere in the middle of Afghanistan. That God had no intention of making a deal with him.

At the end of the week, Jim joined the press corps. He moved into a barracks on the other side of the camp. It had been seven days since the accident in Bamiyan. No reports had surfaced about Ari—no unidentified corpse, no personal items recovered. Every day that passed, the probability that Ari was alive diminished. Jim reread the report written by Stan Chartoff, the MSF worker who had driven him to Anabah. He contacted the Kabul hospital for Stan's whereabouts; surely this man would know something about Ari surviving the accident. The Red Cross in Kabul had no records on Stan, then finally a contact at the State Department e-mailed Simon that Stan had passed through the border and into Pakistan. Simon Bosewall's threats and contacts in London and Washington had come through. Simon wanted Jim to return to Rome immediately; the bureau's resources were limited. Jim refused to leave without Ari—proof that his partner was alive. Or dead.

They sniped and griped and complained and ranted through e-mails and staticky phone calls. Jim could stay at Bagram, on the condition that he was not to leave base and any news reports he would file must first be approved by the military. This was the bargain, the deal, the contract, and the exchange: no sensitive information disclosed, no operations endangered.

Simon refused to jeopardize Ari's chances by announcing on the broadcast that he was missing. No terrorists had contacted the news agency about a kidnapping or a ransom. Ari's family had remained silent. Abdul Ramati was no longer answering Jim's or Simon's e-mails after the initial period of alarm. With access to a laptop and a satellite phone with an amplifier, Jim contacted UNESCO, hoping to uncover more details on the accident and what had happened to Ari. Had the driver been located? The mustached man who worked with Dr. Dupray? Why did no one know who or where he was?

UNESCO had no record of the driver. Nor did the archeological society or Dupray's university. Nor was he part of Dr. Sajadi's team, Dupray's colleague who was working in Bamiyan.

With Simon's help, Jim made fliers that he distributed to any agency—government, civilian, or charity—working in Afghanistan, with the help of the other members of the press corps. At the center of the flyer was a photograph that had been on Jim's desk in Rome that Simon had scanned and e-mailed to him. It had been taken by Philip Bridges while Jim and Ari were visiting him in Morocco. Simon had cropped Jim out of the picture, enlarged and lightened the image of Ari. Jim explained the situation to every press corps personnel, sitting on the side of their bed, or desk, or hovering around their chair, begging that an e-mail be sent to this place or that person asking for information on Ari.

Jim's messages and e-mails to Abdul Ramati continued to go unanswered. He felt sure he was being blamed and punished. Blamed for seducing Ari. Punished for falling in love with him. Blamed for getting Ari his first news job as a cameraman. Punished for training him and agreeing to go with him to Afghanistan. Blamed for keeping him away from his family. Punished because of his disappearance. Blamed for all that would happen. Or punished for all that *had* happened.

Jim spoke to his sister on the phone, explained his plight in a sequence of gasps and words, why he wasn't leaving the country. His sister had met Ari once, had found him intimidating and unlikable. She had urged Jim to move back to Virginia. Their mother was worried. His ear burned and he had to stop the conversation because of the sharp pains that would not go away.

His alliance with Private Baxter grew stronger. Each morning Jim worked with Michael to rehabilitate his leg, sometimes taking a few steps without crutches, sometimes using them to hobble to the medical tent for a follow-up examination. The routine gave him a sense of purpose, the deep concentration could make him momentarily forget his more important mission, finding Ari. He had the young soldier help him distribute the flyers at the mess hall and talk to the drivers who brought supplies in and out of the buildings. Jim was conscious of his fluttery behavior in the presence of Michael—the clichéd racing heart and dizzy concentration. He was conscious of the boy's hands on his shoulders or beneath his armpits helping him balance. He was conscious of the pain which made him drape his own arms around Michael's shoulders for support, then privately, ironically with delight, drinking in the youthful smell of Michael's hair and skin.

Michael arranged for hearing tests—and a hearing aid for Jim's left ear. It hurt and pinched and irritated his skin, but Jim was able to isolate words and sounds better. Michael caught Jim up on the base gossip that Jim was too indifferent to follow on his own—the aborted press conference on Operation Anaconda, the arrival of the British Royal Marines hoping to force the Taliban out of Helmand, the *Daily Mirror* journalist being banned from the front lines.

They talked of other things, too, as new friends would, looking for things to keep them polite and connected to each other: the humidity of New Orleans, if okra was better fried or in gumbo, the rigors of basic training versus ineffective athletic requirements for a college degree. Jim saw fear in the young man's eyes. Michael seemed to have emerged out of the army's basic and specialist training without an allegiance to his corps or a buddy, becoming, instead, a free-floating do-gooder and angel of mercy.

One afternoon, while driving Jim back to the press tent, Michael said, "There was a bomb scare this morning at the front gate."

"Isn't it well patrolled?"

"Yes, sir, but there was a protest demonstration. About a hundred Afghan. It caused a bit of a disruption. There was a sort of panic reaction."

"Is it easy to get in and out?"

"What do you mean?"

"On and off the base."

"If you've got clearance."

"I have to get to Bamiyan."

"Sir, you can't get across base. You could never make it to Bamiyan on your own."

"Could I get an escort? A jeep? A driver? I just want to go back to see what happened."

"Sir, you don't have clearance to leave."

"Don't call me Sir," Jim said. "It makes me feel old."

"We have reports from there," Michael said. "No one has been located."

"How could I get clearance? Who do I need to contact?"

Michael rattled off a list of names. Jim wrote them down on a notepad. He would get Simon to pressure the politicians to pressure the military. He asked Michael if there was a way the young man could be reassigned from the hospital to the press corps to help him out with his reports. "I could put in a request, but that would take months."

"Who could I contact?"

"Sir, no disrespect, sir, but I was trained for triage."

"No disrespect, soldier," Jim answered. "But stop calling me Sir."

"Yes, sir. I mean, sir. Mr. MacTiernan."

"Jim. Please call me Jim."

Wade teased Jim about finding a new boyfriend to help him locate his old one. It was a light-hearted remark intended to dispel Jim's rising frustration over finding out nothing and not being mobile enough to leave the base and return to Bamiyan. Jim took the comment to heart and defended himself.

"He's a source," Jim said. "A friendly insider. I'm not doing anything unethical."

"Ari's going to be pretty pissed off when he finds out your tactics," Wade said. "And you're going to break this young man's heart."

Nine

I did not possess my brother's personality—his ease with people, his sexual curiosity, his focus on activism, his campiness or wanderlust. Philip was a joiner—in high school, Key Club; in college, Young Democrats for Change; in Manhattan, ACT UP and Queer Nation and Out Professionals and Gay & Lesbian Democrats. By the time he had graduated college he had been to Europe and Mexico on his own. By the time I arrived in Manhattan I did not believe I was yet a fully formed person, always stepping into a situation where I knew nothing and was required to react—Didn't I think Ellen was more courageous than funny? Was Larry King homophobic? Who knew the backstory on Russell Crowe? Chris had instilled a yearning in me to connect with another guy on an intimate one-to-one level—but I didn't know how or where to meet someone, was awkward on the two or three dates I had managed to accept because I knew so little of how to be a gay man with opinions and criticisms and likes and dislikes, didn't really know if I was a top or a bottom or "versatile" or understand the multiplicities of fetishes. I was intimidated at the gym, at gay bars, at the dinner parties Eric and Sean would invite me to where the barbs and quips about the newest this or that in the city would fly across the table. And I could not respond to questions on the aftermath of 9/11 without choking through an answer about how daunting everything was—from the randomness of when a subway train arrived at a station to an entrance of a public building being sealed off and being faced with a suspicious security check before it could be entered.

I was thankful for the night job at the video store—guys were never there to flirt with the clerk at the counter—I was invisible, an obstruction to walking out the door with an impulse selection or the reason why a specific title was not in the store. I was only a database, a hand moving along a shelf, swiping a credit card or counting out cash. But I was absorbing things—what movie was *fab-u-lous*, what actor was *hot*, what look was *in*. I studied the way guys groomed their hair and goatees, what colors they were wearing, what sort of bags were slung over their backs or what neckties or sneakers they wore, what kind of lube was the bestselling one and which was the most requested dildo. I worked the last two hours alone—Jack or Ian would lock up the novelty counters, though I could ring up whatever items a customer could still choose—magazines, condoms, cards and the like, and I would blush as personal items passed through my fingers to the scanner beside the register. A few minutes after midnight I would pull down the metal gate and lock it and walk up Eighth Avenue the few blocks to my brother's apartment building. There were always guys out on the street, clusters of them heading out to a bar, couples out on dates. I had discovered that the database at the store had a record of every movie a customer had ever rented, and at the end of my shift, from the list of my brother, who had been a long-time customer of the store, I would select a movie to take back to the apartment to watch, hoping there might be some new clue I might discover about who my brother had been. So far I had watched *Auntie Mame, Stagecoach, Midnight Cowboy, Lawrence of Arabia, Breakfast at Tiffany's, Annie Hall,* and *Maurice*—some of these I remembered seeing in my childhood and teenaged years, but I had never imbued them with the cultural significance that I found was so relevant to the gay men I was now meeting.

My father was not pleased with my new job or the aimlessness that suddenly seemed to have infected my life. In December I went home to spend the Christmas holidays, but it was a difficult trip—I seemed to remind my parents too strongly of my brother's passing and I could see the pain in my mother's expression every time I tried to explain the process for government assistance or city hearings. I couldn't help but feel as my brother might have felt, oddly disconnected and unable to express the direction his life had taken. My father urged me to catch up on law school—he had not spent four years of paying my way through college for me to end up as a video store clerk—but I was too far behind to go back and the economy had stalled and I was thankful I had a job, and I told him I had already emptied out my dorm room. My father no longer believed that New York was the right choice for me, and he suggested that I move home for a while to "help out your Mom," but I knew at this moment that home in St. Louis would be the worst place for me to be, a step backwards, even if I was only treading water right now in Manhattan to stay afloat. "Get out of that city," he said. "It's an unhappy place right now."

But I wasn't unhappy, even though I wasn't happy, and I had been welcomed into my community of neighbors even though I was struggling to define who I was myself. Eric had continued to show up at my door with questions and a creased forehead over my state of affairs and he was genuinely concerned about setting me on a right and proper, good gay path. He had a list of guys he thought I should meet—some for romantic possibilities, some because they were my brother's friends, some because they were "too funny to refuse," and others because he felt I "might learn something new." I e-mailed and chatted with them on the phone or online, but I continued to seal myself off from almost everything except for work and my neighbor Joe's cocker spaniel Inky, which I would walk in the afternoons or the evenings when Joe was out of town. I enjoyed having her follow me from room to room of the apartment, from the bed to the couch to the kitchen table, always looking at me ready and needy for a walk or a treat or a cuddle and a hug. I hated giving her back when Joe returned from wherever he was—it was all a blur to me—but I was also oddly thankful to be thrown back into solitude and loneliness and misery in hopes of trying to figure myself out once again.

It was early January when I made my way one afternoon to a hearing that my father wanted me to attend about compensation for victims and survivors. I had arrived late and the room was packed; attendees were seated on folding chairs in a hotel ballroom. I stood in the back of the room until I noticed an empty chair, then made my way to the aisle and squeezed my way down the row. I heard a few "uuhhhs" and "tcks" as I passed by those who were annoyed by my tardiness. *New Yorkers are never finished complaining*, I thought. *No one is on time, nothing is ever perfect to them.* The empty chair was between a woman with gray-streaked hair whose eyeglasses were held up by chains, and a young Latino guy wearing a rust-colored hunting jacket. I nodded apologies to both of them, settled in my chair and listened. I was aware of the attractiveness of the young Latino man—dark eyes, close-cropped hair, a tan complexion—but I didn't want to attempt a conversation and be hurled into a new tornado of grief. He shifted in his chair a few times as the hearing went on, rolling into a tight funnel the paper handout that had been given to everyone by a volunteer at the door. He left before the hearing ended—squeezing down the row and garnering as many moans and groans as I had.

At the end of the meeting, I noticed him at the back of the room and I was struck by how young he was—it occurred to me then that he might still be a teenager. As I headed towards the door I caught his eye while he was talking to a young woman I thought he was trying to pick up. We both nodded at each other and as I passed him he said, "Who'd ya lose?"

I paused and answered, "My brother. You?"

He nodded and said, "Sister."

The tide of the crowd pushed me along and away from him and out the door. On the sidewalk, I lingered for a moment, hoping he might follow behind and want to talk about something, but he didn't exit the building and I thought it was for the best and headed towards the subway entrance. *I didn't need the sympathy*, I thought, *and I've got nothing to give to someone else right now.*

I was lost in thought on the uptown platform when I realized he was standing beside me saying, "They just drown you in paperwork, man. Can't get anywhere. You?" He was my height but with a slimmer build and it was still hard to tell how young he was—there were no age lines on his face. He had a round smile that showed an even row of lower teeth and a plump lip that protruded slightly. He looked as if he were ready to lean in and kiss me, or perhaps it only seemed that way because it was hard for me to resist kissing him. There was also something troubling about him, a mischievous quality in the glint of his eyes and the tension of his smile, as if he were the kid in school who said, "Let's put a rocket in Mr. Eaton's seat and see it explode in his butt." That made him all the more endearing to me—and interesting—someone I wanted to know better because I was never the bad guy myself—and I wondered briefly if this was how my brother navigated his sexual urges. Look for something different, something remarkable in a guy, and you won't be disappointed.

Rico—that was his name—was headed uptown. We introduced ourselves and he told me his sister had gone for a job interview at the Marriott, the hotel located between the Towers, the morning of the terrorist attack, and hadn't returned home. "We had to piece it all together," he said. "No help from anyone. There's no compensation from the firm she was interviewing with, because she wasn't an employee, and the agency that sent her there, forget it, they want nothing to do with us. We might have to sue them."

I wasn't sure that he was gay, except for the intensity he seemed to direct at me—but that could have been from the connection to the terrorist attacks. I had little chance to talk about Philip. The train arrived and I had let the Fourteenth Street stop pass to have more time with him, trying to get the courage up to ask for his contact information and to see if he was as interested in me as I was in him. When I motioned to get off at Twenty-third Street, he said he would get off at the stop too; there was a card store he wanted to go to that sold great T-shirts. "Shit you can't find anywhere else," he said, and

I wondered if he was headed to Bang, where a small selection of "Chelsea Boy" shirts was located in the back of the store.

But this didn't appear to be the case. At Nineteenth Street, we shook hands. His grasp was eager and tight. I had casually mentioned that I worked at the video store a few blocks away and that my shift started in a half-hour. I knew that would put a damper on a quick hook-up with him if that was even in the mix of things and I was thankful the job could prevent that possibility. It wasn't what I wanted from him or any other guy for that matter. I wanted something more substantial, more fulfilling—to get to know the guy a little better before I jumped into the sack with him—and in that respect I believed I was different from my brother and a lot of other guys. I wanted a boyfriend. A lover. A partner. Not a fast trick or a one-night stand.

"Maybe we could hang out together some time," he said. "Network about agency crap and stuff."

"Sure," I answered and gave him an awkward smile, awkward because I wanted to write down my name and number and e-mail address on a piece of paper to give him but was still too intimidated by the task and uncertain how he would regard it. I had hoped that he would broker this issue first, and when he didn't, I added, "I'm at the store every evening, except Mondays and Tuesdays."

"Cool," he said and turned to leave. "Check you later."

I forgot about him, or, rather, I fantasized about him and then forgot about him. The sexual intensity between us made me uneasy and restless and I was glad when the next morning his strong grip on me had lessened. Instead, I once again assumed the identity of my brother, logging onto a chat room as ChelseaPup, seeing what guy wanted to "spank another silly," or hook up with "any guy who won't give me his bio." I tried to unhinge my brother's psyche—understand what this all meant to him—games? adult playtime? role playing? assuming another identity? I was now more comfortable—in a perverse way—that I was acting as someone else and not myself—or my brother. But it would all end in an uncomfortable tease, as the closer and closer someone came to wanting to get together or to hook up, the more readily I would disconnect the chat and masturbate in an effort to knock everything out of my head.

It was Saturday evening when Rico appeared in the video store, dressed in the same jeans and T-shirt and rusty brown hunting coat, with a knit cap on his head.

He startled me at the counter—I hadn't seen him in the store or approaching the register, and I looked around the aisles to see if he had come in with someone else, but he appeared to be alone. He seemed a bit out of it, wasted, looking for trouble, his eyes wide and glassy. He asked me if I had been to any of the clubs in the neighborhood. There was a bit of a snarl to his tone, as if he hadn't been to any either and wouldn't be caught dead in a place where guys danced together. "A couple," I answered. "But not really my scene."

I looked in his eyes to see if he was buzzed on something, but they were large and brown and it was impossible to tell from where I was standing. "You're probably a great dancer," he said. "Don't be so uptight."

Chris had also called me uptight and conservative. The one time I had gone with him to a sex club on West Twenty-ninth Street, a storefront room with blackened walls and a boarded up window, I had been unable to strip down to only my socks and shoes and left before I had paid the entry fee. I knew what I was walking into—I had certainly read enough accounts online of what to expect in a backroom and what would happen. But I had always had inhibitions in a locker room. I suppose I had always felt awkward in a room of nude guys. I had matured faster than most of my other classmates— by thirteen I was covered with dark hair on my arms and chest and groin and legs, and teased by the other kids because my voice was deepening and my face was succumbing to blasts of acne, and it had turned me into something of a loner, especially after my disastrous season on the football team. Rico's cocky, condescending attitude was a turn-off and whatever charm he might have possessed before, now slipped away from me. I wanted him to leave. He was messed up on something and I didn't want to babysit him or see him create trouble in the store. But since I wanted him to disappear, that only made *me* more interesting to *him.*

"Not uptight," I answered him calmly. "Just don't like to get fucked up, and then feel even more fucked up the next day."

"Yeah, bummer," he said. "Know what you mean." He looked around the store. It was moderately crowded for a Saturday evening, a lot of couples looking for something to watch together. Every now and then a hustler would canvass the store, lingering to meet one of the older gentlemen, but Rico didn't seem to have their savvy or clarity. Ian was at the other end of the store where the magazines, dildos, and leather goods were located and we were always within view of one another, in case there was any trouble in the store from a customer. I noticed Rico take Ian in, regard the merchandise, and turn back to me.

"Lot of shit in here," he said.

"Yeah," I nodded.

"Any good movies?"

"Lots."

"Cool."

He looked at me and then said, "Wanna watch a movie together?"

I knew that was code for, "Do you want to trick? Have sex together? Can I come back to your place and see what happens?"

"I'm on the clock for another three hours," I answered.

"Cool," he answered and looked at the watch on his wrist. I doubted that he had any sense of time. "I can come back," he said. "You pick out the movie?"

"What kind you want?"

"Surprise me," he answered and smiled.

"Sure," I answered.

I thought that once he left the store he would forget about me—he'd be looking to score some other drug, or guy, and I was just someone to flirt and tease and annoy within the haziness of his drugged state. He would probably stumble into a bar or a club and get drunk and pass out. And if he came back I knew I would only be an easy trick. My only concern—if he did come back—was whether it would be safe—whether I was a target to be mugged or robbed. *But his sister died in the attacks*, I thought next. *That makes him someone like me. Well, let's get it over with, let's have sex, and we can both move on to something else. Or someone else.*

Honestly, I didn't expect that he would show up, but ten minutes before closing time he was at the counter. "Hey," he said softly. "What did you pick?"

I flipped him the cover of *What's Up Doc?*, the next movie in my brother's queue. He took it from me and looked at the photo of Ryan O'Neal on the back cover and said, "That dude's hot, man," and that made me laugh. It also relieved the anxiety that it could be a set up for a mugging. And in another strange way, his commenting on Ryan O'Neal's attractiveness seemed to verify to me his "gaydar," though I knew from my friendship with Eric, Sean, and Joe that his lack of comment on Streisand *could* be an indicator for worry. Eric worshipped Barbra Streisand, Liza Minnelli, Cher, Bette Midler, and "any other oversized diva who was ever channeled by a drag queen."

Lock-up went easily. Rico was not part of a drive-by gang out to rob me or the store, but it was an awkward walk back to Philip's apartment; I was silent and looking about with affected interest at the traffic and shop windows and full of embarrassing doubts about what I was doing. We passed a group of men who were probably headed to the clubs, who detected my self-consciousness and tried to set me at ease with their campy calls of "Have fun boys," and "Call me later when you get tired of each other," which seemed to momentarily annoy Rico until I noticed that he was struggling to maintain his balance, because he stopped and smiled and twirled in a drunken circle and then continued to follow me.

We stopped at the deli to get chips and beer, and as we walked along Nineteenth Street, he placed his arm on my shoulder momentarily, then removed it out of worry. I wanted to ask him where he had disappeared to for three hours, but I knew I really didn't want to hear the answer because it would disrupt my own arousal and infatuation with him.

At the apartment, we settled onto the couch to watch the movie—he at one end, I at the other. The movie was funny and engaging—Barbra Streisand and Madeline Kahn were funny, Kenneth Mars and Austin Pendelton were endearingly goofy, and it was true, Ryan O'Neal was a hot dude even dressed up as an academic geek, but Rico was asleep when the movie ended. I rewound the tape, confused about what to do next. Chris had once advised me, "Don't ever let a strange dude spend the night. You wake up, he's gone, your shit's gone, or you wake up and he doesn't want to leave. Make sure he's out the door before you close your eyes."

I nudged him on the shoulder. "Rico, you should go."

"Man, it's late. I'm cooked, can't I crash here?"

"No, you should go. You have money for a cab?"

"Plenty," he answered. He stood up, blinked in the light of the room, seemed to come alive and said, "Piss first."

I waved to where the bathroom was located and immediately worried about Philip's prescription vials in the medicine cabinet. I made a quick decision that I could not prevent him from lifting any of them, but I could stop him from taking anything while I was within watching distance.

In a minute he was back out in the room, slipping on his hunting jacket and knit cap. At the door he lightly shook my hand which ended as a tap on my arm and said, "We can do this again."

He seemed to regard me as a younger brother would, as if I were the older and more experienced of the two of us and that whatever I suggested he would easily agree to do.

"Okay," I answered, wishing he had leaned in to kiss me, but my answer was more to get him out of the apartment than a real desire to hook up again. He seemed at that moment to me to be a fucked-up teenager, wasted and troubled, and I was not the right solution for him because I had a thousand issues of my own. I was relieved when he left and I closed and locked the apartment door. I thought that because I had tossed him out, hadn't let him crash in the apartment, he probably wouldn't want to seek me out again. My suspicion and inhospitality would keep him away.

In the morning there was a rapid, rapping knock at the door, an urgent ring-ring-ring of the doorbell, and some kind of commotion happening in the hallway—voices talking outside my door. I jumped out of bed and found Sean at my door, asking me if I knew who the guy sleeping in the hallway was.

Rico was standing beside Sean, his hands sheepishly in the back pockets of the jeans. Sean was red-faced, asking me, if he should call the police.

"Man, don't call the cops," Rico said. "I fell asleep waiting for the damn elevator."

"Do you know him?" Sean asked me.

"Yes, I know him. He was here watching a movie with me last night. Rico, I thought you were getting a cab."

"I must have just crashed."

"Sean, it's fine. Rico, come on in. You can sleep it off here."

"Teddy, you have to be careful. There are other tenants—"

"It's just a mistake, Sean."

"Dude, I'm sorry. I was blitzed."

"No, no, my fault," I apologized to both of them. "I thought he was catching a cab."

I apologized to Sean again, knowing the encounter would be repeated to Eric and circulated throughout the building, with a note eventually taped to the bulletin board in the lobby—"Tenants—Be Sure Your Guests Leave the Building! No Sleeping in the Hallways!!"

Rico wandered into the apartment and crashed on the couch. I went back to bed, slept a few more hours, and when I got up Rico was looking at one of the gay magazines that my brother had subscribed to, the page open to a guy wearing a white swimsuit at the beach, and talking to someone in a whisper on his cell phone.

When he saw me, he abruptly hung up and said, "I guess I didn't make a good impression on your neighbor."

"Nope," I answered.

"It's not what you think. I'm not a druggie. I just got fucked up this once. It was a bad week."

"You should probably go soon. I've got errands to do."

"I thought we could get something to eat," he said. "I'm starving."

"Not a good idea today," I answered, because I was ready for him to be out of the apartment. I wasn't certain that I was still on safe ground. "I've got a lot of things to do."

"I missed going to Mass with my dad. I thought we could get something at the diner. Brunch?"

"Not today."

"Is this how you treat all your dates?"

"It wasn't a date."

"What was it then?"

"A spontaneous pick up?"

"Did we fuck?"

"No."

"Then it was a date," he said.

I didn't want to argue with him over semantics because then I was engaging him in conversation. "You should go now," I said.

He stood and walked sheepishly to where I stood, adjusting his baggy pants and reaching for his jacket. "Gimme a chance," he said. "You're a nice guy. I'm a nice guy. What about later?"

"I work tonight."

"Then afterwards. I'll meet you at the store. We'll do it right this time."

"No, not the store," I said. "I'm off tomorrow night. We can do dinner."

"Deal," he said. "And I bet you'll have a good time."

The date went smoothly. Rico showed up on time; we ate at a Mexican restaurant on Fifteenth Street, which Rico pointed out was not authentic Mexican cuisine, explaining how his mother made the tortilla casings for fajitas and burritos, pounding the flour into thin, flat sheets with her hands and rollers. Afterwards, we walked north towards my apartment building, our heads bent to the sidewalk because of a chilling wind. Oddly, I was happy. The restaurant had been quiet and warm—ceiling fans lazily rotating above us. Our conversation had been polite and informative—I talked about growing up in St. Louis, the high school I attended where every kid wore expensive clothes and did drugs, my math phobia, my college years struggling to understand computer-programming code but spending time in my dorm room stoned and listening to Eighties pop music. Rico talked of quitting a job as a busboy at a restaurant on Ninth Avenue to be a day laborer—one of a number of guys who hung out in the Garment District looking for construction work—only to give it up when he got a job as the alternate morning manager of a Starbucks near Columbia University, which meant he never got to sleep enough. His father was a janitor at a building on Park Avenue South. His mother worked as a piece-cutter on Thirty-eighth Street. The family was originally from Colombia, though they had aligned themselves with the Dominicans in Queens because it had been a cheap place to crash two years ago when they immigrated to the United States. His mother had gotten her green card first, though Rico was evasive when I asked if he—or his family—were trying to become American citizens. He was surprised to hear that I had given up law school. I liked the way he smiled and scratched his chin, his lower lip itching to be kissed. He touched my wrist several times during dinner, gathering up the hair in a small twist of his fingers, and I smiled at this unusual display of public affection. When I asked him his age, he said he was twenty-one, though I could tell by his smile he wasn't telling me the truth. When I told him I was almost twenty-four, he smiled and said he thought I was older, in my late twenties, "because you always look so serious, dude."

I reached for the check, expecting to split it, but he took it from me and paid it in cash. Walking uptown, I was certain he would follow me home, but at my block he stopped and said he would take the uptown train. I tried to hide my disappointment; I had straightened up the apartment and gotten another movie for us to watch, and I'm sure he detected my feelings. "Your turn, now," he said to me before he left.

"My turn?"

"Ask me out."

I looked at him, ready to kiss him in the cold night before he left, and said, "What are you doing tomorrow?"

"Let's see," he said, with a shy smile. "I think I might be free."

The following evening I got tickets to an off-off-Broadway play written by a man who lived in my brother's building and who had posted a flyer on the bulletin board near the tenant mailboxes offering free tickets for the performance. I met Rico outside the theater on Forty-second Street, but something was off when I went to give him a kiss on the cheek as he approached and felt him tense as we ended instead in an awkward hug. It was as if he had had a conversation with someone who told him I was leading him on a path to Hell. In the lobby I ran into the playwright, a tall, striking man with a suave, sophisticated manner, and thanked him for the tickets, while Rico scowled at my side and glared at him. When we were seated in the theater, he asked, "Who was that guy?"

I explained the ticket arrangement—Rico had trouble believing that the tickets were "comps"—gratis, freebies—saying, "Nothing is free. There's always a price. How do you know this guy? Is he one of your boyfriends?"

I told him I had only met Peter in the lobby a few times, that he was more friendly with my neighbors Eric and Sean, and that he knew me from the times I had walked Joey's dog. Rico was then suspicious of Joey. "Who's Joey? How long you know him?" and I was thankful that discussion was cut short by the dimming lights.

The play was not good. It was long and talky and I could sense Rico's attention wandering because my own had lost interest in the characters. I looked for the playwright in the lobby after the show but was thankful that he was not around. Outside in the cold night, Rico awkwardly explained that he had to get uptown for a "family matter," and I tried to kiss him good-bye but was sidetracked into another handshake and arm punch.

On the subway downtown, I began to distance myself from the date and Rico in order to navigate the disappointment of us not being able to connect in a stronger or deeper manner. I didn't expect it would go anywhere now and I was writing him off. At home, I fell into watching *Bringing up Baby*, another one of my brother's films, and was asleep sometime before midnight.

The week roared by, some of it stressful—new reports on 9/11 were released—the Red Cross was losing files, the city medical examiner announced that DNA samples recovered at the site were too small and so severely decomposed that it was too difficult to properly identify them—and some of it good—Karl stayed at the store one evening balancing the accounts and we fell into a nice conversation about our mutual love of Thai food, of all things.

"Never tastes as good the next day," I said.

He nodded and smirked and answered, "Nothing ever does."

He had owned the video store since "the late Seventies," but was worried that business was off because of the terrorist attacks. "Nobody is spending any money right now," he said. "And realtors are circulating the building. The landlord has an offer to turn the lot into a high rise."

I didn't worry too much about my job eventually disappearing because it had always seemed a temporary thing for me to do, but I was alarmed by Karl's dismay and frustration; he was clearly concerned about what would happen next. I had developed something of a crush on Karl, watching him come and go from his office, checking stock, putting a new CD in the stereo system—a special dance-track mix that a guy had dropped off for him to play, or taping up a poster to the counter about tickets to a dance party or a drag performance or a special concert.

He had the kind of life that I imagined Pup had—many admirers, an active sex life, a group of close friends who wandered in and out of the store telling him jokes, tweaking his arm muscles, tapping his butt. I'd come to realize that every guy who wandered in and out of the store had an active fantasy life, and many times Karl had wandered in and out of my own.

Things with Rico might have fallen to the wayside except for the fact that one of Pup's co-workers called one morning to say that there would be a memorial service that weekend for another employee of my brother's firm whose remains had recently been identified. I wrote down the address of the church, but did not commit to attending, and after a day or so called Rico's cell phone and left a message asking if he would attend the service with me. I left him the time and date and the address of the church. I felt as if I were stretching my soul out on a limb by asking him to join me—if he refused, it would be a way for me to put closure on any hope of a budding relationship with him.

Saturday afternoon, the day of the mass for my brother's co-worker, I stood outside the church on West Thirtieth Street hoping Rico might show, but he didn't. He hadn't even had the courtesy to return my phone call and decline the invitation.

The church was airy, damp, and cold, and the service was strident and impersonal. I occasionally turned my head towards the entrance in hope of seeing Rico arrive, but I continued to be disappointed and I tried to keep my thoughts away from Rico, as well as above the waves of grief around me. Over the past five months I had sat through so many memorials and vigils for Pup's co-workers and other victims of the office towers that I had had too much time for internal ruminations. I knew what my problems were, but I had never let religion—or faith—be one of them. I had lost my faith long before the terrorist attacks—it was hard for me not to see all the fallacies religions presented to their followers. I suppose I could argue that I was an educated agnostic. Where was God? He wasn't around here. Who was Jesus? Jesus was a creation of folk tales and myths, recorded years after any real man might have lived. Whatever was written about him could never have been faithful to the true man—they were stories embellished to make a point. And what was a church? Nothing but an association of men who collected taxes, tithes to psychologically berate the uneducated. Disbelieving in organized religion or believing in its evils didn't mean that I had no regard for justice or ethics. In fact, I had high regard for them, which was one of the reasons why I had sought out law school. I understood that there had to be determinations on how to live our lives, a blueprint for rights and wrongs, but rights and wrongs which were fluid and changing and evolving and decided by circumstances and reason and logic. I had once tried to argue with my philosophy professor in college—without much success because he had a narrow, unbending mind—that if the Supreme Court asked for tithes in the way that the church did, then I would be willing to give them something in return for the determination of justice, but since the government already collected these taxes from us and funneled them into services that included the establishment of justice, then federal and state taxes made sense to me in a way that tithes to a church did not. My professor firmly felt that the abandonment of faith in God meant the initiation of chaos.

I was surprised to see Rico waiting on the other side of the street when I left the church an hour or so later. He waved and jogged through traffic to meet me. When he was beside me he said, "Chico, I could not make it."

I nodded and smiled. Rico had begun calling me "Chico," in part out of affection, but also because he found me determined to define our friendship. I was nonetheless glad to see him. I suggested we get something to eat nearby—and then I would have to leave him and go to work.

Some of his hesitancy surfaced over our meals. "Chico, I feel so strange when I'm around you."

"Strange?"

"I can't keep you out of my head."

I was flattered and tried to think of an appropriate response, but he seemed so young at that moment and now I was his tempter.

"I think about you," he added. "Us. Together. It's not right."

"Why not?"

"The Bible says it's sinful."

My attitude turned more contemptuous and cynical. I warned him that I was not the person to provide him sympathy because of the Bible. "It is all a fairy tale," I said. "Myths. Like Zeus and Ganymede and Cupid and Peter and the Wolf."

"You're wrong," he said. "It's the word of God."

"No, it's man's interpretation of the word of God."

"Then why did God destroy Sodom?"

I was surprised that he was so religious—and well versed in the Bible. He had never struck me as this sort of boy before. "What concrete proof do we have about Sodom other than a passage in a book of myths? It's no different than Atlantis. And you can interpret the Bible many ways. Did God destroy Sodom because of sexual morality or because it was inhospitable to his angels?"

He turned red faced and I expected him to call me blasphemous and a heretic—or just plain foolish. "I can't believe that modern society has created so many problems around the Bible." I added. "Where I grew up, Baptists wouldn't let teenagers dance. Mormons wouldn't let their kids drink soft drinks with caffeine. That's ridiculous to impose that kind of power over how someone should live their life."

"Chico, you've got some serious issues," he said.

"*Me?* Because I have an opinion? You're saying that you don't believe in free speech, which means you don't believe in democracy."

He brooded and I restated many of my theories on religion, justice, and sexuality. I suppose I turned critical and shrewish. But I suddenly realized that I was a man with strong opinions about *something*, in a way that I had not been before. An hour later I left him on Sixth Avenue, feeling doomed and spiteful because of the cold January day and Rico having thumped me with more mental anguish than I wanted to confront. I just wanted to be an ordinary guy who happened to be gay and in love with another gay man. My desire about who I wanted to become was finally taking shape. I had asked Rico to come over to the apartment for a beer and a movie later, after I got off work, to make up for being so harsh on him and his God, hoping that we might move beyond this impasse and into more comfortable, co-existent territory, but he declined and I knew it was to be the end of us—before we even had a chance to begin *anything*.

But he showed up later at the store, his eyes dilated and buzzed from some drug. When he approached the counter he asked, "Chico, what movie did you pick out for us?"

"Rico, you can't show up like this," I said.

"Like what?"

"Stoned. Whatever."

"I'm not stoned."

"You're high on something."

"You're such an angry dude. I lost someone too, you know. I got pain, too."

The evening was a replay of the week before. We returned to my apartment, watched *The Third Man* from opposite ends of the couch, and Rico was asleep at the end of the movie. This time I did not kick him out of the apartment. I went into the bedroom and fell asleep, trying not to feel disappointed or frustrated. Sometime in the early morning, I felt him slip under the covers beside me. He was fully dressed, still wearing his baggy jeans and T-shirt. He snuggled around me and pressed his lips against my neck. *Well, this is a start*, I thought, rising out of slumber. *At least we are going somewhere now.*

He was back in the main room when I woke hours later, watching television, and left when I told him I was not going to join him for brunch or a late Mass.

"You're making this harder," he said to me while I watched him wait for the elevator. "I can't give up my family."

"No one is asking you to. Does your family even know you're here?"

"They *care*," he answered.

"But do they know you're gay?"

His expression showed he didn't like being labeled gay—or, perhaps, that he wasn't.

"Papi would beat me," he finally said. "Throw me out of the house. Why you preaching at me when you ain't out yourself?"

"I'm working on it," I answered. "It's not like I'm not thinking about it."

"You think you're the only one thinking? I got plenty of thoughts, too."

And thankfully the elevator that never arrived opened up its doors. He left and once again I was both glad and miserable to be alone.

Ten

And so began a tug of war with a boyfriend who was not a boyfriend. Rico would call me some mornings when he got off work—he had an early shift behind the counter at Starbucks—wanting attention, conversation, or to hook up later and hang out together. Sometimes I would agree to meet and we might eat lunch together or see a movie at one of the multiplexes on Forty-second Street, but the relationship remained platonic; oftentimes I felt like an elderly shadow following him through the events of *his* life. It was as if he wasn't attracted to me and then he was but wouldn't act on it, and he would occasionally get phone calls on his cell phone and step aside, away from me, and speak in Spanish to someone, looking at his watch. When he hung up I knew he would leave me within minutes, and I believed that he was getting some kind of illegal work on the side, which I would seldom question him about because I knew it might prevent me from wanting to see him again. I had my own strange and tenuous life and I would often leave him and head to the subway feeling more discouraged than when I had arrived. Nothing in my life made sense to me, so it made sense that I would accept this nonsensical behavior from a pretend boyfriend as well.

And then I turned passive-aggressive and stopped answering Rico's calls, walking to the gym in the bitterly cold mornings after I woke up and doing a spinning or power ab or yoga class in the hopes of meeting someone more like myself. I had reactivated my brother's membership and at times I tried to emulate him as I moved from one machine to the next. I fooled around with a guy in the Jacuzzi and felt horrible and guilty afterwards, as if I had broken some kind of public code of ethical behavior even though I knew others had broken it over and over and over and over, and on another occasion I followed a guy to his apartment on Seventeenth Street where he wanted to fuck me—something I had had no experience with—and left feeling inadequate and frustrated because I had not been able to accommodate him as he desired.

Eric, of course, threw in his opinion about all these matters. He had called me one morning and said, "I know a guy I think you might like to meet."

I mumbled and stuttered and said, "I don't think I'm boyfriend material."

"Nonsense," he answered. "This guy is perfect for you."

The guy was not perfect for me. He was like Sean. Tall and elegantly groomed, Liam had just broken up with a lover of seven years and seemed to have years of experience of being a campy gay man or a man who loved campy gay humor. I sat silently through another one of Eric's dinner parties listening to conversations about tattoos and piercings and steroids and obesity and bioterrorism and the acoustics at Alice Tully Hall at Lincoln Center knowing that I would never hear from Liam about a future date because I had come across as too sullen and unenlightened.

And then two days later, after a heavy snowfall, the phone rang and it was Rico asking me to meet him at Central Park. I looked out of my window and realized I wanted to see the city covered with snow, wanted to be out of the apartment, wanted to have some kind of life of my own and I was oddly missing being with Rico.

I met him at the Upper West Side entrance to the park. As I approached him I noticed he was holding two large flattened cardboard boxes. He lifted them up in the air to show me, his smile as dazzling bright as the snow, and said, "There's more fun in here than you can imagine."

The city was enchanting beneath drifts of snow, the park even more so. We made our way slowly along a slippery path to reach a slope that was being used as a makeshift slide. Kids and adults and even dogs were sliding down atop expensive sleds, plastic trash can tops, and flattened boxes. I watched as Rico did the run first, then followed behind him, amazed at the speed with which the thin cardboard could carry me down the hill. We did this several times, then joined our boxes to make a bigger sled and went down together. Each time we completed the run, Rico would pop up and hug me—not romantically, of course, but the kind of bear hug appropriate for two sportsman who had just qualified for the Olympics. The next time at the top of the hill, Rico wanted to ride down on top of me, and he stretched his body over mine and pressed his lips to my ear and said, "Go."

It took on a thrillingly erotic feeling to have him lying on top of me as we raced down the hill, and at the bottom he lifted me up and threw me into another hug. We did this a few more times, with Rico also "bottoming," and then we began to offer rides down the slope to some of the younger kids, having them lie on top of us. There was an energy and enthusiasm radiating around us—two older guys sharing their wild rides with the younger boys. They chanted our names as if we belonged together—Rico!—Teddy!—Rico!—Teddy!—exploding into laughter as they demanded we watch them and praise them, and made us feel as if we were an unshakable unit.

After a while, we tired and our boxes, now soggy from the melting snow, began to disintegrate and become useless. Exhaustion and exhilaration tinged our lungs; our fingers and earlobes and noses were bright pink from the cold. We walked to another hill, watched the fun, and I looked at my watch and said I had to leave to go to work.

"Call in sick," Rico said.

"I can't do that," I answered.

"No one will be there. It's too cold. Too snowy."

"No, it will be packed. All those guys housebound for a day, restless to hook up."

"What do you mean?"

"It's a very cruisy place some nights."

"You're not screwing around, are you?" he asked. His expression turned part angry, part jealous.

"I'm invisible," I answered. "They're interested in hooking up right away."

"That's crazy," he said.

"It happens everywhere."

"You're not doing stuff like that, are you? You're not screwing around?"

I let it remain unanswered, in part because the two of us were not screwing around, but Rico did not let it drop and asked again.

"I'm not celibate," I answered.

"What does that mean?"

"It means that I am free to do what I want."

"You can't do that—"

"But we're not doing anything—"

"I told you I wanted to keep it slow—"

"Rico, are you gay?" I asked him, my frustration showing in quick misty puffs of cold air. "Honestly?"

"Why do you have to pin me down?"

"You're not, are you?"

"Can't we just keep it slow?"

"Slow? Or nonexistent?"

"You've got some serious issues," he said to me. "Pushing me too hard."

"Me?"

We had reached the subway entrance and I had no desire to continue the conversation. I made an effort to reach the stairs but he grabbed me by the hand.

"You can't just walk away. What kind of friend are you?"

"Friend?" I answered. "I'm a friend leaving you so you can go find whatever else it is you need to find."

It was Saturday night when Rico showed up again—this time at the store. High on something. A few minutes before I was locking up for the night.

"Will you be my boyfriend?" he asked, startling me as I was typing some info into the computer for a customer.

"If you were serious about it, you wouldn't always show up like this," I answered him.

"Like what?"

"Like this."

"I'll be your boyfriend," my customer answered. He was an older gentleman, alone, renting *Double Indemnity* and two porn films.

"Who are you?" Rico answered him, a little harshly.

"No one," the man answered lightly, with a laugh, to deflect the hostility. "Just a fan."

When my customer left the counter I suggested to Rico that he should leave the store because I was locking up.

"I'm not a druggie," he said.

"I didn't say you were."

"Let's watch a movie."

"I have plans tonight."

"No you don't."

"What if I did?"

"But you don't."

This sort of playful and irritating banter continued as I locked the register, cut out the lights, pulled down the gate, locked it, and headed up Eighth Avenue to the apartment, Rico tagging along behind me. Finally, I could take no more of it, and I stopped and waited for him to stop beside me. I leaned into him and kissed him and he pulled abruptly away. "See. You don't want to be boyfriends."

He looked uncomfortably around to see who was watching. Traffic had stopped down at Fourteenth Street and the sidewalks were almost empty where we were. I turned away and continued along Eighth Avenue, yelling back to him, "Don't make me have to call the cops to pick you up."

He grabbed my hand and yanked me into place, slipped his hand forcefully around my waist and pulled me into a kiss. A deep, heartfelt one which he would not let me pull away from.

Nor, at this moment, did I want to. I could feel his lips breaking into a smile. He took my hand again and pulled me into the direction of Pup's building.

"We're watching a movie," I said. "That's all. I bet you can't even remember my name."

"I know I want to know your name."

"You're too high to do anything."

"I'm not a druggie, I told you that."

"I can't keep seeing you if you're always like this."

"Okay," he answered. "You're the boss."

I'd love to say that it began as soon as we were inside the lobby and progressed in the elevator and that it was hot and heavy and full of passion, because it was—and wasn't. There was tenderness and confusion and awkwardness because of our inexperience and his drugs. We had made it into the apartment, frantically undressing each other, tossing off our coats and caps, clumsily sliding out of sweaters and boots as we tried to kiss and grope each other. I made it to the couch where Rico stood in front of me. I unbuttoned the top button of his jeans and squeezed his crotch, intending to give him a blow job. His hips were impossibly thin and the jeans slid easily off them and around his buttocks and settled at his ankles. He was wearing low-rise white briefs and his cock was enlarged and straining to be released from them. He wobbled with excitement and I tugged the briefs away and they slipped to his knees. He stepped out of them and his pants and I cupped his balls admiringly. His cock was thick and uncut and too large for his slender body, as if he were indeed a boy who had not finished growing to catch up with the size of his adult equipment. I slid my hand up to the shaft of his cock and he tensed and gasped and suddenly ejaculated, sending a warm spurt dribbling around my wrist.

He laughed and said, "Oh, Chico!"

I left him to rinse my hand and find a towel and when I was back I found he had put his briefs back on and he was lying on the couch asleep. I was disappointed but not surprised, I knew that this was not the relationship I had envisioned having with someone, but I was already smitten, aroused, attracted, and addicted to him. I let him sleep, watching him as I went about the apartment doing the nighttime chores I usually did—putting away glasses, brushing my teeth, checking messages on my cell phone, hanging up our coats.

I wanted to wake him and bring him into the bedroom, but I was confused as to whether to proceed or stifle my affections for him. I draped a blanket over him—there was a chill in the apartment—and in the bedroom I watched the TV, hoping the sound might wake him, but I soon fell asleep myself. I woke feeling him slip into the bed beside me, hours later, as the dark of the night was slipping into an early winter gray light. His hands and feet were cold and he encircled my body to gather in my warmth. I snuggled in closer to him, pretending to sleep, but his fingers played with the elastic band of my briefs as if to gather up more heat and it was difficult for me to hide that I was semi-hard. His fingers lightly touched my cock, as if testing or teasing me to awaken. I let him explore. His other hand had found its way beneath my waist and was grazing the hairs between my stomach and chest. He gathered my cock in his hand—now fully erect—and he squeezed and measured the length of it. His lips were now pressed against my neck, warm, moist impressions. He held me tight, not wanting me to move, as if to torture me with pleasure, and when I could take no more of it I struggled out of his embrace and twisted in the bed to face him. Our lips met and we fell into a kiss, sloppy and wet and sour from sleep. I had wanted to kiss him like this for such a long time that I wouldn't let him break away, keeping him in position by cupping the back of his neck. His hands fell against my buttocks, fondling the hairs at the base of my spine, and I slipped my free hand around his cock and balls, his breath pulsing and pausing as he gasped with pleasure.

He kissed the raw stubble of my chin and jaw and I shifted him in the bed so that he was beneath me; he seemed so young and boyish, his eyes wide with fear and pleasure. I held him in position as I regarded his body, dark and hairless except at his groin, lightly muscled at the arms, flat and ridged at his stomach not by exercise but because he was so lean, the details of his rib cage rising and expanding with his breaths. I rubbed our cocks together, held them both in my hand, then nibbled the small brown circles of his nipples. I kissed him from his neck to his navel, leaving a wet, chilly trail. When I reached his groin, I licked his cock and teased him with its slickness before I took him in my mouth and brought him to release. I stroked myself to a climax as I kept myself hovering over him, rubbing our sticky fluids together against his skin, as if it were an exotic, expensive oil.

We kept this up for some time, and I don't mean in minutes or hours, but in days and weeks. Rico became a lover and now when he called to hang out together we spent our time in my bedroom experimenting, exploring, and expanding our sexual repertoire. We were both eager students, playful but determined with butt plugs, dildos, and porn movies as our teaching aides. I remember the first time he entered me, the painful rush of pleasure as I kept him still inside and then made him withdraw, then pulled him back inside and felt a flush of pride at accommodating him. He was awed and euphoric, and I kept up with his gentle, rocking pulse. It was innocent, pure lovemaking, radiant with desire.

I was obsessed with his body, his lean musculature, his bristly black scalp, his larger-than-should-be endowment. He was amazed by the dark fur of my chest and arms and legs. We watched each other to mimic moods and moves. This physicality continued beyond orgasms, as if we were each afraid the other would float away into space and it would mean an end to our happiness. He held me as I looked into the refrigerator for food; I held him as we watched movie after movie; he held my thigh as he sat and watched me shave. This brotherly possession could escalate into a rougher affection, wrestling each other to the floor or to the couch or the mattress, one of us pinning the other, taunting with kisses and licks and rubs until we laughed and pleaded for more. We showered together, stroking each other until we were red and raw. We would stand and kiss in the doorway when one of us had to leave the other, unwilling to part unless we could carry the raw energy away on our lips. It was as if our initial sexual tentativeness with each other had never existed.

And several things happened simultaneously, among them Rico becoming more interested in me—and in my brother Pup. He wanted to know if Pup had one boyfriend or many ("Many, and I have yet to meet them all."), when Pup came out ("Much younger than me. I think he was active in his teens."). What was his birth sign? ("Sagittarius. Probably why he liked to travel so much.") I always believed his inquiries were genuine and without ulterior motive. His questions soon evolved to asking for details of Philip's job and the aftermath of the terrorist attacks, and I willingly gave him information because I had spent so much time sharing this with others who were not intimate with me—the name of Pup's firm, how long he had worked there, his job position and description, what I knew of his co-workers.

This was not all handled as bluntly as I have laid down, but arrived in moments of compassion and affection. I refused to be suspicious of Rico, but I was also aware that he was not as forthcoming on details of himself, his sister, or his family. I could not verify his real age ("I am only a few years from you, more or less."), the age of his sister ("She was too young for this to happen to."), where in Colombia he had been born ("Only a small village near a mountain."), why he had quit his job at Starbucks ("I had a better opportunity and wanted to spend more time with you.") and where he was working now ("Freelance, you would call it. Temporary work. It pays me too much. I get it in cash and spend it with you."). He would not reveal any details of his sister's death that had come to him: Had any remains been recovered? How did his family handle the burial? Where was the Mass said for her? I tried to emphasize that these details of his life mattered to me, but most times he would shy away from my questions by shaking his head and saying, "I am no good for you, Chico. I cannot tell you these things."

"And I am no good for you?" I would answer.

"No, you are no good for me," he would tease me, though there was still a faint belief behind what he said. "What we are doing is not right in the eyes of God."

"I think God would enjoy watching this because you seem to be enjoying it."

"Chico, I must go to confession because of you."

"And I hope you learn that there is nothing wrong with this," I would tell him. "What we are doing is natural. Okay. Nothing to be ashamed of."

"Chico, I am no good for you. And you are no good for me."

And I knew within these new boundaries of bonding he was also seeking comparison to his own loss, not only of grief and its endless grip, but in matters of compensation. When his questions came about Pup's insurance payments, the amounts received from the city and the government, the Victims' Compensation Fund, and assistance from other agencies, I could sense his anger when I told him that I did not handle all of these matters, that I received no compensation and that anything that was due to us because of Pup's death would go to my parents.

"Because my sister was not American, we are not eligible for any of this," he would say and shake his head angrily. "My family will not see any benefits."

Eleven

"The world doesn't think kindly of Americans," Sean said. "They think our morals are loose."

"They're quick to criticize us," Eric added, "but quicker to take our money."

The dinner party was not going well. Rico sat opposite me at the table, silent, his eyes averted to the table. I moved my silverware, hoping to catch his attention and mouth "I'm sorry," but he wouldn't look at me because of his anger and discomfort.

Eric had not been supportive of my growing relationship with Rico. "You can do much better," he had told me more than once, but I had defended Rico as much as I could to him, even suggesting that Eric and Sean get to know him better. Ever since Sean discovered Rico sleeping in the hallway he had thought of him as "street trash" and uneducated, especially since there was no sign of higher education or even literacy and I could not provide an adequate job description for him. Eric felt that in time it would play out, "once the novelty of the sex was through." He did not see any reason to invite him for dinner, but I persisted, even knowing I would also get resistance from Rico.

"We are not like them," Rico protested, when I told him of the invitation. "Chico, there is no need to do this."

"They're my friends," I answered. "They've been helpful to me. I want you to get along with them."

"They will look down on me," he said. "Because I am not like them. White Americans with too much money."

"You're wrong," I said. "They just need to get to know you. And then they will treat you like family."

There was another couple at dinner that night—Scott and Josh—a forty-something pair who knew our hosts from a Caribbean cruise that they had taken together a few years before, and two other men, single and unattached, whom Eric was hoping to match up together—Liam, who I had met before, and Gary, a thirty-something journalist who Eric knew from his magazine work.

Gary seemed more interested in Rico than Liam, asking Rico questions in Spanish, which Rico would curtly answer. Gary had spent considerable time in Mexico and his Spanish was fluent, and he was questioning Rico on his theory that most Latino men were bisexual and that they felt no shame fucking another man but kissing him on the mouth was taboo. I didn't think it was appropriate dinner-party conversation, but I don't believe that Rico had had much exposure to other openly gay men and couples, either, and he was trying to avoid a conversation with Gary, in part, because there was some sexual goading from Gary. Gary was handsome and meticulously groomed and had a snobbish air of superiority about him, as if he had been raised in boarding schools and academies, which, of course, he had. His questioning did not seem to want to get at the heart of a matter but instead to expose some ridiculous misconception as a fraud. It was also clear to everyone that he was attracted to Rico's discomfort, and that he would have no shame about hooking up with Rico, in whatever position Rico wanted. Both Liam and I seemed nonexistent to him.

I count this evening as the beginning of the end of things with Rico, though I had no idea how wickedly it would disintegrate. Eric saw what was transpiring and tried to monopolize and steer the conversation, mentioning how a bus trip to the see the Mayan ruins of Altún Ha passed right through the impoverished neighborhoods and villages of Belize. Sean nodded and began discussing with Gary how the poverty of the Caribbean nations was largely uncovered in the media.

"It would scare away the tourists," Gary said. "Right, amigo?" he nodded to Rico. "Without the tourists there would be no income at all."

Rico responded in Spanish, which I took to be an offensive remark, given Gary's expression, though it did little to deter his persistent interest in Rico, and Rico would no longer speak in English to the rest of us. I could sense our hosts becoming annoyed and the other couple confused, but there was nothing I could do to prevent the train wreck which seemed to be approaching.

"Tourism has emasculated the cultural world," Gary explained to the rest of us. "Men who would have become farmers and providers are now peddlers selling bad souvenirs, begging American tourists or cheating them with dusty trinkets passed off as relics and antiques. The only alternative is drugs. Working in the drug trade, right, amigo?"

Rico answered in Spanish and gave me a stern look and I pretended to feel nauseated so we could leave the dinner party early. Later, that night, back at my apartment, Rico said to me, "Chico, they are no friends," and he drank as many beers as he could stomach before he passed out on the couch.

The next morning when I tried to apologize to Eric, his response was equally terse, "Teddy, it might be great sex, but you have to let him go. I think you're going to get caught up in something you shouldn't be caught up in. Sean doesn't even think he is of age—he's still a kid—and acting like one, pouting all night—doesn't make a good impression."

Rico and I did not officially break up, but I felt him pulling away. I did not see him as often and he seldom returned my phone calls now.

But I honestly liked Rico and desperately wanted to love him and be loved back. I liked his laugh, going with him to a store, seeing his expressions, hearing his opinions and worries, and I think as he began to escape me I began to fall in love with him more. I was willing to cut him a lot of slack. "Compromise," as Eric had always told me. "A relationship is all about compromise."

I could always itemize what I was conceding, but I never felt I got any respect from Rico in return. When he materialized he would say his work kept him busier now and his time with me could only be short. I never felt that I got an honest explanation about anything and details of who he was and what he was up to were always at a bare minimum. For a few days he made late night visits—three or four a.m. He would call me on my cell phone and buzz my apartment, show up at my door handsomely dressed in a tuxedo explaining that he had been nearby working a business function where he had been a waiter and wave a large wad of cash he had just earned, and when he would slide into bed beside me for a few hours I could smell the smoke and cooking in his hair, so I believed that there could be some truth behind this. I wanted to protest this invasion—what if I had made other plans?—but I couldn't because in essence I was waiting for Rico to appear in just this way. And the truth of the matter was, Rico had become a good lover—the pendulum had swung the other way and sexually he was open and aggressive and willing and wanting. We had worked through the complexity of shame and religion and in sex we lost all of our awkwardness and confusions. I looked forward to the warming days of spring, enthralled, breathless, really, with being in love with a guy, with being happy and out in the sun with someone who wanted to be with me—and I saw Rico as part of this dream. Yes, it was all complicated, but wasn't that the way it was supposed to be?

But I think there were also many unfortunate elements at work in our relationship, one of which was the timing of it, on the heels of our individual tragedies. In February, as preparations were announced for the six-month anniversary of the terrorist attacks, I had received an invitation to do one of the cruises of the Hudson River Bay to watch the twin towers of light memorial—high powered projections of light in the place where the Trade Towers once stood. I knew Rico would not have received an invitation, and I invited him to attend the event with me because I had been given a pair of tickets—and I left a message on his cell phone service describing the event.

Rico reappeared at the store, glad to be thought of and to have someone to hang out with, and for a few days—maybe even more than a week—we seemed to be reconciled, the disastrous dinner party behind us—he showed up for lunch and sex, met me after work, slept overnight, and we fooled around more before he left in the early morning. But then he once again stopped returning my phone calls. And on the anniversary boat ride he was a no-show, even though he had told me he wanted to be with me for this because it would be a special event for both of us—"a memory." I stood at the dock at Battery Park waiting and waiting and was so upset when he stood me up that I left and did not take the cruise. I couldn't understand his lack of communication with me and the disrespect. And I couldn't brush away my hurt.

So when Gary called me, I accepted his date.

"We met at Eric's not long ago," he said. "Eric said you were no longer seeing that other guy. I thought you might like to get together."

I didn't tell Gary that Rico was an on-again, off-again problem and I answered that I would be glad to get together, that I remembered him well, but I worked most evenings, so my schedule was awkward and limited. I thought this would deter him and the date would never materialize because of scheduling problems, but he suggested dinner the following Tuesday night.

When I met him at the restaurant on Twenty-third Street that evening I knew immediately we were headed for sex. I had learned that some guys like to hook up anonymously, others like to flirt their way into the sack. Gary was a flirter and he seemed up to the challenge of wooing me, knowing of my resistance to him due to the dinner party disaster. He asked me what it was like living in Chelsea, what gym I went to, how long I had known Eric and Sean. I tried to keep the storyline of Pup out of the conversation by asking Gary about himself. He confessed to loving chocolate too much and being addicted to potato chips and that he would usually have to spend an extra half-hour a day on the treadmill to keep it from showing.

There was a lot of passion behind his opinions, but he was condescending and over-educated. I tried to keep Rico out of the conversation but Gary was interested in him. I also needed and wanted a sympathetic ear to unload all the miseries I was experiencing, and he seemed to be eager to hear the despair Rico had caused me.

"If you want to get over a guy, you have to fuck him out of your head," Gary said glibly, after I had repeated too many details about Rico to him. Emotionally, I had wound myself up into a little tornado and it was not easy to calm down into a chatty breeze of a fellow.

"You know this from experience?" I asked.

"More than once."

"More than one guy, or more than one fuck?"

"Same answer."

We ended up back at my apartment and into the bedroom quickly. He was patient in explaining what he wanted to do, mostly kissing and stroking, until he announced that he wanted me to fuck him. In some perverse way I could tell he was using me as a stand-in for Rico, that in his mind my fucking him was a fantasy that Rico was fucking him. Or at least happening by one degree of separation.

And in my own perverse way, I had a lot of pent-up animosity over my inadequate break-up with Rico, and I gladly pretended that I was who Gary was probably fantasizing about. He was a talker in bed—moaning, growling as if we were appearing in a porn movie—and I was thankful it was so different than what I had come to experience and expect with Rico.

I had just wiped myself off with a towel and thrown the condoms away when the apartment buzzer rang.

I wasn't expecting a visitor, and when I checked the intercom I heard Rico saying, "Chico, let me up!"

"Not a good time," I said into the speaker.

"What's up?" he yelled back.

"I've got company. Not now."

I knew that this would not deter him. It would only make him want to show up quicker. Rico was oddly possessive, even in his absence. He buzzed again, but I ignored him and I knew he would wait until someone left the building and walk in through the opened door.

"Who's that?" Gary asked.

"You should go," I said. "It's Rico. I think he might create a scene if he finds you here."

"I'm not afraid," Gary said.

"I am, so you better go."

"I thought it was over between the two of you."

"It is. Only he forgets about it now and then. You better go. And take the stairs."

"Sure," he said, and I followed him to the door.

I stood by the door, listening to see if Rico had met Gary on the stairs, but Gary's steps faded away and I stood and listened to the faint shifts and hints of life in other rooms. A few minutes later, the elevator landed into place and the doors phflumped open and Rico was at my apartment door knocking and ringing.

I was relieved that Gary was gone and had not had a stupid idea that this was his opportunity to win more brownie points with Rico—which would have only provoked a bigger confrontation. I opened the door and said, "Rico, you can't—"

He pushed me aside and walked into the room. "Who's here?"

"No one."

"You said you had company."

"He just left."

"Who you messing around with?"

"Messing around?"

"You can't do this," he said. He was suddenly in front of me, red faced and bug eyed. I could tell he was coked on something. He took a step back from me and threw a punch which landed in my stomach.

I reeled back from the shock and doubled over.

"Get out," I said, when I had caught my breath.

"I don't want you sleeping around, Chico."

"I'm not your *chico.*"

"*Puta!*" he shouted.

And then he landed another punch. This one grazed my eye.

I tumbled to the floor and when I pulled myself back up, the burning pain at the side of my cheek, I saw blood running into my hand.

"Chico," he said, suddenly on top of me. "I didn't mean it. Chico, I'm sorry."

"Get out," I said. The blood was bothering me. The amount of it. I put a hand on the counter and pulled myself up. In the bathroom I grabbed a towel and pressed it against my eye. Was it my eye that was bleeding? I almost fainted from the fear of it being true. Rico was still in the apartment, a few steps behind me, saying, "Chico, I didn't mean it. Let's get you help."

I grabbed my keys and pushed him out of the apartment. He went to get the elevator and I took the stairs down. He was suddenly behind me when I reached the third floor, saying, "We'll go to the emergency room. We'll get a cab."

I pushed him away. "Leave me alone. Get out of here."

He followed me out into the street. I headed east towards Seventh Avenue and found a cab at the end of the block. He pushed his way in behind me, and told the driver to get us to St. Vincent's.

The bleeding was slowing, but the pain had now increased. I leaned my head back, tasting the blood in my mouth. In the emergency room, Rico paced as we waited, and when a nurse came to take me back to an examination room, I turned to him and said, "Go away. Or I'm calling the cops."

Another nurse appeared. An intern walked into the small curtained-off examination area I had been led to. The eye was fine. Bruised and blackened. The blood was from a cut that sliced through my eyebrow. The intern said that if he stitched it together, I would lose part of my eyebrow, so I asked him to bandage it and I was given a pain prescription and sent home. I was glad that Rico was gone when I left the hospital, but I was also worried about when he would show up next.

At the apartment was a note taped to the door that read, "Teddy, call me.—Eric."

I crumpled it up and threw it in the trash. Eric only wanted details and I wasn't ready to share them. If he hadn't heard the commotion in the hall then Gary must have phoned him. I wanted no part in any of it anymore. I lay on the couch and fell asleep.

"You reported this to the police?" Eric asked me, when he saw me a day later. My eye was swollen and puffy, the black bruises with yellow edges. I had called the store and told Karl that I would be out for a few days because of an accident. I had been fighting pain and headaches since I had made my way home from the hospital.

"No," I answered weakly.

"I don't know what you saw in him. Well, I probably *understand* what you saw in him."

"Don't make me cry," I said. "It hurts more."

"Has he been calling?"

"No," I answered. "I think I scared him away."

"Scared him away? With what?"

"By threatening to call the police."

"Honey, you gotta flush that man down the toilet right now. I know it hurts, but you have to do it. You're just going through a bad time. Wrong guy. We can get you whatever help you need. Sean can get a referral for you. A therapist. Or get one through one of the 9/11 agencies. Someone to help you."

That, of course, made me cry. I curled myself into a tight ball and sobbed. I didn't want help. I wanted to be my own little island. Self-sufficient and sustaining. As my brother had been.

"Talk to me," Eric said. "What can we do? Your brother was not always a good judge of character either," he added, as if reading my mind.

"Pup? He had these kind of problems?"

"Trouble chased your brother," Eric said. "But he learned how to brush it off."

I could feel the changes happening around me, the air becoming stronger and warmer, the earth pushing itself out of a freeze. I now experienced an aching ennui and an incredible rush of desire to hook up with a guy for sex. I sat in front of the computer hour after hour until I was numb from looking at photos and trying to chat with strangers, disconnecting from one guy, shunning another. Finally, late at night, high on pain medication and a couple of beers, a fellow arrived at the apartment and left a few seconds later after he had taken a look at my eye.

I went back to work two days later. Karl was distressed by my appearance, but more worried that Rico might show up at the store and cause more trouble. He tried to convince me to file a restraining order, but I told him that I didn't even know where Rico lived. I went through the next few days always looking over my shoulder, expecting him to materialize out of the shadows with a baseball bat or a car jack or something more sinister and vile and punish me because I was not on the slow, right path that he was.

But he didn't appear and didn't phone. I was just at the point of relaxing, letting down my guard, when I got a phone call one morning from my father.

"Tad, a claims investigator called the house this morning."

"Why? What happened?"

"Someone filed a claim on behalf of Pup. They used your name and an address in the Bronx."

"The Bronx?"

"Whoever filed it had a lot of information right. His birth date. Social security number. Your social security number."

"Mine?"

"You haven't had anything stolen, have you?"

"I had an accident," I admitted. "But nothing stolen."

"An accident?"

I realized that I had given my father too much information and I now had to come up with a story, fast. "Someone tried to mug me, on the way home from the store," I lied. "He didn't get anything. But I got socked in the eye."

"You didn't lose your wallet?"

"No, sir."

"Nor your keys?"

"No."

"Are you okay?"

"I went to the hospital to make sure my eye was okay. It is. Just a shiner. And it hurts like crap."

"I think it's time you come home for a while, Tad. Then decide what's next."

"I want to stay in the city a little longer," I said. "I don't want to leave it like this."

"I think you need to come up with a better plan."

"I will," I promised him. "I will."

I refused to admit that I had made a mistake with Rico, that I regretted becoming involved with him, in the same way that I had let Chris storm in and out of my life. I knew all along that Rico was not right for me and that we were not right for each other, but I always felt that at the core of him was an honest man because I had trusted him and I had seen his trust in me—in his eyes. I was not convinced that he was behind the false insurance claim because of the Bronx address—Rico had told me he lived in Queens and I could not make that connection to another neighborhood of the city—or another name and life, but after my conversation with my father, I began to check other accounts for possible fraud—both mine and Philip's. There had been a few occasions when I had left Rico alone in the apartment, sleeping, and gone out to the bodega for a newspaper or bagels or coffee or snacks— and times when I had awakened and found him in another room, reading a magazine or watching television. I couldn't believe that he would have used any of that time to write down Philip's information, look through his bank statements, log onto the computer to find out his passwords. But he must have. I found that there had been several withdrawals from one of Philip's money-market accounts over the last month—four of them to be exact, each for a thousand dollars.

I did not tell my father of this. I called the bank and put a freeze on the account and changed the account number and passwords, not an easy task since the account was in Philip's name, but when I mentioned fraud behind the withdrawals the bank was more cooperative, though confused that I did not want an investigation or to prosecute anyone behind the transactions.

I thought that Rico might call with an explanation when he could no longer access the account. But then I thought he might call to see if I was okay and how my eye was healing. I waited and waited to hear from him but he never called. I thought about calling his cell phone and leaving him a message, asking why he had done it, but I couldn't get up the courage to do so. I knew I would probably give in, want to see him again. I wanted to touch him, find his body amazing and attractive, take his cock in my mouth and put mine inside him. I wanted to see his grin as he rose into an orgasm, smell his odor and be pulled into a sleeping embrace. And I know if he had asked me for money, needed it, I would have easily given it to him. I suppose a stronger and more experienced man than I could have shrugged off the loss—both financially and emotionally—but I felt, in those days, as if my self-respect had been demolished and I had been raped. I moved as if I was a victim, in slow motion, aware of my pain, conscious that I was invisible to others.

And as every day passed, I changed a little more. Moved pieces aside, covered them up. Hardened the shell. There was a lot of truth in the advice that Gary gave me—the best way to get over a guy is to fuck him out of your head. And I was able to do things I had been too intimidated to do before. I chatted online, hooked up with guys. Some nights, after locking up the store, I would walk to a bar and meet a guy. Other nights, I would go to a club, check my clothes at the door, stay as long as I could. I thought about Rico a lot. What I would say to him if he called or showed up again. And I thought about Pup. What it would have been like to spend time with him.

It was only by chance that I saw the news about Rico and his dad, though the story rattled through the newspapers and television and Internet for several days. Two men—illegal immigrants from Guatemala—were arrested for insurance fraud relating to the terrorist attacks. The men, father and son, had initiated claims on behalf of the older man's daughter—reportedly missing since the collapse of the two towers. The photograph I saw on the Web was certainly Rico. His real name was Enriquez Suarez. He was seventeen years old. His older sister had reported the fraud when authorities had tracked her down in Guatemala. Both men were expected to be deported.

For weeks afterwards I expected the phone to ring—Rico calling for help, an investigator calling to ask me questions, a reporter tracking down a new element to the story. But it never happened. One day he was no longer in my life, vanishing as quickly as my brother had, a painful memory that would take more time to heal and I would never be able to unravel any of its mysteries and motives.

Twelve

Ari outlined a meticulous itinerary. There would be footage of the airdrop from the plane and footage of the packages landing on the ground and being distributed at a village. There would be facts about the population and the education and health of the local Afghan population, mixed in with reports about the ethnic clashes within the country, the impact of the war, and the fall of the Taliban. He asked Jim to research a piece that they could do about the lost antiquities of Afghanistan and the fate of the Kabul Museum. The National Gallery had just been reopened, after the Taliban had destroyed half of its collection, but the Kabul Museum, once one of the great museums of the world, was now an infamous, almost empty structure. Jim was impressed that Ari thought it warranted an in-depth piece, exactly what Ari had hoped Jim would think.

The museum's collection had spanned more than fifty thousand years—from artifacts of the cave-dwelling tribes that lived along the Oxus River to the elaborate jewels of the early Hindu, Buddhist, and Islamic dynasties. The museum had been inaugurated by King Amanullah in 1924 at Koti Baghcha, a small palace built by the founder of Afghanistan's royal dynasty, Amir Abdur Rahman. In 1931, the museum was transferred to a building in Darulaman, six miles south of Kabul, the exhibitions enriched by the work of the Délégation Archéologique Française en Afghanistan, which had begun excavations in the country after a treaty was signed with France in 1922. After the Second World War, archaeological missions, including those by the

Italians, Americans, Japanese, British, Indians, and Soviets, had added more items to the museum. Soviet troops withdrew from the country in 1988. As the mujahideen factions fought to take control of Kabul, the museum was on the front line. Each time a new group triumphed, the museum would be looted.

In 1993, a rocket slammed into the roof of the museum. Artifacts were transferred to steel-doored vaults on a lower level. In 1994, the United Nations bricked up the windows to prevent looting, but for years Jim had heard of antique dealers and private collectors purchasing many of the stolen items from the museum's collection. More than seventy percent of the museum's collection had been destroyed, pillaged, or illegally sold abroad. A few items had found their way to Bubendorf, Switzerland, to an Afghanistan Museum, a safe haven created by the Taliban and the Northern Alliance in the late 1990s and supported by grants from UNESCO and other organizations.

"There's file footage from the Swiss museum," Ari mentioned to Jim.

"We could use it in a piece about the Hoard of Bactrian Gold," Jim said. "Whether the collection has been looted—or is still hidden away somewhere."

The status and whereabouts of the Hoard of Bactrian Gold, a collection of more than twenty thousand gold, silver, and ivory objects that had been presumably stored in a bank vault under the Arg—the former royal compound and the presidential palace—remained unclear. On the eve of the 1979 Soviet invasion of the country, a joint Soviet-Afghanistan team found the items in five tombs at Tillya Tepe in northern Afghanistan. Jewelry and sculptures in the shapes of cupids, dolphins, rams, dragons, and even an Aphrodite-like figure were discovered—all dating from 2000 B.C. to the third century A.D.—reflecting the remarkable intermingling of Hellenic, Indian, and Chinese cultures north of the Hindu Kush mountains and along the Silk Road. For years it had been believed that the hoard had been spirited away to Russia, sold on the black market, or melted down.

"Muhammad Najibullah ordered it to be hidden," Ari said. Najibullah had been Afghanistan's last Communist president.

"That was 1989," Jim said. "There was a report in 1991 that the collection was seen at the Arg. Najibullah was trying to stop the rumors that he had shipped the collection to Moscow. It hasn't been seen since then. I've heard that it was returned to an underground vault for safekeeping. That's the last anyone has heard of it."

Jim uncovered another source who said the Taliban had tortured a security guard who refused to give up the secret location of the vault. He pored over maps of Kabul and renderings of the Arg buildings. He made lists of people and organizations to contact prior to their trip and once they were in Kabul. Ari, excited about the potential news value if the relics could be found in the Kabul vault, prodded Simon about the logistics and possibilities of doing a live broadcast (which was nixed because of equipment and expense and the possibility of failure).

Jim spoke with a representative of UNESCO, who instructed him on the health issues and customs he and Ari would confront on their Afghanistan junket. Ari began growing a beard, hoping to avoid appearing as a foreigner. He made lists of items they should bring for comfort and trade: cigarettes, toilet paper, dexamethasone, aspirin, Flagyl, ciprofloxacin, chewing gum, batteries, plastic combs, and mints. Jim made a list of other antiquities missing from the Kabul Museum: carved ivories of the Kushan Empire discovered in Begram; a statue of Kanishka, the Kushan ruler; marble Hindu sculptures from the sixth century A.D.; ancestral wooden effigies from Nuristan; fragments of gold and silver vessels dating from about 2500 B.C.

From Rome they flew to Switzerland, where they interviewed the director of the Afghanistan Museum in Exile and shot footage of the museum's recovered relics. Ari had decided that the file footage looked too dated to rebroadcast. From Basel, they drove to an airbase in Germany where they met up with other journalists, from CNN, BBC, LCI, ZDF, and Sky News. A military cargo plane flew them to Manas Air Base in Kyrgyzstan, where they were briefed and assigned translators and military escorts while on base. They were given tours of the barracks and hangers and informed about the various deployments on base and operating in Afghanistan. Updates were given on the Northern Alliance, the War on Terror, and the hunt for Osama bin Laden. They were reminded of the four journalists who had been murdered on the road between Jalalabad and Kabul: an Italian and a Spanish reporter, an Australian cameraman, and an Afghan photographer.

"This is a world response," a press spokesman tried to make clear to the reporters. "A humanitarian mission to Afghanistan."

"In cooperation with the military," Ari whispered to Jim.

"Don't stir up trouble," Jim answered. "We have to play by the rules on this."

"Whose rules?" Ari asked. "The terrorists'? Or the politicians'?"

Jim and Ari arranged profiles on two soldiers—one, a slow-talking Italian-American corporal in the Army from New Haven, Connecticut, and another, an energetic thirty-something British pilot from Scotland.

Ari was more at ease and sociable than on other junkets. Jim was more cautious, worried that Ari's enthusiasm might lead them into unexpected confrontations or towards harm. For all intents and purposes their personal relationship was nonexistent, though their bond was stronger than it had been in months. They did not wander too far one from the other without explaining their whereabouts or their intended mission. Professionally, they did not reveal their intimacy and their relationship. They were out of sync with Muslim morals and the American armed forces' homophobia. They both saw the irony of the boys-club-like atmosphere of the military. And the number of other gay journalists traveling in the press corps. The reporter from the German-based ZDF news service—a lanky, bald-headed fellow who liked to dress in black—kept commenting on the youthfulness and posture of several soldiers, chuckling to Jim in a whisper, "I've got to get to know that guy... And that one... And that one...."

Ari took the opportunity to start a discussion with the fellow about gay men and lesbians serving in the armed forces.

"Of course they can't just blurt it out," the reporter told Ari, an annoyance in his voice. "They would lose all order and rank and support."

"Initially," Ari said. "But over time it would grow to be accepted."

"You're wildly optimistic," the German newsman said. "But the reality is that it is far from practical."

"We should canvass the men for their opinions," Ari suggested. "I don't think it would be as difficult as you suggest."

"Drop it," Jim interrupted the discussion, trying to assert some control. "Not a good idea. You'll get us all booted out of here and where would we be? In *deep* trouble in the middle of nowhere."

The airdrops of food and medical supplies were coordinated as if a Hollywood film were being shot on location. The soldiers were positioned by cameramen and photographers so that they could be "candidly" caught loading the cargo hold of the plane. A kit was opened and demonstrated. The nutritional value of the food was explained by a UNESCO spokesperson. A military official was interviewed. The terrain was explained. The climate was analyzed. In the air, Ari filmed the soldiers tossing the kits out of the plane. Jim strapped himself to a seat, worried that Ari was a little too eager to catch the rations dropping through the air, expecting him to leap out of the plane at any moment and follow a kit to earth. Jim, aware of his own disappointment in all of the officious and coordination of the junket, thought Ari must be feeling disappointed too. Ari, however, felt alive from the adventure, empowered with a hope of capturing an important news story along the way, relying on his images to find any story Jim might want to try to avoid reporting.

Hours later, in a village in the Baharak Valley in Northern Afghanistan, Ari filmed the food and medical packages of another airdrop landing. Jim reported on their efficient distribution by local NGO workers.

The piece took two days. They edited it at Manas and uploaded it by satellite phone to Simon Bosewall in Rome. The next morning they were flown to Kabul and sat through briefings, before meeting more officials from UNESCO. They were introduced to a guide who would drive them into Kabul and serve as their translator for their three days and nights in the city. Omar Desai was gray eyed and gray bearded and would have seemed washed out altogether were he not so stocky and quick. He was always in a hurry, dismissing Ari's questions because Ari now blended in too well with the country—since leaving Manas, Ari dressed as an Afghan soldier would—in long tunic shirts and heavy work boots, with a deep blue turban atop his head.

"We want to find this route," Ari said to Omar, pointing to a map as they followed Omar to his car, a battered and dust-covered Audi.

"We go safe way, M'sheem," Omar said to Jim.

"This way," Ari insisted to the Afghan. "We want to film it."

Omar and Ari were already skeptical and suspicious of each other—as if either one might suddenly be revealed to be a Taliban spy. This left Jim to find out details from Omar in hushed asides he would often have to ask to be repeated because of Omar's poor English. Omar called Jim "M'sheem" because he could get it out of his mouth quicker than Mr. MacTiernan or Mister Jim. "M'sheem, sir, see that wall of Ratbil Shah," he pointed out on the rowdy drive to the hotel. "M'sheem, sir, down there is Ka Farushi. Where bird fight bird." He would briskly wave his hand out the window and repeat when Jim asked for an explanation. "Ka Farushi. Where bird kill bird."

Their brief day in the Baharak Valley had not prepared them for the bleakness of Kabul. Ari remarked that it was like being in one of George Lucas's science-fiction movies, roaming through a transportation hub of dust and mud-like buildings, rubble piled everywhere—in the streets, in the shops, in doorways and rooms.

Omar drove them first to Darulaman Boulevard, once a broad tree-lined avenue laid out by King Amanullah when he was building his new city during the 1920s. Once, trolley cars had run along its length from the heart of the new city to the Shah-do-Shamshira Mosque. The trolleys and poplars of yesteryear were gone; in their place, a shallow ditch paralleled the wide, barren road of potholes and cracks and litter. Ahead, at the end of the boulevard and backed by the snow-capped Hindu Kush mountains, was the heavily-damaged Darulaman Palace, still picturesque in its shattered state, the exposed steel girders of its towers resembling a giant, unoccupied birdcage.

Ari shot footage of the outside of the Kabul Museum, across the boulevard from the palace. Jim did a short report in front of the entrance and beneath a small white banner with Arabic script and a bold English translation: "A NATION STAYS ALIVE IF ITS CULTURE STAYS ALIVE."

"It's hard not to feel depressed about this," Jim said.

"I wish there was some kind of counterbalance to justify it," Ari added. "If living conditions had improved. If the Taliban had improved the roads and health systems and eradicated poverty, but they didn't. This country is a wasteland."

Inside the museum, Ari filmed the dark, empty rooms. Omar spoke with a guard who sat on a folding chair guarding nothing but the timber braces criss-crossed to prevent the ceilings from collapsing further. Jim introduced himself to Talat Khan Rehman, a hopeful, white-haired, white-bearded gentleman who had recently become an associate director of the museum. Rehman gave them a tour of the museum, explaining where specific artifacts and exhibits had once been displayed and how they had been damaged or plundered.

"Our collection was one of the finest in the world," he told Jim. "But anyone can walk in through this rubble and take what they can find. We're struggling to contain what we still can."

Jim asked him if any of the museum's items had been recovered on the black market. "We don't have the kind of money to buy it back," he said. "And our demands hardly carry any weight at all."

Rehman brought up the subject of the Bactrian gold first. "It is very difficult for me to predict if it will ever be revealed to the public," Rehman said. "They are very delicate pieces. Gold pieces constitute most of the treasure, and they doubtlessly have great value in shedding light on the history of Afghanistan and its elegant arts. It would be a national shame if they were not found. But first we must be certain the government is stable."

"Then the relics are still in the bank vault beneath the presidential palace?" Jim asked.

"There is no reason to believe that they are not there. But the exact location of the vault is not known. Only a few have been trusted with the whereabouts."

"I heard a recent anecdote," Jim said, "that when the Taliban were destroying much of the country's cultural heritage, a staff member of the bank deliberately broke a key in the lock of the vault because he thought they were getting too nosy."

Rehman's reaction was a bit of surprise. His eyes widened and his forehead creased. Jim guessed that there must be some sort of truth behind the anecdote.

"I truly enjoy foreign journalists enlightening me on the latest gossip of the whereabouts of our national treasure," Rehman said.

With this footage Jim had enough for a solid "what if" story. The following day he was hoping to interview a government official he had contacted before leaving Rome. He had proposed questions concerning the current excavations in the country and what sites had been looted or destroyed during the Taliban regime, and from there he hoped he could inquire about the Bactrian artifacts. Ari was hoping the Minister might reveal details of the bank vault and allow filming beneath the Presidential Palace. If time permitted, Jim wanted to spend their third and final day in the city working on a news piece about the black-market activity in Afghanistan: bootlegged DVDs, opium, heroin, alcohol, and antiquities.

On the drive to the Red Cross Hospital, their next stop, Omar fidgeted and spoke about petrol prices, carjackings, and the fear of bombs. "I fight with the mujahideen and never worry," he said. "Now I am this close to death, M'sheem." He pinched the tips of two fingers together. "This close. There is more worry here every day."

At the hospital, UNESCO had arranged for Ari and Jim to meet with the Red Cross staff and film the inpatient ward. They were greeted by Sarasah, a slender Afghan woman wearing a white lab coat and a lime-green headdress, who spoke English in a clear, clipped accent. Jim tried to engage her by asking how life was different without the Taliban control, but she responded with a thin and weary smile and spoke only about the new changes and programs at the hospital. They were given a tour of the pharmacy and the outpatient clinic, the funding for the new operating room equipment was proudly explained, and the two men were paraded from room to room, one bleak bullet-scarred dark beige wall after the next, over the jumble of cords running across floors and windowsills to outside generators.

With three other foreign reporters, they sat in on a paramedic training class—instructions being given to three new ambulance drivers—where they also met Matthew Rolley, a sharp, rugged American journalist from *Time* writing a piece on the establishment of a blood-transfusion center. Before arriving in Kabul, Matthew had been in India for several weeks, working on an article on the rise of AIDS in Asia. After visiting Pakistan, he had arranged an escort through the Khyber Pass and into Afghanistan, on the lookout for his next big story.

Matthew mistook Ari for a local Afghan newsman. When Ari had finished filming a bandage-wrapping demonstration, Matthew asked him if he was available to translate an interview of a patient who recently had the lower part of his leg amputated.

"Only if he speaks French," Ari answered.

Jim, on the fringe of their conversation because he was getting facts from Sarasah, was aware that the conversation was becoming more personal between the two men. In a hushed tone, Jim overheard Matthew asking Ari where he was staying, how long he was to be in Kabul, and what his plans were for the rest of the day.

Ari drew Jim into the conversation at the earliest opportunity, explaining that Matthew wanted to hitch a ride with them back to their hotel, because he was staying nearby.

"Dinner?" Matthew asked Ari, clearly not interested in Jim's presence. "I know a few places nearby."

"We don't have any other plans, do we?" Ari answered, looking to Jim to make sure he was not to be excluded.

Jim nodded, trying to deflect the inevitable feeling that he was losing Ari—that sooner or later a job—or another man—would pull them permanently apart.

In the car, Omar took an immediate dislike to the American journalist, particularly when he teased the guide for the whereabouts of a local Chinese restaurant.

"Not in Kabul," Omar yelled at the American, his face bright red with anger. "No such thing, here."

"No Mandarin Palace?" Matthew continued in a condescending sing-song voice. "What about Szechuan cuisine? Some chow mein? Egg foo young?"

"M'sheem, sir, I know a good place," Omar said to Jim. "You trust me. I know of good place."

Over dinner, at a tea house that Omar had promised M'sheem would be the best in Kabul, Matthew explained his Chinese restaurant request to Jim and Ari. Omar was seated deeper into the room, next to the owner, his second cousin's son.

"I've been hearing about cases in Kabul where Chinese restaurants are fronts for brothels," Matthew said. "Strictly for expats. Men. And not with Afghan women. Since there's no legalized sex industry here, I'm thinking this is more about coercion, exploitation, and fraud. *Slavery.* But I have trouble convincing my editors back home to go with the story. I can't even get them to touch the idea of how gay this country is."

"Gay?" Jim asked.

"Men holding hands everywhere," Matthew laughed. "You'd think you were in Chelsea."

"It's a different culture," Ari said. "I don't think they believe that they are acting gay. Homosexuality isn't the same concept here that it is in the West. It's not the basis of an identity."

"True, but it doesn't mean that it doesn't exist, nor does it dispute the theory that the Muslim world isn't aware of how Western culture views them. Mohammed Atta is a case in point. The religious right was quick to point that he was a self-hating homosexual and was compelled to slam a plane into the Twin Towers to prove his masculinity, and there is some truth to that statement. In Western eyes he appeared weak and effeminate. In most Muslim societies men are very affectionate with other men in ways that would seem appalling in smalltown America. I'm told that Kandahar—where I haven't been yet—is one of the gayest cities in the world. In Mazar-i-Sharif, to the north, young boys are solicited to dance in drag at weddings and have sex with their patrons."

Matthew's recent story of AIDS in India had centered around *kothis*—young boys who were sex workers on the streets and at train stations throughout the country. As the food arrived, he elaborated on the mythology that adult Muslim males initiated younger boys sexually. "But that would be another impossible story to write for my magazine. No one will speak of it on record. The true problem here isn't the sex trade or whether a homosexual identity exists, however, it's drugs. Poppies. Opium. *Heroin.*"

"It won't be the next big story," Ari said to Matthew, trying to impress the journalist. Jim had tried not to engage Matthew in conversation, instead watching the dynamics of the flirting between the two men continue. "After the war it will be about women. Women tossing away their burqas. Getting equal rights. Voting, getting elected. Their positions in society restored and elevated."

"There's still a lot to be done about medical facilities improving," Matthew added. "Poverty. Third world issues. And the rise of AIDS is certain to be among them. But you're right, Ari, it'll be about women. And the culture being restored. History being put back into place. I'm off tomorrow morning with a guide who says he'll show me an excavation south of here. A new site at Kafir Kot. A Buddhist complex."

"I heard of a Japanese collector who is very interested in what they find there," Jim said flatly, a half-hearted attempt to break the eye contact between Matthew and Ari.

"This country has been raped many times," Matthew said. "And not always by foreigners."

After the meal, Jim thanked Omar and reconfirmed the plans for the following day, then met Ari and Matthew outside the building for the walk back to the hotel. Jim was sure that, given the opportunity, Ari would ditch him to spend more time with Matthew, but he was surprised when they reached the entrance to their hotel, and Matthew shook their hands and said to Ari, "Sure I can't interest you in something else? A drink somewhere?"

"We've a busy day ahead," Ari explained.

"What was that about?" Jim asked, as they checked the front desk for messages and made their way through the hallway to their room.

"I told him I was with you and not interested in fooling around," Ari answered. "I told him we were together."

"Are we?" Jim asked.

"Yes," Ari answered. "We always have been."

They were able to overlook the inadequacies of their hotel room in Kabul. Jim, because he knew it was temporary. Ari, because he knew they would spend little time in it. After cold showers the next morning and a bag of stale potato chips that they bought from the young boy who worked at a tiny stall inside the lobby, Omar drove them to the Arg, where they began a slow procession through guards and checkpoints in order to speak with a government official.

Inside the compound, they were led from one building to another, one corridor to the next, to a set of chairs that were lined against the wall of an empty hallway. Jim sat and made a few notes. Ari placed his camera on a chair, asking Omar about the delay. "We had an appointment. Letters of introduction. Everything was arranged."

Omar spoke only to Jim, "M'sheem, it will be fine. Everything will be soon."

They waited close to two hours. They studied the water stains on the ceiling, the flaking plaster, the cracks and the unevenness of the floor. Jim began to feel weak. He sent Omar away to find bottled water and food, giving him more money than the task required.

"That's throwing money away," Ari said.

"You have a better way?"

"We could just walk in?"

"Where? Where are we walking to? The only place we'll walk into is jail. For all we know there could have been some kind of coup while we've been waiting."

It was forty-five minutes before Omar returned. He had a warm can of Pepsi and a chocolate candy bar which Jim and Ari split.

They waited another hour and began to display their restlessness. Ari took the snub personally and displayed his annoyance to Omar, asking their translator repeatedly, "What's going on? Is someone coming to find us? Do they know we're here?"

Jim went through a list of other sources he had contacted for the story—an archaeologist at the University of Pennsylvania, Fredrik Hierbert, who worked with the National Geographic Society; a writer in Peshawar, Nancy Hatch Dupree, who had helped organize SPACH, the Society for the Preservation of Afghanistan's Cultural Heritage. Both had given him quotes he could use. He had found archival photographs of the Bactrian Hoard from the 1980s. There was stock footage of the Oxus Treasure of the British Museum which could be used for comparison.

"We've got enough for the story," Jim said. "But if you want another news piece, we could skip Chicken Street and contact CARE or AHDS. I've got several names."

"I promised my uncle I would visit a rug merchant," Ari said. "And I think the black market is important to cover. Simon doesn't want a piece about a blood transfusion."

They decided to leave the Arg, which bothered Omar considerably. "But sir, we must wait!" he yelled. "He will want to speak with you. He is the government. We cannot do this to the government!"

"But we've decided not to speak with him," Ari said. "We want to do something else besides wait."

They spent the afternoon at the BBC bureau in Kabul, editing footage and doing a voice-over, contacting Simon Bosewall on the progress of the stories, then left to do feeds of UN press briefings in front of Kabul University. With the help of an AP reporter and Omar, they interviewed two female university students—one nineteen years old and without a burqa who spoke English—about the changes that were taking place in the country and what their life had been like when the Taliban were in control. They followed the English-speaking student, Baasima, to her home north of the city, where she lived with her father, mother, grandmother, younger sister, and her father's second wife and new baby son in a cramped four-room apartment.

The family invited Jim, Ari, and Omar to eat with them. At first the father said that they had no family photographs—because it was forbidden and illegal under the Taliban—but the ease of the girls with the journalists soon rubbed off on the parents, and photographs of the girls as babies and children were soon displayed to Jim and Ari.

Ari was also allowed to film the segregation of the women and men in the household without interference—men, seated on the floor of the main room, eating; the women, huddled in the smaller kitchen behind a door, concealing their faces from Ari's camera. The father, whose brother ran a stall on Chicken Street which sold carpets and rugs, spent most of the meal admonishing Ari for wanting to meet a notorious dealer who might supply his American uncle with locally made rugs, much to the delight of Omar, who translated the disapproval. The food was warm and plentiful. Jim was full of questions about ingredients, though hesitant to hear the facts within the answers.

The father—Majd—agreed to introduce Ari to his cousin the following day. The next morning Jim and Ari shot footage of the bazaars on Chicken Street and its visible black-market items— bootlegged DVDs of American and Bollywood movies, contraband cigarettes from India, pirate-produced Coke from Pakistan. Omar translated the prescriptions of a spice merchant and his sacks of dried herbs, roots, fruit, and tea. It was an unsettling experience for both newsmen—Jim felt on display, stared at by the Afghan men as he moved from stall to stall. Men held out their hands to touch him, one shopkeeper offered him a bouquet of dusty flowers, telling him, through Omar's translations, that he had beautiful green eyes.

"He wants you to stay with him," Omar said, smiling and bowing to Jim. "To give up America and the West to be his favored guest forever."

Jim tried to politely dismiss the compliment, but Ari broke in and said jokingly, "No, no, no, tell him you are mine."

Omar did not understand the joke. He reacted with surprise, looked to Jim for an explanation, but Jim smiled and shook the merchant's hand, took the flowers from him and tried to hand him a coin, which was waved away.

They moved slowly from stall to stall. Jim showed another merchant a photograph of an ancient gold coin, hoping he might be led to a back room and shown such an item to purchase. No such luck. Jim was too Western. And Ari was too suspicious-looking with his camera.

They met Majd at noon. He led them beyond the stalls of prayer rugs and teapots and sunglasses to an alley where there was a large storeroom of rugs. Ari introduced himself to the owner and gave him his uncle's business card. Two teenaged boys appeared from behind a row of rugs and offered them stools and cups of tea, then set about unrolling carpets for them to look at. Ari, using Majd as a translator, asked prices and shipping routes to Pakistan and took pictures of the carpets with a camera to send back to his uncle in New York. Jim inspected the backs of the rugs and examined the colors—after living with Ari long enough he knew how to tell talented art from shoddy workmanship. Perhaps there was a feature they could do on this—how this rug merchant had survived the Taliban and appeared to be thriving while the rest of the city struggled.

As he outlined the potential story in his mind, Jim lost track of the activity in the room and realized he was staring at one of the teenaged boys, who was leaning against a rolled-up rug, watching Ari. Jim sat at an angle where he thought his stare wasn't obvious, but the boy, youthfully athletic in the way he handled the rugs, turned towards Jim and caught his eye. Silently, he glanced from Jim towards Ari and back to Jim. The boy cracked a lopsided grin that worried Jim. In less than a second, the boy had detected their relationship. Jim had not been cruising the boy—only admiring his attractiveness, thinking how much more handsome he would become as he aged, in much the same way Ari had grown more distinctive. But these internal thoughts were enough to make him guilty—or at least suspicious of his interest in the boy. He reddened, turned, and stood up, walking down an aisle of smaller rugs, his heart beating rapidly with anxiety. Jim heard the boys resume unrolling the carpets, but there was a series of taunting laughs, as if the handsome boy had revealed a secret to the other one. It was enough to unnerve Jim and make him eager to leave.

Jim and Ari said good-bye to Majd a few minutes later and returned to the BBC bureau to finish editing their pieces and upload them to Simon. Ari wrote an e-mail to his uncle about the rug merchant and his storeroom and promised that the photos would be sent when they were back in Rome. Jim confirmed to Simon that they would be leaving Kabul for Rome the following morning. They had accomplished as much as they had set out to do on the trip. They could leave the next morning for Manas with their consciences clear, though Jim knew that Ari was not satisfied or ready to go.

"One of my UN sources says that a mass grave has been found near Bamiyan," Ari told Jim on the ride back to the hotel. "Victims of a Taliban massacre. We could stay and cover this."

"It's not why we're here," Jim said. "It's not a reason to stay."

"You could do a follow-up piece on the destruction of the Buddhas. You can show where they were."

"It's not a strong enough story," Jim said. "And it's old news."

"They're relocating the refugees who live in the cliffs," Ari said. "I heard they're building a new village."

"We've made plans to leave."

"What about Kafir Kot? You could try and link them."

"I heard we should stay away from there," Jim said. "I warned Matthew about it. We should go back as we planned. Aren't you satisfied? You saw what a miserable place this is. What people are trying to do to get back on their feet. Isn't that enough?"

"Nothing happened," Ari said. "Nothing became news. We're not near any of the news. This was all too safe."

"Are you crazy? Why do you have this death wish?"

"You don't understand."

"I understand why you want to get a good story. What I don't understand is why you are putting *us* in jeopardy."

That evening they visited the hotel bar. It was a large room which must have once served tourists meals at Western-style tables and chairs but that evening was barren of all guests and any liquor. No bartender or booze in sight. Jim gave Omar money to go buy any sort of alcohol he could get his hands on—Uzbek vodka, Armenian brandy, wine imported from Iran. Again, Ari told Jim the money was as good as lost. Jim reprimanded Ari for his lack of faith in their guide, convinced that Omar would return with something. Even if it was a decade-old bottle of warm Pepsi.

Other foreigners staying at the hotel wandered into the room, asking Jim and Ari what was happening—first in their native tongue, then in English or French when they were met with Jim and Ari's shrugs—Why was the bar was closed? Did they serve any food here? They wandered in and out, saying they were going to find another place and asking Jim and Ari for their recommendations. Everyone complained about the cold water or the lack of water or the erratic electricity or the lack of phone service or the lack of sleep or the lack of comfort or the fact that all of the snacks found in the hotel's tiny gift shop were old and stale and lacking any sort of nutrition.

Jim gave up on Omar and admitted to Ari that he was wrong. Just as he and Ari were leaving to go find something to eat and drink elsewhere, a pudgy man with white hair walked into the bar accompanied by a tall, scowling companion with a dark, thin mustache and a black turban. Intuitively, the white-haired man said to Jim in accented English, "What's truly barbaric about this place is their prohibitive stance on booze. You can't ever find a decent drink in this country. Alcohol tastes like gas and gas runs like it's alcohol. The Persians didn't shy away from beer. Even Jesus was smart enough to turn water into wine."

Introductions followed. The white-haired man was Dr. François Dupray, a French archeologist headed for Bamiyan the next morning. His mustached companion was Nasser, his local driver. "I know of another place not far from here," Dr. Dupray said to Jim. "Come. Come. We must all be famished and parched."

They followed Dupray out of the hotel, around a corner, down an alley, into another street, to a door with a small blue light overhead. The driver said he would be waiting across the street if the professor needed him. The professor thanked him, said something in Dari, and pushed the door open. Inside was a large dining room full of foreigners, all seated at tables and chairs, smoking cigarettes and drinking from glasses that contained ice cubes.

"Paradise," Dr. Dupray said. They took a seat at a small table and ordered drinks—Dupray bold enough to order American bourbon, which the nervous waiter assured them the bar had but which the professor told Jim would be Russian bootleg at best.

"This is what we should be doing," Jim told Ari. "Talking about all these underground places. The places even the locals don't know about."

"Simon would never let us get away with it," Ari answered. He asked Dr. Dupray, "Have you heard of any good Chinese restaurants in town?"

The doctor smiled, "Fortunately, my tastes run elsewhere, as I gather do yours?"

Ari took the comment in stride. "You see through us rather well."

"It's my profession to see as much as I can with as few facts as I am given."

"Why Bamiyan?" Jim asked.

"It's the Valley of the Gods. *Très incroyable.* Once one of the most inspirational places in the known world."

"Are you hoping to rebuild the Buddhas?" Jim asked.

"It would be a great achievement if that were possible," he answered. "There are professionals now sorting through all the rubble. A Japanese fellow wants to do some sort of laser projection recreation. I have bigger ambitions. I want to find the third Buddha."

"The third Buddha?"

"Bigger than the other two. 'Mahapari nirvana.' A reclining Buddha in a state of ultimate enlightenment. Nirvana. More than one thousand yards long."

"Xuanzang wrote of this?" Jim asked.

The archeologist was impressed that Jim knew something of Afghan history. He widened his eyes and said, "Yes, in detail. You should join us. Scoop the *National Geographic* team on it."

Jim knew immediately this was the story they should not ignore. A third Buddha. Undiscovered. Three other stories that they could file while in Bamiyan raced through his head: The relocation of families out of the caves. The mass graves the UN had reported. The restoration efforts underway for the giant Buddhas.

Ari answered for both of them. "We're ready and packed," he said. "What time should we meet you in the morning?"

Thirteen

"There are only two reasons for a foreigner to be in Bamiyan," Dr. Sajadi said to Barâdar in French. "As a relief worker or because of the Buddhas."

Estelle had arranged for Barâdar to meet the archeologist, avoiding the line of men waiting to be picked for jobs at the excavation site. Barâdar spent his first day digging, his hands and fingernails the color of clay and swollen with blisters from the handle of the pick, before the professor pulled him aside and explained the project to him in French. "One could spend an entire lifetime studying only this place," the professor said. They were beneath the tent which the professor used as an office. "The caves, the Buddhas. What we don't know. But what we do know is that it is impossible to remove the politics from religion. The labor to build the Buddhas was presumably done by slaves. The Buddhist scriptures were written in a court language which the people were unable to speak. The Buddhists succumbed to the Muslims, the British brought in Christianity, and now the Muslims decide one faction of their religion is better than the other. We're lucky, I suppose, that even in modern times this site is so remote."

"Has religion always tried to harness man?" Ari asked the doctor.

The doctor laughed. "Perhaps you are a philosopher? A nomad seeking enlightenment. My friend, religion has shackled the faithful and enriched culture and given greed and power respect, but where would we be without it?"

"The slaves lived in the caves then?"

"No, they must have lived in less glamorous dwellings, easily demolished. The caves were reserved for the holy men."

Tariq Sajadi was from a Muslim family who had lived in Bamiyan prior to the Soviet occupation in the late 1970s. The family fled to France when the Russians arrived and converted to Catholicism. The professor could speak Hazaragi, Dari, and Pashtoo dialects. Now in his early fifties, he was thick waisted, with gray hair and a sparse beard, preferring to wear an explorer's khaki outfit and cap than the native's shalwar kameez and turban. For years he and his colleague and mentor, the elder Dr. Dupray, had lectured on the giant Buddhas of Bamiyan, waiting to return to Afghanistan when it was safe to do so, first to study the giant statues and now to look for a hidden one. Sajadi believed Barâdar was an acquaintance of Francois Dupray—because Barâdar's French was so good, he must have studied with the archeologist at the Sorbonne. That evening Barâdar joined the professor and his young assistant, Danil, at a tea house near the professor's house, a rented compound of rooms on the plateau above the old village where the NGO workers also lived. The portions of food were large and delicious, and Barâdar's stomach swelled and ached from eating so greedily.

"Here, in Bamiyan, was where Buddhism met the art of Alexander's Greece," Dr. Sajadi explained. They were seated on the floor in front of bowls of rice and meat, the owner treating the professor as an honored guest because the professor had hired his brother and cousins to dig at the site and the professor settled his bill every night with cash. "You must know this."

"No, sir," Barâdar answered. "It's not familiar to me. Was there a war then? Did one religion defeat another?"

"Buddhism began four centuries before Christianity. It first spread south, from the Buddha's birthplace in Nepal across the flat Gangetic plain to Sri Lanka," the professor said. "It took a millennium to reach China. Instead of crossing the Himalayas to get there it followed a parabolic curve east-northeast. As Buddhism moved, it changed. In

Tibet it incorporated the preceding Bon-Po religion and spawned new demonologies. In eighth-century northern India, it became scholastic; among the forest monks of Sri Lanka, pragmatic; and in Japan, Zen devotees contemplated minimalist paradoxes. For the first five centuries after his death, few statues of the Buddha were made. For five hundred years the Buddha was shown only as an empty space—or as empty footprints or a riderless horse, or an empty saddle or an empty throne—or sometimes as a wheel. It was not considered proper to make images of the Master. After seven to eight hundred years of theological development, however, the portrayal of the Buddha in human form was considered appropriate. Missionaries carried the humanized Buddha along the trade routes to China and beyond. Buddhist craftsmen began to mix together Indian, Persian, and even Greco-Bactrian traditions, and gave birth to the art of Gandhara. We have found sculptures and reliefs fusing Eastern and Western motifs throughout Afghanistan, including *les grands Bouddhas*. The Bamiyan Valley became a sort of religious theme park with the giant Buddha statues decorated with gold and precious stones. Does any of *this* seem familiar to you?"

"I can't recall any of this," Barâdar answered. "I can only remember some prayers."

"*Prayers?*" Danil, the assistant, asked. "Are you Catholic?" A young man in his late twenties, Danil was fair skinned and clean-shaven and wore clear-rimmed eyeglasses. He had sat quietly through the meal and conversation, letting the professor do all the talking.

"I'm not sure. I don't know. I recall passages in French and English. But they are not from the Bible. Or I am told that they are not from the Bible."

"Christianity underwent a similar transformation over the centuries, as the Church became wealthy," the professor said. He was a teacher who liked hearing himself talk, using his education and experience to both entertain and inform his listeners. "The Pope now wears gold and jewels. Surely, you know what the Pope looks like?"

"I know there is a Pope, yes—in the same way I know of the Buddha. But I don't understand my relationship to either."

"You're hardly different there. Man has always been trying to understand his relationship with God and the invention of religion."

Barâdar was more interested in France. He asked the professor questions about the classrooms of the Sorbonne and the neighborhoods of Paris.

"How can you not know Paris if you speak French so well?" Dr. Sajadi asked. "*Incroyable.* Listen to the words and you will see the city. *La Ville-lumière.*"

"The Eiffel Tower?" Danil asked. "The glass pyramid at the Louvre?

"No," Barâdar answered.

"Montmartre? Sacré-Coeur?"

Barâdar remembered nothing. Instead of the blocks of Paris or library of the Sorbonne, he recalled a small sign above a door, the lettering in Greek and English for "deli." The professor laughed and told him this could be anywhere—he must sit and meditate—search for something deep within himself to find out who he was and where he came from.

"I don't believe the core of who we are ever leaves us," the professor said. "If you are not a philosopher, *mon ami*, then you are some kind of thinker or concerned citizen. Maybe a doctor perhaps? Here to help the poor and ill?"

"I don't remember why," Barâdar said.

After the meal, Danil walked with Barâdar to the path that led to the cliffs. They sat on the rocks. The black sky above them was splattered with stars. Barâdar was not ready to give up on remembering something from his past. Danil offered him a cigarette.

"Do you smoke?"

"I don't think so."

Danil lit a cigarette and tossed the match into the dirt.

"Did you know me before?" Barâdar asked.

"No," Danil answered. "*Pourquoi?*"

Danil was from Belgium and had once been the professor's student. He could speak French, German, English, and Dutch. He had spent the evening studying Barâdar and Barâdar had spent the evening noticing it.

"Something you are not telling me," Barâdar said quietly. "The way you look at me."

"You remind me of someone, that's all."

"Did you know Dr. Dupray?"

"*Oui*. He was a good man. *Très intelligent*. It is a great loss. Professor Sajadi is lost without him."

"Will he find the third Buddha?"

"Of course not."

"What do you mean?"

"It is a silly legend. A myth. Unsubstantiated."

"But you are here, looking for it."

"I am here with the professor."

"Pardon?"

"We have … an arrangement."

"Arrangement?"

"He permits me … indulgences. I assist him."

"I don't understand."

"He is my patron and I am his."

"*Pourquoi?*"

"It is a long story," Danil said. "*Très miserable*. Once I was hurt. The professor saved me from this. I am indebted to him."

"I don't understand this hurt. You were beaten?"

"No. Pained. Pained from love. Unhappiness."

"A woman caused this?"

"No," Danil said. "A man who loved a woman."

The following morning the professor showed Barâdar pictures of Dr. Dupray and ancient maps of the valley. Together, they thumbed through notebooks with sketches of the cliffs and photographs pasted on the pages of the Buddhas, but nothing jogged Barâdar's memory. In the professor's files were maps of France, airplane tickets, and

European magazines, though none of these stirred anything familiar and personal to him.

"You are a mystery, I see," Dr. Sajadi said. "As anonymous as the sleeping Buddha. I hope that you will reveal as many tremendous secrets. If this Buddha does exist, it would be the world's largest statue in human history."

Jim wrote about laser binoculars, global positioning JDAMS, remote-controlled predator surveillance drones, and the events of the war in Afghanistan being watched via satellite images and video at MacDill Air Force Base in Tampa. He filed the kind of war stories Simon would use, knowing this would keep him at Bagram and searching for Ari. He was so close to Bamiyan and yet so far away, frustrated by his lack of mobility and the inability of technology to conquer the isolation of this region of Afghanistan.

"How does MacDill see all of it?" he asked Michael Baxter the next time the young soldier was visiting the press tent and helping with Jim's audio reports. Jim already knew the answer to his question. He was flirting because he enjoyed the young man's company. Michael's presence calmed him, made him feel less frantic that he might already be defeated; he always felt as if he was not doing enough to locate Ari.

Michael tapped the monitor and explained the diagram Jim had up on the screen. Michael was young enough to be Jim's son. Jim studied the soldier's appearance as an older man would—admiring the long, spidery eyelashes; the prominent Adam's apple; the waist that did not sag or hang over his belt. At Michael's age, Jim had still been in college in Virginia, avoiding political science texts and art history classes to smoke pot and watch John Waters' films. At that age he understood little of sex except that some boys were attracted to girls and others were not, and he was one of the latter. He inched into his sexuality question after question, following his openly gay friends to discos and bars in D.C., always an observer and never a participant, waiting on the sidelines to meet the right person until one night frustration overwhelmed him and he went home with a man who told him exactly what he wanted to do together.

Michael had a girlfriend back in Mississippi. Carole, a brunette with a long face and large white teeth. Michael had shown Jim her picture, and Jim had given her a compliment even though he had not found her pretty. "I never seem to do the right thing with her," Michael said. "She thinks I don't think of her enough."

"My girlfriend said the same thing," Jim answered. "Long ago, when I had a girlfriend."

Michael took the statement in stride, not asking for any further details. Anyone on base who wanted to do a little homework could have easily uncovered Jim's relationship with Ari—they worked together, traveled together, lived together, shared the same address, phone numbers, and telecom bills. The press corps was treating the loss as a professional one, though they all understood how the despair and uncertainty was creating an unbearable stress for Jim.

"Do you think he knows?" Jim asked Wade, during a visit when they were talking about Michael—and Ari. "Do you think he understands?"

"Would it matter? He's so young he might not get it. And if he does, it could mean trouble."

"I don't want to lead him on."

"What are you talking about? It's not like he's going to ask you out on a date."

"I don't want him to think that I'm straight. That Ari and I are just friends."

"Tell him."

"I'd be too upset if he backed off. I need his help. And his company."

"Maybe he's gay too and has figured it all out already. My gaydar certainly goes off around him."

"That's so unreliable when it comes to younger men."

"And men in uniform."

"*Young* men in uniform."

A light scar was prominent on Michael's chin. Jim wanted to ask the soldier how it had happened—did he fall off a bike? Or a skateboard? Did it happen at school? At home? He couldn't do it, however. He was full of questions he could not ask Michael. It would be crossing a line Jim knew was best to avoid even seeing.

Michael described the surveillance techniques. It was hard not to be caught up in his enthusiasm. Jim had never been the kind of reporter who took copious notes; he deconstructed complex items to their simplest level and offered a layman's explanation. Once, in Manhattan, he had inventoried his ex-lover's medicine cabinet when Frank's health took a turn for the worst. He meticulously listed the medication, dosage, and frequency as if he would need to summarize it later to a grieving party—"six pills a day, and none of them vitamins."

"What?" Jim interrupted Michael. His attention had drifted away.

"When did you decide to be a reporter?" Michael asked again.

Jim had started writing about lost artifacts and overlooked art about the time Frank announced he was HIV-positive. They were living together, but as roommates not boyfriends, though neither of them had lovers or anyone else waiting in the wings. Jim found the research and writing therapeutic, a deflection from too openly worrying about Frank. He couldn't confess this to Michael, either.

"My family has always worked in the news business. My great-grandfather was a typesetter. My father was a pressman because his father was a pressman," Jim said. "When my grandfather was a baby he had scarlet fever and lost his hearing. He never went to college or was in the service. Right after school he started working at the presses of a newspaper in North Carolina because the sound didn't bother him, then later in Virginia, where my father worked the presses, too. I remember visiting them at the printing plant when I was six and watching the newspapers being printed. The sound was horrific. Like thunder that wouldn't stop. I wouldn't let my father leave me alone. My grandfather had taught me ASL so I could sign out words to him over the noise. I hated the press rooms. But I loved the smell of the ink and the way the newspapers came out folded and bundled. I wanted to be a writer because I wanted my grandfather to see my name in the paper and be proud of me. It's ironic that I have to rely so much on sound now to do my job. To be a reporter. The kind of journalist I want to be."

"Teach me one of the words," Michael said.

"What?"

"Sign language. Show me something I can say in sign language."

Jim interlocked his right and left hands at the index fingers, separated and changed the positions of his hands so that they came back together. "Friend," he said and demonstrated the movement again. "Friend."

At night, Jim could not disconnect himself from the news. He worried that Ari had been kidnapped and was being tortured, and he could not shake the fear from his mind of Ari being flogged or stoned. He read the wire reports, sat with other journalists, or worked on e-mails to Simon or Abdul Ramati or his sister or Stan Chartoff or Matthew Rolley. Abdul had spoken to Simon on the phone in an attempt to coordinate assistance from the State Department, though he refused to respond to Jim's e-mails. It only made Jim more determined to stay in touch, a response he knew Ari would have had as well. At the end of each day, Jim always made a list—how many phone calls he had made and to whom, what he had heard and who was the source, who he hadn't heard back from and who he needed to try. He examined the casualty lists. He read through military briefings for some kind of sign of Ari's whereabouts or another name to contact and ask for details and information. He would not allow himself to grieve, or to look for closure. Ari was alive as long as there was evidence that he wasn't.

He felt in many ways responsible for what had happened. He saw the chronology of his life as a chain of choices—cause and effect, as it were—with Ari's disappearance arriving at the end: if he hadn't moved from Virginia to New York, if he hadn't lived in Chelsea near Eric, if Frank hadn't died, if he hadn't found the bureau job in Athens and then been transferred to Rome, if he hadn't covered the Cannes film festival, if he hadn't met Ari, if he hadn't pushed Simon into giving Ari a freelance assignment, if Ari had taken another job, if he had only been more adamant about wanting the anchor job in London and turned down the trip to Afghanistan.

Wade said that with that sort of rationalizing, Jim could blame himself for everything. "Why not factor in your father's mistakes and your mother's unhappiness. Do a Eugene O'Neill guilt trip and accept the blame for *generations* of wrong turns."

"I can deconstruct the happiness just as easily," Jim defended himself. "I resisted falling in love with Ari because I didn't want to be hurt again. There was my first boyfriend, John, who told me he wanted an open relationship—we were college roommates and I didn't even know what an open relationship was, but I learned that I didn't want it. There were a couple of hundred guys between John and Frank—who only wanted to trick, or to go out on one date and not a second one, or were already in an open relationship and wanted something else on the side. And there was Frank, who wanted a non-sexual relationship when he became ill. And from Frank giving up to the time I met Ari there were another hundred or so dysfunctional men, so that by the time I met Ari, I didn't want a relationship with a guy. And Ari was Ari—beautiful and hotheaded and an opinionated activist. I didn't even want to *try* to have one with him. Ari broke down my resistance. And what happened? I loved him effortlessly, faults and all. Okay, he wanted to come to Afghanistan and I resisted and I thought he was wrong, but I didn't stop loving him—or wanting to love him. And if I hadn't put up that resistance, we wouldn't be where we are now, because I thought if we came here together, things between us would be better—and they were."

"Be careful," Eric wrote Jim about Ari on the back of a postcard that landed on his desk in Rome with the rest of his office mail. "He will rattle your cage and then break your heart."

That afternoon they met for the first time for lunch at an outdoor café on the Croisette that Jim had suggested when Ari had phoned Jim's hotel room in Cannes. The Mediterranean that afternoon was a beautiful light blue. Baie de Cannes was crowded with speedboats, yachts, and publicity-seeking starlets and reporters. Ari arrived wearing a camera around his neck, trying to mimic a tourist—or a fan. Jim wished there was a way they could skip lunch and he could invite Ari back to his hotel room, though he believed it was a hopeless path of obstacles. He was scheduled to be at a screening in less than an hour—he'd only agreed to lunch to appease Eric. And even with Eric's warning, Jim doubted the attraction was mutual. Ari's gaze flickered away from the table, his attention drawn towards the other diners or passersby on the sidewalk. He played with the camera, snapped some shots of a man emerging from the surf.

They avoided talking about Philip Bridges. Jim knew from Eric, their mutual friend, that Ari had been involved with a man who didn't want to be involved in a relationship with him. Ari asked Jim what he was covering at the festival and Jim talked of how easy it was to get around town without having a car.

"Democracy has done little to erase the aristocracy of this country," Ari said, after a waiter had left their table after placing forks and napkins and water glasses in their proper positions. "All this luxury and beauty here, but the wages of almost every worker are substandard. I've even heard of slavery in Monaco. You should do a report on this."

"It's not why I am here," Jim said flatly.

"Isn't the media supposed to keep government responsible?"

"But it is not my job to do it," Jim answered. "I'm not paid to uncover this. I'm paid to report on other things. And you? Where are you staying in this Mecca for the rich and entitled? A shack on the beach?"

"A tiny room on the Rue des Serbes," Ari answered. "Top floor and rather stuffy."

"Overdecorated?"

"Hardly. A thin mattress and no ventilation. The one window seems to be an afterthought. 'Oh, let's put something right here, through the ceiling, to let in the heat.'"

Jim laughed and said that his own accommodations were hardly stellar. "The bureau's budget is worse than my own."

After lunch, Jim offered to try to get Ari into the screening. Ari suggested that they stop by his hotel so that he could pick up his press card; before leaving for Europe, he had been doing freelance work for a cable news channel in Manhattan and if he liked the film, he might be able to do an on-camera review back in New York City. It was a ten-minute walk in the wrong direction, and they walked briskly around the shoppers and tourists on the sidewalks as if they were on deadline.

They did not make the screening. Jim was winded by the walk and the six-story climb to Ari's small hotel room. He stood beside the narrow bed laughing, trying to catch his breath. Ari was sweating and searching his knapsack for his press card. One tap of apology was followed by another. A gesture lingered. The press card was found and Ari handed it to Jim to see if it could get them into the screening. Jim complimented Ari's picture. Ari thanked Jim. The kiss happened spontaneously and the room was filled with more heat.

Jim was relieved that Ari was not the kind of young man who kissed and groped and then shook his head about going farther. It was exactly what he needed at the moment it arrived. Ari fumbled with Jim's fly, slid down his pants, and tipped him back onto the small bed.

Jim tugged off his shoes, watching as the young man slipped out of his shirt and jeans, a cruel but delicious torture that was out of reach. Naked, Ari's skin was dark and smooth about the chest and furiously hairy at the groin and legs. He was not self-conscious about his body as Jim was. Jim hid his erection with his hands. Ari's cock was raised for attention. Jim could not remain on the bed. He stood and moved his arms around Ari's waist, pressing their bodies together into a kiss.

They were gentle and slow, smiling as they stroked and nibbled at each other. Their bodies fit well together—Ari's taller, longer; Jim's thicker, more developed. The small bed in the hotel room didn't encourage a lot of movement and they soon found themselves on the firmer and more spacious ground of the carpet, though they did not need any more room beyond the physical space of their bodies together. Their skin shone with sweat. Ari clasped their cocks together as if they had always belonged that way and brought them to a release.

Afterwards, they napped on the floor, holding each other, barely whispering a word, occasionally shifting and teasing each other to a rise which they would stroke and then let deflate. Jim felt that there was nowhere else he belonged but here, with his arms around Ari. He lay still and listened to Ari's light snoring, matching their breaths in and out. The room was stuffy, just as Ari had said it was. Quietly, without disturbing Ari, Jim removed Ari's hand and got up from the floor. The air cooled his damp skin.

Ari rolled over, stretched his arms and legs, and looked up at Jim dressing and said, "Eric warned me about you."

"Of what?" Jim asked with surprise.

"He told me you would be brutally honest," Ari explained. "That if you liked me, I would know it right away."

"Am I really that transparent?"

Ari nodded and asked, "When can I see you again?"

Jim looked at his watch and thought briefly about his schedule. "A little later if you can find a black tie."

When Jim saw Ari next, Ari was dressed in a tuxedo. He looked like an exotic prince out of a fairy tale. The occasion was a gala at the Grand Palais. Jim nearly missed his interview with a Greek actress because he was so delighted to have Ari's company. His cameraman for the event, a freelancer from the Paris bureau who had too much to drink, made a pass at Ari, and when he was rebuffed, made a pass at Jim.

Later that evening, after they had sent the drunken cameraman in a cab back to Nice, they walked together back to Jim's hotel. A light rain had fallen while they were inside the gala; the streets were slick and shiny with the reflections of light. Jim felt the happiest he had been in years, though he believed it was only fleeting and temporary. Ari would be gone before Jim was hurt that a one-night stand was not something more.

But the next morning Jim put himself out on an emotional limb. He invited Ari to return to Rome with him. It was irrational and impulsive and he had not entirely thought the consequences through. He was relieved when Ari said he could not go. "I have to go to Paris for a few days," he said. "To work off the price of the tuxedo."

Jim gave him an expression that must have indicated he wanted more explanation. "My uncle fronted the money for it. So I have to do a few errands for him."

"You're not in some kind of Mafia, are you?" Jim asked lightly.

"No," Ari answered. "Just a large, demanding family."

An archeologist from Japan arrived with a team of assistants. With them were a filmmaker and his cameraman. The archeologist was hoping to restore some of the frescoes in the caves and grottoes not far from the excavation site for the third Buddha. The foreigners were staying at the same neighborhood compound as Professor Sajadi and Danil. Since Barâdar's English was better than Danil's, Barâdar assisted with the interview the Japanese filmmaker wanted to do with Dr. Sajadi.

"*Tragique*," Dr. Sajadi said while filming. "All that remains of these once majestic statues, which can now only be seen on postcards, are their outlines and some rubble."

The professor was standing in front of the niche of the large Buddha. Beside him was the Japanese archeologist. "The Buddhas were covered in red, blue, and gold," the professor explained for the camera. "Their niches were covered in frescoes depicting scenes from the Buddha's life. The little and large Buddhas are a quarter mile apart. The figures were carved out of the face of the sandstone cliff and then covered with a mixture of mud and wheat straw in which the features and drapery were modeled. This in turn was smoothed over with a very fine plaster which was painted. The robe of the small Buddha was once blue. The face and hands were yellow. This would perhaps account for early eyewitness reports that the figures were gilded."

Barâdar watched the cameraman adjust the lens to tighten the shot. The camera was a digital Betacam. The cameraman's movement was familiar to Barâdar in a way he could not identify. The cameraman followed Dr. Sajadi as he talked and approached the niche. "The niche was once covered with paintings, including one of a heroic sun god riding in his golden chariot pulled through a dark-blue sky by snow-white horses. The sun god was dressed in a long cloak with a sword attached to the belt and he carried a scepter. The chariot was flying through the clouds. Above it, there were flying geese and busts of women wearing pointed caps and holding billowing scarves over their heads. They represented the breezes at sunrise and sunset. On either side of the sun god were two half-bird, half-human sirens, representing the deities who directed celestial music. Below them there were two winged female figures wearing helmets, each holding a shield and a spear. These were thought to be Night and Dawn or the wives of Surya."

The group walked along the base of the cliffs towards the professor's excavation site. Barâdar asked the Japanese cameraman about his camera and if he traveled with any playback and editing equipment. The cameraman did not understand English or French and relied on the director to translate any requests or questions for him. The director was not interested in anything Barâdar was asking. Assuming Barâdar was an aggressive local hustling for money, he ignored the questions. As they walked to the excavation site, Danil told Barâdar that a villager had tried to sell a camera lens to the professor a few days before.

"It was from a camera about the size of Ly's," Danil said, referring to the Japanese cameraman. "But it was useless. It was only a piece of something."

"Where did he get it?" Barâdar asked.

"He wouldn't say. Tariq thought it might have been used when they filmed the Buddhas being destroyed."

At the excavation site, the cameraman continued to film while Dr. Sajadi sifted through trays of dirt at the bottom of a ditch. "Xuanzang, the Chinese pilgrim who visited Bamiyan in 632 A.D., reported ten monasteries and over a thousand priests in attendance," the professor said. "Most of them were probably located between the two standing figures. Where are those monasteries? We're here to solve that mystery. We're here to uncover these sleeping treasures."

Jim was working late in the press tent when Cates from AP yelled across the room that Jim had a call on the satellite phone. It was Simon Bosewall in Rome. Simon had heard from his contact at the U.S. State Department that Ari's passport had been presented at the Pakistan border two days before. Jim was full of questions: Who had it? How did the man get the passport? What did he know about Ari? Why did it take so long for the State Department to inform the bureau? Did this have anything to do with Stan Chartoff?

Simon had already posed those questions to the official who had contacted him. The man, Hamdi Al Kassem, was a suspected member of Al Queda. He had purchased the passport in Kabul from a source he would not identify. He was trying to get to Karachi. He was with five other men, two of them also with stolen passports. They were being detained in Peshawar—there was also a truckload of contraband arms and floor plans to an embassy in Africa.

"Can you get me to Peshawar?"

"We don't have the resources. The Pakastanis are handling it."

"There's a trail. I can follow it back to Ari."

"It's not your story, Jim. Stay where you are. Ari is not in Peshawar."

"I can't stay put," Jim said. He was shouting because it was hard for him to hear Simon on the phone. And he was also exasperated.

"Then you should come back to Rome," Simon answered. "The trail is cold."

"I can't leave without him. You know that."

"You've got to start facing the possibility that Ari might not have survived the accident."

"I know he's alive, Simon. I know it in my gut... my *heart*. I know he's not dead. I've got to go to Peshawar and talk to those men. They might know where Ari is. What happened."

"My guess is that it won't lead anywhere. It was a deal on the black market. Ari was not even involved. It's circumstantial."

"Simon, I've got to do it. For my own sanity."

"Then work it out on your end," Simon said. "I'll send you some of our contacts. And don't try to get around the U.S. military. Make them work *with* you."

"It took them more than two weeks to destroy the Buddhas," Danil told Barâdar.

They had followed the Japanese filmmakers up the cliffs and into the caves. They were in one of the larger grottoes. The archeologist and the professor were being filmed nearby in a smaller one. Their voices echoed against the stone walls.

"The smaller Buddha was the first to fall," Danil said. "The bigger one required greater explosives."

Barâdar was standing at the cave's opening. Below, he could see the top of the white canvas tent beside the excavation site. Danil used the toe of his boot to kick through the rubble on the ground of the cave.

"First, they used tanks and artillery," Danil explained. "They hit the statue with tank shells and rockets, but they couldn't destroy the entire statue. They ran out of dynamite and TNT. The local Taliban leaders refused to carry out the order to destroy the Buddhas. The final explosions were carried out by Pakistani and Saudi Arabian engineers. They were standing at the top of the cliff with their rifles. I asked a mullah who was there, and he said bin Laden and Mutaqi, the Minister of Defense, were here. Four airplanes came to the airport. And about three hundred Taliban were here. The explosions all went off together, all at once. The Taliban shouted '*Allahu akbar!*' The whole valley shook. They were all laughing and happy, like they were at a wedding or it was the end of Ramadan. They celebrated by slaughtering a cow."

"Why?" Barâdar asked. Danil was standing behind him, watching the workers below in the valley at the archeological site carefully pick at the dirt and lift it out of the ditch. Barâdar wanted to turn and study Danil's expression, but he was worried about what he would see. And feel. "Why do these people live like this?"

"It is hard for one man to beat an army," Danil said.

"But not impossible," Barâdar answered. He felt that because Danil understood more about him than anyone else he should expect to understand everything.

"Politics," Danil answered. He moved closer to Barâdar, as if he were going to place a hand against his shoulder. Barâdar waited for the touch to arrive. When it didn't, he turned and looked at Danil. He thought they would kiss instead and the need and desire of intimacy confused him, but the sound of footsteps through the caves distracted them and they parted, rushing from one cave to the next to catch up with the professor and the film crew.

"Big mistake," Wade said to Jim. "Simon's right. Ari's not in Pakistan."

Jim had spent hours arranging a trip to Peshawar. He'd gone to the base commander, phoned the State Department, and arranged to have two U.S. soldiers drive him to Kabul, where an Afghan soldier would escort him through the Khyber pass and into Pakistan. He had been practicing walking with a cane, trying to get out of the habit of using the crutches, but would take both along on the trip for as far as he could.

Simon had cautioned him. "The moment you're recognized as a journalist, you're putting yourself in jeopardy," he had e-mailed to Jim. "There's little anyone can do, if you're discovered. It may be one of the most dangerous places in the world right now. You have to be crazy to go there."

"I am crazy," Jim answered. "And you know why."

Jim shook with fear as he packed a small travel kit. "What else do I have?" he said to Wade. He saw each hour, each delay as another opportunity for the prisoner's release before Jim could question him. But each element was also a certain misstep he would not be able to prevent.

"I could never live with myself if I didn't go," Jim said. "There would always be the 'what if' at the back of my mind—what if this man knew the guy who had sold him Ari's passport?—how did this man know the other man?—what if they knew Ari?—what if they *took* the passport from Ari? I have to see them to know if what they are saying is the truth."

"What about your own passport?" Wade asked. "Didn't it disappear too?"

"It hasn't surfaced," Jim said. "There's no lead there."

The State Department had issued Jim an emergency replacement which the military had been reluctant to pass along to Jim.

"What about Ari's family?" Wade asked. "What if they're doing the same thing you're doing?"

Jim's investigation had turned up correspondence from Ari's uncle to the U.S. consulate in Pakistan. Jim had continued to e-mail Abdul Ramati, even though Ari's uncle had not answered any of his e-mails. He had notified Abdul about Ari's passport being discovered and the arrangements for his trip to Peshawar.

"I hope he has the same kind of luck I'm going to need myself," Jim said. "And I hope we both find the same answer—that Ari is still alive."

A new restlessness haunted Barâdar. He could no longer sleep soundly in the cave. Insomnia plagued him. He was overwhelmed with the feeling he was lost. He went through the facts about himself that he had recovered. He didn't smoke. He was not Afghan. He had once lived in a book-filled apartment. He could read and speak three languages. He could type—he'd done so using the professor's laptop. He knew how to tell time and tie a shoe. He wanted a toothbrush. A hot bath. And a clean pair of socks.

He tumbled and tossed and shifted and listened to the breathing of Haatim and his family. His bruises were healing but his hands were sore from their new fissures and blisters. His back ached from being hunched over all day, sifting through the dirt and dust with the professor. Even in his exhaustion, his mind wandered, searched, looked into his emptiness and found only a dark, hollow shell. He prayed that he could find out who he was. *Let me be who I am supposed to be.*

The prayers. Were there any clues here?

He imagined the large outspread wings of a bird flapping, flying across the valley. He followed the journey across rivers, villages, and farmlands. If he were airborne, flying, searching, he thought he might see something familiar. He saw only the dusty cliffs and the hollowed-out buildings of Bamiyan, Roonah washing clothes in the stream, Haatim smiling and offering him tea, Danil at work at the computer at the edge of the white tent. Maybe God did not want him to go any farther than where he was. He imagined the bird balanced on the cliffside, curiously watching the movements below. He tossed and shifted on the hard cave floor, pulled the thick blanket to his neck for warmth.

He thought again about Danil. A man who loved a man who loved a woman. He tried to imagine the ache of leaving someone behind and felt something in his past was unfinished.

He imagined an embrace, someone holding him. He thought of Danil sitting on the rocks, studying him when he wasn't studying Danil. In his memory he found the image of an arm circling his waist at night—a pale arm that brightened against his darker complexion. It was softened by blond hair which he could stroke and touch as if it were covered with feathers. It was a man's arm. He was certain it was not the arm of his father or brother. But who? Or was he imagining the future? What he wanted from Danil?

Barâdar held the arm in his mind, felt it, touched it, stroked it. It gave him both comfort and jealousy. *Jealousy? What did this mean?*

Queer. Homosexual. Warmer brueder. Faggot. Finocchio... These words came into his mind and stayed there with the arm. They took shape as the arm and hand moved across his body. He was a man lying with a man. One body with another. There was a kiss, a scratch of stubble, a warm rush at his groin. Was this what he had forgotten or what he instinctively remembered?

There was a man, somewhere there was a man, Barâdar was certain of it. Somewhere there was a man looking for him. He could feel the firmness of a man clutching his body as if at any minute he would float away.

What divine being had permitted this? This love? This hurt? This separation?

Allah? Buddha? God?

For Ari, it began with a feather of arousal. Something about the way Jim's cheek dimpled on the left side; the even row of bottom teeth; the faint, almost imperceptible, cleft in his chin; the green eyes that seemed to hold as much intelligence as they did curiosity. Ari was used to this tug of lust and imagination, had, in fact, been with several men on this trip away from home—part vacation, part business, part job prospecting—a waiter in Paris, a guy he had met at a dance club in the Marais, two lovers on a guided tour who were interested in a threesome. At lunch on the Croisette, Ari had studied Jim as though he was about to take his portrait, lifting the lens of his camera and zooming in to a yacht in the bay and playfully swerving the camera around to focus on Jim's face. Jim had responded with a nervous laugh and held up his hand to stop Ari's scrutiny.

"No, no, that's so unfair," Jim said.

"I thought you'd be used to it. You're always in front of a camera."

"Not *always*. I hate being so public. If I had my druthers, I'd only write all my pieces. I hate seeing myself on television—almost as much as I hate hearing my voice."

"Your *druthers*?" Ari asked.

"My druthers," Jim answered and smiled. "What a silly expression. I must have picked that up while I was working in Athens with all those Brits."

Everything that first day—that lunch, that afternoon, that evening with Jim—was effortless. With Pup, Ari had always felt awkward and unpolished. Pup had always cast himself as the patron and teacher. A daddy. "I wouldn't wish my life on you," he would sometimes say to Ari when they were together. "My opinions, yes. My life, *no. Not at all.*"

With many guys—mainly the usual crowd of Gay White Men at clubs and bars—Ari felt cheap and stereotyped. Jim was neither judgmental nor condescending; he had folded his hands together and listened to Ari go on and on about his relatives back in the States, and why he wanted to work in broadcasting.

"I respect my uncle very much," Ari said. "He gave me my first job. He paid for my schooling. No one works harder than he does, except maybe my cousins, who don't ever get enough credit for having to work for my uncle."

"And your dad?" Jim asked. "Does he work with your uncle?"

"My father is from a Italy. Third generation from the Veneto. Working class. Dock workers, teamsters. My grandmother always believed that he had married beneath him when he married my mother, whose family was Persian immigrants, and wealthy. My mother did not want to convert to Catholicism, but she did and we lived in New Haven for a while, but when she found out my father was having an affair, she left him. They never divorced, because my grandmother would not allow it, but they never lived together again. My younger sister and I were tugged between them. Queens and Connecticut. I was the only one of my father's family who went to college and for a while that kept me out of having to work in my mother's family business, which my uncle runs. Carpets. Oriental rugs. Importing."

"Were you raised Catholic?" Jim said.

"I know all about Catholicism," Ari said. "I was sent to a few parochial schools. But my mother's family is Bahá'í. My grandparents— my maternal ones—wanted something more tolerant."

"Tolerant? I doubt they feel that way about homosexuality."

"What religion does?"

"And how do you feel about religion? Catholic or Bahá'í?"

"Many lessons were learned," Ari said. "Hopefully they are useful. But religion is useless without faith in change."

"Chocolate?" Danil asked Barâdar. "You must remember chocolate. Bittersweet? Bakers' squares—my mother would buy large blocks of it."

"No," Barâdar answered. They were working inside the tent and talking in French.

"Croissants? The smell of rolls?"

Barâdar shook his head, and smiled.

"I'd love to clear my brain of all the crap," Danil said to Barâdar. "Just remember how to type. Or tie a shoe."

Danil was sorting through pottery fragments that had been discovered in the dig, dusting away the dirt with a feathery brush. They had become good friends quickly. Barâdar had described his loss of memory and the family who was taking care of him. He had told Danil that he was proud that he had learned to speak enough Hazaragi to tell Roonah that he was grateful for the food she gave him, even though it went against the customs of purdah for them to associate.

"What would you want to forget?" Barâdar asked.

"A mother who cried. A father who beat me," Danil said. "A lover who doesn't care."

"What do you mean?"

"It does not matter if I am hot or hungry or thirsty or lonely," Danil said. "Only what I find in a pile of dirt."

Barâdar felt suddenly uncomfortable. He was concerned that Danil was unhappy but did not feel it was appropriate to continue talking about it. Or to ask for any more details. The professor had been good to him. Had fed him meals. Given him work. The money had helped his Afghan family. He did not want to put any of this in jeopardy by becoming too close to Danil and risk angering the professor. But he also wanted to help Danil, if it was needed.

"He is not unkind to you?" Barâdar asked.

"Unkind?" Danil answered.

"Abusive?"

"*Non. Non.* The opposite. Too kind. Smothering."

Barâdar worked quietly the rest of the day, moving between the professor in the ditch and Danil in the tent. At the end of the day, he waited in line for his wages with the local men and followed them back to the village. Danil caught up with Barâdar when he was almost at the bazaar. He was going to buy sacks of nuts and dried fruit to bring back to Roonah.

"The professor is happy with your work," Danil said. "We both are. Come join us again for dinner."

"I should spend time with the family," Barâdar said. "I must help them out for helping me."

"Will you think about joining us?" Danil asked.

"Yes," Barâdar answered. "Another time."

"We have room for you at the hotel," Danil said. "The professor enjoys your company. We both do. You can leave the cave. Live with us at the hotel."

"It would be such an imposition," Barâdar said.

"It would be a pleasure," Danil said. "Our pleasure to spend time with you. Know you better. Please think of joining us."

"Another time," Barâdar answered. "Let me discuss it with the family."

The following day an official from the French embassy in Pakistan called Jim. They were inquiring into details of the death of Dr. Dupray at the insistence of his wife and daughter in Paris. Jim explained meeting Dr. Dupray in Kabul, and the long ride in the van to Bamiyan, and the details of the accident as they approached the village—what he recalled of it. He told of his own survival, the trek to Anabah and then to Bagram, and asked Monsieur Hermance, the French official, if Dr. Dupray's family had been contacted by Afghanistan government or anyone from an NGO agency.

Monsieur Hermance seemed more interested in the recovery of the professor's personal items. A watch, his journals, and his wedding ring were missing. Jim had also lost his wallet and passport, all of his identification, press credentials, and credit cards. He explained that he had no knowledge of anything belonging to the doctor that had been left behind, and that as of yet, he had not heard back from any of the other archeologists he knew who were working in Bamiyan.

When he hung up, Jim finished writing an e-mail to Stan Chartoff. The MSF worker had been located in Paris, en route to the States, and he had begun a steady correspondence with Jim when he learned of the reporter's survival, though he had nothing to add to the fate of Ari. "Tomorrow, I'm leaving for Pakistan. I've met with reluctance and resistance from everyone about the trip. I know in my gut that nothing from it will lead to finding my cameraman Ari Sarghello, but it is the only thing that I can attach some hope towards. I am hoping that by going to Peshawar, I will somehow be able to return to Bamiyan, as illogical as it sounds.

"I can't thank you enough for all that you have done for me. Someday, I hope that you might visit me in Rome, and I can entertain you and thank you in person, though right now Rome seems like another lifetime to me. I don't know when or if this e-mail will reach you, but if you remember anything else that might help me on this search, please write to me as soon as possible."

That evening there was an argument in the cave between Nadeem and Roonah. Haatim had brought home a seven-year-old girl whose mother had given birth to a baby boy that afternoon at the hospital. The woman's husband had been killed by a mine five months before. Ghatol, the girl, and her mother had been hiding in the mountains with other refugees and had walked three days to reach the village and the hospital.

The argument had nothing to do with Ghatol. Roonah yelled, *"Khâneh! Khâneh!"* She pointed at the floor and the walls and the stove and the barrels of water and dung. The candles flickered angrily because of her movements in the cave. The men shifted and hung their heads, lifted their chins and fought back. Siraaj and Haatim tried to convince Roonah of the same thing Nadeem was telling her. She slapped the back of her hand against her palm. She hugged her chest and moaned and shook her head. The evening ended in retreat and silence, Roonah turning her back to her family and shepherding the girl close to the stove, where Ghatol was fed and pampered with bowls of rice and doll-like figures Roonah made out of twigs and straw.

The girl slept next to Roonah and stayed at the cave the next morning when the men left. Haatim led Barâdar to the hospital office to speak with Estelle. She translated Haatim's plea for help. The men wanted the family to be relocated to the new village settlement. A small house would be better than the cave. It would be safer for them in the winter. They had a better chance of being assigned to a house if the family was large and there was a new baby to take care of. They would take in Ghatol and her mother and the new baby boy. They'd have a diesel generator for a few hours of electricity in the evening. Haatim wanted Barâdar's help. Roonah was stubborn and old and set in her ways. She didn't want to leave the cave. She didn't want to move again. She considered the hillside her home now.

Barâdar didn't know what to say. How could he help convince Roonah without speaking the language? Haatim explained he must stand beside them, help the family move to the new settlement.

The men told Roonah that one day they would be forced to leave the cave. A house in the village was better than nothing, better than returning to the mountains, which had been worse than the cave. It would not be taken away from them. Haatim asked Barâdar to help them. He was a smart man. He must show Roonah that they would be better off in the village than in the cave.

When Haatim walked across the courtyard, Barâdar asked Estelle if the mother and her new baby boy would live.

"Yes," she answered. "They are doing fine. But Haatim is right. Where will they go? Back to the mountains? A house would be best for all of them."

"When will this happen?"

"Soon, we hope. Until then, they must stay in the caves. Haatim will bring Zaina and Moji back tomorrow. I will send some more food for Roonah. And goat's milk for the baby."

"I can stay with the professor and Danil," Barâdar said. "Near the NGO compounds."

"Is that wise?"

"It will give them more room."

"For you, I mean. I've heard talk that the mullah is unhappy with the professor. It's quite possible there will be trouble."

"What kind of trouble?"

"It's hard to say. He's not Taliban, but he could be just as dangerous."

"I should warn them."

"You must look out for yourself. Remain with the family. Help them move to the new village. It's best they leave the caves as soon as possible, so they are not moved outside the valley."

Back in Paris, Ari found the city painfully beautiful—the trees along the boulevards, the stalls along the banks of the Seine, the giggling clusters of tourists pointing to the Eiffel Tower and Sacré-Coeur. Each day his memory of Jim grew fonder and he felt the ache of inertia. He worried that Jim would find him callous or cocky, showing up at his office and asking for a job. And how could he possibly move to Rome without help? Already he owed his uncle a fortune. Graduate school. Years of graduate school. An unemployable doctorate.

He invented the notion of visiting Rome to see his father's distant cousins—a ruse no one in his family believed to be sincere, but it got him out of Paris with his family's blessing and assistance. He stayed with them a day and then moved into a small pensione near the Coliseum, waiting three more days before contacting Jim.

The interview with Simon Bosewell and Jim at the network office was awkward and uncomfortable, and Ari believed that the possibility of a position was out of his reach. Before Ari left, Jim walked him down the hall, introduced him to several other editors and producers, and suggested that Ari could pinch-hit as a freelance cameraman if needed. Simon indicated that there was an event the following day at the Vatican that had not been assigned. Jim agreed to cover it if Ari could handle the filming.

Jim waited around while Ari filled out some paperwork for the network and discussed labor arrangements and filming equipment, then asked where Ari was staying as he escorted him to the elevator. Jim knew of the pensione Ari had found and suggested a few alternatives, one of them being the couch in Jim's apartment, if Ari was hard up for cash.

"If you're comfortable with that," Jim said.

"Would you be?" Ari asked.

"Yes," Jim answered. "I'd find it comfortable having you around."

"You have a visitor at the front gate," Michael said to Jim when he arrived at the press tent. It was the morning Jim was leaving for Pakistan. He was waiting for the soldier to drive him first to Kabul.

"A visitor?"

"Afghan fellow. Young guy. Said he drove up from Kabul."

"Did he say anything about Ari?"

"He only wants to speak with you."

Jim could still not walk without the help of crutches. The cane was useless. Michael drove Jim across the base to the front gate where, a few minutes later, Jim found the teenaged boy from the carpet warehouse in Kabul. Jim's face reddened as he approached. The young boy suspiciously glanced from Jim to Private Baxter and back to Jim, exactly as he had done before with Ari in the carpet warehouse in Kabul.

"Sir, I am Yazeed Ali-Khan, son of Muhammed Ali-Khan and nephew of Manno Ali-Khan. I am to drive you now to Bamiyan. Hurry, we must go."

The boy was as tall as Ari, dark eyed and dark haired, with the same chiseled features. If Jim hadn't known better, he might have imagined that the boy and Ari were related. He appeared to be eighteen or nineteen, but his voice was younger. His complexion was not darkened by the stubble of a beard; instead, fine wisps of black hair lined his upper lip where one day a moustache would likely grow thicker.

He was dressed in Western clothing—shirt tucked into his pants, and a jacket, though he wore a brown pakol cap on his head and a blue-and-green striped vest over his shirt.

One of the soldiers working at the front gate handed a piece of paper to Jim and said, "He had this on him." It was a print-out of an e-mail message dated the day before. The paper appeared to have been folded and unfolded many times. It was from Ari's uncle in New York. It read, in English: "Jim, This man will help you find Ari."

"We must hurry and leave now, sir."

The boy's English was choppy, but with the help of an Afghan soldier, Jim learned that Yazeed had been given his uncle's van to drive Jim to Bamiyan to search for Ari. Yazeed was impatient to leave soon—it was a long journey, close to five or six hours through the mountains. His uncle would be impatient if they did not return the van as soon as possible. "There are many deliveries," he said. "Many customers to be lost."

Yazeed showed the soldiers and Jim his documentation. Jim asked the boy a few questions, trying to banish any suspicions or reluctance. Jim was ready to leave. He'd been waiting for a chance like this to happen. He asked Yazeed to wait while he went and got his kit. He asked Michael to drive him back across the base to retrieve it.

"Sir, you're not going to go with this boy, are you?" Michael asked. "What about Pakistan?"

"Ari's passport is in Pakistan. But if Ari's alive—and he *is* alive— he's still in Bamiyan. I would have heard something if he wasn't."

Had his prayers been answered? He was both elated and fearful of this new turn of events. Jim got his travel kit, canteens of water, and his pain medication. Michael drove Jim back to the front gate where Yazeed was waiting.

On the floor of the front seat of Yazeed's van were empty soda cans and the ground-out butts of cigarettes. Yazeed shrugged his shoulders and pitched the cans into the back of the van, where two rolled up carpets were lying. Before they drove away, Michael asked Jim, "Are you sure you want to do this, sir?"

"I need to find out what happened to him," Jim said. "It's why I've stayed here. So I *can* do this."

He still did not confess to the young man that Ari was his lover. But he detected something in Michael's eyes that indicated he understood Jim's mission.

Michael told them to wait. Yazeed was impatient, gunning the engine of the van as though he was on the starting line of a race track. Michael returned with three flak jackets and helmets.

"Keep in touch," Michael said. "Let me know where you are."

He signed the word "friend" for Jim as Yazeed drove towards the front gate.

Jim tried not to feel that he was making a mistake. He waved as the van disappeared through the gate, his fingers hooked together to sign "friend."

Fourteen

Outside the airbase, the road was rutted with potholes. Yazeed tried to speed past the merchant sheds that were near the main gates, but the slow-moving traffic prevented him. Cars and trucks were parked at odd angles in front of food stands. Cyclists pushed their bikes around clusters of Afghan men. Jim pressed his hand against the door and then to the ceiling to steady himself as the van rocked and dipped along the uneven dirt road. Each lurching movement sent a small shiver of nervous pain up his left leg.

Ahead, a mist shrouded the snow-capped mountain peaks. Each slow, painful dip of the wheels of the van along the ruts in the road made Jim want to tell the boy to turn around, take him back to base. This was a mistake. He was ready to give up, admit defeat. Ari was dead and it was time to return home to Rome without him. The journey was useless.

But it wasn't. Ari wasn't dead. Jim was more sure of this than anything else. *But what am I doing? Is this boy even old enough to drive? Is this another mistake in a string of mistakes?*

When they reached the outskirts of Bagram, the road leveled out and Yazeed picked up speed. He also lit a cigarette. Jim cracked his window for ventilation.

"You have American smokes?" Yazeed asked him.

"No," Jim answered bluntly, and shook his head. His eyes teared and his ear stopped up from the change in air pressure inside the van. A sharp, stabbing pain ached in his damaged ear. A sudden rise of nausea moved into his throat, and he stretched out his hand to the dashboard to steady himself. He turned away from the boy and studied the passing dusty landscape. It was a bleak scene. Why was he here? Why had he given in to the assignment—to prove to Ari that he could be an admirable journalist or to prove to Ari that he didn't place himself first in the scheme of their relationship? A squeeze of pain rippled through his chest. He had never stopped loving Ari, even as he, himself, pursued other career options. In interview after interview he had hoped he would fail so that there would not be a reason to leave Ari. Jim knew he would be more miserable to step away from Ari and let him go.

In the distance an abandoned caravanserai, brightened by the sunlight and outlined by the blue sky, made Jim squint and feel sleepy. He was too sick to reach for the sunglasses in his shirt pocket to deflect the intense glare of the sun so he closed his eyes. *If the situation were reversed, would Ari be doing the same thing? Would Ari be looking for him? Would Ari be submitting himself to the mercy of a boy recklessly driving a car across the bleak landscape of Afghanistan? Would Ari take his life in his hands in an attempt to save Jim?*

The boy did not wear the flak jacket Jim had offered him. A helmet sat on the front seat between them. Jim held another helmet in his lap. Yazeed finished his cigarette and tossed the butt out of the car. He reached inside his chest pocket and lit up another cigarette with his lighter. Jim wanted to tell the boy he was too young to have such a habit, but he was too intimidated to speak out. The boy's attractiveness appalled him. He found it hard to think and speak to him because of it. And Jim's interest in the boy's sexuality unnerved him. How could these curiosities float to the top of his consciousness while he was hoping he might finally find Ari? This trip was a mistake, he was sure of it, as sure as the Peshawar plan had been. Something bad was going to happen. Or was this simply Jim's subconscious preparation for a worst-case scenario? What if Ari hadn't survived? What then? What would he do? *How will I go on?*

A few miles beyond the base, the boy slowed the van down and stopped on the edge of the road. He opened the door and stubbed out the cigarette with the toe of his boot. Jim didn't question the delay. He opened his door and shifted his legs to be more comfortable. The crutches were in the back of the van, but the boy did not reach for them to offer them to Jim. Yazeed walked around the back of the van and out into the flat field of dirt. He unzipped his pants and pissed on the dry ground.

Jim watched the backside of the boy and told himself not to watch him any longer, to avoid a comment or a confrontation. He looked at the patterns of snow creasing the tops of the mountains. The morning mist had disappeared. The sky sat above him like a giant blue ceiling. Yazeed walked back to the van and stopped at the rear wheel. He squatted and reached his hand up and beneath the rim of the wheel well and withdrew a handgun that had been concealed by tape. He removed the tape and shoved the gun in the back of his pants. He reached deeper behind the rim and brought out another gun and positioned it at the front of his waist, which offered Jim a quick view of the boy's underwear and a slight trail of pubic hair. Next, he opened the back doors of the van, pushed aside the rolled-up carpets, opened a compartment that ran along the side of the van, and pulled out a rifle.

The boy put the rifle in the front seat between himself and Jim. Jim pretended it wasn't there—that nothing had changed—though he was aware that the boy had waited till a deserted stretch of road before unveiling his weapons. Jim knew there was no way they could make the trip without them for their own security, and that the American military wouldn't have allowed Yazeed through the front gate with them obviously displayed. Jim had spent hours watching soldiers—young men with guns—parade and practice and drill and escort him around the base, but the young Afghan's ease with them unnerved him more. "War loves to seek its victims in the young," Ari would have reminded him. "Because it is the business of cowards."

Yazeed slid open the back door and found a pale blue patterned scarf on the floor which he twisted around his head into a turban. Jim thought it made him look older, even though the wisps of his unshaven beard were light and sparse and betrayed his youth. Yazeed lit another cigarette and started up the van.

"You live in America?" he asked Jim.

"Italy. *Italia.*"

"*Italia?*"

"Europe. *Europa.*"

"I know. I study map," the boy answered. "I thought you American."

"I am. I live in Rome. I work in *Roma.*"

"*Roma,*" the boy echoed. "One day I see it."

Jim wanted to offer to show it to him—*if we find Ari alive and healthy, I would take you around the world to celebrate, no strings attached*—but he was worried it might be both an empty gesture and an impossible task. He was at the mercy of Fate and this young man's driving skills.

"You like *Roma?*"

"Very much."

"Your friend. He like *Roma* too?"

"Yes."

"He *Italia?*"

"American. *Americano.*"

"He not live in America? I don't understand."

"It's where we work. *Roma.* We like it." *Most of the times we like it,* Jim thought, but he didn't say that. He didn't want to confuse the boy. *Our lives are complicated.*

The road narrowed and climbed as they reached the first range of mountains. Jim shifted his position often, keeping his weight off-balance and his leg from hurting. Yazeed smoked and talked about learning English from American action movies—*Die Hard, Lethal Weapon, Terminator.* "Hasta la vista, baby," he said, and mimicked shooting something ahead on the road.

Jim smiled and corrected the boy, "It's not English."

"Not English?"

"No, not really. *Spanish.*"

"Why is this Spanish?"

"It means good-bye. *Khoda hafez.*"

The boy asked Jim if he liked John McClane best, and it took a moment for Jim to realize that he was referring to Bruce Willis's character in the movie *Die Hard.*

"Too vengeful," Jim said, trying to smile. "Too hotheaded. Do you like Indiana Jones?"

"Ah yes," Yazeed answered. "But he does not like the mujahideen."

Soon, they ran out of action movies to talk about. Jim leaned his head against the window and made more bargains with God: *If Ari were safe and healthy, he would spend more time volunteering for the relief agencies, campaign for contributions, recruit others for the organizations. If Ari were alive he would thank Ari's uncle, thank his family and offer to help out in their family business, even if Ari still could not make that offer himself. Maybe he would quit the bureau, do anything to repay what needed to be repaid.*

As the van ascended along the unpaved mountain road, Jim's prayers became short naps. The rocking was easier to handle with his eyes closed, but he was jolted awake by the sound of voices at a checkpoint. Yazeed was talking to an Afghan soldier and pointing at Jim and the crutches in the back seat, making it obvious that Jim was a foreigner who needed medical attention.

The soldier looked into the van at Jim, nodded, and waved them along. The van bumped and lurched over the road. Yazeed grinned at Jim and reached for a cigarette in his chest pocket.

"I like American smokes best," the boy said. "These okay, too," he added and waved the cigarette towards Jim.

◆◆◆

Whenever Barâdar prayed, which on most days seemed to be minute by minute, he would always ask God for the same thing. *Lord, please help me find out who I am. Lord, thank you for those who are watching over me now. Lord, watch over those who are worried and looking for me.*

The search for his identity continued. Danil was able to take his photograph and make copies with the professor's computer printer, which Barâdar now distributed after work to the foreign military officials he found in the village—American, French, and Italian soldiers. There had been no answers from the Red Cross, UNESCO, DDR, Aga Kahn, or the other non-governmental organizations, but Estelle warned him to wait before approaching the local Bamiyan mullahs and Afghan officials for help, worried there might still be a possibility of kidnapping or punishment. She helped him with memory exercises—questioning him with maps and foreign phrases—and helped him meditate and visualize moments from his past. Within the blank spaces of his memory came more images—a taxi ride through Manhattan, an explosion on the Bamiyan cliffs where the large Buddha statue had been—the billowing tunnel of gray smoke and brown dust that seemed to spread across the valley like an alien attack.

He had no memory of the Taliban, however—the mass graves which were on the west side of the cliffs, nor of the refugee camps to the north or in Iran. Nor of being inside any building in New York City—Rockefeller Center, a Broadway theater, the lobby or observation deck at the World Trade Center. He could remember a bed and the warmth of a body beside him when it became cold, though he did not tell Estelle this or his belief that it had been another man.

At the hospital, he would stare at his reflection in the cracked mirror above the sink. It was a good solid face, a hint of gray in his beard but generally unweathered. His teeth were in good shape. Even. White. A cap on a back molar. Somewhere there was a dentist with a record of this. *Where? Where had he lived?* He continued to look for his mother in his eyes. Or his father. But all he could see was a man still looking for himself.

At night, after eating with the family, while the men sat talking and praying, Barâdar continued to say his own prayers and search for other memories. He stared at the black and gray walls, trying to imagine patterns within the shadows cast by the soft glow of the gas lamp. He looked for messages within the rim of the ceiling where the arch of the dome began, but his eyes always traveled to the faint remains of the outline of the sitting Buddha's body on the western wall of the cave, which on some days would catch a bright patch of morning light but at night remained hidden unless a flicker of a candle leapt up high enough to reveal its folded legs, soft limbs, and large broad head and halo. *Dear Buddha,* he prayed, *Gracious Buddha, grant me wisdom, grant me peace. Grant me enough memory to keep everyone around me safe.*

Jim was the center of attention whenever they were out together on assignment, the one immediately recognized, ushered into a private room and introduced first while Ari waited in the background. But there was usually a moment when something changed, a shift of attention by the spokesperson or celebrity towards Ari, a glance that betrayed a curiosity to know better this other handsome guy holding the camera, a sort of sexual intrigue that seemed to glow and burst into flame. Ari was always aware of this moment, never failing to seize the opportunity to show off his intelligence or interject politics or human-rights issues by asking a question that could put everyone on edge. Ari's combination of attractiveness and political arrogance made him immediately loved or despised—there was seldom any in between. Jim had endured interviews abruptly ended because of Ari and awkward moments when his partner was pulled aside and slipped phone numbers and e-mail addresses for later hookups.

They were improbably unbalanced. There were differences in their ages, their heights, weights, and physiques. Ari came from a wealthy family yet was always at a loss for money for even the basic necessities such as toothpaste, razors, and clean laundry. Jim had been born to a family who always struggled, but he had reached a level of personal comfort that allowed him to be generous to his relatives, helping his niece pay for her college tuition and his sister with a down payment on a house. Their tastes in men were also different. Jim was drawn to the types of guys he had hung around with in college, smart, shy, quirky but non-threatening bookish men. Ari preferred the rowdy pretty boys—handsome surfer dudes and frat boys and runway models—those guys with long legs and thin shoulders, tousled hair and day-old stubble, but he found them as insubstantial as bubble-gum and soon grew to want to be with men who were older, educated, and opinionated.

Jim had never believed that their affair would last longer than a few weeks and was surprised every day that it had continued. He was always ready to let Ari go. He believed that Ari did not love him as strongly as he loved Ari, another imbalance, that Jim was, in fact, the one who loved, not the one who was loved. It had been the same way in his relationship with Frank, and he wasn't looking to repeat the loss or depression or the emotional breakdown when things ended with Ari. Jim's scheme was to emotionally disconnect from the young man, divorce himself from Ari's social issues and extracurricular sexual activities, to bequeath the young man his independence, give him a set of keys to the apartment and let him come and go as he pleased, which always seemed to backfire when he would find Ari at home waiting for him. "Don't you care about what we do together?" the upset younger man would ask the astonished older one.

Ari had come to believe that his attractiveness was a stronger curse than his politics. He allowed himself to be an easy prey, and regret usually followed. A trick usually had no interest in discussing chemical additives in food distributed in third-world countries, the lawlessness in Senegal, or the government suppression in Venezuela. And even if they did it was empty talk. No action. No follow through. "All I was was a toy," he told Jim during their first month together in Rome about his four-year on-again, off-again involvement with Philip Bridges. "Emotionally, I was very young and needy, but it left me feeling like I was always abused. The day I got my Ph.D. was also the one I finally walked away from him."

But Ari also liked to play, and he played well with Jim. In bed, they were an ideal combination—assured, exploratory, experimental, gracious, and aggressive. Jim believed that their sex together was a tenuous link and that once Ari tired of *him* they would be forced to navigate a way to remain colleagues at work. Simon had even cornered Jim in the hallway of the bureau and asked, "When this plays itself out, are you still going to be comfortable working with him?"

"What would I do without you?" Ari would ask when he found Jim in the kitchen most mornings hunched over notes and outlines, a pot of coffee already made, a question that Jim had come to ask himself about Ari.

They stopped when Jim became nauseated. The smoke and a loss of balance had overwhelmed him. The air had thinned as the van ascended the mountains. Jim asked Yazeed three times to pull over, then opened the door while the van was still going and made the boy stop. His head was burning with pain. He leaned out of the van and vomited on the rocky ground. He wiped his mouth with the sleeve of his shirt and stepped outside and found that his right leg was stiff. Blood had seeped through the fabric of his pants and dried against the hair of his leg. He pried away the pants from his skin, rolled the fabric up to his knee and dabbed his scabs with water to keep his skin clean. He rinsed his mouth with water and felt his forehead. He was fighting off a fever. Or was it just a headache from tension? He could feel his heartbeat throbbing at his temples and neck because of the rising altitude. He touched his right earlobe to make sure he was not bleeding through his ears. He wondered if he would survive this trip, if this would be a fatal last lark.

In the kit he had brought there was a type of protein bar that the soldiers ate while away from their base. He took a bite out of the corner of it, the texture rubbery and tasteless in his mouth. He chased it with a small gulp of water and offered Yazeed the rest.

Yazeed waved it away, lit up a cigarette, and they were on their way again. The road was narrower in the mountains. The breeze through the window made Jim feel better. They passed a man riding a donkey, and a family who carried baskets and rolled up carpets on their backs. Jim wanted to stop and find out their story, something Ari would have insisted on doing—not from a journalistic perspective, but from a humanistic one. Where were they headed? What were they carrying? Why were they leaving? Who caused their exodus? Who refused to help them out?

A few miles later, as Yazeed drove through a pass between two mountains, Jim recognized a chaikhana where he and Ari had stopped when they had traveled this route with Dr. Dupray three weeks before. The professor had been full of local tidbits—pointing out the abandoned Russian tanks, the gutted village of sandy-colored mud walls that had once surrounded their rest stop, the sense of lawlessness and feudalism of this region that did not begin with the Taliban. "A gun is more important here than the Koran," Dr. Dupray said. "But God has not abandoned this land. He has filled it with the startling kindness of a beggar helping another beggar."

"Beggars because of an extremist conservative religion," Ari had responded. "What kind of religion strips a man of his dignity and self-worth and prevents him from doing what generations of his ancestors have been able to do—make a living for himself from his local resources—from items God has provided him?"

"This land was bleak long before the Sunnis," Dr. Dupray said, not wanting to argue with Ari. "I doubt the Mongols were better."

Ahead, a muddied jeep approached from the other direction on the single lane road. Instead of veering to the side to allow the van to pass, the driver angled the jeep so that it blocked the passageway along the narrow mountain road. Two men wearing black turbans and dark shalwar kameez sat in the jeep and waited for the van to reach them. Jim knew immediately it was a shakedown—that it would cost them something to make it past this illegal checkpoint—*if* they made it past.

Yazeed slowed down as he approached the jeep and removed the gun that he had kept hidden in the back of his pants, resting it on his lap. There was no way for the van to make it around the jeep. On one side was an ascending cliff, on the other a descending one. Yazeed braked and leaned out the window and shouted something to the two men.

The men raised their rifles and shouted something at Yazeed, obviously relaying their bargaining points or price for passage. Jim slipped off the wristwatch he had bargained off a soldier at Bagram and showed it to Yazeed. "I've got this," he said to Yazeed. "We can give them this." The watch wasn't worth much. Jim had never developed a taste for expensive items because he was always leaving something behind while out in the field—a cell phone, a watch, eyeglasses, his notes.

Yazeed gave Jim an irritated look and shifted the van into reverse, using the rearview mirror to back up along the mountain road. Jim thought certain they were headed for trouble—either Yazeed would lose control of the van and they would be stuck on the road, or the two men in the jeep would decide to pursue them. Neither happened. Instead, Yazeed quickly braked the van to a stop and shifted again into forward, driving towards the jeep at a fast and reckless speed. Jim immediately understood the boy's strategy, but he was also aware that there was a greater probability that it wouldn't leave them all unharmed. He tensed his back and pressed his hand against the dashboard to brace himself for the crash. Yazeed drove the van towards the front end of the jeep, steering the larger vehicle close to the ascending cliff of the mountain and hoping that a crash would do minimal damage to the van and push the jeep off the road and the cliff.

The two men in the jeep saw the approaching van and jumped out of the jeep, waving their rifles and yelling insults at Yazeed. Neither man aimed or pointed their guns at the van, which immediately showed their bluff—they had guns but no ammunition.

Yazeed slowed the van but butted it against the jeep, pushing it off the road. The men responded with furious shouting and hand waving and stomping their feet into the muddy road. Yazeed leaned out his window again, this time pointing his gun at one of the men and yelling instructions to the other to move the jeep out of the road. The behavior was extraordinary and Jim wondered where in this young man's life he had acquired such guts.

The men hopped in the jeep and now it was their turn to back up along the mountain road. At a wider passage, they pulled over at the cliffside. Yazeed stopped the van and had both men get out of the jeep. With his gun pointed he ordered them to walk away from the jeep and down the road, so that they could not cause any trouble while he was attempting to navigate the van around the jeep—by trying to push the van over the cliff.

Yazeed hopped back into the van, talking to Jim now in Dari, as if he understood everything he was saying, and drove the van around the jeep. As they passed the two men, who had stopped walking and were watching the van approach, the boy yelled something again at the two men.

Then he turned to Jim and said something else in Dari, and ended with, "Hasta la vista, baby," and smiled, then added, "That's Spanish. Not English."

It took Jim four months to admit he was in love. They had traveled to Munich to do a report on the Christmas market and it had rained constantly since they had landed at the airport. They had tried to do interviews in front of the shopping stalls, but many were closed because of the weather and few shoppers were to be found. They sprinted to a nearby building, thinking they might be able to film an establishing shot from the rooftop, but once they had climbed the winding stairs and were overlooking the square they were again thwarted by random gusts of wind. They had gone to a large restaurant and interviewed tourists, only to have one teenaged girl retch on Jim's shoes because she was drunk. Next they tried to film a segment in the lobby of the Konigshof Hotel before the management asked them to leave because of a private reception being held.

Back in their hotel room they had laughed and undressed and dried off and turned up the heat and cuddled under the covers, buoyantly recounting the obstacles and the certain-to-be-snide remarks they felt they would receive from Simon.

Ari fell asleep quickly, but Jim was too giddy and restless to relax. He flipped through the cable channels of the television, then turned it off to listen to Ari snore and the rain tap against the window. In the bed, Ari was curled into the spot where Jim had been sleeping, embracing a pillow as if it were Jim. The room was littered with their drying clothes—socks on the backs of chairs, shirts hanging on the cabinet doors of the armoire, Jim's necktie draped across the desk—everything they owned intermingled. The tripod was leaning in the corner, but the camera sat on another chair as if it were a sleeping pet, waiting to be awakened to play again. At that moment Jim wished this feeling could be captured on film—his desire to be nowhere else in the world except where he was now.

There was another argument when Haatim brought Zaina and her new baby to the family's cave. Roonah slapped her hands together, hugged her chest, and spoke harshly to Haatim and his uncles, pointing to the dirt floor and the blackened walls. It was easy for Barâdar to understand that Roonah believed that this was no place to be raising a new baby.

Haatim fought back, his voice as demonstrative as Roonah's. He pointed to the cave's opening and the village below and then back to the cave and the fire in the stove. The uncles chimed in with their opinions, and Barâdar thought this must be the moment that they were revealing their plan to move to the new settlement. Estelle had told Barâdar that the family might be able to move soon; she had helped Haatim with the agency handling the relocation of families still living in the cliff caves. Roonah's face turned hard as she listened, her eyes flickered around the cave as if this were the most safe and sacred spot in her world.

The argument subsided when Roonah settled Zaina and the baby near the stove. Zaina, pale and weak, clutched the baby, unwilling to let Roonah take him away. Roonah's displeasure at this was further directed at the men. The girl, Ghatol, Zaina's seven year-old daughter, huddled close to her mother, teary eyed and confused, trying to curl herself up into a small ball of nothing. Roonah shielded the new mother from the view of the men when she breastfed the child. The men sat by the opening of the cave smoking and looking at the view of the dark valley below. Haatim continued to direct the conversation, probably arguing the finer points to his relatives of a move to a new house for their growing family, the fact that there was an heir now, a baby boy to keep their family growing and prospering. Siraaj and Nadeem offered grunts or small phrases as asides, which Barâdar decided must be advice or warnings from the family's past experiences. Haatim spoke and gestured at the young girl, probably pointing out to Roonah all the advantages she could have at a new house, a home that wasn't in a cave on the side of a cliff. Barâdar wished he could understand and participate in the discussion; he wanted to ease the concerns of the women—Roonah who was stubborn, Ghatol, who was frightened, Zaina, who was exhausted and unwell. His inability to communicate made him draw more inward and wonder about his own family—his real family—and where he had come from and where he had lived. Why he could still not remember who he was. Estelle had convinced him that his health might not be in danger—if the brain damage was more severe, he would be convulsing, unable to stand, prone to fits and pain, which was not the case. His eyes flickered around the walls, just as Roonah's had, but instead of finding her sacred space, he thought,

This is no way to live in the modern world.

The modern world. Yes, I am a foreigner. A stranger out of place. Why can't I remember who I am when I can clearly see that this is no way to live?

Roonah's displeasure rose again when she brought the men their bowls of food. "*Khâneh!*" she shouted at them, as if they should all be ashamed at their behavior in front of a stranger, a young girl, a new mother, and a baby. "*Khâneh!*" she said to Barâdar as if he was her last chance at reason.

In Morocco, Jim and Ari were houseguests of Philip Bridges. Philip had taken Chris Radnor to northern Africa where they visited Casablanca before renting a house for a week in Tangier. Jim and Ari had flown from Rome to spend a long weekend with them at the house. Jim had met Pup before, in New York, but had not met Chris, and though Ari had a history of animosity with Chris, he was willing to overlook it because he wanted to see Pup again—and wanted to show Pup that he was happy in his relationship with Jim.

"Chris is nothing but a big baby," Ari told Jim. "Who can't stay out of trouble."

"We don't have to go," Jim said.

"I don't know when we'll be able to get to New York again," Ari answered. "And Pup is doing this just so he can see us."

"You," Jim said. "To see *you*."

"I worked through my issues with him long ago," Ari said. "So you should too."

"But what if he hasn't worked through his issues with *you*?"

"If that were the case, then Chris wouldn't be tagging along."

The house was large and airy, in the northern part of Tangier, and had come with a houseboy and a cook. Jim and Ari had arrived on a morning flight and went for a tour of the markets with Philip. Pup had wanted to play tour guide and Ari had a list of vendors he was checking out for his uncle.

When they returned to the house later that afternoon, Chris was high. He had arranged through "one of the guys on the block" for a large sack of hashish to be delivered to the house and he had smoked a bowl full in a hookah that he had gotten the houseboy and the cook to demonstrate for him. Chris was now on a food binge, looking for snacks to eat. The cook had found a sack of potato chips through one of the markets, but Chris wanted something "more special." "You know," he tried to explain to the cook. "Local stuff. Nuts, raisins, dates. Something hot and exotic."

Philip was a calming influence on the rush of strangers in and out of the house trying to solve Chris's appetite issues. The cook finally prepared a meal, which they ate sitting on cushions on the floor. The food was hot and dry, but there had been plenty to drink—more local stuff Chris had managed to get strangers to provide.

After dinner, Chris was ready to demonstrate the hookah, which neither Jim nor Ari wanted to try.

"I've a reputation to maintain," Jim said and added a light laugh. "I could lose my credibility if word got out that I was doing this."

"Or enhance it," Chris said. "Everyone loves a scandal."

Ari was not so concerned about his reputation and changed his mind, and the three men passed the hookah pipe between them. There were some personal remembrances between Ari and Pup, about the winter they went to Aspen and tried to learn to ski after smoking dope, which made Jim feel shut out. Chris offered Jim a massage—to unwind and "not be so stiff"—but Jim declined. Chris massaged Ari's shoulders to demonstrate his talent so Jim would change his mind, which was when Jim sensed something pass between Ari and Pup that all between them was not entirely over. He imagined that Ari would want to spend some time privately with Philip and it was probably only a matter of outlasting Chris.

But Chris was also territorial. As he massaged the back of Ari's neck he said, "You know I love that guy."—indicating Pup. "I'd do whatever he'd want me to do. I'd go to the ends of the earth for him."

"As long as I was willing to pay," Pup said and smiled.

"Okay, I'm a loser," Chris said. "But I love you, man."

"And I love you back," Pup said.

"That's a bold statement from you," Ari said to Philip. "You never freely admitted such things before."

"The older you get, the more theories you make up about things," Pup said. "No one loves the same. Each person is distinct so the love you express to them is distinct. Like a fingerprint. My love for Chris is not the same as my love for Jim—or for you," he said to Ari. He took a toke from the hookah pipe and added. "And when two people express their love for each other, a third entity is created."

"No," Ari said, "not if everyone expresses love differently. There would be two different entities created, not one."

"But the love they create together would also unique. A third love. Which would only confirm that that space—or love between them—is owned by God."

"God?" Jim said. "I think you have been smoking too much."

"Or not enough," Pup answered.

"But what about hate? Or jealousy?" Ari asked. Chris had abandoned the massage to play more with the hookah and refill the bowl. Ari stretched out his body over a pillow, leaning his head near Jim's lap. Jim looked down and studied Ari's eyelashes, watching his stare subtly shift towards Pup. "What if one person expresses love and the other doesn't?" Ari added. "Is God in the space where there is a partial absence of love?"

"What is jealousy but another form of desire?" Chris said and they all turned to him, surprised to find him adding to the philosophical discussion. "What is hate but a darker fear of love?"

"Or a fear of losing it," Jim added, realizing his head was both light and dense from inhaling the nearby smoke and that it had taken him an incredible amount of time to speak because he was tiring. He let out a nervous laugh, which echoed around the room as the others mimicked him.

"You cannot lose love," Pup said. "Because it is not something you can own. It is only something you can appreciate and, well, accept and *love*."

"And God?" Jim asked. "What about God?"

"Ah," Pup answered and smiled. "Sometimes God is *forgotten*."

Time seemed to freeze. Or pass slowly. Finally Jim asked Pup, "Are you defining love or lust? Sexual attraction is a desire, not an emotion."

The houseboy was now passing around small glasses of a strong liqueur. Jim chugged his at once and the burning in his stomach was immediate.

"Another reason why there should be no fear," Pup answered.

Ari had readjusted himself on the pillow to drink the liqueur. Chris was standing behind him, and he stretched his hands and began to massage Ari's shoulders again.

So this is how it begins, Jim thought. *The beginning of the end. Lust into love. Or lust into the desire for new love.* He stood and felt his heart rearranging the circulation in his body and he mumbled some sort of thanks and good-night. As he made his way slowly across the large room, the thought occurred to him that perhaps Ari was headed into a threeway. Perhaps Chris had no intention of abandoning Pup for Ari—that this had been the plan all along.

Then Jim felt someone lifting his hand. It was Ari, flushed and wide-eyed before him.

"I'm fine," Jim said. "Stay with them. It's okay."

"No," Ari answered. "I'll stay with you."

"You must tell them all to stop," Barâdar told Danil. "The men must be allowed to rest."

"I will speak to the professor about it," Danil answered.

They were working at the archeological dig and one of the local men, a short, wiry fellow with bad teeth who had been an eager worker for days, had brought along an older man that morning. The older man was his father-in-law, a gray-haired man with a scraggly beard and an unstable footing.

The professor had told the local man that there were enough workers, another one was not needed, but the local man had persisted, telling him, "We will work for the price of one."

Finally, the professor had consented, and the elderly man had helped with the removal of dirt from the ditch, carrying pails of earth from the dig to a small but growing mound not far away. The two men worked tirelessly, the local man and his father-in-law, as did the other workers, not wanting to take breaks to rest or eat. Barâdar had noticed the elderly man struggling with the weight of the pails and the uncertainty of his steps, which was when he approached Danil with concern.

Danil went to speak to the professor, but the work did not stop. Barâdar went to the professor to complain that the treatment was unfair and express his concern over the health of the elderly man. The professor was in the ditch, inspecting the pails of dirt before they were carried out.

"Sir, these men must rest," Barâdar said. "I am concerned that they will be too tired."

"I want to see this corner," the professor said. "When we get this corner done, they can stop."

"Then let me do this," Barâdar said. "Let the men rest. Let me do this work."

The professor stopped sifting his fingers through the dirt and stood and stretched his back. He looked at Barâdar and nodded. "Yes, you are right. The earth has been there for many centuries. A few more minutes will not harm anyone."

The professor stopped the work in the ditch and had the workers rest. Barâdar and Danil distributed water to the men, ladling out drinks to open palms or into the small tin cups of those who had them.

"We must stop early today because of this," Danil said. "There is not enough water."

The water was also needed to clean off items recovered from the earth—thus far only shards of pottery.

"You must allow the men to rest," Barâdar said. "I will bring more water from the stream. I will tell the professor that I will take some men to get more water."

"No," Danil said. "I will speak to the professor about this. We will use the jeep. We will bring more water tomorrow. We will stop for the rest of the day. The professor is tired too. He is trying too hard and too fast to find something no one is certain even exists."

The road became more dramatic—steep climbs and uneven descents. At the bottom of one cliff was a large puddle of mud that stretched across the road and flowed into the stream that paralleled the path. It didn't seem to be a formidable obstacle and Yazeed slowly skimmed the van directly through it instead of driving around. It was a mistake. The rear wheels struggled to find traction; the left one became submerged in sludge near the opposite side of the puddle.

Yazeed floored the gas pedal, shifting the van between drive and reverse. The van rocked a small bit, then dug deeper into the mud. Yazeed got out, gathered up some twigs and brush from the hillside, waded through the puddle and tried to put the brush he had collected beneath the wheel. The twigs floated to the surface. Yazeed motioned for Jim to sit at the wheel and rev the van while he pushed from behind. Jim floored and rocked the gas pedal and gear shift and steering wheel, which only dug them deeper into the mud. Yazeed dramatically wiped his brow and pointed back towards a village they had passed ten minutes before.

"I am going to service," Yazeed said, by which Jim understood that Yazeed was leaving him to find help. Yazeed adjusted the turban on his head and reached into the van and got the rifle and slung it across his shoulder. He pulled the gun from behind his back and offered it to Jim.

Jim was not strong enough to make the walk. He nodded and waved Yazeed away, reassuring him with hand gestures that he would be safe and did not want the gun. They had not passed anyone along the road for almost an hour. Yazeed offered the gun again, and Jim shook his head no. The boy stuffed the gun back behind his belt and walked away.

Yazeed said something to Jim as he left, which Jim didn't catch. The boy stopped to light a cigarette before he continued on. Jim lifted himself out of the van, hopped to the side of the road, and sat down on a rise of the cliff where he could stretch out his legs. He was tired but restless. He looked at the splashes of brown and gray mud that covered the side of the van and the wheels deep in the puddle and felt annoyed by another obstacle. *Why? Why this, Lord?* His shoes were wet and muddy. His fingernails were deep with dirt, the skin of his palms cut and cracked. He studied the hills to see if he could find a large piece of wood or a boulder he could drag into the puddle—something Yazeed might have missed, but knowing he might not be able to accomplish the task even if he discovered something. Desperation surfaced first in his chest and then rolled up into his eyes. He watched Yazeed's figure grow smaller and smaller and then disappear around a curve of the mountain road. He felt the immediate silence, the absence of Yazeed's boots scraping along the rocky road. The air was still and chilly as it grew quiet. He blew air across his fingertips to warm them. An eerie calm descended upon him as he looked around for some kind of movement and saw nothing. He sensed danger and trouble until it dawned into a realization that he was too far away for anyone to find him. Even a stranger would not stumble upon him. He closed his eyes and the tension lifted from his shoulders. His forehead relaxed.

Above, large buzzard-like birds arrived and circled the van and squawked. Jim sat up, more alert. No doubt the buzzards were looking for bones or blood or freshly killed meat. A few alighted and sat on the slope, their necks twisting and their eyes shifting towards Jim, as if testing his breathing. As long as he stayed awake, Jim had no fear of them. For a moment he wished Yazeed had left behind a cigarette and his lighter—smoking would have given him something to do, though he knew it would not stop his thinking. Another flash of thought arrived—what if he had been abandoned? What if Yazeed did not return? Willingly or unwillingly? How would he survive? Would he be able to kill one of these birds before they could kill him?

If he did not survive this trip to Bamiyan—if he were to die here, now, it would not be a terrible spot to have it happen. God had led him here with a plan. And God was here. He felt His presence all around him. He could see Him in the landscape—the rocks and cliffs and bright blue sky. In the valley below, a flowery field was nestled where it met the tributary of the brook, the same source of water which had caused the mud hole. He was doing what he wanted to do—looking for Ari. Keeping Ari alive, even if only for a little while longer.

And God had given him Ari at a time when Jim did not think a relationship was possible. Every day now without him, there was the fear that his memories of Ari were becoming more faint. The way his hair felt. The tight skin of his thighs. The large dark brown circles of his eyes. The sound of his voice. The smell of his feet and his groin and his stale morning breath. The taste of his stubbly chin as they kissed. Jim imagined Ari in bed, waiting on the subway platform, reaching for a jar on a shelf at the deli around the corner from where they lived. He thought of all the easier places he and Ari had been to—in Sorrento, their only drama had been whether to take the ferry to visit Capri or Ischia first; in Venice, it was what restaurant to eat at; in Paris, it had been whether or not to meet with Ari's uncle or lie and say that they had to cancel to cover a breaking assignment. Yes, Jim decided, this was a perfectly respectable place to die, if this was God's plan for him. Out in the world, searching for the man he loved. Far from his home and past.

Or was he wrong? Was he being too naïve? Had God abandoned him now? Had He abandoned Ari? Or was there even really a God?

"God's plan is not always obvious to us," a curator at the British museum had once mentioned to Jim years ago during an interview. The remark had been directed towards a lost religious item—a saint's relic—but the quote had remained with Jim because at the time he was trying to sort through the troubles in his personal life. Frank was dead. And something in Jim's life had been unable to survive.

God's plan. *His* God's plan, so different from the other gods of other religions. Or was He? Was the God of Christianity the same God of Islam and Buddhism? Over time Jim's God had even become different from his own family's God—his God was not a destroyer, a weapon, or a judge. He did not punish or discriminate or withhold or prevent. Still, Jim's God had not left his life without disappointments. Like many journalists Jim had collected his own turning points into a list of Great Moments and Tragedies of My Life, those forks in the road where he could wander back in time in his memory and wonder what if, what if I had gone another direction, what if the one-two combination of choice and fate had been different?

Still, they were there for him to re-examine now as he waited for Yazeed—the broken arm in second grade which prevented him from playing baseball, the girlfriend in junior high who broke up with him in a written note, the professor's threat in college that he was an underachiever, his first kiss with another man, the death of Frank a decade later. Frank was only one of his many friends who had died of AIDS when he lived in Manhattan but was the one who had hit Jim the hardest—the Godless months of coughs and infusions and hospital stays—the catheters and prescriptions and stumbling in the dark to find the bathroom light before a bout of diarrhea disrupted everything.

And all this was a road map to here. This hillside in the remote corner of Afghanistan. If he could reduce his life to a map of right and wrong directions, then couldn't he do the same with religion? Faith. Prayer. God. There it was. Three bullet points he only needed to list. Is this where faith in God begins, when life is at its lowest point? "Wherever there is love, there is God," his mother told him when he was seven or eight. It was a simple lesson, one of many that a mother passes along to her child, but somehow that was the one that stuck with Jim. His mother was a simple woman who had devoted her life to her husband and their family. If love was faith and faith was God and God was in the moments Jim shared with Ari, then Jim would sit on a hillside in the most desolate place he had ever been and pray for the safe return of Yazeed with help to get the van out of a puddle of mud. All he wanted to know was that Ari was alive and safe. And if he wasn't, Jim wanted to begin walking around another corner himself. He was tired and frustrated and losing patience, a virtue he had never possessed. He wanted to find the next fork in the road. He wanted to close this chapter and start a new one.

That morning men were running from the village towards the excavation site. Barâdar knew something was different—as he approached the tent, he could see a circle of men surrounding a man on horseback who was yelling at the crowd. The man had a rifle slung across his back and he was angrily gesturing at someone below.

Danil pulled Barâdar aside when he reached the site. "The professor has closed down the site," Danil said. "At the request of the Consulate."

"Why?"

"Dr. Dupray's passport was used to get into Iran. *Stolen*. From the accident. The family of Dr. Dupray has requested the return of his personal items stolen from the accident. Dr. Sajadi will not pay the villagers for any more work until these items have been returned. Important, personal things stolen from the accident—the professor's journals, books, wallet, his wedding ring. The professor is doing this out of respect for Dr. Dupray and his family."

At the center of the crowd, speaking to the man on the horse, was Dr. Sajadi. The doctor was wearing a cap and shielding his eyes as he tilted his face up to talk to the man on the horse. The sun was very bright. Occasionally a man in the crowd would throw in an angry comment. The man on the horse would turn and look in his direction and shout angrily back.

"The man on the horse is Shabir Misraddin Ayub, the mullah who oversees the village," Danil said. "He is angry that the men are not working and not being paid, because then he is not being paid, but he is more angry that they are being called thieves. The village men are not happy either. They want to work. And they do not want to be called thieves."

"What will happen?"

"We will wait a few days. See if items are returned. Tempers cool down. Then we will hire a few men. Then more. It will put us behind schedule. Disappoint the professor."

"They will not fight, will they?"

"No," Danil answered. "They could seize all our work, but what would it bring them? What would they gain?"

"What will these men do?"

"What they did before we arrived. There are other programs."

"I will see Madame Estella about work," Barâdar said.

"Why? You may work here. You are not one of them. There are many items already we can process."

Barâdar looked at him strangely. "It would not be right."

Danil stretched out his hand, and clasped Barâdar at the wrist. "Do not leave," he said. "*Stay.*"

"I must work like the other men," Barâdar said. "I must not bring any harm to my family."

Two hours later Yazeed arrived with a truck and three Afghan men with rifles. Yazeed introduced Jim to them as M'sheem, as Omar had done when he and Ari had been in Kabul. The men were Sayif, Kamil, and Mikko. A father and two brothers.

The men stood their rifles against the cliffside and walked into the puddle. The water was deep and slippery. The three men pushed the back of the van while Yazeed pumped the gas pedal. The van rocked back and forth but was not dislodged.

The men stopped to smoke and argue amongst themselves, shaking the water out of their boots. Mikko, the taller Afghan brother, went to the truck and found a coil of rope. He tied one end around the front bumper of the van and the other end around the back bumper of the truck. This time Jim sat in the van and pumped the gas pedal while Yazeed joined the two brothers at the back of the van. The father sat in the truck and tried to pull the van out with the rope by attempting to drive the truck.

There was a cloud of smoke as the truck's wheels spun round. Rocks and gravel shot out and landed against the front of the van. One man shouted orders or opinions and another responded with grunts or yelling. Sayif had a higher-pitched voice than his sons, and he spoke rapidly to the younger men, giving them instructions. Finally, the van edged out of the puddle. Jim drove a few feet ahead and parked. Mikko helped Jim out of the van. All of the men clapped him on the back as if he had done all the work.

Yazeed sat with the men and smoked a cigarette. They passed around a wine bottle, filled at the bottom with an amber sludge, which they sipped and wiped clean with the back of their sleeves. They offered a sip to Jim, but he refused with a shake of his head. Jim was surprised at the open display of alcohol, so forbidden and untolerated elsewhere in this country. The men sat laughing and pointing and whispering remarks to one another. At one point Jim knew they were talking about him, probably making fun of his leg or crutches or his speech, but Yazeed yelled, "M'sheem! M'sheem! They are blue, no?"

Jim smiled, trying to ignore the men by lifting his wet pants leg away from the stitches and scabs.

"M'sheem! M'sheem!" Yazeed continued. "Blue, no? My friends want to know how you describe."

Jim lifted his head, nodded at the men, and yelled back, "Green!"

Yazeed repeated the word and the men nodded and yelled "Green! Green!" back to Jim.

Mikko, the taller brother, yelled "Green! I like!"

For a moment Jim wondered how this would escalate—was it simple boyish rowdiness, or would he now be a target for trouble? He kept himself tense, ready to fight if necessary, his ear tuned to the inflections of the men's phrases, but the Afghans grew tired of the word, and soon began speaking of something else, and Jim rolled up his pants leg to let his wounds and skin dry.

The bottle was finished and the men hugged and clapped each other on the back and lifted their rifles and returned to their truck. Yazeed arrived at the van smelling of alcohol and mud and smoke. He waved good-bye to men and drove on through the mountains, now swerving around dry potholes as well as muddy ones.

Hours later, when the red and pink cliffs above Bamiyan came into view, they seemed to float above the horizon, a giant carved box placed on a span of flat land. Jim briefly studied the niches where the missing Buddhas had once been as they made their way west into the valley and towards the village. On the road, a man came along on a donkey, just as before. Jim's eyes darted nervously to the road in front of the van. "Careful," he said to Yazeed. "Don't go off the road."

Jim did not relax until they had reached the edge of the plateau and had parked in front of the tiny mud-walled building with a sign that read in English "Hotel," but even then he was eager to continue the search for Ari.

Fifteen

Yazeed spoke to the hotel owner—a lean, bearded man wearing a long white shirt, black vest, and a racing cap—and after a period of reluctance or negotiation, Jim wasn't sure which, showed him a photo of Ari which Abdul Ramati must have supplied to the boy's uncle. (It showed a young and freshly shaven Ari, nothing like how he had looked when he and Jim had started their Afghanistan trip.) Jim was frustrated that he could not understand their conversation—he assumed the young boy was being cautious that the hotel owner was not a member of the Taliban. Because they were strangers, he and Yazeed had attracted the attention of several villagers, who approached and looked briskly at Yazeed's flyer, all shaking their heads as if they had never seen Ari before. The town consisted of a wide street and a scattering of one-story mud and brick compounds. There were no other cars in the vicinity of the hotel, but three bikes leaned against the side of the wall and a donkey was tied up in a courtyard behind the hotel. In the distance the cliffs rose like the backdrop of a stage set, the grotto openings like tiny black keyholes in a giant scrim.

Helped by his crutches and two small boys who tugged at his pants leg, Jim started towards the area where the hotel owner pointed, along the dusty road to a group of mud-brick buildings. It was midafternoon, the sun was dizzyingly bright, but the sunglasses Jim had been using in the van now made everything seem dim and indistinct and he set out with them perched atop his scalp. There was a strange vibration to the air, as if it was rumbling, which got deeper and louder as Jim progressed down the road. From behind one of the buildings a large helicopter—a Chinook—emerged, its rotating blades lifting it up into the sky. Jim stopped and shielded his eyes, watching it rise and move out of the valley.

At the second compound of walls, Jim noticed three American soldiers and a group of men at work in a large building set back behind a larger wall. He approached them cautiously, speaking English and shouting ahead that he was from Bagram Air Base and searching for a lost journalist.

Two soldiers approached him with their rifles pointed and sternly asked him in English, "Who the fuck are you? What are you doing here?" They were broad-chested and towered over Jim, their cheeks and necks flushed from a potential confrontation.

Jim identified himself again—a journalist, from Bagram—and he showed the soldiers his press credentials and the flyer which he had made using a news-bureau photograph of Ari. A third soldier arrived from out of the building and looked at the photograph and said Ari did not look familiar to him.

"I was traveling with an archeologist to do a story on Bamiyan when our van hit a landmine," he explained. "My cameraman has been lost since then."

The taller soldier had a nervous smile, but it was the shorter one who relaxed his grip on his gun and asked Jim about his journey.

"We've just arrived," Jim explained, gesturing towards Yazeed, who had followed Jim and was now talking with two Afghan men who had come out of the compound when Jim had come to the soldiers' attention. "We're trying to locate my cameraman."

The taller soldier asked about the accident—he had heard some of the details from the villagers—but hadn't realized that there were any survivors. "Two Frenchmen were jacked out of here pronto," he said. "Both dead and identified."

"No," Jim said. "I was one of them. But my cameraman—Ari Sarghello—has been missing since then. No one has seen him since the accident."

The soldiers studied the flyer again, but one of the local Afghan men was excitedly telling Yazeed, "Barâdar! Barâdar!" and pointing at the large empty niche at the eastern end of the cliffs where the giant Buddha had once stood. The boys, still along for the adventure and eyeing the soldiers and strangers suspiciously, echoed the man, shouting "Barâdar! Barâdar!"

While Yazeed talked with the men, Jim asked the shorter soldier how long he had been in Bamiyan, and the soldier answered that he had been in the village since the spring, when the relief missions had geared up. His name was Mark and he was from Kentucky—and his taller companion was Jeb from Rhode Island and the third was a lieutenant from Billings, Montana. Mark explained that the military was trying to restore the landing strip for the airport, help get the hospital back up and running, and turn the building where they were working now into a decent hotel. Neither he nor Jeb had recognized Ari from Jim's photograph. The lieutenant, not recognizing Ari either, returned to the interior of the compound, uninterested in Jim's plight.

Yazeed, finished with his conversation with the local men, began walking away, down the road towards the cliffs, turning back only for a second to yell at Jim, "M'sheem! M'sheem!"

Jim thanked the soldiers, finding their sentiment in their strong, brisk handshakes, and followed Yazeed slowly on his crutches, trying to teach a few words of English to the little boys who still tagged along with him. "Allo! Allo!" he said and wondered if he appeared patronizing because his voice had become loud and high pitched, as if it would help the boys understand him better. One boy touched Jim's fingers, twined his in between them as they walked. It was awkward with the crutches, but it filled Jim with hope and energy. Yazeed had found someone who had recognized Ari. That meant he must still be alive. Jim smiled at the boys and thanked them for their company and relaxed the grip on his crutches and showed them his empty palms. The sunlight was still bright and the dust made Jim thirsty and his eyes itch but he wasn't ready to stop because he was convinced, now, that Ari was close by.

He tried to walk faster, but pain seared up from his leg and he found it hard to breathe. He tried to keep his agitation from flaring into annoyance as the boys taunted him for gifts. *Ari, Ari, Ari,* was all he could think. When they reached the fringes of the old village settlement, the boys lost interest in Jim once they realized that he had no money or food or trinkets to give to them. The shells of the abandoned buildings reminded Jim of one of those haunted frontier towns in a Western film. Jim tried to keep up with Yazeed's pace, following behind the young man along a path that led to the foot of the eastern end of the cliffs and the niche where the smaller of the two large Buddhas had once stood.

It was a glorious valley, mountains so spectacular they seemed like vast curtains to a theater. To the east there was a rise of white tenting. Not far away a group of five men were working with shovels and picks in a ditch, lifting their rocks and dirt out in flat baskets and tossing it onto a growing group of small hills. It was an archeological site—roped off with wooden stakes in the ground and a fence of string. A stocky, gray-bearded man wearing a Panama hat and khaki shirt and pants met Yazeed, shook his hand, and looked at the photograph the young boy had presented to him. As Jim approached, the bearded man looked up and began speaking to him in French, which Jim only partially understood, something about "*Monsieur Barâdar*" and "*médical*" and "*travail*" and "*l'hôpital.*" Jim, thinking that Ari had become sick or had been more seriously wounded in their explosion than he had first thought, repeated back to the man in a concerned tone of English, "He's been taken to hospital, right? The hospital in the village?"

The man, realizing that Jim spoke English and not French, answered in a heavily accented English. "He is not worker here, but worker at hospital now. Monsieur Barâdar has been waiting for someone to find him. You must be him. He will be relieved."

Yazeed, finding out the same information from the local diggers, had already turned and was headed back into the village, but Jim stayed a few minutes longer, anxiously introducing himself to the archeologist. Tariq Sajadi, as the man identified himself, was looking for the sleeping Buddha which he believed ran from the base of the large niche of *"le grand Bouddha"* to the base of the smaller niche at the eastern end. They had already uncovered shards of clay figures and sculptures of Buddha heads and a wall which was believed to be a part of the ancient Buddhist monastery.

Jim hastily explained that he had originally come to Bamiyan with Francois Dupray, the archeologist who had been killed when his truck hit a landmine. Jim and Ari—or Barâdar, as he was being identified by the villagers—had been traveling with Monsieur Dupray and were journalists who were going to do a news piece on the search for the third Buddha, before the accident disrupted all of their plans.

"Ah, *oui*," Dr. Sajadi said, shaking his head, "that explains Monsieur Barâdar," and he described, in his broken English, Ari's loss of memory—*"l'amnésie"*—and his living with a local family until his identity was discovered. "He is a strong man," Dr. Sajadi added. *"Bon homme*. Full of convictions and devotions."

Jim tried to contain his happiness—he wanted to fall to the ground and thank God that Ari had survived—but instead he let his eyes tear and he asked the professor whether Ari was physically hurt or suffering, trying to gather as many details as he could before he caught up with Yazeed.

"Bon homme," Sajadi answered. "A miracle that he is alive. I see he has been missed. We will miss him. My assistant Danil has been very fond of him. He will be sorry to see Monsieur Barâdar leave. He must be with him now. I have not seen him all day."

"I am sorry about Professor Dupray," Jim said. "He spoke passionately about this trip. About finding the third Buddha."

"It is a great loss. To me. To history. We would not be here if not for him."

Jim thanked the archeologist, apologizing for not being able to stay longer and hear more of the archeology project, and promised that he would revisit the idea for a news piece as soon as he had a chance to reassure his bureau that Ari was alive and safe and well.

Yazeed was already out of sight. Jim walked faster, more urgently, hardly relying on the crutches to keep himself upright. Ari was alive and waiting for someone. Jim's heartbeat raced and sweat gathered in his armpits and rivered along the sides of his cheeks. He stopped to dry them, felt the tears collecting in his eyes and spilling over. His nose began to run. He coughed and choked, bending down to the knee of his good leg. *Thank you, Lord, for keeping him safe*, he said to himself. *Thank you, Lord, I owe you for this.*

The young boys from the village arrived again, tugging at Jim's sleeve as if he were a new arrival, asking him for money or trinkets. Jim stood and adjusted the crutches beneath his arms and flashed his empty palms again to the young boys. He tried to display his relief and happiness this time, to convey it to the children. But Yazeed was nowhere to be seen and a small flare of annoyance surged through Jim's mind because the young Afghan was so determined and headstrong and blind to the fact that every step for Jim had now become a struggle. As he stood and brushed himself off, he was aware of his self-pity and he tried to laugh at himself because things were finally turning around, getting better. Ari was alive. That was his mission. Find Ari.

Jim's leg throbbed from the weight he had been putting on it as the crutches burned beneath his underarms and where he gripped the side handles. He felt a tightness in his chest and he knew he was pushing himself too hard. But there was no way he would stop until he found Ari. He had the strong impression that Ari was just around the corner. He could see Ari squatting and running his hands through the soil, the empty niche and cliffs behind him. He could see Ari walking through the village with the other workers at the end of the day, arm in arm with another man, trying to convince him that there was a better way to collect water or import food or dig in the soil for artifacts. He could see Ari returning to the hospital to offer patients water or a shoulder to lean on, helping volunteers lift a patient from a gurney and onto an examination table, pressuring a doctor for something to help a poor soul's pain. In Jim's mind Ari was alive and well and only waiting to be found. God. Allah. Buddha. They were all watching over him. He could sense it in the air and the sky and in the pink stains on the rocks of the cliffs. Ari was alive. *Thank you, Lord. I owe you for this. Bless you, Allah. Praise Buddha.*

There was work to be done at the hospital. Military trucks arrived with two hundred sixty crates of equipment for the hospital donated by the Norwegian Red Cross and Afghan Ministry of Public Health—examination tables, beds, cabinets, chairs, heart monitors, fire extinguishers, blood-pressure cuffs, a heart defibrillator, thermometers, surgical gloves, antibiotics, and emergency medical kits. The hospital was filled with workers—soldiers, NGO organizers, and local men. Haatim had found extra work for a few days for Siraaj and Nadeem and other villagers to help sweep and mop and unpack. Barâdar helped Estelle inventory the medicine—his handwriting was precise and legible. UNESCO workers arrived with advice and more back power. The debris left over from the Taliban burnings was piled in the courtyard and set afire. Walls were patched and painted. Bed frames were assembled. The pay was considerably less than the earnings at the archeological site, but Barâdar was grateful to be of assistance, to have something to fill his days.

One of the young Afghan men who worked in the pharmacy, Ali Hassad, went room to room, speaking with each of the new workers who had arrived with the crates of equipment. "Stan Chartoff?" he asked them.

"*Non*," they answered, shaking their heads. "*Nu*." "No." "*Nein*."

"Who is Stan Chartoff?" Barâdar asked Estelle, when the young Afghan had left the room where they were assisting with workers from the Red Cross.

"MSF," she answered. "He was part of the team that set up the clinic. He left the night of the accident that killed Professor Dupray. They drove a patient to Kabul. Stan and Ali Hassad were good friends. It has disappointed him that his friend did not return to Bamiyan."

"Why? Why did he leave?"

"He was ready," she said. "His work was done. He did not want to become too involved."

"A doctor?"

"No," she answered. "He was like us. A worker. Someone who cared."

"Was he frightened? Did something frighten him to cause him to leave?"

"No," she answered. "It was complicated. Ali Hassad misses him deeply."

Danil arrived late one afternoon and told Barâdar that work was resuming at the archeological site and that the professor intended to use more men to catch up on his schedule.

"I will stay here," Barâdar told him. "As long as there is something for me to do at the hospital."

"The professor wants you to help," Danil said. "We both want you to help."

"I must stay here," Barâdar explained. "I must repay the kindness I received."

"The professor will pay you more," Danil said. "You will help with special assignments. Things we need of you."

"I cannot repay everyone at once," Barâdar said.

Danil persisted. "Then join us for dinner tonight," he said. "Dine with us."

"Another time," Barâdar said. "There are more mouths to feed—Haatim has brought a young woman and her baby and her daughter to the cliffs. I must bring food and wood when I return tonight. I cannot ignore their kindness. You must understand that."

"Of course," Danil said. "Then you will join us tomorrow?"

Barâdar gave him a smile and said, "I cannot promise, but I will not say no."

His answer pleased Danil and the young man waited while Barâdar and Estelle spoke to an NGO worker who had arrived in the courtyard. Danil walked with Barâdar from the hospital to the bazaar, where Barâdar bought small sacks of fruit and nuts and a piece of candy for Ghatol. The sun flooded the western sky behind a large bank of clouds and the two friends stood arm in arm, shoulder against shoulder, breaking apart only to point out items to merchants. They nodded and smiled, offered each other a taste of a piece of dried fruit or a handful of seeds. Barâdar was comfortable with the bursts of affection because Danil was agreeable to it as well—they were acting no differently than the closeness many Afghan men displayed themselves as brothers or friends.

At a stand Barâdar looked at selection of small blankets and scarves—something he could give to Zaina for the baby—and he bought a small blue blanket and then, impulsively, selected a bright yellow scarf to give to Roonah.

"She will complain to me about this," Barâdar told Danil. "But she will love it and wear it, I know!"

Siraaj and Nadeem were sitting at the base of the cliffs when Barâdar and Danil arrived. Beside them were plastic jugs full of water. Danil again told Barâdar that he was welcome to return to the dig whenever he wanted. They shook hands and embraced to say good-bye. Siraaj interrupted them, speaking rapidly and motioning for Danil to join them at the cave. Danil offered an awkward protest and a wave indicating no, but thank you, but Nadeem tugged his sleeve and Barâdar added, "They want you to join us. Join *us* for dinner."

"But there's not enough," Danil said. "I couldn't do this."

"You cannot insult their kindness. Come, join us. All you must do is climb. We will make you work for your dinner. And you will make us happy. You will make *me* very happy to have you as a guest."

Danil followed Siraaj and Nadeem up the steep stairways of the cliffs. Barâdar was pleased that Danil would join them for dinner. He would have someone to talk to during the evening who could understand him and respond and he was filled with a new warm and grateful feeling.

Zaina was pleased with the blanket Barâdar brought, praising its warmth and color to Haatim and Siraaj, though Roonah protested at Barâdar's gift of the bright yellow scarf—just as he had expected. Barâdar was glad to have Danil as a witness to the scene she created and which ended in her smiling and tying the scarf around her shoulders.

Dinner that evening was a warm bowl of rice and raisins and small knots of bread. The men prayed and Barâdar and Danil sat silent and respectful.

Ghatol decided to save the hard candy that Barâdar had brought her, and after the meal she tried on Danil's eyeglasses to the dismay of Roonah, walking around the cave and peering closely at the walls and the stove to bring things into sharper focus. She pointed at the ancient drawings at the top of the walls of the cave, and Barâdar lifted her to look more closely at them, causing her to giggle. Roonah was distraught that she was so friendly with the men and foreigners and she spoke harshly to Zaina and Siraaj, though Haatim chimed in with his big smiles, comically waving any concern away. Danil taught the young girl a few words in French—just as Barâdar had done with the family not long ago—and Barâdar knew he was growing fonder of the young man. Danil had a good heart, he understood that. He only wanted what Haatim wanted, someone to share his life with, someone to create a family with, someone to share their experiences.

When the men grew quiet, Barâdar rose and said he would walk Danil to the base of the cliffs and return with more water from the stream.

Barâdar led the way slowly down the cliffs, using a torch from the hospital Estelle had given him one night. Danil walked with him to the stream where they sat on the rocks. Danil placed his hand on top of Barâdar's.

"You know how I feel," Danil said to Barâdar.

"I do," he answered.

"Does it bother you?"

"No, it reminds me of something. Someone, maybe."

They were quiet for a moment, both leaning their faces closer together until they moved into a kiss. The kiss was brief. Barâdar felt his body change and he slipped his face to the side and pressed it against Danil's back. He had moved from a man without a memory to one who had found something familiar. He broke away from Danil and clasped his friend by the neck, their eyes locking. Danil searched Barâdar's face for some kind of reaction—disgust, lust, a desire to continue or rush away.

"There is already someone," Barâdar said. "Someone who means this to me. I don't know who he is, but I know he is there. Do you understand?"

Danil nodded and his eyes welled up with tears. "Stay with me till then," he told Barâdar. "There is plenty of room at the guesthouse. More than you have here. You will be happy there. Let me help you."

"You help me? Or me help you?"

"Both," Danil answered and smiled. "Stay with me till then."

"This has nothing to do with love," Ari said.

"That's obvious," Jim replied, not attempting to hide his bitterness.

They were at the hotel in Istanbul, packing for the flight to Rome.

"You can't take this personally," Ari added.

"And how am I supposed to take it?"

"I want to tell this story. This is a story *I* want to do."

"I'm holding you back, is that it? All of a sudden, I am standing in your way?"

"No, you're twisting it out of context. You've been a good teacher—the best, you know that. But I don't want to be a shadow. I want to chase the story. I want to do my own stuff. That doesn't mean I don't want anything to do with you. I do. I want to keep what we have going. Don't you understand that?"

"I understand you're walking away. You're breaking things off."

"You don't understand. You never try to understand. Sometimes you can never see around the edges of that little box you work in."

"Ari, you can't solve the world's problems on your own."

"I'm not trying to solve anything," Ari answered. "I learned that long ago. But I can make a difference, can't I? Or at least try."

Jim ignored the plea. He was moving his bags to the door, ready to walk down to the lobby and begin the journey back to Rome.

"It's not the end of us," Ari said. "I don't want this to be the end of us. This shouldn't change anything about *us*."

"Then what is it?" Jim asked. "This is not something we're doing together."

At the building that housed the hospital, Yazeed was nowhere in sight. Jim made his way across the courtyard to where there was an open door. He stopped midway and looked up at the shadows a wall created in a corner of the courtyard, an eerie memory of having been here before floating to the surface of his consciousness. His leg seemed to respond with throbbing and at the doorway he leaned in and spoke to an NGO worker who was trying to repair the legs of a chair, a squat, well-built man with a barrel chest and closely cropped brown hair. In English and broken French Jim asked for "Monsieur Barâdar," or "Ari Sarghello," and showed the man the flyer with the photograph of Ari.

"*Non*," the man answered, shaking his head back and forth and continuing in English. "There has been many workers here, but I do not see him. This man. There are others who have been here longer. Please, we ask them."

Jim thanked the man and there was more small talk, questions about where Jim had arrived from and why he was in Bamiyan. Jim lobbed questions at the worker in return and discovered his name was Brian Perré and that he was from Strasbourg, France. He had been part of a Catholic ministry in Kandahar that had left him behind when the Taliban escalated their attacks the year before and he had gone to

Kabul. From Kabul he had made his way here a few days ago with the new equipment that had arrived at the hospital. As they were talking another man entered the room—a tall, dark young Afghan teenager in a white shalwar kameez with a short black vest. He looked at Jim suspiciously and said something to the NGO worker in Dari. They both turned to Jim and continued their conversation as if Jim were a corpse that had sprung to life. Their conversation rose in pitch and speed—particularly the Afghan's—and finally, Brian said to Jim, "My friend Ali Hassad thinks you have been here before," he said.

"Yes, that's right," Jim answered, and he described his memory of the accident on the plateau but that he knew very little of what had followed at the hospital. The NGO worker turned and translated Jim's explanation and Ali Hassad, with the help of Brian, told Jim that he had driven the van from Bamiyan to the Panjshir Valley with Stan Chartoff. Jim stood and hugged the Afghan boy, thanking him by shaking his hand and clasping him in an embrace of gratitude, then awkwardly described the surgery and therapy he had endured to his leg as Brian translated.

"You go to America?" the young Afghan asked Jim.

"Yes," Jim answered. "But not right away."

The young man looked at Jim in the eyes, as if he hadn't understood what Jim had said. "You speak... Stan Chartoff?" he asked.

"I hope to meet him some day, yes."

"Stan Chartoff," the young man repeated. "You tell Stan Chartoff, 'Ali Hassad.'"

The young man pointed to his chest and his face moved into a memory. "You tell Stan Chartoff, 'Ali Hassad. Ali Hassad...'" The young man turned and spoke to Brian in Dari, or Hazagari, Jim could not quite tell which. Jim watched the conversation, Brian's nodding, and his absorbing what he already knew Ali Hassad was trying to say. Then Brian said to Jim, "They were great friends. He misses him a lot."

Brian offered Jim tea, which Jim accepted and drank slowly while leaning on a crutch, looking out at the courtyard for Yazeed to appear. Ali Hassad would not leave the room, circling Jim and telling him "Miracle! *Allahu akbar!* Miracle! You speak Stan Chartoff. Stan Chartoff, Ali Hassad."

"You are a true friend," Jim answered the young Afghan. "Allah will reward you many times."

Jim showed Ali Hassad the flyer of Ari and pointed at the picture. "Do you know this man?"

"Barâdar," the Afghan man said. "Gahd mahn. *Bon homme.* Brah-durh."

Ali Hassad spoke to Brian, and the NGO worker translated. "My friend says that your friend here lives with a family in the grottoes. The caves in the cliff near *le grand Bouddha*. The biggest Buddha."

"Is he okay?" Jim asked.

"Okay?" Brian asked Ali Hassad.

"*Malade?*" Jim asked.

"*Nu, nu.*" The Afghan man shrugged. "*Grottes bouddhistes.*"

Jim sat on a small ledge on the outer wall of the hospital building. He used the sleeve of his shirt to wipe the dust and sweat from his face. He did not want to sit too long—it would make his leg cramp and it would be even more difficult to walk—but he needed to rest. He could feel his heart beating in his ears.

Ali Hassad pulled Jim by the sleeve and walked him to a hallway at the back of the hospital. The Afghan waved his hands back and forth along the wall, as if offering a bed, and Jim realized that this was where the professor had been brought to die and where Jim had waited for Ali Hassad and Stan Chartoff to lift him up into the van. Again he said their names and mimicked driving a steering wheel. "Stan Chartoff. Ali Hassad."

Yazeed walked out of a doorway of the hospital and saw Jim with Ali Hassad. He lit a cigarette and looked at the bright blue sky. Jim said to Yazeed as he approached, "*Grottes bouddhistes?*"

Yazeed nodded and said, "Come M'sheem. We go. We go."

But first Jim introduced Ali Hassad to Yazeed as "the man who saved me."

Ali Hassad bowed proudly and he and Yazeed talked in Dari for a short period, then Yazeed said to Jim again, "Come, M'sheem. We go. We go."

Jim had Ali Hassad write his name down on a scrap of paper—both in English and Dari—and he folded it and placed it into his pants pocket. "Tell him there will be a reward one day," Jim said to Yazeed. "God will repay him for his kindness if I can't."

Yazeed stubbed out his cigarette and blurted something quickly to Ali Hassad.

"No, no," Ali Hassad said to Jim. "Stan Chartoff. Ali Hassad. *Allahu akbar. Allahu akbar.*"

Jim's energy was fading. They walked from the hospital to where they had left the van and drove to the western side of the niche where the large Buddha had been located and where they had been told Barâdar was staying with a local family.

The wind picked up speed as Jim and Yazeed climbed the cliffs. The chill numbed Jim's fingers but oddly made the pain in his leg more bearable, though the crutches were proving an awkward hindrance, dragging them behind him as he worked his way up the steep stairs step by step, one foot carefully placed after another. Jim refused to abandon the crutches on a shelf of rocks as Yazeed had ordered him, worried that they would not be there later when they returned. Yazeed climbed the cliffs in bold bursts and stops, reaching a point and yelling down to Jim to hurry, then waiting on a ledge of rocks and smoking a cigarette as Jim caught up to him. All Jim wanted was to stop, take off his right shoe, stretch his leg out, and slip into a warm bath. *Yes, a bath. That would be nice.*

No. They had to find Ari first.

He stopped and felt the cold air in his lungs. This was what he would remember of Bamiyan. The thin air. The chill. The bright light and dark shadows. Had the Buddhist monks struggled on their own pilgrimages to reach the cliffs? He cast his eyes down to the valley.

The sun was yellowing, lengthening across a field of green grass and
trees that somehow he had missed seeing while they made their way
through the village. The cliffs were a stark contrast—dusty, beige, and
devoid of vegetation, the grottoes before them empty and dark, like
dangerous, gaping mouths. There was no sign of life in any of them
and a memory came to Jim from the recent Kabul trip that there was
an effort underway by one of the organizations to relocate all of the
families who had once been living inside them. But to where? Where
were they if they weren't here? Where had they been relocated? Jim
was worried that they were running out of time. So was Yazeed. That
explained the boy's manic bursts up the mountainside. It would be
dark soon and then what? Where would they sleep if they didn't find
Ari? In a cave? In the van? Was there room at the hotel?

They reached a series of steps that led down into a grotto opening.
Yazeed helped Jim down the steep stairs to where the floor leveled
off into a hallway. Yazeed bolted ahead into the dark opening, yelling
"Allo? Allo?"

It was warmer inside the first cave and Jim stood and rubbed his
hands together and blew hot air over his fingers. His eyes adjusted to
the darkness and he looked at the slick black walls, the dark, dusty
ground, and the bright light pouring in from the opening of the cave
on the side of the cliff.

Yazeed continued to yell as he moved deeper into the cells and
rooms, "Allo! Allo?"

Jim limped to a hallway and into another cave. A damp stench
hovered in the air. There was a series of niches carved near the ceiling,
where the ceiling itself rose into the shape of a dome. Jim continued
to hear Yazeed's voice echo against the stone walls, "Allo? Allo?" while
his eyes searched across the blackened stucco of the cave. Near one
of the upper niches was the outline of the Buddha's body surrounded
by waves or auras—or were they halos? The face was gone, and Jim
tried to imagine the benign smile of the god. What was in store for
him now? Would God open a window if this door was closed? Jim
limped a few feet closer to the wall so that he could get a better look

at the missing Buddha. The figure was seated, cross legged, and there was a garment draped only over one shoulder. Again, he imagined the face—a light smile—crumbling off the wall. He reached an arm up as if to touch the Buddha's face—an ear or a tip of the nose—he had heard somewhere long ago that it would grant a believer good luck and good fortune. Jim thought that if he could imagine the face he could also imagine the blessing—or benediction—or hold it as a reason to continue and to go on.

Jim heard Yazeed's voice again—this time he was yelling to someone—speaking loudly and deliberately in Dari—the sound both loud and faint—and Jim realized that he was talking through the opening of one of the grottoes to someone who was standing at the opening of another. Jim walked to the cave's opening and looked out. He could see Yazeed above him at the opening of one of the other cells but he could not see to whom the boy was talking.

The conversation stopped and Jim knew instinctively that the caves had only been recently abandoned. A pile of ashes was near the opening of the cave—soot that a broom might have missed or that might have been carried from the deeper and darker part of the room. He walked slowly to the hallway where he leaned against the wall and waited for Yazeed. Yazeed appeared moments later, his footsteps arriving first, then his body bursting through the darkness and into the hallway opening where Jim stood.

"Shahr-e-Nau," Yazeed said to Jim. "Come, M'sheem. We go. Your friend at Shahr-e-Nau."

They had taken a cab from Midtown. They had spent the day working together on a piece on the lack of tourists in the city, using the Christmas tree at Rockefeller Center as a backdrop, and interviewing tourists in Times Square.

Eric and Sean were at the restaurant when they arrived. Ari was only joining them for drinks, before taking the subway out to Queens to have dinner with his cousins. Jim had hinted at the disappointment he would have to bear alone if Ari did not make an appearance.

"The apartment's vacant?" Jim asked Eric.

"Philip's brother is staying there," Eric answered.

"How is he handling it?"

"He's lost too," Sean said. "The city's overwhelmed him. And he knew very little about Philip."

"They weren't close?"

"Philip was older," Eric said. "Ten or eleven years, I think. The brother dropped out of law school."

"It's a sad time," Ari said. "Full of awful stories. I know I would be lost if something happened to Jim."

"Me?" Jim answered. He was surprised by the sentiment coming from Ari at a time when they were having trouble staying together.

"Yes, you," Ari said and then turned to Eric and added, "He never gives me credit for how deeply I feel for him."

"Ari, you don't need to pretend," Jim said. "Eric knows what we've been going through."

"See, he thinks I am pretending," Ari said. "What do I have to do to convince you how I feel?"

"And do you know how I feel without you?" Jim said. "Give me some credit, too. Do you understand what it is to feel lost?"

"Perhaps you were a botanist," Danil said to Barâdar.

"Why do you think that?"

"Calluses," he answered. "You have rough patches on your right hand."

"They are from working," he answered and laughed. "Digging for the professor. You have them too."

Danil had walked to the hospital again that afternoon to find Barâdar. They had gone together to the guesthouse where Barâdar could bathe in a small room where the cold water of the well was

pumped through a spigot. Danil had given him some soap to use to
wash and a large sheet to dry himself off with. Barâdar had dressed
and joined Danil in the room he shared with the professor, who had
not yet returned from the site. The room held a thin narrow mattress
on a cot, another mattress on the floor, and a chair. Suitcases were
open and overflowing with clothes. Danil was seated at the edge of
the bed as Barâdar toweled his hair and beard dry.

Barâdar lifted the wet sheet to his nose and smelled. "This is
clean," he said. "I remember this. Or I remember that I missed feeling
this. *Clean.*"

"You will stay?" Danil asked.

"There is more room with the family," he answered. "And that is
where I belong right now."

"There is nothing to be ashamed of," Danil said. "It is perfectly
natural. What you should feel. What we should feel."

"I am not ashamed," Barâdar said. "But I do not want you to have
a wrong impression of me. What if I am not available? What if what I
feel for you would hurt someone else?"

"You may go when you need to go," Danil said. "And you may stay
when you need to stay."

"Why are you so kind to me?"

"I am only offering what I would also wish," Danil answered.

There was not much to carry down the cliffs—a sack of utensils and
pots, which Barâdar helped Roonah collect, the broom, a bag of rice
and nuts, and the bundles and baskets of clothes. Nadeem and Siraaj
rolled up the carpets and strapped them to their backs. Haatim had
moved Zaina, Ghatol, and the baby boy the day before to the new
house in Shahr-e-Nau—settling them in a tiny room with a stove that
would serve as both a kitchen and a living space for the women and
the baby. Roonah used the broom to the end in the cave, sweeping
the dust to the opening of the cliff and out into the sky. Her back

was tensed and hunched, her brow creased with anxiety and her eyes welling up with tears. She frequently chided Nadeem and Siraaj, most likely, Barâdar imagined, because of the worry of leaving a stable home for an uncertain one.

Nadeem led the way down the cliffs. Barâdar followed Roonah, watching her tentative and unsure steps and her glances back to the caves as if she knew her family was making a mistake. Siraaj took up the rear of the single-file journey down the slopes, a steady stream of words hurled over Barâdar's head to reassure Roonah that the family was doing the right thing.

Haatim was at the base of the cliffs with another Afghan man Barâdar recognized from his work with an NGO that was relocating the families out of the caves. Both men had rifles at their sides as they waited for the family to arrive, a fact that Roonah did not let go unnoticed, her voice rising in pitch and anger as she approached Haatim. Haatim stubbed out the cigarette that he had been smoking, said something to Nadeem and Siraaj, and took one of the rugs from Nadeem's back, the fringe shaking in the morning breeze. Haatim made another remark to Roonah and this time she remained silent, and she took the yellow scarf that was wrapped around her head and neck and used it to screen her face.

Haatim now led the way, or, rather, he followed the NGO Afghan man, and the family continued their single file march along the base of the cliffs. The journey was silent, punctuated only by their shoes sliding and gripping a position on the dirt and stones. Barâdar studied the back of Roonah's head as if he might be able to detect her fear or a rising hysteria, but he was weighted by an unstable bundle of clothes and the neck of a sack that burned his grip. A man on a horse with a rifle thundered up to them and spoke to the NGO Afghan. The family stopped and Haatim offered an explanation and the man and the horse cantered away.

As the family approached the village, they were met by the boys, who ran up to them, stared, and then ran away. The new house was another fifteen-minute walk which Roonah bore in silence, veiled and with downcast eyes. When the new settlement came into view, Haatim began his chattering again, pointing to one compound after the next, explaining the buildings and the lanes. Roonah did not react—she kept her eyes pinned to the dirt—but Barâdar searched out the doorways and windows, the fluttering blue curtains and shaded courtyards. He said something in English to Roonah to reassure her—"It will be a safe place to live. You will be happy here."—but she did not react to this either.

The Afghan man led them down a lane between several houses and into a courtyard where Ghatol was waiting, her eyes brightening as the family arrived, though she bowed her head to the ground and quickly disappeared into the house. The men began to help each other unhook the rugs from their backs. Estelle appeared at the doorway and said to Barâdar in English, "The baby is fine. We've set up a nice space for him."

Zaina appeared behind Estelle. Siraaj said something sharply to Roonah, who still stood veiled and with her downcast eyes, and Zaina took the bag of pots from her and led her into the house.

Estelle spoke to Roonah in English, as if the old woman would understand everything she told her. "We've hung curtains," she said. "Come see. And we can put shelves where you need them."

Roonah cautiously followed the younger Afghan woman, nodding to Estelle. She went to the room where there was a small stove and a shelf and began unpacking the utensils, remembered her face was veiled and rearranged her scarf. Near the stove, the baby lay atop a bundle of clothes that formed a pillow. Roonah's fear seemed to dissipate as she began to get her bearings. She said something to Zaina, and they began gathering up the empty plastic jugs and pails. She stopped and yelled something to Haatim—most likely a question about where the women could collect water—and when she was satisfied with Haatim's answer, she returned to instructing Zaina on what they should do next.

◇◇◇

It was dark when they reached Shahr-e-Nau, the new settlement of buildings in Bamiyan which had been built after the defeat of the Taliban. They had returned to the van and the hotel where they ordered food; Jim knew that Ari's uncle had supplied Yazeed with enough money for a recovery mission that also included food. He was impatient and exhausted and wanted someone to talk to who could understand his mood, but it felt good to be eating and off his feet, though sitting on the floor meant he had to contort his posture to prevent the pains and cramps in his leg.

Yazeed spoke to several of the local men about Barâdar and Shahr-e-Nau, so that when they left the hotel the young man seemed to have a clear sense of direction.

Yazeed walked more slowly now, more out of deference to Jim and his leg than his own tiredness, or so Jim believed. The mystery of Ari's disappearance was slowly unraveling for both of them. Ari, with amnesia, had been living with a local family in the caves until the family was relocated to the new settlements. He had worked at both the hospital and professor Sajadi's archeological site in the weeks since the accident. Amnesia and a lack of his identity documents had prevented him from finding his way elsewhere and the locals had called him "Barâdar," or brother.

From the tea house it was a twenty-minute walk to the new settlement, a cluster of small buildings surrounded by mud brick walls and narrow lanes. The purr of motors from the diesel generators hummed in the background, rising and then diminishing as Jim and Yazeed approached and passed the homes that used electricity. A warm, flickering amber light spilled out of the windows and doorways and onto the gold mounds of dust and sand. At a gate Yazeed yelled, "Allo! Allo?" and a man stood silhouetted in the doorway and looked out at the darkness. "Allo? Allo?" Yazeed said softer, and began to speak to the man about "Monsieur Barâdar." A young girl came into view behind him, looking out at Jim and Yazeed in the courtyard.

The man led Jim and Yazeed inside the gate and into a room of the house, which was warm from the cooking on a stove and where a young woman was seated on the floor with a baby. An older woman turned away from the visitors and covered her face. The man ushered them into a larger room where two men were seated and the girl—about seven or eight—appeared behind the standing man. The room was clean, the smell of fresh paint clung to the air, and the floor was covered with several small carpets. A radio was playing music. A small kerosene lamp glowed in a corner, but elsewhere there were candles. The man standing appeared to be in his thirties. He introduced himself to Yazeed and Jim as Haatim. He knew of Barâdar and kept nodding and waving his hands in the direction of the bazaar, saying "American! American!"

Jim felt his disappointment arrive immediately. Ari was not here. The change from the cool air outside to the warmth inside the house had made him break into a sweat. Jim recognized the word "Kabul" when one of the older men seated spoke and Yazeed turned to Jim and said, "No Bamiyan. Kabul. Kabul."

Jim looked at Haatim and asked, "Monsieur Barâdar alive? Monsieur Barâdar okay?"

The men looked at each other and Yazeed answered for them, "Okay. Okay. Kabul. Kabul."

Yazeed shook the standing man's hand. The boy was ready to leave, waving away what appeared to be an offer to join the family for tea. Jim knew his own frustration and depression showed in his face. He nodded and thanked the family, but before he left the room his vision grew blurry and he bent to a knee to keep himself oriented. He thought he was going to cry but he was already drenched with sweat. As he tried to lift himself up, he blacked out and lost consciousness.

He awoke a few minutes later on the floor. His heart was beating rapidly. The bearded man was lifting the back of his head, trying to get him to drink something from a small tin cup. Another man was trying to unfold his leg. Jim shook his head and lost consciousness again. The next time he awoke there was an old woman above him, pressing a cool, wet cloth against his cheeks and forehead. Her eyes met his and she said, "Barâdar? Barâdar?" first as a question and then again, softer, as if she had seen the answer in Jim's eyes. "Barâdar. Barâdar."

She said something to the other men about Barâdar and next about the bloodstains on Jim's legs and the thick visible scars on his right arm. She tapped his pants leg and one of the men used a knife to slit it open from his ankle to his thigh. Her voice took on a sharp edge—instructions, Jim thought.

Haatim dampened a rag with water and cleaned the wounds on Jim's leg, rinsing the fresh blood out in a small tin. The water and the chill in the air made Jim's exhaustion overcome him. He closed his eyes and felt the fabric being parted from the scabs and matted hair on his leg. The old woman said something to the young girl, who ran out of the room and returned with a bright yellow scarf. The old woman used a knife to slit it into pieces, and gave them to Haatim, who wiped Jim's leg dry and wrapped the scarf around his wounds and tied it into place at the base of his leg as a bandage. Jim lay there and thought about what he could do to repay such kindness. He felt his body being covered by warmth—a blanket. He fluttered his eyes open briefly and said, "Thank you... Thank you."

He slept soundly through the night, lifting his head only once to orient himself. He was sleeping in a room with the other men, their snores nearby. Yazeed was asleep close to the door of the room. A wave of gratitude washed through Jim's consciousness, followed by a prayer that Ari might still be safe and alive.

They slept together entwined. Jim, smaller, older, the circulation a little slower, embraced by the taller, younger, warmer body of Ari. Hours later the arrangement would shift. Ari, rising into consciousness, his arm pinned beneath Jim's head, would roll over on his side. Jim would stir, feel the cooler air on his skin, and follow Ari's body, his turn, now, to embrace his partner, his arm slipping around Ari's waist and tucking his fingers against his hip.

They could stir each other further at any moment. Jim pressing his lips against Ari's neck and the raw stubble of his chin. Ari slipping a hand to Jim's genitals to test the firmness of his cock. Some nights they would tease each other, more and more, kissing, tweaking, caressing, till they both sensed the moments before the alarm clock would ring and their movements became more urgent, deliberate, passionate.

Other times, they would display their affection towards each other in a light kiss or a pat while passing in the kitchen, or the hallway, or while one was working at a desk. This never failed to stir the other partner deeper. They carried this contentment throughout the day as each made their way through wire reports, assignment ledgers, transcribing notes and editing videos, a secretive balance they continued to maintain as professionals while out in the field, interviewing, reporting, filming, broadcasting. Their desire for each other had never played itself out.

Their ease together left others baffled—Why does Jim put up with a cameraman who mouths off during interviews? Why is Ari hanging out with that older guy? They did not attempt to explain or offer excuses, their answers a succinct and precise, "Because it is right."

That afternoon a group of physicians arrived from Kabul to tour the hospital and assess the progress and the new equipment. They were joined by several journalists. Ali Hassad had greeted each one, asking them if they knew "my American friend, Stan Chartoff."

Barâdar was working in a small supply room when they arrived. Estelle had sent Ali Hassad back to the pharmacy.

The group stopped at the doorway while Estelle explained the arrival of the new supplies that they had been awaiting. "Bandages and surgery tools," she said. "Needles and syringes and proper disposal canisters. Things that were never here before the Taliban."

As the group moved on to another room and followed Estelle's voice down the hallway, Barâdar noticed that one of the men in the group had remained behind and was staring at him. He knew at once he was found.

"Ari?" the man asked. "Ari Sarghello?"

Barâdar stared at the man, trying to recognize him, but he was coming up blank. "Tell me," he said to the man. He was tall and good looking and dressed in a blue cotton shirt and khaki trousers. "Do you know me?"

"You've been thought dead by everyone," he said and introduced himself, shaking Barâdar's hand and clasping him on the back as if they were old friends. His name was Matthew Rolley and he was a journalist for *Time* magazine. He had met Ari recently in Kabul. "Jim MacTiernan has gone mad looking for you."

"Mad?"

"He's at Bagram, trying to locate you. He was hurt, you know that?"

"Hurt?"

"Injured."

"How?"

"Ari, what happened? Don't you remember? *Jim.*"

"I've lost my memory," he said. "Tell me who I am."

Sixteen

They woke early and said their good-byes to the family; even Yazeed was impressed by their graciousness and hospitality as Roonah pressed him to have a small cup of warm, weak tea before they left. While Jim used his crutches to move slowly through the courtyard, Yazeed spoke to the men at the doorway, offering Haatim a pack of cigarettes as a parting gesture as he shook their hands, then jogged to catch up with Jim.

Yazeed followed Jim along the narrow lane of houses, then took the lead as they headed back to the village. In the distance the cliffs towered above them, making their movements seem slower and smaller. A sharp morning chill hung over the plateau, their breaths icy clouds. Yazeed's impatience began to show as the distance between them grew wider and wider. As Jim's head began to clear of its sleepiness, his leg began to throb. He tried to walk without putting pressure on it, his foot twisted outward to alleviate the pain that now burned at his ankle, then stopped to reach down and adjust the tightness of the bright yellow scarf the Afghan man had tied around it. He tried not to let his frustration over not finding Ari show. They had traveled this far only to discover that Ari was elsewhere—but at least there was confirmation now that he was alive, that he had survived the accident that had killed Dr. Dupray and sent Jim to the hospital. The family had said that Barâdar had returned to Kabul the day Jim and Yazeed had driven to Bamiyan; he had found a spot in a cargo chopper that was flying back to Kabul.

Jim's strategy that morning was to find the service men he had spoken to the day before in the village—to get them to take him to their operating base where he might be able to send messages to Simon or Abdul or Michael that Ari was alive and send more messages to alert the officials and NGOs and consulates in Kabul that Ari was still missing but reported to be in the area.

Yazeed wanted nothing to do with the military. He wanted to leave for Kabul right away. There was a small disagreement between them as Yazeed headed to the van still parked near the hotel, as Jim made his way towards the village.

"I have to send messages," Jim said. "It's *important!*"

"M'sheem! M'sheem!" Yazeed yelled. "We must go now. Kabul, sir. We find friend in Kabul."

"I want to send messages *first*," Jim yelled, though they were the only two people on the street except for a woman leaving the hotel carrying an empty pail. If Jim didn't find the Army men from yesterday, he'd search out the UNESCO workers that Ari had found, or he would walk to the archeological site where Dr. Sajadi might be able to send messages or phone calls.

"M'sheem, we must hurry," Yazeed said. "We must find friend and give uncle back auto! We must go now!"

"Soon," Jim said.

The distance between them grew. Yazeed was standing his ground by the van and Jim was making his way farther into the village. Jim was already planning what he would do if Yazeed left him—he'd hitch a ride with the military—someone would surely be headed back to Bagram or Kabul—or he would stay with the professor and wait for another ride—he'd make the military retrieve him, airlift him out of Bamiyan. But first he wanted to send out the messages—Ari was safe. Alive. Keep looking for Ari.

Jim had reached the compound where the soldiers had been working the day before, but it was empty except for two Afghan men sitting on the stoop.

"Soldiers?" Jim asked one of them. "Americans?"

The older man with a long dark beard pointed a finger out into the street. Jim thanked him and slipped the crutches beneath his arms and made his way deeper into the village, shouting "Officer Mark! American? Army?" when Yazeed came up behind him and grabbed his shoulder.

"M'sheem, sir! We must go now!"

Jim was sweating. His forehead was burning. He felt his chest was ready to explode. He struggled to argue with Yazeed and discovered that he was choking. He took a step away from Yazeed, tried to continue walking, when he suddenly felt the crutch slide out from under him and he lost consciousness.

He awoke hours later, his throat dry, his neck sweating from a fever. He was lying beside a long, rolled up carpet that was bumping against his body. He pressed his hands down against a cold metal platform to steady himself and realized that he was lying in the back of the van. Yazeed must have carried him back. Jim tried to lift his head but his neck was stiff and his head felt thick and groggy. He tried to roll over and prop himself up by an arm when the throbbing returned to his leg. He gave in to his helplessness at once, thinking again of Ari. *Please God*, he prayed. *Keep me alive. Keep me alive till I find Ari.*

It was a quick recap. Facts written down on a sheet of paper Estelle provided Matthew Rolley, who was leaving almost immediately for Mazar-i-Sharif to cover another story. His name was Ari Sarghello. He was a cameraman for the IBN network, based in Rome. "Jim MacTiernan," Matthew said to Ari. "You worked with the reporter Jim MacTiernan. You remember Jim, don't you? Your partner?"

Ari shook his head no, his forehead creased with thought. Matthew flickered his eyes towards Estelle and pulled Ari out of the room and into the hallway.

"*Jim*," Matthew said. "Your lover. You two are together. You came here together. You were covering a story about the Buddhas."

He shook his head, trying to remember.

"You don't remember at all, do you?"

Again, he shook his head no.

"Come with us to Mazar-i-Sharif. I'll get you in the van as part of the press."

"I can't."

"The army will get you to Jim. Or Jim to you."

"I can't just leave."

"Why not?"

"There have been people here, helping me. I can't just walk out and leave them."

"They'll understand."

"No, I can't just leave without telling them thanks. I cannot leave them so quickly, they will worry. No, I must stay."

"It's a cruel world that doesn't allow me to openly show how I feel about you," Ari said. They were in the back of Omar's car in Kabul, driving from the BBC bureau to the university. A yellow-gray haze hung over the city. The camera was placed on the seat in the space between them. Jim thought that he could detect a slight facetiousness in Ari's comment—the fact that Ari hadn't been feeling so strongly about Jim until this trip to Afghanistan emerged.

"You do know how I feel, don't you?" Ari said. His manner was more sincere now, as if he had realized his tone and Jim's impression of it. "That hasn't changed."

He lifted his hand over the camera and placed it on Jim's thigh. Jim glanced at Omar in the front seat to see if there was a reaction from him, then smiled when he had noticed it had gone undetected.

But Ari was never content with offering a simple gesture. It was always caught up in a bigger struggle. "At the Vatican we would be excommunicated," he said. "In China, we would be thrown in prison. In Nigeria, we would be stoned. In Saudi Arabia we would be beheaded."

"Ari, I'm converted. You don't need to preach to me."

"But you do understand what I am willing to risk for you?" His hand had remained on Jim's thigh.

"And your uncle is quick to reprimand us," Jim said. "Individually." Months before, after a display of affection between them during a business gathering in Paris, Ari's uncle, Abdul Ramati, had drawn each of them aside and asked that they show more respect to those who weren't as tolerant as he was.

Jim had been appalled at the reprimand, but Ari's reaction was quick and outspoken. He had lifted a wine glass and offered a toast to his "life partner"—Jim—in front of his uncle's guests. Jim had been able to graciously smooth out the confrontation, but it had left a deep resentment between Ari and his uncle, something that Jim wondered if Ari had carefully orchestrated in order to break the grasp his family had on him.

"Four years ago, the Taliban toppled a wall on top of three men accused of sodomy," Ari added. The word "Taliban" had caught Omar's attention in the front of the car, and Jim noticed his eyes in the rear view mirror seeking out their conversation in the back seat. "I doubt that the reaction would be any different today. Homophobia rules."

"I'm not going to argue with you on this," Jim said.

"We could do a piece on it," Ari said. "Showing that theory."

"Simon wouldn't air it. You know that."

"Simon is a prude. He's against public sex."

"Most people are against public sex," Jim said. "You were pretty unhappy with the couple at Sitges last year."

"They were *straight*," Ari answered. "There's plenty of places for them to show off their affection for each other that they don't have to do it at a nude gay beach."

"I think that argument could be taken by many straight people too, about gay behavior in public."

"We've never had the kind of public spaces straights have enjoyed," Ari said. "Or public acceptance. Which was why everything went underground."

"And into the toilets."

"You sound like Simon, now."

"No, I have my preferences like any other gay man," Jim said. "Or any individual, regardless of sexuality. I prefer intimacy to be intimate."

Ari moved his hand away from Jim's knee but stretched it along the top of the back seat so that his fingers dangled at Jim's shoulder. "Then you understand how I feel about you," Ari said. "The risks I'm willing to take to show you and to keep us together."

"You shouldn't travel anywhere now until we can get your paperwork in order," Estelle said to Barâdar. "It would be too much of a risk. You could be stopped anywhere. I know you must want to know more about who you are, but it's best to be cautious, not impulsive. Be patient and let the paperwork come and the Americans arrive to get you out of here."

"But the Red Cross is sending a truck to Kabul tomorrow for supplies," he answered. "I could try to get a ride on it."

"But the Americans wouldn't allow you into Bagram without any identification."

"But the Red Cross could get me in."

"Not necessarily," Estelle said. "Only if they could convince them you are an American. And you don't remember enough about yourself to be sure of that."

"I could try the landing strip," he said. "Someone flying in will be flying out."

"They're mercenaries," Estelle said. "They will want to charge you. Where will you get the money? And once you land in Kabul or

Bagram or Kandahar—it is all too risky. Be patient. Wait. We will get your papers in order and get you to the place where you belong."

"You don't want me to go, is that it?" Barâdar said. "You'd rather I stay here."

"I want you to be safe," Estelle said. "That's always been my main priority. I'll be sad to see you leave, yes, if that's what you mean. Many of us will. We think of you as one of us now."

Barâdar remained quiet.

"Do you remember anything more?" Estelle asked.

"Flashes," he answered. "Small things. But nothing adds up to anything yet."

"You were traveling with the archeologist," she said. "The accident. Do you remember anything of it?"

"No," he answered, then said, "Yes. Something. I remember someone—or something pulling me across the dirt."

"The American?"

"I'm not sure," Barâdar said. "He was different. His face was covered with dust. Brown. Black smudges. It was very... upsetting."

"One of the men who brought you here?"

"His eyes," Barâdar said. "His eyes were green."

He awoke with a cramp in his groin. He yelled to Yazeed to stop the van, but his voice was not loud enough to carry over the rattling and jostling movements. He waited a moment, gathering his strength, propped himself up on an elbow and yelled, "Yazeed!" and motioned for the boy to pull the van over to the side of the road.

Yazeed turned around, surprised, "M'sheem? M'sheem? You hungry? Eat now?"

Jim waved again, and the young man brought the van to an abrupt halt.

Jim lay back down again until Yazeed opened the back doors of the van. He was in an awkward position and accepted the boy's help getting out and retrieving the crutches. The boy stood before him, wide eyed, waiting for a sign of what to do next. Jim waved him back to the driver's seat, while he made his way a few steps away from the van to a small ditch that led to the side of the road and turned his back to Yazeed.

His head was thick with sleep—he wanted a cup of coffee or something sweet to jolt him awake, make him more alert. He unzipped his pants and let out a long stream of urine. He tried to find the humor and irony in it—what had pulled him awake, kept him alive and ready to go on, was the body's biological need, the natural urge to piss.

Finished, Jim turned and adjusted the crutches beneath his arms. The young man was instantly beside him, smelling of smoke and dirt, his arm around Jim's waist, helping him walk back to the van.

They were close to Bagram. The mountains were behind them, the road now a level stretch of dust. Jim lifted himself into the front seat and handed the crutches to Yazeed, mumbling a raspy "thanks." The boy tossed the crutches into the back of the van where Jim had been lying beside the carpets, shut the doors, and started up the van. Jim leaned his head against the window and tried to fall back asleep, thinking, *What now? Who do I have to contact to find Ari?*

It was too difficult to be patient. To wait for messages. Documents. Papers from an embassy. What if there was a snag? More complications? He began to think that he had made a mistake, not leaving immediately for Mazar-i-Sharif with the American journalist. The most important thing now seemed for him to be somewhere else. He went to the room in the hospital where Haatim was working, helping another Afghan worker stabilize the legs of an examination table.

"Haatim, I must go," Barâdar said. He reached out and used both of his hands to shake Haatim's.

"I must thank you," he added and embraced him in a hug.

Haatim registered surprise and confusion.

"Kabul," Barâdar said. "My name is Ari Sarghello." He tapped himself several times at the chest so that the name would register. "Ari Sarghello. American. I am Ari Sarghello, an American. I go to Kabul now. *Kabul.* Thank you. Thank you. *Allahu akbar.* Thank you. Kabul now."

Haatim understood and pulled Barâdar back into another embrace. "Kabul," he echoed and nodded. "*Allahu akbar.* Kabul. Kabul."

Confusion followed Barâdar as he left the hospital and walked out into street. He tipped his eyes towards the dirt path because of the bright sunlight. He was elated over discovering his identity but worried over how to reach Jim MacTiernan and the network where he worked as a cameraman. He was distressed by his impulsive need to leave so quickly, without proper good-byes to those who had helped him in Bamiyan—Roonah, Siraaj, Ghatol, Zaina, Estelle, Danil, Dr. Sajadi. He simply wanted to shout for joy, but it was not that easy. His memories were still absent and vague. What if he could not remember who he used to be? What if the Americans refused him? How would he feel someplace new? *Home?*

Ari Sarghello. Jim MacTiernan. Ari Sarghello. Jim MacTiernan. Ari rolled around the names on his lips as he began to pick up his pace, jogging, then running through the old village, trying to recall something else from his past life, but all he could find was a noisy, dusty tumble through the desert.

The accident?

He remembered the pain on his shoulder. A hand, pulling him through the dirt. Dust. Swirls of dust. The blackened face. The creased brow. The eyes. *Green.*

Barâdar was an American. An American citizen working abroad in Italy as a cameraman for a news organization. Ari Sarghello. Jim

MacTiernan. Ari Sarghello. Jim MacTiernan. *Could I convince one of the NGOs to take me with them to Kabul? Would the American soldiers help me get out of here?*

A plan materialized, and he began to run faster. He ran onto the road that led to the Buddhas. He was sweating and breathing hard when he reached the archeological site. The professor was inside the pit, using a trowel to remove a line of dirt from the interior wall.

Barâdar avoided speaking to the professor. Instead, he found Danil beneath the white tent, working at the computer, and pulled him aside.

"Ari Sarghello," Barâdar said to him. "My name is Ari Sarghello. I must go to Kabul as soon as possible."

"Kabul?" Danil asked.

"The embassy," Barâdar said. "I have to go to the embassy. Or contact the Americans at Bagram. But I need your help."

"Yes, of course," Danil answered.

"I will pay you back," Barâdar said. "Everything and more."

They had returned to the hotel in Kabul. Ari had rebuffed Matthew's advances and was feeling cocky. Jim was feeling cranky and annoyed, ready to leave and return home to Rome.

"M'sheem, M'sheem," Ari mocked Omar's voice. "Let me kiss your shoes."

"You're just jealous," Jim said and laughed. "That he listens to me instead of you."

"And you're just jealous because Matthew clearly wanted to split us up for a while."

"He wasn't the first, and I doubt he will be the last," Jim said. "The translator at the hospital had his eyes on you too."

"M'sheem, M'sheem," Ari continued, playfully taunting Jim. "I love your green eyes. So beautiful and strange. You are special friend. I will never leave you."

He caught Jim and held him in place, whispering "M'sheem, M'sheem," into his ear.

Jim laughed and tried to pull away. He was already in a better mood. But Ari wouldn't release him. He smothered Jim's neck with kisses. "M'sheem, M'sheem, what would I ever do without you?"

It was easier than they both expected. They walked together from the tent to the landing strip behind the hotel. A Chinook was being unloaded—supplies to be used by the engineers working to stabilize the grottoes in the cliffs.

Barâdar introduced himself to the pilot, an American who worked for a subcontractor of the Pentagon, a short, tough-looking fellow named Adam Birch from Millheim, Pennsylvania. He would be returning to the airstrip at Bagram. He quoted a price to Barâdar for a lift in the chopper back to the base.

"Do you need clearance first?" Barâdar asked.

"You're buying your clearance."

"And I'll be on the base, right?" Barâdar confirmed.

"Right," Adam said.

"Without papers," Barâdar added. "No passport."

"You'll be on base," Adam explained. "How you get out of it is not my problem."

"Euros?" Danil asked.

"Dollars," Adam answered.

"Euros," Danil added. "It's what I have." Danil counted out the money which he pulled from a belt that had been hidden beneath his pants.

"Euros it is, then," Adam said, and counted the amount out when he received the bills.

Barâdar and Danil sat on a hill while the chopper was unloaded. "You will thank the professor for me?" Barâdar said.

"He will be sorry to see you go," Danil answered. "We both will."

"He will be worried when he sees you are not in the tent, at work on the computer, where you should be."

"I will explain," Danil answered. "He will understand."

"I was worried you wouldn't help," Barâdar said. "Because you would want me to stay."

"I do," Danil answered. "But I must not think of only myself. Someone has missed you a lot, I'm sure of it. I know I would be upset to lose someone like you. You must get back to where you belong."

"I will find you again," Barâdar said. "I will return the money. I will thank you properly."

"You do not need to speak of this," Danil said. "I am glad to help. I will see you again soon, I know."

The flight was as he had imagined it from the opening of the cliffside grotto—the deep folds of the mountainsides rising up from the outlined patches of farmlands and villages. The Valley of the Gods. *Très incroyable.* There was no attempt to talk to the pilot—the chopper vibrated with a thunderous roar and made it impossible. Barâdar sat and thought about who he was leaving behind as the thick sound and cool wind of travel made him forget.

A hovering presence arrived, a memory, the shape of a man's body, his eyes, and then a tumble of images: a donkey, a hand, the sand, and again the sea-green eyes of a man.

Then he thought of what he had lost—a life in America? But where? Matthew's outline had been sketchy one—a journalist working in Rome—but for how long? And as a cameraman? On assignment in Bamiyan? He only had a few facts to work with and only scattered images to remember.

And Jim MacTiernan? "Your partner," Matthew had whispered. "Remember? *Your lover.*"

Lover. He rolled the word around in his mind. He held the image of being loved, protected, wanted, sought after—a contained elation of knowing he was headed to someone. A *lover.*

Who are you? Who am I? Who are we when we are together?

He was taken directly to the medical unit where he was examined by a staff doctor. There were questions about his vision, his heartbeat, his general health—did he know of any allergies, pre-existing conditions? The doctor did not detect any visible physical damages or injury to his skull but said more tests were needed. Ari asked about Jim MacTiernan. "Is he here?" he asked the doctor. "Can I see him?"

The doctor wasn't interested in relaying a message and said he would send someone in shortly with more information. Ari waited in an examination room for another doctor, who asked him questions about his memory and headaches and twitches and fits. A pin light was shined into his eyes and ears. Again, Ari asked about Jim MacTiernan. "Can I see him? Can you get a message to him?"

"What unit is he in?" the doctor asked.

"He's a reporter. For IBN."

"I'm not sure if we can get a message to him," the doctor answered.

Ari noticed the hesitation and added, "He knows me. He was in the accident with me. He's somewhere on base. He knows all the details. Everything. I need to talk to him."

"I'll send someone in to speak to you."

A soldier arrived who asked Ari for facts—his name, address, social security number, and other information. Ari stumbled at every question. "You've no papers," the soldier said. "We've got messages out."

"Jim MacTiernan? Can you contact Jim MacTiernan. He's a newsman. He's somewhere on the base."

"Mr. MacTiernan is not on base today," the soldier answered. "We're not sure when to expect him back."

The soldier left and another arrived with a set of hospital clothes. Ari was led to the shower, where he bathed and changed, then to a row of beds in a large infirmary, where other men—most with injuries worse than Ari's—were billeted. By now it was dark outside and Ari had found out nothing new about himself. "Take this," the soldier said when he had shown Ari his bunk. "It'll help you sleep."

"I need to reach Jim MacTiernan," Ari said. "Do you understand that?"

"I do, sir," the soldier answered. "He'll be notified as soon as he's back on base."

"I leave here," Yazeed said.

He had stopped the van at the merchant stalls outside the gates of Bagram. Jim offered a half-hearted protest for the boy to accompany him. "Food?" he asked. "Something to eat before you go to Kabul?"

"No, Kabul," he said. "I must go. Uncle's automotive very important to him. I must go now."

Jim nodded and offered his hand out to the boy to shake. "Thank you," he said. "And thank your uncle."

"Your friend, he wait for you inside?"

"No," Jim answered. "But I will find him soon."

"You can walk?" the boy asked. There was a touch of sincerity there.

"Yes," Jim answered.

He wanted to give the boy something more, something to show his appreciation for the extraordinary effort and journey they had shared. He slid off his watch, and held it out to the boy and said, "You want?"

"No, M'sheem," he answered. "You keep. You need."

Jim nodded and slid the watch back on to his wrist. "God bless you," Jim added and turned away before he grew too sentimental for comfort. "I'll send you some American smokes."

"*Allahu akbar*," the boy answered, smiling. "I like American smokes best."

His sleep was heavy and undisturbed, but hours later he was lifted into a dream about the yellow scarf, the gift he had given to Roonah. He replayed his gesture of handing her the gift, watching the stern, solemn lines in her face lift into a smile, her coy gesture to hide her teeth, the push of the scarf back to Barâdar, and his push back to Roonah. She waved her hands, hid her smile again, a beautiful smile of crooked, dark teeth of an honest woman, but she accepted the scarf, and he watched her unfold it and tie it around her shoulders. The dream shifted to the cave and the dark walls—they were not in the new house at Shahr-e-Nau—and his eyes focused on the rubble of stones, the thick ends of the twigs of the broom, the flickering candlelight as it leapt up the wall, the faint halo of the ancient Buddha painted on the stone, suddenly the same bright yellow as the scarf he had given Roonah. And then he was awake—the infirmary active, a soldier in the bed beside him eating from a tray.

Another soldier approached his bunk and said, "Sir, your papers are in order. You'll be shipped out to Manas at eleven hundred. Let me know if you need any assistance."

"Manas?" Ari asked. "Why Manas?" His head was foggy and it was too early to have a conversation.

"More tests and debriefing, sir. From there you'll be sent back to the States."

"The States?"

"Yes, sir."

"But I can't," Ari said.

"I can help you get ready, sir."

"No, you don't understand. I can't leave. I must speak to Jim MacTiernan."

"Sir?"

"Jim MacTiernan. You must help me locate Jim MacTiernan."

"But the orders are that you ship out today at eleven hundred."

"Then change them," Ari said. "Or find me someone to talk to."

The young soldier found Ari an hour later in the rec room. Ari had showered and changed into fatigues the Army had given him for the trip to Manas. He felt useless and restless because of it. He was tired of waiting. He wanted answers. He had been waiting too long for answers to who he was.

"Sir, you know Mr. MacTiernan?" he said to Ari.

"Yes," Ari answered, though he could not remember Jim's face at all. "We work together."

"The cameraman?" the young solder asked.

"Yes," Ari answered.

"Ari Sarghello?"

"Yes."

"Mr. MacTiernan will be glad to see you," the soldier said, with a big smile. "He's spoken highly of you."

"You know him?"

"Sir, yes sir. He's a good man. He left the base yesterday in spite of warnings."

"Warnings?"

"An American, traveling without military escort. And his leg."

"His leg?"

"Yes, sir. An injury sustained in the accident. He went to Bamiyan with a young Afghan to find you."

"He's back?"

"Not yet, sir. But we've heard from some troops who had contact with him yesterday, circulating your picture."

"My picture?"

"Yes, sir. He's been looking for you for some time. I know he'll be pleased to find you're safe. He'll contact you in Manas when he arrives back on base."

"Manas?"

"Yes, sir, that's right."

"Private...?"

"Baxter. Michael Baxter, sir."

"You know Jim, right?"

"Yes sir."

"Then you know you can't send me to Manas. One day is all. Keep me here one more day. I have to find *him*."

"Sir, I'll do what I can."

"I know Jim will be grateful. I know I am."

It was a slow and lonely walk to the Bagram gate. Jim's foot throbbed. The yellow scarf was pasted to his leg by sweat and blood and was beginning to itch. At the gate there was some delay with his press credentials and access to the base, but he was soon found on a list of approved personnel and admitted. He asked the soldier on duty if he could message Private Baxter about a ride to the press corps, but Michael wasn't responding to the pages, so Jim decided to walk, making his way slowly, hoping he might be able to flag down a ride from another a passing soldier.

It was growing dark. Jim knew his frustration was showing on his face. He was defeated, for now. Disappointed. He wanted a shower and a clean set of clothes and to stretch out his leg so that it would ease the pain.

Ari had been able to stall his deployment to Manas, thanks in part to Michael Baxter and Wade Quinlan, a journalist on base who said he would vouch for Ari. Ari had spent the morning with a psychiatrist. His preliminary diagnosis had been dissociative amnesia—repressed emotional memory from stress and trauma—and the doctor had questioned Ari for answers and images of the accident in Bamiyan—the explosion of the van, the aftermath on the plain, the travel to the hospital, the numbing pain he had woken to. The psychiatrist had said what Estelle had told him, that the memory would possibly return slowly, bit by bit, the memories had been stored as fragments not as a whole unit, but that there were other alternatives to help—meditation, hypnosis, therapeutic exercises, some medications might be useful. But the base was not equipped for this sort of long-term treatment— Ari needed to be sent elsewhere. And he needed to be more thoroughly examined for internal injuries with X-rays and CAT scans. A neurologist should be consulted.

In the afternoon, Michael had driven Ari to the press corps building, where he had spent time with Wade, asking questions about his past. Little snippets of memory returned, like photographs, and Ari, seeing a photo of Jim for the first time since the accident, the light circles of his green eyes, began to find longer stretches of his memory—Jim at work at the computer on his desk at the bureau, the light dusting of hair at his collar where it spilled up from his chest, the old gray-white sneakers Jim wore around the apartment with holes worn through at the toes. Ari had a short satellite conversation with his Uncle Abdul, who insisted that Ari return immediately to the States.

"Not yet, sir," Ari said through the static.

"Your family is concerned," Abdul said. "I have heard from a doctor that you do not remember the accident."

"Nor much of anything," Ari answered. "I need to see if I can find some details first. *Here.*"

It was twilight when Michael returned to the press corps to escort Ari back to the infirmary, where he would spend another night before being airlifted to Manas. Wade walked with Ari to the jeep, where they shook hands to part.

Michael noticed the man on crutches first, but it was Ari who sensed the greatest change in himself. He had seen the yellow fabric moving through the darkness, then the crutches and the man's downturned head. Then again the yellow scarf. Roonah's scarf. The bright pattern he had bought at the bazaar in Bamiyan. He saw the scarf wrapped around a man's leg, a man who was slowly walking towards the press tent.

Instinct told Ari to run ahead. He heard himself yell "M'sheem! M'sheem!" without even having to think that the man could be anyone else or what the words meant.

Jim only heard the noise of the shouts, not the recognition of his name, but something equally instinctive told him to stop and look around. He was there. Ari. Rising out of the dark night and running across the space that Jim was slowly trying to reach. He dropped a crutch he had been using and cried "Ari, my Ari" and he was lifted off the ground as his arms wrapped around Ari's neck.

They hugged and kissed and embraced and swung before each other without a shred of embarrassment that someone else might be watching them at their most intimate display of emotion. Ari remembered only that this was the most important person in his life. Jim was overwhelmed with relief. And suddenly, as easily as they were separated, they were together and happy again, both grateful to be alive.

Seventeen

At the end of August, my parents arrived with my cousins, Seth and Luke, and my aunt Janice, my mother's sister, and we began to pack up Pup's apartment. I had decided to leave New York, but it was still a toss-up where I was going to land. I had told everyone that I was going to live in Los Angeles, but I was toying with the idea of moving to San Francisco after Eric had mentioned he had a friend who lived in the Castro who was looking for a roommate. We donated a lot of Philip's belongings to a nearby charity thrift shop run by an AIDS non-profit group, my cousins and I renting a van and dropping off boxes of clothing and kitchen utensils and a few larger pieces of furniture. A neighbor purchased the leather chairs and sofa, which we carried down three flights, and we donated the money he gave us to a gay rights foundation. Other neighbors appeared at the door, fretted and moaned and asked us questions, which would cause my mother and aunt to tear up and hand them something to remember Pup by.

My parents had driven from Missouri to New Jersey, where they were staying at a hotel in Bergen County and riding buses into the city daily to attend meetings and events surrounding the one-year anniversary of the terrorist attacks. My mother had been invited to be one of the announcers at Ground Zero to read from the list of names of the victims. I don't think that she had understood the intensity that would be focused on her because of the loss of her older son. She met with several reporters, talked to an author who was writing a book on the Towers, and was filmed by the camera crew of a documentary in a suite provided by a Midtown hotel. She did not speak openly of Pup being gay, in part because it was never asked of her, nor was I certain that it was a fact that the media was aware of, but she was also fragile—I could see how the exhaustion and depression had settled on her face and I could tell people were being respectful of her grief. I could not bear to be caught up in it again, and I remained stoic and undaunted because I was now an old hand at pushing it away, guiding my cousins to tourist spots around the city—places I had not even been to—the Museum of Natural History, Rockefeller Center, and a cruise around the harbor. I had timed my big move for the following weekend, staying in the empty apartment on an air mattress with a suitcase of clothes. My family's caravan of cars was departing the day after the memorial service and my father tried several times to get me to join them, stay at the house in St. Louis a while, before heading out again. I was too polite to tell him that I was tired of living in the shadow of my brother, but I know he must have understood this. I also said that it was important to say good-bye to a few friends who had helped me out, before I gave up the city for good.

It was late morning when I heard a knock at the door. It was the day my parents were leaving, and I thought it was the super checking on my whereabouts and when I planned to drop off the keys. Instead, it was a man I had met the day before at Ground Zero at the memorial service who had said he had known my brother well—an out-of-town television news producer. I had forgotten that he had asked if he could stop by and see the apartment before I moved out—he knew Eric well, and his partner, Jim MacTiernan, a reporter, had lived in the apartment before Pup moved into the building.

His name was Ari Sarghello and I had heard bits and pieces of his involvement with Pup from Sean and Eric and Chris and other friends. From Stan Chartoff I had heard the account of an accident Ari and his partner had suffered while working in Afghanistan. I doubted that Ari knew of my own brief dalliance with Stan unless Eric had gossiped about it, and I was too young to understand that it would be one of a number of random events that would continue to link our lives.

"Things come back to me in many ways," he said, as I waved him into the empty apartment. "Hypnosis has helped. I think I have about eighty percent back now." He was shockingly handsome, masculine in the way movie stars are, and I understood the sexual draw my brother might have felt for him. "There was a poster on the wall there," he said, and pointed to the shadow of the frame that had once hung on the wall. "Of Vienna."

"He got that in college," I said. "He was an exchange student there one summer."

"He loved traveling," Ari said. "He took me on some wonderful trips."

He walked to the window and looked down on the street. "You look just like him," he said. "I'm sure you've heard that a lot."

I nodded, though I don't know if he detected it.

"Where are you moving to?"

"Not certain," I answered. "Los Angeles, maybe. San Francisco."

"We have a bureau in L.A. But it's cutthroat. Everybody thinks it's a stepping stone to something else. But I also think San Francisco would be too intense for me. *Très gai.*"

He walked to the bedroom door and looked inside the room, at the mattress on the floor, the wild pattern of the sheet that I was using, the box that was supporting my laptop. "Your brother was very private," he said. "I loved him deeply. He was the first guy—"

He was unable to finish or to look at me. "What happened?" I asked.

"I tried to use him to come out to my family. My parents had separated but never divorced, and that was a big taboo in my family, but being gay was a bigger one. I thought if I introduced him to my family as my lover I might get their respect—or I would be able to break away from them."

"I'm sure Pup wasn't happy with that."

He smiled, recollecting something of my brother. "He refused to meet my parents. Well, he refused to meet my parents so I could come out to them. He told me to do it on my own. So I did. My father stopped talking to me. He told me I was wasting my life. I was finishing my masters at Columbia and was about to start the doctoral program. My mother thought I should move home and see a therapist. My uncle picked up the slack and paid a lot of my bills for me. He was always more of a man of the world than my father was."

He went back into the main room, returned to the window and sat lightly on the sill. "We were in a small town in Turkey the day the Towers were hit. I remember feeling a heaviness in my chest that day, because that evening I helped out at a clinic and I still felt this burning sensation. I remember that burning weight—it's still so clear and vivid to me now. A woman was giving birth and I did what I could to help, but I was also worried about myself. Something was wrong but I tried to push it away, out of my mind. I went back to the hotel exhausted. When Jim woke me up with the news, I knew immediately Pup was dead."

"I think my mother did too."

"Your mother was very gracious yesterday. I spoke to her a while. I told her we had talked on the phone many years ago. I used to answer the phone in the mornings when she called here. I wanted my mom to be like her. She was always a pleasant, faraway voice."

I laughed lightly. It was an ironic laugh. "That's because she wasn't your mom."

"Yes, I suppose—"

"I haven't told her anything about... myself."

"Well, you shouldn't wait. You should do it as soon as possible. She must know. Mothers usually know. It might be a shock to have it actually confirmed, but then it will stop being one. You are not her *gay* son. You're her son. She just needs to work through the psychology of it."

"And your mom?"

"She came 'round. But there're still scars. She's very cold to Jim, my partner. But then she's still cold to my father, too."

I offered him a drink—soda or water, which he declined. I had some paper cups that I would use until I left. I went into the kitchen and poured myself a glass of water. On the refrigerator were the pictures of my brother's friends. They would be the last thing that I would pack, and I intended to take them all with me. Ari stood in front of them admiring them. He pointed to one in the upper left corner. "That's us. In Hawaii."

I looked at it and realized I had seen it many times without ever really seeing it.

"You look happy."

"I was. Most of the time. But I was so envious of your brother. It was so easy for him to be gay. I wasn't a club kid and I think that was who he wanted me to be. I was trying to be serious about school and serious about your brother at the same time. I was jealous of all the other guys he fooled around with. Wildly, insanely jealous. I just wanted a husband. And he had this one friend who just hated me—big fellow—this guy..."

He pointed to another picture.

"Chris?"

"Yeah, that was him. He was a mess and he made me feel like a mess. I wanted a husband and Pup wanted a playmate. We spent time with them last summer. In Morocco. It was the last time I saw your brother."

"Did he have a good time?"

"Pup?" Ari asked. "Pup was always having a good time."

"And you? Did you have a good time then?"

"Yes," Ari answered. "And no. My partner has always been jealous of my past with your brother. But we had a lovely tour—and a great dinner one night—and we drove out to the desert one day—which was amazing. I'm grateful we had that experience—all four of us."

He looked again at me—this time meeting my eyes. "You must have a lot of boyfriends."

"No. I'm certain I am doing it all wrong."

"Unfortunately, there's no guidebook," he said, and now it was his turn to add an ironic-sounding laugh. "You just have to learn from your mistakes."

There was another knock at the door. It was Eric with Jim MacTiernan, who had been visiting two doors down. I had also met him the day before, along with Ari. We shook hands and Jim said to Ari, "Well, does it look the same?"

"You tell me," he answered.

Jim stepped briefly over the threshold of the door and eyed the empty main room. "Not really," he said. "There was a wall in this room—a partial wall that rose almost up to the ceiling but not quite. Free standing. It separated my room from Frank's."

"Jim lived here with Frank, before Pup took the apartment," Eric said.

"Let's not be maudlin," Jim said. "If I stay here I will become weepy. These two are going out to lunch together, but I have to go to a screening up by Lincoln Center. Why don't you come with me?—I have an extra ticket because this one only wants to commiserate with Eric about me."

"I should probably—"

"I won't take no. It's the new Meryl Streep film and I can't bear to have to watch it myself. She might even be there..."

"Well, all right," I said and went to find a light jacket in the jumble of my suitcase.

Meryl Streep was not at the screening, but the movie was good. Afterwards, Jim suggested a pub near the park to get something to eat. "Or drink."

I offered a small protest, but he responded with, "It's never too early to have a cocktail," and the pub we walked to seated us in a quiet booth in a darkened room that made it look like it was already past midnight.

After the first round and polite, awkward recaps of the movie, Jim asked me why I was moving away from New York. "Because I don't belong here," I answered.

"Nonsense," he said. "This city embraces you and challenges you. You can never be bored here. And you are part of a continual living, evolving organism. Of course you belong."

"Then why did you leave?"

"Same reason as you. I was running away from myself."

"I'm not running—"

"Yes, yes you are. That isn't a bad thing. Sometimes we have to step outside of ourselves to understand our lives. You've reached a point where your life makes no sense to you here, so you need to look for it elsewhere. Don't disparage the city. There's nothing wrong with the city. It's us that needs work. I understand what you are going through. When Frank died—he was an early boyfriend of mine—after a long battle with AIDS—I had to move away and have a meltdown—take out all the pieces of my psyche, repair and polish them, and put them back together. I spent a year in Athens, thinking that I loved the place, doing massive amounts of research on stories—overreaching and ambitious, but it was all part of a meltdown. And it wasn't just from Frank dying so slowly and all—it was the entire dysfunctional mess of our relationship—he was never 'into me'—whatever the hell that means—but he 'loved me.' I mean, our lives are complicated enough to have to settle for something like that."

Another round arrived and I began to unload the tale of my woes with Rico. Jim was a good listener, prodding for my feelings as I presented the facts. "It's sad about losing your brother this way," he said. "And never really knowing him. And then having a guy like that shit all over you. God will reward you for putting up with it."

"God?"

"That's right. It's all a system of checks and balances. Doors and windows, opening and closing."

"What if I don't believe in God?"

"Nonsense," he answered. "Been there, done that. You believe there *isn't* a God, right? Deconstruct that. That means that you believe there *is* a God."

He asked me what kind of career I was looking for and when I told him of abandoning law school, he said, "I once wanted to be an actor, though I hadn't a clue of how to act in any circumstance."

We laughed. Drunken, oversized laughs. "Is that how you became a journalist?" I asked him.

"No, that was all accidental. I got a part-time job as a fact checker and I was pushed into writing. I never had any desire to be on camera, so it was a surprise to see that happen. And what does it get me?" he laughed again. "A trail of scars."

He rolled up his pants leg and showed me the scars from the bombing of the van in Afghanistan. He spoke a little of that day, the hearing loss, the pain, but said the true misery was the thought that he had lost Ari. "We have our own issues—what relationship doesn't? And I love him in a way that I didn't love Frank. It's weird how there are so many people that are inside of us."

"Yes," I nodded.

He talked some more of the events in Afghanistan, hunting for Ari in Bamiyan with a chain-smoking young boy, his prayers that Ari would be safe and his bargains with God. "I owe *Somebody* for the way things turned out," he said. "Which I must interpret should mean that I owe *Everyone* for everything. So I should try to pass along the good that has happened to me. That's my responsibility as being part of this planet."

I was just about to confess my one-night stand with Stan Chartoff when Jim's cell phone rang and he excused himself and answered it. It was Ari, checking on Jim's whereabouts.

"I'm here with my new best friend Teddy," Jim said. "And we are getting sloshed."

We had another round of drinks, and then another round of drinks. I can't remember if I told him of my time with Stan or not. I remember Jim's cell phone ringing again and Ari and Eric arriving and refusing to join us for another round. When I stood the room swam around as if I were in a helicopter trying to land on the roof of a carousel. Eric led me out into the night. I remember giving Jim a hug. Ari too. And then I was in the cab and we were speeding downtown— the windows of skyscrapers twinkling as if they were stars.

Eighteen

Onward

I lived for two months in an apartment in San Francisco with a roommate named Kip. I wasn't unhappy there, but I also felt disconnected. I went out on job interviews to a number of places—a video store that was beginning to downsize, a yoga center cum spa that was decorated in only beige tones, a restaurant that was hiring waiters who would sing show tunes—but was never offered anything. I was not part of the bar scene, not interested in meeting guys via a chatroom or on the street for a half-hour quickie, nor was I interested in participating in a fetish scene of "leather and other kinks." "What do regular guys do?" I asked Kip. Kip was a hustler turned poet, who performed at venues around town talking about his body and the bodies of his clients and friends and tricks. Kip suggested I try the backroom of an adult bookstore on Mission Street or one of the toilets at the public library. He responded to my display of dismay with, "Well, at least he might be well read." It was a novelty to see him perform the first two times I did so—his ego and self-deprecation worked well on stage, but the continuous deconstruction of life within the apartment—"Why should soap be only something good?—smells are natural, my body is rank with desires to be released"—grew irritating.

In January, I went to live in Los Angeles, with a guy who was advertising for a roommate who would neither be "seen nor heard." The building was located in the hot flat plain of streets south of West Hollywood. I stayed in my room and read book after book, interviewed for various intern positions here and there—jobs that offered no pay, nothing in exchange for the experience of being overworked by an officious celebrity-climber. I registered with a temporary employment agency and began being sent out for various word-processing jobs, landing a gig with a law firm in Burbank where I could come and go as silently as I did my apartment.

In May my cousin Seth asked me to join him for a week hiking in Vancouver with three other guys. It was his own silent way of coming out to me, though I didn't think he expected that I would say yes to his invitation. I landed at the Seattle airport and rented a car to drive north. I knew that day, as I drove through Seattle, that I would be back. Sometimes a person or a place just seems right, and this was how I felt here, as if it were the place I had been forever looking for. I gave up Los Angeles and settled into an apartment just south of Fifth Street and began a job as a paralegal with a law firm. Within three months I was taking night classes to finally earn a law degree. Slowly the plan of my life began to emerge.

The spring that I turned fourteen my brother came home for a long weekend, a surprise visit to take our Mom out for her birthday. Pup picked me up at the high school and drove me to the abandoned parking lot of the elementary school we had both attended.

"Dad said you want to learn to drive," he said, and we switched seats so that I was behind the steering wheel. "I'm not the best teacher," he added, "but the best way to learn is to practice at it."

He was patient as I started up the car and lurched through the parking lot, adjusting the rearview mirror and trying to back out of a parking space. I was nervous to be driving and to be with my brother, until he put me at ease with a tale of when he had scraped into Dad's car one night while trying to park Mom's car in the garage. That day was one of only a few times that I think I ever connected my brother to being my brother.

After the lesson we drove to a restaurant where we met our parents. My mother was radiant because the family was together to celebrate her birthday. Afterwards, Pup left us to go somewhere downtown for the night. I saw him the next morning as he arrived back at the house. I was headed to the bathroom while he was headed up the stairs and to his bedroom. His eyes were shining and there was a tired, scraggy beauty to him. "Where you been?" I asked as our paths passed.

"Dancing," he answered and disappeared into his bedroom.

Pup was thirty-six the day the Towers fell. He was five foot eleven, one hundred seventy-two pounds, wore size ten shoes, pants with a thirty-one-inch waist, and a forty-regular jacket. His shirt size was fifteen and a half at the neck with thirty-three inches length at the sleeve. His hair was black. His eyes were brown. His locker combination at the gym was his birth date: 11-29-65. His favorite e-mail password was "chelsea." He was HIV-negative, blood type A.

In a newspaper eulogy of my brother a co-worker noted that Pup was "always smiling" and "the center of an ever-expanding circle of friends." I can't help thinking that some lives are bigger than others, but that does not diminish the regret that I never knew my brother better.

The following year at the Ground Zero memorials, Ari Sarghello said to me, "Your brother loved being gay. He was always going to a show, or a cabaret, or a gallery, or a bar or a dance for this or that cause. And there are always a million gay things to do in this city. And he had a great sense of the discrimination and injustices we face as gay people, but we often argued a lot because I thought his view of the world was too narrow."

"Too narrow?" I asked him.

"Too gay," he added. "It's amazing how you can totally isolate yourself in this city—at the same time you are being out and open in the world."

The following day when Ari visited Pup's apartment, I asked him, "What did you love about my brother?"

His eyes dimmed as he moved through remembered thoughts. "His voice. His hair. The way he smelled," he answered, then added,

"The way he walked into a room. His laugh. His chest. His thighs. There was nothing I didn't love about him. When I was with him I felt as if I were a part of something, a unit—a couple—in love. His attention was always focused on you until it wasn't, and when it wasn't focused on me, I was wildly upset."

On the second anniversary of the terrorist attacks, there was a documentary shown on the public television channel which contained accounts from survivors who had worked in the two Towers. I had not planned to watch it, but I could not bear to miss it. I waited for the image I knew I wanted to revisit. The second plane hitting the South Tower. The ball of fire that shatters windows and blackens into a gaping hole. I've always expected that I would find my brother in those repeated moments, but as the black cloud grew larger I shifted my eyes to the crazy beauty of the blue sky that morning.

Somewhere after the first half hour, I had to walk away from the television set because of the heaviness that had settled in my chest. I washed dishes and cleaned the kitchen counters. When I came back into the room a woman was talking about being trapped with two other workers in a stairwell on the sixty-seventh floor of the South Tower. She was about late forties, nicely dressed, and had worked as a secretary in one of the firms. She told of two men breaking through a fire exit door and leading the group of three to another stairwell. The men were not firemen or police—but two guys with white shirts and expensive ties covered with soot and oil, looking like "soiled Wall Street Prince Charmings." "One man was an absolute dreamboat, the kind of man you would always think would appear just at that moment to save the day—perfect white smile and shiny black eyes, sort of grizzly looking, and he told me his name and what floor he had come from and what was happening, but I was hysterical so all I could make out was "ripped edges." I remember holding this insanity in my head—*ripped edges?—ripped edges?*—as we followed him through a smoky floor and into another stairwell. Another woman said that after they had gotten to the other stairwell, two floors below, they encountered a man who was yelling that there was a group of people still in a conference room and they couldn't get out. The two men in ties disappeared with the other man to help the people trapped in the conference room, while the women continued down the stairwell.

"That was the last I saw of them. If those two men had not led us to the other stairwell—well," she choked up. "There were many heroes that day."

I knew in that moment that the women had described meeting my brother. I was certain of it. *Ripped edges—ripped edges*—Philip Bridges—*Pup Bridges*. The documentary had moved along to another anecdote and as I tried to step away from the television again, the phone rang.

"Teddy?"

It was my mother.

"Were you watching this—?"

"Yes," I answered her. "It was Pup. I know it was Pup."

"Yes," she answered. "I know it was Pup too."

One night on my way home from an evening class at law school, I discovered a cell phone in the parking lot outside the grocery store that anchored a nearby shopping center. When I made it back to my apartment with my groceries, I called a number titled "Home" which had been stored in the phone's memory. I left a brief message that I had found a cell phone and my own contact information. An hour later a woman named Cassie called to say that the phone was hers and that she had probably lost it while struggling to get her three-year-old son in the back seat of her car. I made arrangements to have Cassie's brother Allen pick up the phone from the reception desk of the law firm where I was working as a paralegal.

The next morning, I left the cell phone with Sandra, the receptionist, and forgot about it, until Sandra buzzed me around noon and said that there was a guy in the lobby to see me. Allen introduced himself with a strong handshake and eye contact, and I found myself immediately attracted to him. We made small talk, all of which I have long forgotten because there was a mind-numbing ringing in my ears that this sort of man might step into my life. Allen was about six feet tall, with a slender, athletic build and close-cropped light brown hair. He had a sexual aura that reminded me of Karl. When he left with the phone Sandra looked up to me and said with a laugh, "Well, that was a nice, cool drink of water, wasn't it?"

By the time I made it back to my desk I had put the meeting out of my mind because there was a crazy number of things I needed to accomplish for work. But late in the afternoon, my phone rang and the caller said to me, "My sister said that I should have offered to take you out to lunch."

It was Allen and my heart raced and I began to sweat. I felt uncomfortable talking to him because my cubicle was surrounded by other cubicles and it was impossible to muffle my half of our conversation, so I hastily agreed to meet him for lunch the following day at a diner not far from my office.

I was more relaxed and sociable at lunch. By that time, I had knocked the fantasy of Allen out of my mind and was able to ask him about his sister and his work. Cassie, his younger sister, had recently divorced and had two children, the older in second grade. Allen was an architect and something of an artist. He did renderings for an architectural firm of potential building projects—shopping malls, office complexes, apartment buildings—he loved the work but said it often left him exhausted because it had to be imagined with such precision and detail. He mentioned that to unwind he went to yoga classes or to the movies—or on occasion hiking in one of the parks north of the city. I mentioned a few trails my cousin Seth and I had done and we talked about a few recent movies I had seen. I told him about my job and going to law school in the evenings—I was in my third year by then and would graduate in the summer and I hoped to pass the bar in the fall and land a better position where I was working now or move to another firm. I felt a quiet connection with him—our meal was full of smiles, compliments, and gentle probings, though neither of us gave any hint of homosexuality to the other. At the end of the meal, I suggested that if he wanted to catch a movie together I would be glad to abandon my studies for a few hours. He politely nodded and seemed to take the invitation in stride, as if it were merely a pleasant way to part.

On Friday, as I was scanning the movie reviews in the newspaper, I saw a film that interested me and impulsively called Allen's office and asked him if he wanted to see the movie the following afternoon. I expected I would be rebuffed and I could then file away any hope of a friendship with him. He declined because he said he had a houseguest in town for the weekend, but suggested that if I wanted to see the movie Sunday evening, he would be free then. We agreed on a time and a place to meet and I again felt a rush of pleasure, even though I had no idea of how to proceed with Allen.

As it happened, it proceeded naturally. We met for the movie, the movie was funny and satisfying, and afterwards, we had drinks at a bar not far from the theater. We talked of many things, mostly safe topics—the weather, the movie, my classes and his job, until we ordered another round of drinks.

"I've not been entirely honest with you," Allen said, after a waitress had dropped off our drinks. "I'm trying to get over someone right now."

I nodded, giving him space to continue, because I felt a stronger attraction to him with his intention of honesty.

"It's complicated. We've been breaking up since we started dating."

"This was your houseguest?"

He nodded. "He lives in Portland and he's reluctant to travel to get together. He expects me to keep running to him, which I can't do. We spent yesterday breaking up again."

I thought of Gary's line he had once given me, that the best way to get over a guy was to fuck him out of your head, but I didn't mention it because the fantasies of what Allen might be like as a lover suddenly washed through my consciousness. Instead, I mentioned a guy I had dated when I had first moved to Seattle, but said that between work and school I had little time to pamper a needy boyfriend. I instantly regretted saying it because it made me look shallow and unwilling to be in a relationship.

We parted without a commitment to get together again, so I was surprised when Allen called me mid-week and invited me over to his house for dinner. "I'm not a very good cook," he said. "But I'm very good at reheating good cooking."

His house was simple and nestled at the end of a wooded drive. I liked it the moment I arrived because it seemed as if it were a quiet escape. Inside, the rooms had strong, clean lines and were furnished with dark wood and leather furniture, reminding me of rooms on display in a upscale catalog.

The dinner was nice, not overly romantic, and Allen was careful not to make it look like the date was a seduction. There were small clutches at the shoulder or the arm, to indicate his interest in me in more than a friendly way, and he stayed beside me in the kitchen as I offered to help him clean up. Afterwards, we sat on the couch and continued talking, until I could resist no more and leaned in to kiss him.

It was a short kiss. He clutched me by the shoulders and pulled me away to a stop, his eyes dead centered on mine.

"There's more," he said.

"Okay?" I nodded to him to continue, expecting him to tell me that he was in love with someone else, or that he was bisexual, or married. Instead he said, "I'm positive."

He must have seen the thousand questions that raced through my mind. He relaxed his grip on my shoulders and leaned away from me. "I've been asymptomatic for a long time," he said, and then, as if to add more of an explanation. "I was pretty wild when I was young."

I didn't know what to do next and I am sure it showed. "I don't want to push you into anything you haven't thought your way through. Just stay a while and relax. Let's not rush anything."

He opened his arms and pulled me to his chest, where I held him for a long while without speaking. In his embrace I could feel his heart beating. I thought about Chris Radnor and told myself that this was a different situation. It was getting late—I had to drive back into town and work the next day—and when I finally pulled myself away from Allen to indicate that I should be going, he asked. "Do you want to stay?"

"That would be nice," I answered.

I will admit that I struggled. Things moved slowly, but foremost was the sense of honesty from Allen at every step. Sex with Allen was practical and solid; he had a list of things he was willing to do and a way he found pleasure. Our first few times together were awkward and impersonal. My body was willing but I was filled with hesitancy. The changing point occurred when I began to whisper his name while he was holding me and I knew he was someone I could trust. I suppose I could become sentimental and say that I was lucky that fate brought us together as it did, though Allen, practical, precise Allen, said he was the lucky one that his sister was such a klutz. I did not intend to keep the details of Pup a secret from Allen; in fact, I had mentioned on our first or second date together that I had an older brother who had died, but I remember the first night that Allen spent at my apartment—it was also the first time I felt comfortable with him sexually—how to keep everything safe but still passionate—we had showered together and collapsed on my narrow bed and Allen's embrace, and the dim light of my bedroom and the warm, satisfied glow of our bodies after sex, made me remember the time I had spent with Stan Chartoff. I began telling Allen about how I had met Stan, which progressed into recounting how my brother died and I came to find myself in his apartment in Chelsea.

Allen and I dated close to nine months before I moved in with him. After two attempts, I passed the bar examination and found a position at another firm. Allen's sister and her children easily accepted and incorporated our crazy schedules into their own. My cousin Seth said I had found a perfect guy for me. One morning I woke up and I was a man in love, with a busy life.

For years Allen had harbored a dream of writing a history book of architecture—how Corinthian columns emerged, what defined Gothic architecture, and on and on—all of which would be illustrated with his own sketches—and he had filled many notebooks with his designs, which he began to scan and digitize and explain with captions. His attempts at creating chapters were clumsy and poorly written, so he enrolled in an evening writing class taught through an adult-education extension at the nearby high school. He returned home one night saying the homework for the next class was to write something "about my life."

"Maybe I should write about how we met," he said. "The teacher said, 'Write about something you know.'"

His essay was precise and practical, just like he was, how he had seen one door closing and another one simultaneously opening. It made me remember the drunken night I had spent with Jim MacTiernan and his confession that "Everyone has a book inside of him. A terrific one. All you have to do is connect the dots." Jim had thought I should write a memoir about losing my brother Philip, a man I hardly knew. I had confessed that I was reluctant to invest time in creating another 9/11 sob story. No remains of my brother had ever been uncovered at Ground Zero. Chris had faded into a memory and my scar from Rico was only that—a lesson learned the hard way.

"How can I write about someone I didn't know?" I drunkenly asked Jim.

"That's only an excuse not to write about someone you didn't know," he answered. "People write about all sorts of things all the time, so there is no reason for you not to put your thoughts down on paper and clear your mind. Look at the facts, then write about how you feel. And be honest about everything."

So as Allen began writing little scenes from his life for his class, I began to write down notes about Pup. And Chris. And Rico and Stan. And finally about Jim and Ari. They were all fragments laid down on paper in hopes of seeing their importance and relation and clarity. But my truth and honesty did not bring amazingly clear results—in fact, I had come to worriedly believe I was something of an increasing mess, and this was when I believed the seemingly random events of our lives began to show an interconnectedness, doors and windows opening and closing. Allen had introduced me to yoga and meditation—or, rather, reintroduced me to them; in our early courtship I had followed him from class to group to gathering. Now, as I calmed myself and stretched and breathed and looked into the blackness of my body, moments from my past triggered a new insight about my life—a belief that a spiritual energy does reside in the universe, swirls around us, gives us strength and hope and mission. Was this the presence of God? I still cannot confirm that and I have my doubts, but I do have a belief that there is some otherworldly life force at work around us. I didn't disbelieve, but I didn't wholeheartedly believe, either. I had reached a higher ground so to speak. My belief in God was and continues to be an evolving answer. Certainly there was a god and a spiritual energy at work in the small details of day-to-day life—in Stan rushing to the aid of the fallen messenger, Eric arriving at my apartment with photos of Pup, an Afghan family harboring a lost American journalist. Good begetting good to you and others. I am sure that there was a reason for all that happened to me because now all my dots were connected nicely at last. Ours—mine and Allen's—was a pleasant life and my acknowledgement—and appreciation and awareness of it—was because it had been so hard for me before. My parents had visited and embraced Allen as my partner—sometime between San Francisco and Los Angeles I had blurted out my dilemma over the phone, telling them I was gay and trying to meet someone. I always thought this was also what prompted my cousin Seth to call me—my mom calling his mom, two sisters trying to subtly manage and improve their children's lives. My parents' reaction were more supportive than I could have imagined them being, and I know I owe much of that to my brother Pup for paving the way for me.

But life intruded to prevent me from doing any further work on writing my stories down to a full and satisfying completion—isn't that the way it always happens? My job and clients demanded attention, new friends arrived, and an addition to our house—adding a great room which would also serve as a library—was a big expenditure and learning curve for two gay men honestly trying to carve out their lives.

But Allen was adamant about traveling to visit relatives, as well as giving ourselves vacations. In 2006, after registering as domestic partners, he wanted us to honeymoon in Paris, to celebrate, really, what we were trying to do together, though I knew he was also eager to do some more architectural sketches and that this was another motive to see one of the grand cities of Europe. I didn't mind—I had never been the kind of world traveler my brother had been, and with his absence from my life, I had become envious of what he had accomplished and how much he had seen of the world. Allen had booked a cheap flight for us that winter—it was January 2007 and the travel industry was slow. We stayed in an inexpensive hotel on the Left Bank that neither of us liked the moment we walked up the six flights of narrow winding stairs and into an airless attic room. But we also knew it would be a memory and another story to tell one day.

"If nothing else, we'll always have Paris," he joked, sticking his head out of the small window into the chilly Paris skyline. "A tiny little room at the top of the Left Bank."

And it was a romantic trip, full of wonderful moments. I had never been to Paris before and took to the city immediately—the weather was brutal, even for Europe in January, but the panoramas were clear and spectacular from Sacré-Coeur and the Eiffel Tower.

While we were in Paris, I had noticed a poster for an exhibition at the Musée Guimet. It was never my intention to see this particular exhibit, but the afternoon we had gone to the top of the Eiffel Tower and taken one of the short boat rides on the Seine, we were walking from the Palais de Chaillot when an icy wind blew through the street and the cap of an elderly man walking ahead of us flew into the air. Allen and I chased it down the sidewalk as if we were characters in a silent film comedy and laughingly returned the cap to the man and his wife. But it was too cold to continue any farther, and we followed the man and his wife to the nearest building, which was the Guimet, where Allen suggested we go inside and warm up and see if there was a café. He also thought he could do some sketches of Asian artifacts.

One of the temporary exhibits on display that day on the basement floor of the museum was of ancient items recovered from Afghanistan known as the Bactrian Gold—gold, ivory, glass, and bronze items hidden for many years by a secret society of "key holders" in the vaults beneath the government compounds of Kabul, some of whom resisted threats and torture by Taliban militants demanding entry into the safes where the treasures were kept. The artifacts blended Greek, Bactrian, and nomadic traditions, and reflected Afghanistan's historical position at the crossroads of ancient civilizations. In 2003, Afghan President Hamid Karzai had announced that the boxes had been recovered from the vaults and later, after much negotiation, the Paris museum had been offered an exhibition of the treasures.

Allen suggested we roam first through the exhibits before we sat and ate. The building was a rectangular maze of rooms in the way that only museums can be, one exhibit leading into another and into another, some under dark lighting, some astonishingly bright. Allen was slowly sketching an item uncovered from a tomb, a tiny winged figure of Aphrodite, and I tried not to rush him along with my mounting hunger. We had gone from a dimly lit rotunda into collections from China and Tibet when we found our way to a stairwell and descended into the Afghanistan exhibit. As I was following behind Allen about to make a comment about the absurd layout of the museum, I thought I recognized a man who was moving out of a room and into the next.

"I'll be right back," I said. "I'm not sure—but I think I see someone I know."

"Really? Here?" Allen answered. "Take your time then if you want to catch up. I want to draw this piece. Why don't we meet in the café later?"

"Sure," I answered. I went through the room and into the next where I had seen the man walk to. I was sure I was mistaken, but I recognized the back of his head as he was staring at the elaborately carved ivory figures of river goddesses that had once adorned a chair. As I approached to introduce myself, he looked away from the case and was moving in my direction towards the next case. I was rather mindless of the art on display—some were beautiful and delicate gold jewels and I knew if Allen had the time, he would want to draw each one. For a moment I thought the man had recognized me because he looked up at me and then averted his eyes, but he moved away, and I knew he had not seen me, just as I had not seen the artifacts around us. I was more sure now that I knew the man and I stepped closer as he came to stand in front of another glass case and I said, "Stan? Stan Chartoff?"

The man glanced up at me. He was nicely dressed in a cotton button-down shirt and khaki pants, a dusty jacket draped across one arm. His hair was cut shorter and a lighter shade, and it gave him a sense of elegance he had never had before.

"Yes?" he said.

"I'm Teddy Bridges," I said. "I met you several years ago at a dinner party in Chelsea. I was there with Eric and Sean."

Stan smiled and held out his hand to shake. "Teddy, yes, of course. How are you? What are you doing here—in Paris? Visiting?"

"Yes," I said, "I'm here with my friend. *Lover.* My partner Allen. He's in the next room, absorbed in one of the exhibits. Trying to draw them."

"An artist?" Stan said.

I nodded and I know I was beaming with pride, the sort of pride I had always wanted to feel about talking about my lover. "Do you live here now?" I asked him.

"No," Stan answered. "I have been in India for a long time. Mumbai. I went there not long after we met, as a matter of fact. I was just back in New York for a family matter. I'm only here in Paris for a few days."

"I met Jim MacTiernan not long after I met you," I said. "He and his boyfriend Ari were in the city. Did you know he wrote a book?"

"A book?"

"Yes," I answered. "About his trip to Afghanistan."

"No," said Stan. "I didn't know."

"It's quite good," I said. "You're mentioned in it. There's a lovely dedication—"

He looked embarrassedly at his shoes, which were nothing to be embarrassed about. They were nice, rugged-looking boots. "I'm afraid I've lost contact with him. But how are you? Are you still dog walking?"

"No, no," I hurriedly answered because I was afraid of him walking away too soon. "Lawyer. I finally went back to law school and passed the bar. We live outside of Seattle now."

"Seattle?"

"I can't believe Jim MacTiernan didn't send you a copy of his book."

"I've not been easy to reach," Stan said.

It was then that a tall, young man appeared at Stan's shoulder. He was boyishly handsome, a dark swarthy jaw, deep brown eyes, and blue-black hair. I took him to be Indian only because Stan had just mentioned Mumbai.

"This is Ali Hassad," Stan said and introduced the man to me.

I reached out to shake the young man's hand, felt his strong clasp, and realized that this was the fellow Stan had spoken of on that night we had shared years before. Stan turned and spoke to Ali Hassad in what sounded like a mixture of French and Hindi, and all at once it occurred to me that Stan had left Manhattan and returned to India or Pakistan or Afghanistan to be with Ali Hassad again, navigating an insurmountable set of odds and documents—or perhaps just smuggling the young boy out of the country—to bring them together in India. I heard Stan mention Jim MacTiernan's name to the young man, which was when he directed his gaze back to me.

"We are on our way back to Mumbai," Ali Hassad said. His English diction was precise and sounded out hours of education and practice, and he carried the hint of elegance and contentment that Stan was also displaying. "You must give my regards to Jim MacTiernan when you next see him. He was a great man that I met only for a short time."

I couldn't bring myself to confess to them that I was not close with Jim myself, that we had not shared any more time together than I had with Stan, that we were nothing more than psychically or spiritually connected, so I answered, "I will."

But I was also bathed in the glow of memory and history. "I'm meeting my partner in the restaurant," I said. "Will you join us?"

"We want to see an exhibit upstairs," Stan said. "We'll look for you after that, if you are still here. But don't wait for us. It's best not to wait for us at all. We are apt to linger and forget ourselves."

"Well then," I said, shaking both their hands. "I hope I see you upstairs, but if I don't, I wish you a safe journey back to India."

"And you to Seattle. I'm glad to see you happy."

I left them and hurried to the café, where I found Allen sketching with his pencil in his notebook. I watched him drawing lines and writing descriptions, hearing my own words rattling around in my head looking for a way out of my skull.

"Well?" he asked, when I plopped down beside him. "Was it the fellow you thought it was?"

"Yes," I answered. "And I met his lover. I asked them to join us here, but I don't expect they will."

"Small world," Allen said and nodded, returning to the sketch. I ordered a cappuccino and a pastry and sat eating and remembering, thinking maybe there was a book inside of me too. Allen moved on to another sketch. When he was done some time later, he looked up at me and said, "Well, I guess it's just the two of us then."

"Yes," I answered. "Yes it is."

Acknowledgments

It is a difficult task for me to acknowledge how all the elements of this novel came into place or where the details contained herein were derived—to do so would require me to publish an encyclopedic list of all the news accounts I have sifted through since September 11th, 2001 occurred. This novel began as a short story, and first and foremost I must acknowledge the attention and enthusiasm of Anne H. Wood and Brian Keesling, my long-time writing friends, who championed that early version. The story was originally the final one of a working manuscript titled *The Chelsea Rose*, about the interlocking lives of the gay and lesbian inhabitants of a New York neighborhood apartment building. Readers who might be familiar with my short stories will recognize the background of the character of James MacTiernan in this novel as similar to the one in the published story "The Chelsea Rose." The early short story version of "The Third Buddha" revolved around the stories told at a dinner party, when Jim returns to visit the apartment building post 9/11. I must also thank an unknown editor at a literary magazine where I submitted that short story, whose form rejection letter sent to me contained the handwritten note, "Have you considered expanding this to a book-length work?"

That note sent me drinking and thinking and worrying and working. At the heart of this story was always the desire to recast and retell the story of "The Good Samaritan" during a time of crisis and within a clash of religions and cultures, and as the work grew and morphed and solidified, I knew I also wanted it to represent what it meant to be an articulate gay activist and citizen of the world.

Important formative source materials used on Afghanistan and Bamiyan include Christian Frei's documentary, *The Giant Buddhas*;

Rory Stewart's memoir of walking across Afghanistan, *The Places In Between*; Peter Levi's travel journal, *The Light Garden of the Angel King*; and *Afghanistan, A Companion and Guide* by Bijan Omrani, Matthew Leeming, and Elizabeth Chatwin. Acknowledgement must also be given to Zemaryali Tarzi, the archeologist and professor who has led the search for the reclining Buddha in Bamiyan. Equally important in providing a contextual case of gay men and the Muslim countries was Michael Luongo's anthology *Gay Travels in the Muslim World*, whose introductory note was as significant and as illuminating as his contributors' essays. An important emotional source for the 9/11 portions of this novel was Marian Fontana's book *A Widow's Walk*. Special thanks to Richard Labonté for including the opening chapter in *Best Gay Romance 2011* and to Peter Dubé for including it in *Best Gay Stories 2011*. Gratitude is also due Alex Jeffers, Andrew Beierle, and Raphael Kadushin for their comments that helped shape and polish the narrative.

Once again, my special thanks and appreciation go to Arch Brown, Edward Iwanicki, Hermann Lademann, Kevin Bentley, Andrew McBeth, Steve Berman, and the New York Foundation for the Arts. Long-time gratitude is also still due to many friends who are no longer around, especially Kevin Patterson and David Feinberg.

Thanks are also sent to Sean Meriwether, Greg Herren, Paul Willis, Vince Liaguno, Tom Cardamone, Mark Sullivan, Wayne Hoffman, and Toby Johnson. My list of thank yous for Chelsea Station Editions grows longer and longer every day, but the efforts of fellow authors David Pratt, Felice Picano, Jon Marans, and Andrew Beierle to help the press take its first big steps are especially appreciated. And no thanks would be complete without those to friends I haven't already mentioned, among them Kathy Corey, Ellen Herb, Edward Bohan, Teresa Smith, Deborah Collins, John Maresca, Joel Byrd, Larry Dumont, and Martin Gould.

About the Author

Jameson Currier is the author of three novels, *Where the Rainbow Ends*, *The Wolf at the Door*, and *The Third Buddha*; and four collections of short fiction, *Dancing on the Moon*; *Desire, Lust, Passion, Sex*; *Still Dancing*; and *The Haunted Heart and Other Tales*.

CPSIA information can be obtained at www.ICGtesting.com
Printed in the USA
BVOW080117290313

316754BV00001B/32/P